Change of Heart

Center Point
Large Print

Also by Courtney Walsh and available from Center Point Large Print:

Paper Hearts

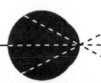

This Large Print Book carries the Seal of Approval of N.A.V.H.

Change of Heart

COURTNEY WALSH

CENTER POINT LARGE PRINT
THORNDIKE, MAINE

This Center Point Large Print edition
is published in the year 2016 by arrangement with
Tyndale House Publishers, Inc.

Scripture quotations are taken from the *Holy Bible*,
New Living Translation, copyright © 1996, 2004, 2015
by Tyndale House Foundation. Used by permission
of Tyndale House Publishers, Inc., Carol Stream,
Illinois 60188. All rights reserved.
Scripture in chapters 42 and 44 is taken from the New King
James Version,® copyright © 1982 by Thomas Nelson, Inc.
Used by permission. All rights reserved.
Change of Heart is a work of fiction. Where real people,
events, establishments, organizations, or locales appear,
they are used fictitiously. All other elements of the
novel are drawn from the author's imagination.

The text of this Large Print edition is unabridged.
In other aspects, this book may vary from the original edition.
Printed in the United States of America on permanent paper.
Set in 16-point Times New Roman type.

ISBN: 978-1-68324-000-6

Library of Congress Cataloging-in-Publication Data

Names: Walsh, Courtney, 1975– author.
Title: Change of heart / Courtney Walsh.
Description: Center Point Large Print edition. | Thorndike, Maine :
Center Point Large Print, 2016. | ©2016
Identifiers: LCCN 2016009443 | ISBN 9781683240006
    (hardcover : alk. paper)
Subjects: LCSH: Life change events—Fiction. | Large type books. |
GSAFD: Love stories. | Christian fiction.
Classification: LCC PS3623.A4455 C48 2016b | DDC 813/.6—dc23
LC record available at http://lccn.loc.gov/2016009443

For Cindy Fassler, my mom.
My cheerleader. My secret keeper.
My guilt-trip inducer. My best friend.
Everyone should have a mom like you.

CHAPTER

1

Evelyn Brandt stood in her kitchen, the sound of uptight laughter filtering in from the dining room.

Hosting the Loves Park Chamber Ladies hadn't been her idea. Christopher told her a good politician's wife had to put herself out there. So she did.

And now she regretted it. It wasn't the first time that agreeing to something she didn't want to do had ended in regret.

She dialed Christopher's work line.

"Christopher Brandt."

". . . is in serious trouble," Evelyn said.

"Evelyn?" He sounded concerned, telling her he hadn't gotten her joke.

"This luncheon is pure torture," she whispered. "You owe me."

His laugh was forced. "I do owe you. Thanks for playing nice."

Of course she played nice. That was the only way she knew how to play. Learn the rules and follow them. Words to live by.

"Evelyn, do you have any more peach tea?" Georgina Saunders appeared in the doorway, took one look at her, and frowned. "I didn't realize you were on a call."

Bad manners?

Evelyn said a quick good-bye to her husband and hung up. "I'm sorry about that. I'll bring more tea."

The caterer appeared to be occupied in the corner of the kitchen. So Evelyn took the empty crystal pitcher from Georgina, president of their philanthropic group, and moved to the opposite side of the room, thankful when the other woman returned to the dining room. If Evelyn had her way, she would've hidden out in the kitchen for the rest of the luncheon.

But the pecan-crusted chicken with chardonnay cream sauce hadn't even been served yet.

As Evelyn refilled and picked up the pitcher, it slipped from her hands. She caught it before it hit the ground, but not before the peach tea sloshed onto her black-and-white silk and cotton dress, the one Christopher had special ordered for this occasion. The one that made Evelyn feel like a child playing dress-up in her mom's closet.

Even after all these years of learning to fit the mold, she still felt uncomfortable in these scenarios.

"Evelyn, do you have that tea?" Georgina returned. "Oh, my. How clumsy of you. You should soak that before it stains."

Evelyn nodded. "I think I'll go change."

"Good idea." Georgina took the pitcher and left the kitchen.

Evelyn hurried upstairs, pulled off the dress, and stood in her closet. What she really wanted was a pair of worn-out jeans and her oversize light-gray sweater.

But that would never do, and she didn't want to embarrass Christopher. She knew how important these ladies were to his political career, both present and future.

She returned to the dining room, wearing a simple pair of black dress pants, heels, and a loose patterned blouse. A conversation was already in progress.

Georgina sat at the end of the table like a queen on a throne, chin tilted ever so slightly downward as always, eyebrows raised in judgment. "I hadn't heard that about Willa Seitz's husband," she was saying.

Evelyn frowned as she took her seat at the opposite end of the table.

"Did you know he was having an affair with Willa's sister, Evelyn?"

Evelyn felt her eyes widen. "I hadn't heard that, no." She should call Willa. Make sure she was okay. They didn't know each other well, but their paths had crossed enough for Evelyn to consider her an acquaintance at least, if not a friend.

And if the expressions on the faces of the women in her dining room were any indication,

9

Willa Seitz wouldn't have many of those now.

"Seems it's been going on for quite some time." Georgina surveyed the rest of them. "We should all say a prayer of thanks for faithful husbands, ladies."

Yes. Evelyn was grateful for that, though she wished her husband was home more often. Being a state senator kept him busy. And away.

But then, weren't his position and his power part of what she loved about him? Her mind conjured an image of Christopher. Handsome and charming with eyes that sparkled and a smile that melted hearts. She'd never met anyone with quite so much charisma, and while she certainly didn't enjoy the days they were apart each month, the wife of a public servant had to make sacrifices too.

The main course was served, and the ladies around her table began eating the catered lunch. Evelyn mostly stayed quiet at these sorts of functions, meant for networking and planning the occasional philanthropic event. Christopher thought it was important she was involved.

"These women decide the who's who of Colorado," he'd told her. "Be charming and wonderful. We need their support."

She did as she was told, and while she never uttered a word of protest, she dreaded these luncheons more than dental work.

"Evelyn, will Christopher be home this weekend?" Lydia Danvers straightened. The woman might have been four years older than Evelyn, but she dressed fifteen years younger. All that time spent in the gym had certainly worked in her favor.

Evelyn shrank under her watchful eye. "He hopes to be," she said, then took a sip of her tea. "His schedule is always up in the air."

Lydia gave a curt nod, then a quick once-over. "Did you change your clothes?"

Evelyn smoothed her blouse. "I did. I just spilled some tea on myself."

The ladies laughed. "Oh, Evelyn, it's a good thing you had this meal catered," Georgina said.

More laughter.

Heat rushed to Evelyn's cheeks. She would tell Christopher she needed a break from the entertaining. She didn't have the gift of hospitality, and it was time she said so.

After this luncheon.

The doorbell rang, drawing all six pairs of eyes toward Evelyn.

"Are you expecting someone else?" Georgina asked.

Evelyn set her cloth napkin on the table as she pushed herself up. She'd never been more thankful for a doorbell in her life.

But when she moved toward the front door and spotted a man and a woman, both dressed in suits and looking quite official, her gratitude slowly dissipated.

She stood motionless on her side of the door, staring at them through the window until they flipped open badges, expectancy on their faces.

"Who is it, Evelyn?" Georgina called from the other room.

She cracked the door as her heart became a stopwatch set on double time.

"Evelyn Brandt?"

She nodded through the half-open door. "Yes?"

"Agent Marcus Todd, FBI. This is Agent Debbie Marnetti."

"What can I do for you?" Her stomach fluttered, and that familiar panicked feeling set in. And just like that she was eleven years old again, waiting for her father to come home, knowing her grades would not meet his approval. Her anxiety had turned to panic even then, and she'd been battling it ever since. Would she ever find comfort in her own skin?

Not now. She needed to keep it together.

"We need to speak to you about your husband. May we come in?"

"Christopher? Has something happened?" Evelyn didn't move from her spot in the doorway, her mind racing back to the quick conversation she'd had with her husband earlier today. He had seemed distracted—well, even more so than usual—but everything else was fine. He would've told her if it wasn't.

"Ma'am?"

Evelyn realized she'd been staring, mind reeling, and she quickly apologized. "I have guests."

The woman—Marnetti—rolled her eyes. The man gave her a warm smile. "It might be a good idea to ask them to leave."

Evelyn felt like she'd just been asked to return to the doctor's office for an in-person explanation of her test results.

"We really do need to speak to you immediately," Agent Todd told her.

"Of course. Come in."

She led them to the living room of their lakefront house. The house Christopher bought without telling her. He said it was a gift for her, but Evelyn knew better. The lake ran through Loves Park, and the homes surrounding it were some of the most desirable in town.

"It's a house worthy of a future governor," he'd told her on their first walk-through, confirming her suspicions.

"It's so big," she said. "What are we going to do with all this extra space?" The ornate fixtures certainly didn't seem like the kinds one would have in a houseful of children.

"We'll be entertaining," Christopher had told her. "Fund-raising. Campaigning. I've hired a decorator to come in and redo everything."

"Can we really afford that, Christopher?"

He pulled her into his arms. "You deserve a

beautiful home, Evelyn. I want you to have the best."

She looked past him to the elaborate staircase at the center of the entryway. "I don't need all of this. I'd be happy with a small house in the country. As long as you're there. You know that."

His phone had chirped in his pocket and he'd excused himself to the other room, leaving her alone in the middle of a house she was sure would always feel more like a hotel than a home.

Now, in spite of the people surrounding her, Evelyn felt more alone than ever. She gestured for the agents to sit on the posh sofa Christopher's decorator had picked out.

"Can I get either of you something to drink?" she asked, trying to remember her manners in spite of her trembling hands.

"We're fine, Mrs. Brandt." Agent Marnetti's tone almost sounded like a reprimand.

Evelyn begged her heart to stop pounding.

"Evelyn, are you coming back?" Georgina appeared once more in the doorway. Her perfectly tweezed brows drew downward.

Evelyn's throat went dry.

"Who are you?" Georgina's superiority permeated the air.

"Georgina, I think it's best if we cut the luncheon short."

"We haven't even begun the meeting," Georgina said. "The others are still eating."

"Georgina, please." Evelyn practically pushed her out of the room, wishing she would just take a hint already. Her mind spun with possible scenarios. Why on earth was the FBI in her living room? And was there any way to get these ladies out without having to answer a million questions?

"Evelyn, I don't like the idea of leaving you alone here," Georgina said as they returned to the dining room. "Ladies, there are two strangers who've just barged into Evelyn's house. I think we need to get to the bottom of this."

Evelyn sighed. "They're from the FBI."

A collective gasp filled the room.

"What do they want with you?" Susan Hayes asked, rising from the table.

"I don't know," Evelyn said. "I haven't found out yet. Please go and let me call you all later."

"We should stay," Georgina argued.

"No." Evelyn's tone was firm for once. "Please go."

These women were really only here to help Christopher's political career, and whatever the FBI wanted, she had a feeling it wasn't going to be very helpful.

Evelyn suspected that before she discovered why the FBI was sitting on her sofa, Georgina and the others would have a litany of false explanations floating around town. She ushered them out, dismissed the caterer, and returned to the room where she'd left the agents.

"Do you know why we're here?" Agent Todd asked.

Evelyn shook her head. "You said it was about Christopher."

"Where is your husband now?" Agent Marnetti asked. She stood near the windows.

"Denver. They're in session. He's a Colorado state senator. He was elected three years ago. He worked hard to get where he is." She was rambling.

Something passed between the two agents in a silent exchange.

"What is it?" Evelyn folded her hands in her lap, feeling a rush of anxiety rise to the surface.

"This is quite the house you have here, Mrs. Brandt." Agent Marnetti walked toward the fireplace. "Is this marble?" She ran a hand along the mantel—a mantel most women would love. Evelyn had never cared for it. She'd tried her best to add personal touches—Christopher had allowed her to give three photos of the two of them to his decorator, a regal woman whose accent sounded like a cross between Britain and the Upper East Side. The photos stared at her from the mantel now.

"How do you suppose your husband paid for such a lavish home, Mrs. Brandt?" Agent Marnetti asked as she picked up a framed wedding photo.

"Would you mind telling me why you're here?" Evelyn stared at the agents. She had a right to know, didn't she?

The two officials exchanged another telling glance. Agent Marnetti looked away.

Agent Todd turned toward Evelyn. "We believe Senator Brandt has been embezzling money from the state."

Evelyn's stomach twisted. "That's not possible."

"We have evidence," Agent Marnetti said. "Lots of evidence. And we think it started long before he became a state senator."

Christopher adored Loves Park. Serving in city government had been a point of pride for him. Surely there'd been a mistake—he would never do anything to jeopardize his future.

Their future.

"I'd like to call my husband."

"There will be time for that, but right now we're going to have to ask you to step outside."

"Why?"

"We need to look around. Determine your involvement in your husband's crimes."

"*My* involvement? I don't even know what you're talking about." Evelyn's fingers were cold, like they always felt when she was nervous.

"Then you have nothing to worry about," Agent Todd said, his tone kind.

It was clear who was who in the whole good cop/bad cop scenario.

"Have you noticed any other elaborate purchases?" Agent Marnetti asked. "I mean, other than the house."

Evelyn frowned. "I don't know. Christopher's family has money. It's not so hard to believe he'd be able to afford the things he's bought."

"He lost all of his family's money a few years ago, Mrs. Brandt," Agent Todd said. "The senator made a few bad investments and lost it all."

"That's not possible," Evelyn said. "He would've told me."

"It seems there's a lot he didn't tell you," Agent Marnetti replied. "Or maybe he's just trained you really well on how to look innocent."

"That's ridiculous," Evelyn said. "Christopher handled all of our money. I never even paid attention." Her voice trailed off at the realization. She hadn't wanted to know about the money. Christopher assured her they were fine, and that was good enough for her.

She trusted him.

"Probably not the smartest choice." Agent Marnetti crossed her arms. "I find it hard to believe you didn't suspect anything. What about the cabin your husband purchased last month up in the mountains?"

"Our vacation home?" Evelyn had thought it was a bit excessive when Christopher bought that place, but she wouldn't tell them that.

"Quite a price tag on a home you rarely stay in."

"He was going to rent it out. Try to make some extra income. Christopher is a brilliant businessman."

"Spare us the rhetoric, Mrs. Brandt." Agent Marnetti pulled a walkie-talkie out of her pocket. "Come on in," she said.

Agent Todd stood. "Why don't we go outside? You don't need to watch this."

The front door opened, and a group of men in suits entered, rushing past Evelyn.

"You can't do this," she said, her voice barely audible.

Agent Marnetti stopped in front of her. "We have a warrant." She snapped open a folded piece of paper and handed it to Evelyn.

Her phone beeped. A new text message from Susan Hayes. **Georgina would like a full report once the FBI leaves your house. We'll finish our meeting at her house. Join if you can.**

"It'll be easier for you if you come with me," Agent Todd said.

"You're just going to go through all of our things?"

"We'll only take what's pertinent to the case."

A man walked by with her laptop.

"That's mine. Christopher has nothing to do with that computer."

"He might have hidden things on it, Mrs. Brandt. We have to cover all the bases." Agent Todd ushered her toward the front door. "You can wait in my car."

Evelyn's head started to spin, her heart raced, and she couldn't get a good, deep breath. *Not now.*

She turned her phone over in her hand. "I need to call my husband."

Agent Marnetti snatched the phone from her. "Not a good idea."

"He won't answer, Mrs. Brandt," Agent Todd said.

"How do you know that?"

"According to our director, he was arrested about fifteen minutes ago."

Evelyn couldn't process what she was hearing. "I just spoke with Christopher. He didn't say anything. Why didn't anyone call me?"

"We couldn't risk you destroying evidence. Now, please, let's go outside." Agent Todd opened the door.

As Evelyn stepped onto the porch, she heard her name being called from the yard. She glanced up and saw four television cameras all fixed on her.

"Mrs. Brandt, did you know about the senator's embezzlement?"

"Mrs. Brandt, are you an accomplice to the fraud?"

"Did you know your husband was a crook?"

Wondering if she'd ever wake up from this terrible nightmare, Evelyn took a backward step into the house and slammed the door. "Get those people out of my yard."

"We're working on it."

Evelyn walked through the house, trying not to pay attention to the way these federal agents were carelessly searching through everything she owned. She went out to the rear patio with Agent Todd following close behind.

"Can you just leave me alone?"

"I'm sorry, Mrs. Brandt. My orders are to keep you in my sight at all times."

"You honestly think I had anything to do with any of this?"

He shrugged. "Stranger things have happened, ma'am."

"Not to me." Evelyn sat on a deck chair and let her head drop into her hands. "I can't believe this is happening."

A rustling in the bushes pulled her attention. She stood just in time to glimpse a man with a camera pointed at her.

She spun around, head whirling, black dots at the edges of her vision. She struggled to breathe. This time she couldn't keep the panic away. It was too strong. Every coping mechanism she'd learned in therapy eluded her, and she dropped into the chair, willing away the worry.

Her heart felt like it was being squeezed. Her airway, blocked. Her mind spun out of control, unable to latch on to one sane thought.

For a split second she was in her parents' house again, hiding under the bed, hoping her father didn't find her. He wouldn't abuse her—not physically—but he would tell her what a disappointment she was. He would point out that she wasn't living up to her potential, that what she needed was hard work and discipline. He would make her feel like the failure she was.

I'll never be good enough.

"Mrs. Brandt?" Agent Todd leaned in. "Are you okay?" He turned to the man with the camera and shooed him away. "Get out of here. I can arrest you. This is private property."

The cameraman rushed off.

"He's gone, Mrs. Brandt." Agent Todd stood a few feet away. "Do you need a doctor?"

Slowly Evelyn's panic subsided. It had been months since she'd had a panic attack, but they never got any easier. "I'm fine. I just want to be alone."

He lingered for a moment as if to assess her condition. "I'll wait over here," he said finally. "By the door."

But knowing she remained under his watchful eye was enough to prevent her from relaxing. That, coupled with the fact that her entire world had just come crumbling down around her, made Evelyn feel like she might never truly be at peace again.

CHAPTER

2

The fence at the base of Whitney Farms lay in pieces at Trevor's feet. He'd been meaning to fix it for months, and last night one of the cows got out, so today it had become top priority. He hadn't spent a fortune raising grass-fed cattle just to have them wander off in the middle of the night.

The whole electric fence needed to be replaced, but the family farm had seen better months. Better years, if he was honest. Sometimes he wondered if there was any point in keeping the old place up and running, but every time the idea of shutting it down entered his mind, he heard his dad's voice clear as day:

"It's not much, Son, but it's ours. Our legacy. And that means something to us. It's yours now. Your turn to carry on the Whitney name."

He shook the memory from his mind and hammered one of the broken slats to the post.

He'd almost finished his repairs when an old blue four-wheeler appeared over the hill. His aunt Lilian stopped the vehicle a few feet away.

"Where's your helmet, Aunt Lil?" Trevor teased, prepared for whatever sarcastic remark she'd throw his way.

When none came, he stopped his hammer midswing.

She killed the engine. "You need to come inside."

Trevor frowned. "Why?"

"Just come on. There's something you need to see." She started the engine back up. "It's important, Trevor."

He didn't like this one bit. Made him feel a lot like he did the day he got the call that his dad had passed away. And again, just two years later, when Mom followed him to heaven. He checked his pocket to be sure he had his phone with him. Had something happened to Peter? Jules? His siblings had chosen to leave Loves Park, but they still checked in now and then. When was the last time he'd spoken to either of them?

Trevor followed Lilian back to the house. She didn't live there, but she might as well for as much time as she spent at Whitney Farms as the organic vegetable grower. Insisted on having her own space, even though the guesthouse out back would've been perfect for her. That headstrong nature ran in their family.

When she reached the driveway, she got off her four-wheeler and went inside.

"Lil, what is going on?" he called after her but was answered with the slam of a screen door.

Inside, he heard the news blaring from the television in the living room.

Lilian stared at the screen, barely glancing up when he entered.

"What is the big deal?"

"Trevor. It's Evelyn."

He followed Lilian's gaze to the screen. The news replayed the same images on a loop. Evelyn walking out her front door, a horrified look on her face, a man in a suit at her side. Then Evelyn on her back patio, head in her hands.

The text crawl at the bottom of the screen read, *Senator Christopher Brandt arrested today on charges of fraud and embezzlement. Authorities question Brandt's wife, seizing property in the couple's Loves Park home.*

"Chris. What have you done now?" Trevor walked in a tight circle around the living room, trying to process what he'd seen. The close-up of Evelyn's face told him she was terrified. His heart sank at the realization.

As usual when it came to Evelyn Brandt, he felt completely helpless.

Trevor went to the kitchen and grabbed a bottle of water from the fridge, willing away the images with no luck.

Lilian followed him. "Sorry; thought you'd want to know." She leaned against the counter. "Did you see her face?"

Yes. He'd seen. More proof of what he already knew. His old friend Chris had left her completely alone. Again. Who was going to clean up his mess this time?

"Why do I feel like you think there's something I can do about it?" He took a long drink. He had a fence to mend—and it had nothing to do with Evelyn. "It's not like I can waltz in there and whisk her away."

Lilian only stared. Her silence always said more than words ever could. He hated that.

"You want me to go over to a house crawling with federal agents and extract their prisoner." Even saying the words sounded ludicrous.

"She's not a prisoner. She's not under arrest. I'll call Casey—he'll know what to do." Lilian had that look on her face—the one that told him she had no intention of leaving this situation alone. She took her phone out.

Trevor had gotten really good at staying out of Evelyn's life. For the past ten years, he'd been nothing more than a blip on the radar of her past. He didn't like it, but that's the way it had to be. He could hardly rush to her aid now that Chris had finally messed up big enough for someone to notice.

Lilian set down her phone. "Casey didn't answer. I'm going to see her." Lilian grabbed the keys to the pickup truck from the hook by the door.

"This is a bad idea."

"She's your friend. At least, she was. And she's

got nobody." Lilian looked like a stubborn toddler intent on getting her own way. His aunt had had fifty-plus years to perfect that stubbornness. He supposed he shouldn't be surprised.

"Fine. I'll go. But I'm going alone." Trevor snatched the keys from her hand. "I don't want you anywhere near this."

"I've handled my share of trouble."

Of that, he was sure, but he didn't need Lilian getting in his head right now. He needed to be alone.

He drove in silence toward town. He dialed Chris's cell but got his outgoing voice mail message. He and Chris might've grown up together, but in recent years their paths had diverged in every way.

Chris was wealthy and charismatic. Trevor was middle-class and introverted. Chris lived a life in the public eye. Trevor much preferred animals to people. Chris had won the most beautiful girl Trevor had ever known. Trevor was alone.

It had been months since he and Evelyn had spoken, so why did Lilian's argument sway him?

He didn't leave a message. Instead he flipped on talk radio, where some newsman out of Denver was explaining what they knew so far about Christopher Brandt, one of the youngest state senators in Colorado history.

"According to the police, they've been building a case against Brandt for two years," the reporter said. "Questions were raised after his brief career in local politics in his hometown of Loves Park. Authorities now have enough evidence to prove he was embezzling money from the state to the tune of three million dollars."

Trevor let out a groan. Leave it to Chris to figure out a way to get rich from a life in public service.

"It remains to be seen whether the senator's wife, Evelyn Brandt, was aware of or complicit in the fraud, but we're told federal agents are at the Brandts' Loves Park home gathering evidence today. We'll continue to report on this story as the details are revealed."

Trevor rounded the bend that led to town while his mind wandered to the first time he'd met Evelyn. He, Chris, and the rest of the Loves Park High football team had just won a game against Dillon, their biggest rivals. The party that night was at Chris's house. His parents were out of town as usual, and Trevor's old friend loved to be the center of attention.

Trevor had walked in, fresh off his game-winning touchdown, feeling on top of the world. Until he spotted that new girl outside by the pool. His mouth went dry at the sight of her.

She sat in a chair next to two other girls, but there was something so different about her. He'd seen her at school a few times—even asked about her. She'd just moved here with her military family, someone said.

He barely noticed the people slapping him high fives, telling him, "Good game." Once he saw the new girl, all he could think about was finding a way to talk to her. And that said something. Trevor hardly ever started conversations with anybody.

But that was all in the past. As he drove through town, Trevor pushed the memories to the back of his mind where they belonged. Reliving his foolish feelings for Evie wasn't going to change anything about the here and now. She was someone else's wife, for pete's sake.

So why was *he* rushing to her rescue?

He arrived at the Brandt house to see that four news vans and six other cars had descended on it. Reporters stood outside. Men and women in suits milled around the porch, some of them entering and exiting, carrying what he could only imagine were Evelyn and Chris's personal property.

He parked his truck up the block and watched for a few minutes from a neighbor's yard, but there was no sign of Evelyn. On the news clip, she'd been outside on the patio.

He got out of the truck and moved toward the back of the house, careful to stay in the neighbor's yard, on the other side of the tree line and out of sight. The patio came into view, and after moving around some shrubbery, he spotted Evie, still sitting in the lounge chair, a man in a suit standing guard by the back door. She looked miserable and humiliated—and who could blame her? Once again, Chris had let her down.

After a few minutes, the patio door slid open and a woman dressed in a black suit appeared. She said something to the man who guarded the door, and the two of them disappeared inside the house.

Without thinking, Trevor moved to the other side of the trees. "Evelyn?"

She looked up, tears in her eyes. "Whit?"

"Come on." He moved toward her as she stood, then grabbed her hand and led her to the other side of the trees and down the block to where his truck was parked.

"I don't think I'm supposed to leave," she said as she got in the truck.

"Have you been charged with anything?"

She shook her head.

"Then we're leaving. We'll talk to Casey." Thank goodness one of his other high school buddies had gone to law school.

Once they were safe inside his truck, Evelyn wiped her face with her sleeve. "Do you think it's true, Whit? What they're saying about Christopher?"

He started the engine and turned the truck around. He didn't want to lie to Evelyn. But how did he tell her there was a side to Chris that she'd never known? She would hate Trevor if she found out what he knew.

Worse, how did he protect her from what he was sure would cause even greater pain? Because if there was one thing Trevor knew about Christopher Brandt, it was that there was more—a lot more—waiting to be uncovered.

CHAPTER
3

"You didn't answer me," Evelyn said after a long and silent drive back to Whitney Farms.

"What do you want me to say?" Trevor tapped the steering wheel with his thumb. "I hope it's not true."

"But it wouldn't surprise you if it was?"

Trevor's jaw twitched. He'd gotten more withdrawn and difficult to talk to over the years and he knew it. He couldn't be sure, but he thought Evelyn had even begun avoiding him in town—which was probably for the best. Now that she was a rich senator's wife, she didn't have time for people like him. At least that's what he told himself.

After a long silence, he finally said, "I know Chris lost a lot of money a couple years ago."

She shook her head. "How is that possible?"

"Bad investments." He kept his eyes on the road. "You know Chris—always has something to prove."

Evelyn stilled. "So what? He got desperate enough to steal from the government? From Loves Park?"

It did sound pretty stupid when he heard it out loud, but then Chris didn't always use his intelligence and political connections for good.

"They think I had something to do with this." Evelyn's voice trembled as she spoke. Did Chris have any idea what he was putting her through? Trevor wanted to drive to Denver, pull him out into the parking lot at the police station, and throttle him.

"You'll be fine. They'll do their search and clear your name." But even as he said the words, he wondered. What if it did come back on Evelyn? What if Chris had implicated her somehow without her knowledge?

This is not my problem.

They turned onto the gravel road that led to the farm.

"By the time they clear my name, all the damage will be done. Everyone in town will think I knew." She wiped a tear.

"So?"

Evelyn shot him a look. "So?"

"Who cares what people think?" He never understood that about women. Always so concerned with what other women thought. It made no sense to him.

Judging by the steeled jaw and tense shoulders, he'd offended her.

"Why did you come for me?" She sniffed, her eyes fixed on him.

He hated questions like that. So many feelings had to be hidden in order to answer. "Thought it was what Chris would want me to do."

Evelyn stared out the window. "You always did watch out for him."

Not lately. Not for years. Not since he married the woman Trevor loved.

And not since watching out for him came to mean covering up for him. Trevor wasn't a liar, but Chris had a way of turning people into something they weren't. Just look at his wife.

Or maybe he'd misjudged Evelyn all those years ago. Maybe she wasn't the kindhearted, thoughtful girl he'd believed she was. Maybe she'd always been caught up in power and money and appearances, and he hadn't noticed. It certainly seemed that way from where he sat now, on top of his John Deere.

He didn't respond. Instead he drove past the farmhouse.

"Where are we going?"

"To the guesthouse. I lived there until my parents moved to the retirement home, before they died. It's small, but it's quiet. No one will bug you there."

"I feel like a fugitive." She stared at her hands in her lap.

He drove around the bend and pulled into the narrow driveway in front of the guesthouse. A smaller version of the main house, the bungalow at the rear of their property had been his pet project for years. Some days, the old farmhouse seemed too large for him, and he considered moving back to the guesthouse, but at that moment it seemed the smaller house had a bigger purpose.

"I didn't even know this was here," Evelyn said as he parked the truck. "It's lovely."

Trevor laughed.

"What's so funny?" She looked offended again.

"Nothing. It's just not a word I hear around here very often."

"*Lovely?*" Her face twisted. "It's a perfectly acceptable word."

He nodded. "It is. For a rich person."

She rolled her eyes. "Maybe this is a bad idea."

"I can take you back to the reporters."

She glared at him.

"Come on. I'll show you around."

Evelyn sat in the truck while Trevor circled to her door, which he opened, waiting for her to get out.

She looked at him for several seconds but didn't move.

"You coming out?"

"Thanks, Whit. I mean, I'm probably going to be arrested for leaving without their permission, but thanks anyway. I couldn't stand to be at that house for one more second."

He shrugged. "Just trying to help."

Evelyn didn't know what to do with Trevor Whitney's unexpected generosity.

She knew better. He didn't have to help her. No one else had come over. Or even called. Come to think of it, there weren't many people in town she'd expect to stop by or give her a call. All she had were superficial friends. The realization made her feel a bit nauseous.

Still, Trevor Whitney was about the last person in Loves Park she'd have thought would come to her aid. She used to find him mysterious yet kind, but in recent years he'd turned cold. Irritable. And he'd made it clear he didn't like her or her lifestyle.

So why was he helping her today?

"Have you talked to Christopher?" She got out of the car and followed Whit toward the front door of the little white house.

"Tried him on the way over. No answer."

"They took my phone." Evelyn felt lost, like a child who'd wandered too far from home. She walked up the steps to the front porch. "You should plant some flowers out here," she said mindlessly, looking at the empty flower beds.

"I'll get right on that." Whit pushed the door open and stepped out of the way so she could go inside first. Evelyn nearly gasped when she saw the open floor plan of the Whitney guesthouse. Thick crown molding encased built-in book-shelves, and a fireplace stretched up to the top of the ceiling. Hickory floors throughout the house kept everything light and bright.

"This is an amazing space." Evelyn actually liked it better than her own house. It was cozy, not the kind of place you could get lost in. She couldn't say the same for the house she and Christopher shared on Brighton Street. Something told her it would be hard to feel lonely living in a place like this.

And she couldn't remember the last time she didn't feel lonely.

"Didn't used to be." Whit opened the curtains in the dining room, letting even more light pour in.

She turned in a circle, admiring the home. A photo on the mantel caught her eye. "What's this?" She picked it up.

"That's my dad standing right where you're standing."

All the built-ins in the guesthouse were new. The flooring had been restored entirely. Walls had been removed. Someone had done some serious work on this house, and judging by the aesthetic, she could safely say it was not Christopher's designer.

"It's like a completely different house."

"It's *lovely,* isn't it?" Whit's tone dripped

sarcasm. Her life was falling apart and he was cracking jokes. Or maybe he was just intent on making her feel foolish. He'd gotten awfully good at that, hadn't he?

She shoved the picture back at him. Never mind that he'd practically rescued her, she knew it wouldn't be long before his grouchy side appeared.

He stared at her for a few long seconds, then finally walked away. "I'll show you the rest of it."

She followed him to the kitchen. Good size for such a small house. "Bumped out the original kitchen a few years ago and added this breakfast nook." Another built-in, this one a wraparound bench edging a table along a row of windows facing the pastures behind the house.

"Who did this work for you?" She admired the butcher block–topped island that stood at the center of the room.

He frowned. "I did it."

"All of it?"

"I'm not going to hire someone else to do this stuff." He made it sound like the most outrageous idea he'd ever heard. How he and Christopher had ever been friends, she would never understand. They couldn't be more different.

It had been a long time since the first night she'd met Trevor. He'd been so kind then—but quiet and humble. A stark contrast to Christopher, who, even in high school, was larger than life. She'd been enamored with his ability to command a room—a talent she didn't possess or understand.

Back then, it was Whit she related to best, but it was Christopher who'd won her heart. He exuded self-confidence and security and everything she craved. Until today, their life had been nearly perfect.

"There are just two bedrooms upstairs," Whit said, pulling her from the past and back into her horrifying present. The realization that this wasn't a bad dream struck her all over again and turned her stomach over with a flop.

Whit continued. "Take the big one. There's a bathroom attached to it."

She nodded as though taking instruction from a teacher.

He stood awkwardly at the center of the kitchen, looking almost too big for the space. Knowing Whit, he wanted to be there about as much as she wanted him to be, and he had no idea how to escape.

Finally he said, "I'll run up to my place and grab you some food."

"I'm not hungry."

He looked away, an almost-wounded expression in his eyes.

Evelyn hadn't expected that. He needed something to do and she was making it hard for him. Why?

"Maybe just some coffee." The reality of her

situation hung heavy on her mind. There was no waking up from this nightmare. She was horrified to realize tears had filled her eyes.

He stared at her, an awkward, uncomfortable look on his face, and she begged her emotions to stay tucked out of sight until Trevor had gone, but the tears didn't ask her permission. They came hard, fast, and without warning. She turned away. How embarrassing. Never mind that this wasn't the first time Trevor Whitney had seen her cry because of something Christopher had done.

She felt his hand on her shoulder. He turned her around and pulled her into the kind of hug that didn't promise to make everything better. After all, the last thing she needed was another empty promise.

He held her while she cried bitter, angry, humiliated tears, anxious to talk to her husband and praying there was some sort of explanation for all of this.

But deep down, she had the most terrible, scary feeling that none of it could be explained. At least not in a way that would ever make sense to her. And the faint knowledge that this might be the case was enough to keep her confined to that very spot for far too many minutes, her shame and sorrow colliding right there in Trevor Whitney's kitchen.

CHAPTER

4

Trevor might've slammed the back door when he returned to the farmhouse. He might've banged a cupboard or two gathering food for Evelyn. It was possible he almost broke a pickle jar rummaging around in the refrigerator looking for coffee creamer.

"Trevor?"

And he knew his aunt was about to call him out on it.

"I don't want to hear it, Lil."

"Where is she?"

"Don't worry about it."

"I can help. The police don't scare me—what they did barging into her house like that was wrong." Lilian leaned against the doorjamb, eyes fixed on him. His mom's youngest sister had become a staple at the farm when her marriage went awry years ago. Trevor had been a teenager then with no plans of ever entering the family business.

But things changed. Some things, anyway. Not Lilian. For as long as he could remember, she'd always spoken her mind without any filter. Some might say she was kind of pigheaded, but they'd never say it to her face.

Truth be told, the farm wouldn't have made it without her. She was a whole lot more than just the lady who grew the vegetables. She was the voice of reason.

Trevor sighed, tossing a loaf of bread onto the table where he'd thrown the rest of the supplies he planned to take to Evelyn. "We need to try calling Casey again. Find out what we're looking at here."

Lilian stilled. "Are you okay?"

"This isn't about me, Lil."

"That's not what I asked."

Another thing about his aunt. She had this weird sixth sense when it came to detecting feelings he thought he'd done a sufficient job of burying. Somehow the two of them were cut from the same cloth, and it gave her the keen ability to read his mail.

He hated it.

Because, no. He was not okay. And he had her to thank for telling him about Evelyn in the first place. It was Lilian's fault Evelyn was now only a few yards away, in *his* guesthouse. Lilian was to blame for that hug—for the nearness of her, holding her in his arms. This was why he'd purposely put so much distance between them.

It would take days to erase the smell of her from his mind.

"Maybe I was wrong." Lilian sat at the kitchen table, letting out a heavy sigh. "Maybe I shouldn't have pushed you to get involved."

Now she was worried?

"It's too late."

He grabbed a cardboard box and threw the food in, then stormed out the door, angry at Lilian for pushing him. Angry at himself for listening. Angry at Chris for allowing it to come to this. He'd done a lot of stupid things in his life, but this was a new low. But that wasn't all, was it? He was mad at himself for still, after all this time, battling raw feelings for Evelyn.

He thought he'd gotten over it. He thought he'd set this one down and told God he was done pining away for someone who would never be his. It was wrong. She was married. To one of his oldest friends.

And he'd done a pretty good job of convincing himself he'd been successful. Until today.

Trevor set the box on the passenger seat of his truck and drove toward the guesthouse. Just as he arrived and got out, his phone buzzed in his pocket. A Denver number he didn't recognize.

Did the FBI know he'd gotten Evelyn out of there?

Against his better judgment, he answered. "Hello?"

"Whit?"

Chris. After all this time, Trevor was still his first phone call?

"Tell me she's okay."

Trevor involuntarily gritted his teeth. If Chris

were anywhere near him right now, he'd have knocked him out cold.

"Whit?"

"What did you do, Chris?"

"I can explain. Trust me. This whole case is bogus."

"The FBI sure doesn't seem to think so. Have you talked to your wife?" Trevor paced outside the truck, keeping an eye on the white bungalow just in case Evelyn got curious.

"No. They're only giving me one call, and I wanted to talk to you. I need you to do something for me."

Trevor sighed. He really wanted to punch something. Or someone.

"It's not really for me, Whit. It's for Evelyn. You've got a chance to spare her a lot of hurt."

Lilian was right. Trevor shouldn't have gotten involved.

"What do you want me to do?"

"I need you to argue the other side of this mess—my side. She's going to hear a lot of stuff about me, and you've got to find a way to put her mind at ease."

"What's she going to hear?" Trevor wasn't sure he wanted to know.

Chris paused. Now Trevor was sure he didn't want to know.

Trevor groaned. "I don't want to get in the middle

of this. It's not like you don't have hundreds of other people you could call."

"No one I trust." Chris sighed. "Whit, I promise. They've got no proof of anything. My name will be cleared."

Trevor kicked the tire of his truck. "They've got no proof, but are you guilty? Did you do this?"

"Trevor, you know me," Chris said.

Exactly.

With his free hand, Trevor took his baseball hat off and raked his fingers through his hair. "You knew this was coming, didn't you? You knew and you didn't warn your wife?"

"It's complicated. You wouldn't understand."

"Then why me? Why get me involved?"

"I knew you'd watch out for Evelyn." Chris paused. "Like old times." Trevor imagined him standing in the hallway of a nondescript jail, tie loose, sleeves of his pressed white button-down rolled to his elbows. "Have you seen her?"

Trevor rubbed his free hand over his stubbled chin. "The whole town saw her, man. It was on the news."

"How'd she look?"

Trevor shook his head. "How do you think, Chris?"

"Keep an eye on her for me, would you?"

"What makes you think I've got time?"

"I'm not asking you to become her best friend or anything. Just check on her. From a distance."

"How much more of this do you think she can handle?"

Chris sighed. "It's not as bad as it looks. Just give her a call. Make sure she's okay."

"They think she's involved in whatever mess you've made."

Silence on the other end.

"Chris?"

"I'll fix it, Trevor. You know me. I always fix it." He hung up then, leaving Trevor with conflicting feelings and a new sense of dread pooling in his gut. Why he didn't tell Chris he'd extracted Evelyn from their mansion on Brighton Street, he didn't know. Why Chris expected him to watch out for his wife, he also didn't know. Or appreciate. Chris obviously had no idea what this was going to do to Trevor's years of resolve. It had been forever since he and Chris had interacted at all—wasn't there someone else in his life to sweep up after him?

He stuffed the phone back in his pocket and picked up the box of food he'd brought for Evelyn. When he turned, he saw her standing on the porch staring at him. He let himself study her for a moment. She wore an outfit that likely cost more than his entire wardrobe, hair pulled up into a loose knot pinned to the back of her head. She looked like what she was—a senator's wife—and nothing about her resembled the Evie he remembered.

Maybe he really had fallen in love with someone who had never existed in the first place.

"Who was that?" She stared at him with glassy eyes.

He couldn't lie. Not to Evelyn.

"Unbelievable. He called you and not me." She shook her head and went inside, leaving the door open behind her.

"You don't have your phone, remember?" Trevor saw no point in telling her Chris had not, in fact, even tried to call her. Or warn her. Or do right by her.

No sense pouring salt on that wound.

He followed her inside and stood awkwardly in the doorway of the living room, staring at her back as she gazed out the window that overlooked the pasture.

"My life will never be the same," she said, her voice quiet.

He wanted to point out that maybe that wasn't such a bad thing, but he swallowed the words. Instead he shifted the box from one arm to the other in silence.

She turned, fresh tears in her eyes. "Thanks, Whit."

He held her gaze for too long, then looked away. "I'll put this in the kitchen."

She didn't follow him. Thankfully.

Get a grip. She is not yours.

He knew that. Of course he knew that, and he

would honor it no matter how difficult it was. But no number of words could convince his heart to stop caring what happened to Evelyn. He'd been trying for nearly fifteen years.

"I'm going to call Casey," Evelyn said from the other room. "Have him tell the FBI where I am and how to reach me."

Trevor pulled the food from the box and began putting it away in the familiar cupboards. Bread in the cabinet above the stove. Crackers and popcorn in the pantry. Coffee in the cupboard next to the sink and above the coffee-maker.

"Do you think that's a good idea?"

He turned and found her standing in the kitchen, that hopeful, helpless look on her face. Was it possible he'd forgotten how beautiful she was? No, he hadn't forgotten; he'd just stopped thinking about it. Which was what he needed to do right now. He'd walked away from her for a reason.

Remember that.

But he couldn't leave her alone. Who else did she have?

He nodded. "Casey will know what to do. Here, you can call him on my phone." He handed her his cell and went back to putting the groceries away.

"You don't have to do that, Whit," she said. "I can do it."

"It's fine. You've got enough on your mind. Go on, call Casey. I'll finish here."

She nodded and disappeared to the porch, leaving him alone with his thoughts, which, he discovered, drifted right onto the porch with her.

CHAPTER

5

Evelyn's conversation with Casey had gone as expected. He'd heard and seen what had happened and he couldn't believe it. He wanted Trevor to bring Evelyn to him immediately, and he'd call the FBI to act as her liaison.

"Can I go home yet?" she'd asked him, wishing she could at least get a change of clothes. Her luncheon attire only served as a tangible reminder of the phoniness of her own life.

"I should have an answer by the time you get here."

Now she sat in the passenger seat of Whit's truck, listening as he hummed the melody of some country song she didn't know and feeling comforted by the fact that in a world that seemed to change in the blink of an eye, some things about Trevor Whitney stayed the same.

Rough around the edges, Whit had always been a man of few words. Even when they were high school kids, no one ever knew what he was thinking. Over the course of their friendship, he'd opened up to her only a few times, and it was those glimpses that told her she was riding down the road with a very complicated man.

Never mind that he'd become irritable and standoffish, especially, it seemed, where she was concerned.

It was like they'd gone from great friends to perfect strangers overnight. She remembered once, not long after she and Christopher were married ten years ago, running into Whit at the grocery store.

She reached the end of the cereal aisle and nearly plowed over him, coming from the opposite direction.

"Hey, Whit," she'd said, happy to see him for the first time since he stood beside her new husband on their wedding day.

He nodded a hello.

"I haven't seen you since the wedding. How's it going?"

"Fine." He shifted.

She laughed. "Fine? That's it? We need to catch up—I'm sure Christopher would love to see you."

He met her eyes then. "You're sure, huh?"

"Of course. You're one of his best friends. Why don't you come over for dinner Friday? I'm taking a cooking class and I'm going to make a skirt steak."

"I'm more of a burgers-on-the-grill kind of guy. Say hi to Chris for me." He pushed his cart past her, leaving her standing in the aisle, confused.

Later, she'd asked Christopher why Whit would be so cold to her, but he waved her off. "Why do you care what he thinks of you anyway?" he'd said.

"He's one of your best friends," she said.

"It might be time to make new friends, friends more like us. People like Trevor Whitney can't understand the kind of lifestyle we're going to live, Evelyn."

From that point, they rarely saw Trevor anymore—and never socially. He became a part of her past. It shamed her how easily she'd thrown their friendship away. He might have originally been Christopher's friend, but she'd confided in him too. In some ways, early on, Whit knew more about her than anyone else in the world.

She glanced across the console at Whit, who wore a pained expression—always. The chip was still securely fastened to his shoulder, but he'd come to help her anyway. Why?

They arrived at the Old Town building that held Casey's second-floor office, right across from Willoughby Medical. Whit parked the truck, turned off the engine, and sat, hands still on the steering wheel.

"I can wait here," he said, eyes focused out the window, a troubled look on his face.

"Do you mind coming in?" Evelyn hated to ask, especially him, but she needed a friend and she supposed he was the closest thing she had right now.

His jaw twitched. "I think maybe you should do this one on your own." He didn't move his gaze.

The words dropped in like a sneak attack and left her feeling cold and alone. "Of course. I'm sorry." She hurried out of the truck, but before she reached the entrance to the building, she heard Whit's door open.

"Evie."

It had been a long time since anyone had called her that. Christopher insisted on full names. Formal and professional. It seemed so unimportant now. She stopped and faced Trevor, who looked like he'd rather be anywhere but there, with her.

"I can . . . I can come with." He slammed the truck door. "Sorry." He moved past her, opening the door that led to the office building, but didn't say anything else.

She didn't protest or say thank you. One thing she did remember was that Trevor didn't do well with thank-yous. Or apologies. Or emotions.

Perhaps that was why the comfort of his embrace had taken her so off guard. Knowing Trevor, they would never speak of it, and that was just fine with her.

They walked up the stairs and entered Casey's

office. Casey came around his large wooden desk and greeted them.

He pulled Evelyn into a side hug, like a brother or a person who felt sorry for her would. What Evelyn really needed was a good girlfriend. Instead she had Casey and Whit, neither of whom she'd spent time with since high school.

Oh, well. Beggars couldn't choose, right?

She sat on one end of Casey's plush tan sofa, while Trevor awkwardly took a seat on the other end, and told him the whole sordid tale. What she knew of it anyway. He listened with only the occasional glance at Trevor.

When she finished, he stood. "You're fine to go home. They got what they needed. I don't think you have anything to worry about."

She scoffed. "Have you seen the news lately?"

"I mean, I don't think you're going to be implicated. I spoke with the FBI—told them you were on your way over here, and if they wanted to charge you, to let me know. They don't have any real reason to suspect you're involved at this point, but they want to know what you know."

"Nothing. I know nothing. What is there to know?"

Casey looked at Trevor, who quickly glanced away.

"What aren't you guys telling me?" Evelyn could feel the heat as it rose from her neck to her cheeks. She felt like she was on the outside of an inside joke. Only no one was laughing.

Neither Casey nor Whit responded.

"Unbelievable. You think he's guilty, don't you?" Evelyn stood, eyes darting between Whit and Casey, then repeated her question. "What aren't you telling me?"

"He took it pretty hard when he lost his family's money," Casey said, refusing to meet her eyes.

"So you think he started stealing from the city? And now the state?"

"Sounds like they think he started stealing long before he lost his family fortune," Whit said.

Casey shot him a look, then returned his attention to Evelyn. "We have no reason to speculate. My only concern is for you. You're my client—not Chris."

"That's great, Casey. You're his friend. If you don't believe him, who will?" She glared at them for a long moment before walking out the door. She knew they were no doubt talking about her, just like everyone else in town, but at the moment she didn't care. Because while she was chastising Christopher's friends, she was thinking exactly the same thing they were.

That her husband might have secrets that were finally coming to light.

She plodded down the stairs and out to the street but quickly remembered she didn't have her car and was horribly at Trevor's mercy.

She wished The Book Nook were still in Old Town. She could slip inside and hide in one of the corners. Instead she turned at the end of the block and found herself face-to-face with three women she knew there was no sense avoiding: Gigi Monroe, Doris Taylor, and Ursula Pembrooke.

They let out a collective gasp and swarmed around her on all sides, making it pointless to even attempt a clean getaway.

"There you are, Evelyn. We've been looking all over for you," Gigi said, pulling her into an unwanted hug.

"How *are* you, dear? You must be a wreck." Doris's wide eyes reminded Evelyn of a close-up photo of a fly. She didn't like being examined like that.

Still, she knew they meant her no harm. In fact, if she was going to confide in anyone other than Whit or Casey, they were probably her only choice.

"Come on, dear. Let's go get some coffee and we'll talk this whole thing through. We'll help you decide what to do next."

Evelyn didn't respond but soon found herself being walked across the street and stuffed in the backseat of Gigi's Buick.

Ten minutes later, the four of them were situated at a corner table at The Paper Heart, Abigail Pressman's quaint business, which she'd opened after The Book Nook closed. The shop, a uniquely converted barn, had recently celebrated its first anniversary and hosted its second annual Paper Heart Ball. Evelyn marveled at how well the new establishment suited the young woman.

Abigail met them with coffee and a sympathetic ear. With the exception of Tess Jenkins, the entire group of Valentine Volunteers had assembled. The trouble was, instead of focusing on bettering Loves Park or making their latest match, they were all focused on her. And Evelyn didn't love the attention.

"I'm sorry, Evelyn," Abigail said. "But we don't know any facts yet. Maybe it's not as bad as it looks."

Ursula let out a scoff from across the table that mocked the comment. "Right. It's probably worse."

"Ursula!" Gigi whipped her head around and gave the older lady a look that *should* have snapped her mouth shut. But this was Ursula, and she had no reason to play nice. Ever.

She mussed her wild gray hair in a quick scratching motion, then took the end of her purple scarf and tossed it behind her shoulder. "I'm just saying these political types are usually guilty. Whatever it is, they're guilty."

"This is not just some politician we're talking about here," Doris said. "This is Christopher Brandt. Loves Park born and raised." She punctuated her sentence with a sharp nod.

Ursula only stared, looking as if she was making up her mind whether to point out that it didn't really matter. Criminals were criminals and every town had at least a few.

Evelyn just wanted to go back to sleep. Maybe she'd wake up and this whole nightmare would be over.

"What can we do, dear? What do you need?" Gigi reached over the table and covered Evelyn's hands with her own.

She shrugged. "I don't even know. I just can't believe this is happening."

"Believe it, sister," Ursula said. "Thanks to that man, your life will never be the same."

Evelyn's jaw went slack as she stared at Ursula, who popped the last bite of a cookie in her mouth and chewed. "Frankie always said there was no such thing as an honest politician." Crumbs fell from her lips as she recalled her late husband's sentiments.

Evelyn frowned. "Christopher is not a criminal. He wouldn't do this."

But even she knew the words sounded trite. She'd become *that* wife, the one who blindly accepted whatever tall tale her husband told her.

How had she let that happen?

No, she loved Christopher. And he loved her. There was no way she was going to presume his guilt without a shred of proof.

None of the others responded. Only the sound of Ursula's chewing broke the silence.

"I'm sure you're right, dear," Gigi finally said.

"Can we talk about something else?" Evelyn turned away. "The new store looks wonderful, Abigail."

Abigail smiled through her pity. "Thanks. I'm hoping to start some art classes for the community. You should come teach."

Evelyn smoothed her hair. How many years had it been since she'd held a paintbrush? "Well . . ."

"Just think about it. You might like the distraction."

"I doubt it. I think I'm going to have my hands pretty full the next few months."

"We could talk about when we're going to have our next meeting," Doris said. "We're in quite the matchmaking slump. Do you know last month was our second Valentine's Day without a wedding since the Volunteers were assembled?"

Evelyn didn't respond. She'd only joined the Valentine Volunteers because of their charitable work in Loves Park. Responsible for stamping letters and wedding invitations with the famous Loves Park seal, the ladies were a staple in their small, romance-obsessed town, but they did much more than decorate stationery. At its core, this small group of women took care of Loves Park. They provided meals for the sick or injured. They raised money to beautify the city. And they prided themselves on their matchmaking skills—and had quite a track record of success. They'd tried to pull her in to their tight-knit circle over the years, but Evelyn always resisted, content to float around its edges.

Sadly, none of that mattered to Evelyn at the moment. "Gigi, can you take me home?"

"Of course." Gigi stood.

"Are you sure it's safe?" Doris wore her standard wide eyes. "I saw on the news they were cleaning out your whole house. Those men reminded me of the crew that took E. T. away from Elliott."

"It's fine now, Doris," Evelyn said.

"Okay, then. We'll be checking up on you," Doris said.

Evelyn didn't doubt it.

The ride to her house was quiet. Too quiet. And Evelyn could sense Gigi wanted to say something. Normally she might've told the older woman to go ahead and say what was on her mind, but not this time. Not when she didn't want to hear any truth being spoken. She wanted to go on believing that maybe, possibly, somehow there was a chance her husband was innocent.

Even though her own mind had begun adding up inconsistencies.

The lake house. The vacation home. The jewelry he sometimes brought back from Denver. The fact that he'd never told her about any bad investments. She hadn't known he'd lost any money at all.

That alone spoke volumes.

"You all right, dear?"

Evelyn glanced up and realized they were sitting in her driveway, which—thankfully—was clear of news trucks. At least for now.

"I'm sorry, Gigi. Yes, I'm fine." She opened the car door.

"I'm here if you need anything, Evelyn," Gigi said as Evelyn stepped out. "I don't know exactly what you're going through, but I'm a good listener."

Evelyn smiled. "I know you are. Thank you." She closed the door and leaned down to the open window. "Thanks for the ride."

"Anytime."

Evelyn stood still while Gigi pulled away, leaving her alone with a too-large house that had likely been turned upside down.

Her heels *click-click-click*ed on the pavement as she walked toward the door, the sound of a light breeze rustling the leaves overhead. It was almost as if Evelyn were outside her own body, like this couldn't be her real life, only a dramatic reenactment.

But as soon as she opened the door, she was whisked back to the moment the FBI intruders had pushed their way in that afternoon.

She stood in the vast entryway, staring into the

living room. The marble fireplace stared back, mocking her.

The room looked like it had been plundered, drawers removed from side tables, their contents scattered about. How could this have happened?

Evelyn forced down the tears she desperately wanted to cry and began picking up the mess left in the wake of the FBI raid. She made her way through the living room to the kitchen. Why they'd tossed the drawers in the kitchen, she didn't understand, but one thing was certain: they weren't careful about it. Evelyn spotted her cell phone on the kitchen counter—the agents must have examined and discarded it already. She dropped it into her purse without checking for messages.

After she returned everything to its rightful place, she entered Christopher's study and gaped at the mess. Of course this room had been given the most attention. They'd ransacked it. What were they hoping to find that they didn't already have? While she couldn't say for sure that her husband was innocent, he certainly was smart, and if he'd been guilty of a crime, he wouldn't have left any evidence of it here.

Would he?

She closed the door, her desire to clean up the mess gone.

Upstairs, she made her way through more disorder into her room, where she found a pair of yoga pants and a sweatshirt. Christopher hated when she dressed like a gym rat, but she didn't care. Silk pajamas had never been her style anyway. Besides, he wasn't here to say anything about it, was he? According to Casey, they'd made a point to arrest him late on a Friday so he'd have to spend the weekend in jail.

Maybe that was good. What would she even say to him if he were standing in front of her right now?

The sound of the doorbell startled her. She glanced at the clock. It was almost nine.

Almost nine on the worst day of her life.

She stayed still and quiet, wishing all the lights were off, but the doorbell chimed again. Next, the house phone rang. She looked at the caller ID. *Whit.*

"Hello?"

"You're home, right?"

She'd left Casey's without telling him where she was going. That probably wasn't the best choice, but did he really care where she was? He was probably happy to be rid of her. "Yes, sorry. I'm home."

"I'm outside. Can you open the door?"

What was he doing here? Had he come to apologize? To tell her he was wrong about Christopher—that her husband couldn't have done those things and he was sure there was a simple explanation?

"Please, Evie?"

She walked to the door, receiver still in her hand, and opened it just as a van pulled into the driveway. He stood on the porch, phone up to his ear.

"Who's here?"

"Just get back inside."

He pushed his way into the house and shut the door, turning off all the lights and drawing the blinds.

"What's going on?"

Whit turned and faced her. "You ditched me after Casey's. I've been looking for you for over an hour."

Why? Why had he come looking for her after he'd made it so clear where he stood on this whole thing? He stopped inside the den, brooding, looking out of place and unhappy.

She frowned at him. "What's gotten into you?"

He glanced away. "I shouldn't have come."

Outside, another van parked in front of the house.

"What is going on?"

Evelyn watched him for several long seconds, then finally turned toward the television.

"Evelyn, don't."

She rummaged through a basket on the coffee table until she found the remote and clicked the TV on, flipping to a channel out of Denver.

Whit let out a groan.

Heat rushed straight to the center of her stomach as she watched in horror. Photo after photo of Christopher—her Christopher—in compromising, horrible positions. A talk show host with short blonde hair spoke, but Evelyn couldn't hear the words she said. It was as if her mind got stuck on the words underneath the image. *Mistress of Senator Christopher Brandt Comes Forward.*

Evelyn's skin didn't so much tingle as burn, as if that ball of anger radiated its heat from her core.

"What does this say about the senator's wife, Evelyn Brandt?"

The host's mention of her name pulled her out of the fog. Trevor reached for the remote, but she held it tightly.

"Either she knew everything and turned a blind eye, or that is one oblivious woman," the other host—a man in a black suit—responded.

"It does seem unlikely Mrs. Brandt was unaware of so many of her husband's indiscretions," the woman said, "especially when he seems to have documented each one."

"Let's keep in mind Mrs. Brandt has often been criticized for never really joining the political community. It's highly possible she knew and didn't care, but it's more likely Mrs. Brandt is the saddest victim of all." The host in the black suit wore a look of pity as he teased the next story coming up after a commercial break.

Trevor walked three steps to the television and shut it off. "Enough."

But the damage had been done. Evelyn had seen images she would never forget—not for as long as she lived.

She didn't even know her own husband.

And here she thought the day couldn't get any worse.

The home phone rang again and her parents' names and number appeared on the caller ID.

The hits just keep on coming.

Evelyn didn't answer, letting the machine pick up the call. She heard her mother's voice from the other room as she left a message.

"Evelyn, we received a very disturbing call from a church friend of ours this afternoon. I thought it was some kind of practical joke, but I'm watching the news. What is going on?"

Maybe, for once, her parents would be on her side. Maybe they'd sympathize. She could do with a little sympathy right about now.

"Who would do this to poor Christopher? Who would frame him like that? We need to get to the bottom of this. I hope you're at the jail trying to get him out of there. It's a wife's duty to support her husband—no matter what."

Her mother's voice faded, or maybe Evelyn simply stopped listening as a knot formed at the base of her throat. Her parents hadn't approved of her marrying Christopher—not at first—but he'd won them over eventually, the way he did with everyone. Now they would never see what she was only just beginning to realize, that there could very well be a side of Christopher none of them knew.

A flash from the yard drew their attention, and Whit quickly pulled down the only still-open blind in the room. "Stay here."

He hurried outside, shutting the door behind him. A few minutes later, he returned, out of breath and even more agitated. "I don't think you should stay here tonight."

She glanced past him and saw another news truck parked in front of her house.

Whit closed the door. "Pack a bag. You can come stay at the guesthouse. These people aren't going to leave you alone."

But Evelyn wasn't thinking about the news or the people outside or where she would finally go to sleep that night. She couldn't think of anything except the image of her husband in the arms of a leggy, half-clothed brunette.

And in that moment she knew Christopher was as guilty as they said he was.

CHAPTER
6

Evelyn lay on the couch, fully aware of the media circus outside her home. She'd practically forced Trevor to leave, but as soon as she was alone, she wished she'd gone with him. His attitude toward her was no match for the knowledge that these men and women were waiting to take her picture or catch her saying something they could play on tomorrow's news.

Not to mention, she hated being in her lavish house alone. She always had, and yet it seemed that's how she spent most of her time. Funny, a part of her married Christopher so young to avoid that very thing.

She tried—and failed—to fall asleep, too many thoughts tumbling in her mind. She thought about Christopher and the night they'd met. The big win on the football field had been reason enough to celebrate, and though she'd met only a few people in town, she found her way to the Brandt home. That night, it seemed like maybe Whit would be the one to eventually ask her out—after all, he'd sat with her most of the evening.

She later decided he must've been gathering information about her for Christopher because it was he—not Trevor—who called her a few days later and invited her to a Broncos game.

Evelyn didn't know Christopher very well, but he was gorgeous and confident, and from the beginning of their first date, he'd made her feel like she was the only person on the planet.

She'd never felt that way before. And they'd been together ever since.

Evelyn rolled over and wiped a stray tear from her cheek. She'd given that man everything. He was the only boy she'd ever loved. She never even looked at anyone else, let alone cheated—and this was how he repaid her?

She glanced out the window. Unbelievable. Still two trucks parked down the street. As if she wouldn't notice. The rest would be back early, she assumed. Everyone wanted to know how she was involved. What did she know? What was she hiding?

Would anyone believe that she was as much in the dark as the rest of the world?

With just an hour before the sun came up, Evelyn did the stupidest thing she could've done. She turned on the television again. She told herself she was going to find some old program to hopefully fall asleep to, but the truth was, she was curious.

"Don't turn the TV back on," Whit had said when he left that night. "Promise."

She hadn't promised, though, and he probably

knew she wouldn't because it might turn her into a liar.

Now here she sat, listening to the playback of an earlier talk show segment—commentators speculating about her husband's sins and her involvement in them.

"Do you really think Mrs. Brandt had no idea? Come on. Is she that naive?"

"Many women don't know their husbands are cheaters."

"But it's not like this was a one-time fling. Senator Brandt had multiple affairs. On an ongoing basis, dating back years. Tell me how Evelyn Brandt doesn't see that. Maybe she liked the money and the lifestyle too much to admit what was going on right under her nose."

Pictures of her house flashed across the screen. Then photos of the vacation home. Christopher in his Audi. Christopher and the other women.

Her heart raced. Everyone was talking about her, speculating about her. How she had become the focus of conversation, she wasn't sure, but did they really think she was in on all of this? That she approved of his lying and cheating and embezzling? No one who knew her could believe she'd actually been involved—could they? How would she ever convince them that all she'd ever wanted was a family of her own and a house in the country?

She looked around the lavish living room. Her choices certainly said otherwise.

She'd tried so hard to fit the mold that had been carved for her—the one that would give her the validation she'd been seeking for so many years—and for what? Now those efforts to become someone worthy of respect and admiration were all exploding in her face.

Evelyn turned the television off and walked through the house, the blue light of the moon mixed with the promise of dawn illuminating her path. She stood in the doorway of the kitchen, and the memory of last year's Christmas party flittered through her head.

In an instant, she could hear the jazzy Christmas music filtering through the sound system Christopher had installed earlier in the week. His colleagues strolled through their home as if it were a museum. Evelyn had spent the evening anxious and worried—about how she looked, about things going perfectly, about appearing like the ideal political wife when all she really wanted to do was curl up on the sofa with her sketch pad and a glass of merlot. But those were things of the past, weren't they? The only wine she drank anymore was the kind served at fancy dinner parties, swallowed with shallow conversation.

Christopher had insisted on the Christmas party.

"A way to give something back to the people who make what we do possible," he'd said. He spent a fortune on a professionally decorated artificial tree. Evelyn hadn't told him, but she hated it. If it wasn't a real tree chopped from the Christmas tree farm out on the edge of town, it wasn't worth her time. Who cared if it was lopsided or a bit misshapen or not the full ten feet he wanted? If it filled their home with the scent of evergreen and dripped spicy, sticky sap, then it won her seal of approval.

But then he hadn't asked for her opinion, had he?

Evelyn moved toward the island at the center of their chef's kitchen. Christopher had decided on brand-new stainless steel appliances. Granite countertops. Beautiful new cabinets.

She'd asked where the money was coming from, and he'd told her to stop worrying about it. They were fine. He'd make sure they were always fine.

So she stopped worrying.

The night of the party, a young guy in a suit had passed through the kitchen. "Anyone seen the senator?" But he snapped his mouth shut as soon as he made eye contact with her.

She smiled. "Jordy, right?"

In retrospect, Jordy had looked uncomfortable as he nodded his reply.

The caterer had everything under control, yet here she was, moving bruschetta from one tray to another. Hiding.

"I think he had some business to attend to in the study," she said, remembering what Christopher had told her. "Do you want me to get him for you?"

70

Jordy shook his head. "Oh no, no, that won't be necessary. It's not important." He glanced around the kitchen. "You have a beautiful home."

"Thank you." She smiled again.

From where she stood, she saw the door to the study open and Christopher emerge. "Oh, there he is now." She turned in her husband's direction. He met her eyes, then quickly looked away, intercepted by another man.

Evelyn finished plating the bruschetta as Jordy fumbled over his good-bye and disappeared amid the throng of people invading her home. Seconds later, Evelyn glanced back up just in time to see the door to the study close again, but not in time to see whom Christopher had been meeting with.

She'd assumed it was another suit.

She'd assumed . . . but what if . . . ?

Evelyn gasped, reality pushing the memory to the edges of her mind. What if the reporters were right? What if she simply didn't want to see what was going on under her nose? Had she been making up excuses for her husband all along, afraid their perfect little life would come tumbling down around them?

A wave of nausea rolled through her body as the walls of her too-big kitchen began to close in on her. She closed her eyes, focusing on slowing her breaths. *Breathe in . . . breathe out. . . .*

The image of Christopher walking out of the study assaulted her mind. He hadn't been in a meeting, had he? He'd been with a woman that night. In *her* home. A woman she'd probably welcomed and shaken hands with. A woman whose coat she'd probably hung by the door and to whom she'd likely served beverages and hors d'oeuvres.

Her pulse quickened as she struggled for a breath. Her head started to spin, and for a moment she thought this might be the end of her. Chest tight, she doubled over, aware that this one was too vicious to stop. She sat on the kitchen floor and inhaled. Then inhaled again and again but still felt like the air wasn't reaching her lungs. The tips of her fingers tingled and she desperately tried to calm her breathing, to keep her thoughts from racing.

How many minutes would the panic have control of her this time?

Seconds felt like hours as she finally—finally—convinced herself that she wasn't having a heart attack, despite the constriction in her chest.

You're fine. Just breathe. No one ever died from a panic attack. Right?

She'd been off her anxiety medication for months. She'd been doing so well. Christopher didn't approve of his wife being medicated.

"People will think you're crazy if they find out. They'll say you're mentally unstable—and that's the last thing I need to hit the newspapers."

She would've much preferred for that "scandal"

to be the only one in the newspapers, given what she now faced.

Besides, maybe she *was* crazy. Crazy for believing a single thing he'd told her since she'd first met him fifteen years ago, since she'd married him ten years ago. Was any of it true?

Just yesterday morning, the community had viewed her as a happily married woman with a beautiful home and a bright future. Even after hearing of the embezzlement, she'd clung to her perception of Christopher, desperately clutching the idea that these accusations were fabricated.

But now even her heart told her otherwise.

Those pictures hadn't been photoshopped. Her own memory hadn't misrepresented the Christmas party. Her husband had been cheating and lying and most likely stealing—for years.

Evelyn's mind quieted, her pulse returned to normal, and she lay on the floor, face pressed to the cool travertine tile.

Her entire life had been a lie. A lie that had her stomach in knots most days. She'd endured the spotlight, the public appearances, the social events because that was what Christopher wanted. What he said he needed. He didn't care that she was painfully shy—the worst kind of introvert. He'd never once asked what she wanted or what she dreamed of.

Worse, she wasn't sure she even knew the answer anymore.

After lying on the floor for too long, Evelyn finally pulled herself up and went upstairs. She needed a shower and a fresh change of clothes. Most of all, she needed to get out of this house. It was filled with Christopher's fiction and follies. The lies crawled out of the woodwork, and she knew they would continue to torment her if she didn't leave.

Maybe if she left early enough, the reporters wouldn't be prepared.

Mind spinning again, trying to land on her next move, Evelyn rushed to get ready and packed an overnight bag with clothing and shoes that might be appropriate for meeting with the authorities at some point.

Of all the women she'd interacted with at social functions, she supposed Susan Hayes was the kindest, the most like her. She quickly dialed her number and drew in a deep breath meant to bolster her courage.

"Hello?"

"Susan, it's Evelyn. I'm so sorry to wake you."

"Evelyn? How are you? I was worried."

She swallowed. "I'm okay. It's just kind of a zoo over here. I wondered if I could stay with you for a few days. Just until I get things sorted out."

There was a long pause on the other end of the line, the kind of pause that made Evelyn instantly wish she could take back her request.

"Never mind, Susan. I don't want to put you out," she said quickly, desperate to fill in the silence.

"Oh, Evelyn, I'm sorry. I hope you understand," Susan said. "I just don't think it would look very good for us to get in the middle of it. For Jerry's sake."

Her husband, also a politician, would certainly want to avoid any affiliation with the Brandts, and Evelyn couldn't blame him, though it stung to know that Susan would put that in front of whatever friendship the two women had.

After Evelyn mustered a "Thanks anyway," she hung up and swallowed a lump that had formed at the back of her throat.

Her mother's phone call replayed in her mind. She couldn't bear the thought of calling her parents in Texas, of admitting they'd been right when they told her she wasn't ready to be anyone's wife, of hearing them defend the son they'd never had.

She considered calling Gigi, but she didn't think she could bear the questions the older woman was bound to ask. Gigi was a fixer, and right now Evelyn didn't want the false hope that anyone could mend what her husband had broken.

She had no one.

She'd spent her life building shallow relationships that had no lasting value. Her only friends were Christopher's friends. Small-minded and judgmental, they would be more interested in the gossip than in her well-being.

Evelyn threw her bag in the backseat of her Lexus and started the engine. She opened the garage, aware of the reporters parked near her front lawn, and pulled away, certain there was only one safe place for her to go.

CHAPTER
7

If Chris weren't in jail, Trevor might've put him in the hospital. After Evelyn had left the office and Casey told Trevor all the media was saying about Chris's liaisons, the only thing Trevor could think of was going to see Evelyn. He hadn't intended on being there when she saw the news reports.

After years of receiving his coldness, she must have felt like leaving with him was a worse alternative than staying in a home that was under media siege, watching images of her husband's infidelity splashing across the television.

Told him a little something about where he stood with her, but whose fault was that?

He'd driven home in silence, wishing there were something more he could do, wishing she'd come with him to the farm—at least there he could keep an eye on her and make sure she was safe. And that might've been good for her, but it would've been downright awful for him.

He was already having a hard enough time figuring out his place in all of this.

God, I promised I'd put her out of my head. I gave this to you a long time ago, so if you don't want me to help her, I need you to make that clear.

He spent a long and sleepless night wrestling his conflicting feelings. He knew he'd been rude to Evelyn. It wasn't the first time. Somehow he'd decided that was better than admitting how he felt.

Morning came quickly, and Trevor needed coffee—and a lot of it. What he didn't need was waiting for him in the kitchen. *Lilian.*

"What are we doing today, Trev?"

"Not in the mood right now, Lil."

She glared at him. "We can't just abandon her right now. Her husband is a liar and a cheat."

She didn't think he knew that? He dumped a few spoonfuls of grounds into the coffeemaker and started it brewing. "What do you want me to do about it?"

"When John cheated on me, the thing I really needed was a friend," Lilian said. It was why she'd ended up at the farm all those years ago. Despite her rough exterior, that betrayal had wounded his aunt. Sometimes he wondered if she'd ever really recovered.

After his parents passed away, Lilian became a lot more to him than the farm's organic vegetable grower. She was like a second mom—the closest family member he had, and while he loved her for it, today he needed her to leave him alone.

"I know she's been hurt, Lil. Chris cheated over and over again."

And I knew it, didn't I?

The words tortured him. He swatted them away. What Lilian asked was impossible. Being Evelyn's friend wasn't an option—Chris had hurt her, sure, but Trevor's actions were also unforgivable.

Once upon a time, Evelyn had considered him a friend. A good friend. What had he done but abuse that trust?

Lilian crossed the kitchen and stood right in front of him, forcing his attention. "Look, I know how you felt about her, but that was a long time ago. She needs your help."

Trevor stared at the coffeepot. *Take your time.*

He had no interest in talking to her about Evelyn. He'd done his best to convince Lilian his feelings for Evelyn had disappeared the day she married his best friend because that's what *should* have happened, but Lilian always saw through him. She was the first one to call him out on his feelings for Evelyn all those years ago, and no amount of protesting on his part could lessen her loyalty to her own gut feeling.

Apparently his aunt had decided Evelyn's dilemma was more important than his.

"Do you think she's guilty?" Lilian asked,

pulling him from the past. "Do you think she was in on all of it?"

Trevor sighed. "I don't pretend to know anything about Evelyn Brandt, and neither should you. We aren't a part of their world for a reason."

A crash in the next room startled them both. Trevor moved through the kitchen toward the front of the house, Lilian close behind. When he rounded the corner, he saw her—Evelyn—in a heap on the floor, looking like a wounded animal in need of a home.

"Sorry," she said, barely meeting their eyes. "I didn't know where else to go." She'd obviously overheard his hateful remark and tried to make a run for it, but the table in the entryway must've tripped her up.

Lilian rushed over and helped her to her feet. "You can always stay here, Evelyn. We have plenty of room."

Evelyn slowly looked at her, then at Trevor, whose heart pounded at the sight of her in his house. He said nothing but instead turned and headed back to the kitchen.

Lilian's voice became downright chipper. "Do you want some coffee?"

He didn't hear Evelyn respond but assumed she nodded because seconds later she was sitting at his kitchen table. He leaned against the counter, holding his mug and feeling claustrophobic. How long was she planning to stay here? Was he going to have to share his morning coffee with her on a regular basis?

And how long would he be able to pretend he didn't want to do everything he could to make sure she was okay?

"I'm sorry to barge in on you guys," Evelyn said, taking a fresh cup of coffee from Lilian. "I was hoping last night's offer was still good."

Lilian shot him a questioning glance. He ignored her.

"Of course it is," Lilian said, sitting beside Evelyn. "We're just so sorry this is happening to you." Funny, he'd never thought of Lilian as the sympathetic type, but kindness overtook her. Where was that tough love she doled out in his direction?

Evelyn's eyes found Trevor's. "I won't stay if it puts you in an awkward position. I mean, you were always Christopher's friend more than mine."

Trevor looked away. If she only knew.

She took a sip. "I think I might need an IV of this stuff today. I hardly slept last night."

Well, they had that in common. But he didn't say so.

"Drink all the coffee you want," Lilian said. "I've got to check on my vegetables, but, Evelyn, if you need anything, let me know?"

Evelyn nodded. "Thanks."

Lilian went outside, leaving the two of them horribly alone.

"I really don't want to drag you into the middle of any of this," Evelyn said.

He fought the urge to tell her she could drag him anywhere and he wouldn't put up a fight.

No, that wasn't true. He'd been fighting it since he was eighteen. He lost Evelyn the same day he found her, and he had Chris to thank.

Now he'd become paralyzed somehow. Thirty-three and still very single. Every relationship he'd had felt wrong, like wearing shoes on the opposite feet. Even Rachel, whom he'd thought he loved, had ended up getting hurt because he couldn't fully commit to her. He didn't like being responsible for someone else's pain, so he'd stopped going out. Instead, he threw himself into the farm, into his work. No one would get hurt that way, least of all him.

"Did you hear me?"

Evie's statement gnawed at him. Wasn't he already in the middle? Hadn't he always been? "It's fine."

She watched him for several seconds, and he finally turned and dumped the rest of his coffee down the drain. "Stay as long as you want."

Evelyn needed someone to be kind to her, but it couldn't be him. She turned the cup around between her hands, staring at the steam from the hot drink, which gave Trevor a moment to study her.

She'd changed since she married Chris. Her

long blonde hair was always pulled up, makeup perfectly applied. Even the clothes she wore now were different. She'd been such a free spirit when they first met. It was part of what he loved about her—her ability to stay true to herself even though it sometimes made her an outsider.

Now there was only a trace of that girl in the woman sitting at his kitchen table.

She fidgeted, looking torn. He'd made her feel unwelcome and he knew it.

"The guesthouse is still empty. You should stay there," he offered.

She glanced at him. "Are you sure?"

"No one will even know you're there." He knew his tone was abrupt. It had to be. She wouldn't understand, but it was what it was. He found the guesthouse keys hanging by the back door and handed her the ring.

She took them and gazed at them for a few long seconds. "Thanks, Whit. I'm starting to feel like you're the only person in the world I can trust."

He looked away. "I've got to run to town. I have my phone if you need me."

What he should've said was that he had to run away. Far away. Because being around Evelyn made him think about things that could never, ever be, and that made him wish he could rewind the clock a day or two, ignore Lilian's dramatic plea to help Evelyn, and never involve himself in the first place.

He wasn't lying—he had somewhere to be. Because no matter what Chris asked of him, there was no way he was going to be able to convince Evelyn there was another side to any of this.

CHAPTER

8

A barrage of unwanted thoughts pummeled Trevor as he drove toward Casey's office. Knowing his oldest friend, he was spending his Saturday working on Evelyn's case. No way this ended well, and Trevor knew it. What was he doing? The second Evelyn said, "I do," every possible chance between them ended. His head knew this, but why couldn't he get his stupid heart to fall in line?

He drove through Old Town, trying to focus on the way the trees were starting to bud again now that spring had arrived or how the streets seemed to be especially full today, as if people had just been waiting for one ounce of warmth before descending on their small tourist town. He ran through a list of which vegetables needed planting and which needed harvesting, though he trusted Lilian to think about those things for him. He reminded himself to consider strategies to diversify the farm, make sure they didn't plateau. He needed new ideas— ways to grow their business.

That's what he should be focusing on. Not on Evelyn Brandt.

Trevor arrived at Casey's office, turned off the engine, and sat for a moment before going in. His reflections turned to his conversation with Chris, who seemed to believe Trevor had the power to convince Evelyn everything they were seeing on the news wasn't true. But Trevor knew Chris well enough to know better. Trevor couldn't even imagine how deep the corruption went.

Mostly Trevor wanted to find out if his old friend had implicated Evelyn in whatever he was mixed up in. Didn't corrupt politicians often use their wives to help hide money?

He shook the thoughts aside and got out of the truck. As he rounded the corner toward Casey's office building, a woman coming from the opposite direction plowed into him, knocking his keys out of his hand.

"I'm so sorry," she said, righting herself. "I wasn't even looking where I was going."

"It's fine," Trevor said, picking up the keys. "My fault."

"Trevor Whitney? Oh, my goodness. How are you? It's been ages."

He struggled to place her.

"You don't recognize me, do you?" She shot him a playful smile.

"I'm terrible with names," he said. *And faces. And people.*

"Maggie Lawson." She stuck her hand out in his direction. "We went to school together."

A vague memory passed through his mind. "Maggie. Right. You were in my sister's class."

She gave a sharp nod. "That's right. How is Jules?"

He shrugged. "She's . . . Jules. She's out in LA trying to be an actress."

"And what about you?"

"Can't complain." Well, he could, but what would be the point? "What brings you back to town?"

She smiled. "I thought it was time for a visit. Didn't think I'd see you, though."

He fidgeted with his keys. "I didn't leave for long."

She looked away. "I heard about your parents. I'm sorry. My mom's kept me up on all the news in town since I moved."

Trevor waved it off. Everyone knew about his family situation over the past several years— how Dad's health had cut Trevor's college career short and brought him back to Loves Park. Who else was going to run the farm? Most people his age wouldn't have to worry about caring for aging parents for quite some time, but his parents had been late bloomers when it came to starting their family, which meant Trevor hadn't had enough time with either of them.

Not long after the Parkinson's diagnosis, his

parents moved to a retirement home because they didn't want to be a burden to the family. Dad's health began declining and he passed away a few years later, leaving Trevor without the constant support and wisdom the man had always offered.

He could use some of Dad's advice right now.

"Where are you headed?" Maggie asked. "Do you have time to catch up?"

Trevor glanced in the direction of Casey's second-story office. Maybe this wasn't the best time to share his many concerns with Loves Park's most promising young attorney. What was he going to accomplish revealing he had more than a few reservations about their fallen senator anyway? Besides, if Evie was involved, he didn't want to risk getting her in trouble.

Maggie played with a strand of her wavy reddish hair, falling loose around her shoulders. "You're probably busy. Forget I asked."

"No. I could use a cup of coffee. And it'll be good to catch up."

She smiled. "Great. Is Barb's Diner still open?"

"Best omelets in Loves Park." He gestured in the diner's direction.

Barb's was a hole-in-the-wall restaurant only the locals knew about. Off the main drag, it wasn't trendy, and it wasn't fancy, but there was little chance of running into a tourist, reporter, or FBI agent, and that was almost as appealing as a meat lover's omelet.

They sat in a booth at the back of Barb's, and Regina Ray sashayed over to take their order. A few years older than Trevor, Regina had never let her age stop her from flirting, but now, as she stood inches from their table, her expression had turned sour.

"Hey, Whit. Haven't seen you in here lately." She filled his mug with hot coffee. Nothing gourmet about Barb's brand—it was black and that was good enough for him.

"Haven't had much time lately, Regina. Do you remember Maggie Lawson?"

"Can't say I do. Should I?"

Maggie's smile faded as Regina Ray sized her up. "Probably not. I was a few years behind Trevor in school."

The waitress wore a suspicious expression. "Why are you visiting now? Did you hear the latest scandal and want to get in on the town gossip?"

Maggie frowned. "What scandal?"

"Never mind. Regina, can you give us a few minutes to look at the menu?" Trevor gave her a nod of dismissal and turned to the menu that hadn't changed since he was in high school.

"You're awfully quiet." Maggie folded the edge of her paper menu.

"Usually am." Trevor didn't look up.

"I did hear about the scandal. My mom likes to talk. I just didn't want to make a thing of it, and the waitress seems like she's looking for more gossip," Maggie said. "I'm sorry about Chris. I know you two were friends."

He glanced up and found her eyes fixed on him. "Doesn't bother me any. Chris and I sort of lost touch over the years. We don't exactly run in the same circles anymore."

"Come on, Whit. You, Chris, and Casey. You ran the school your senior year." She rested her hands on the table. "All the girls loved you guys. I'm sure you still talk sometimes, right?"

Trevor didn't want to talk about Chris. Or Evelyn. Maybe this was a bad idea.

"Sorry," Maggie said. "I don't mean to pry. Just know if you need someone to talk to, I'm here."

He nodded, but he was pretty sure there was no way he was going to talk to Maggie or anyone else about what was really troubling him.

"So tell me about you," Trevor said, anxious to change the subject.

She leaned back in the booth. "Now *that* is a boring topic."

He couldn't help but smile. He noticed the freckles on Maggie's nose. They were cute. How long had it been since he thought anything about anyone was cute?

"But since I know you're not much for conversation, I'll keep up my end." She smirked at him. "I just moved to Denver last year. I work as a journalist for an environmental magazine. I'm like a hippie who happens to understand writing." She took a sip of coffee.

He wondered if she was choking it down to humor him. She had to be used to the gourmet stuff in the city.

She focused on him. "You?"

He shrugged. "Not much to tell. I run the farm."

"Still the same old Trevor." She shook her head.

He frowned. "What's that mean?"

The look on her face said she knew something he didn't. "Nothing."

But it wasn't nothing, was it? And while he couldn't pinpoint what she was getting at, there was something playful in her tone that made him curious. How long had it been since someone had flirted with him?

He'd perfected the fine art of keeping everyone at arm's length. No one but Lilian had dared come closer in years.

Before he could say anything, she covered his hand with hers. "I think you've gotten better-looking."

He held her gaze for a long moment.

She sighed. "It's good to be home."

The way she said it sparked something inside him. Something that had been lying dormant, and for the first time in ages, he wondered if this could be the second chance he'd been asking God to grant him.

Oddly, he didn't feel altogether uncomfortable with that idea.

CHAPTER
9

The bungalow at the top of the hill at Whitney Farms had an easy way of feeling comfortable to Evelyn. Probably more comfortable than it should've for as few hours as she'd been there.

A part of her felt like an intruder, especially given what she'd overheard that morning. Whit was only allowing her to stay because of his friendship with Chris, but that didn't mean he liked it. Still, she'd returned to the white guest-house to find a distinctly feminine selection of shampoo, conditioner, and body wash in the shower, and hanging on the faucet—a new loofah.

The whole place must have been recently cleaned and now smelled fresh, like cotton, masking the faint scent of bleach.

Evelyn reasoned that Lilian was probably responsible for the additions to the guesthouse. Who else would care to make it feel like a home?

She probably should've taken Trevor up on his offer to stay there the first time, but the whole situation seemed awkward, and she didn't want Whit caught up in any of this. Especially since she knew he didn't like her. Still, his cold shoulder was a welcome change from the paparazzi on her front lawn.

But Whit used to be one of Christopher's best friends. If ever there was a conflict of interest, this was it. If she'd had any other choice, she would've taken it, but something had drawn her back to the cozy guesthouse in the middle of nowhere. Something she couldn't quite put her finger on.

Her cell phone rang. She'd found it on the kitchen counter when she went back to her house, though a part of her wished she hadn't. She didn't much feel like talking to anyone.

She fished it from the bottom of her purse and saw it was a blocked number. Maybe Christopher had finally decided to call her?

"Hello?"

"Mrs. Brandt, this is Agent Marcus Todd. We spoke briefly yesterday."

"I remember. I believe you need to speak to my lawyer, Agent Todd."

"I've already spoken to him. We just need you to meet us at his office later this morning. We have to clarify a few things."

"It's Saturday." Evelyn didn't like this one bit.

The call waiting signal beeped. Casey. *A little late, buddy.*

"It's important," Agent Todd said.

"Just get the details to my lawyer and I'll meet you there."

"Great. Thanks." He hung up.

Evelyn switched lines. "Casey, why is Agent Todd calling me? On a Saturday?"

Casey sighed. "I told him I would handle it. I think they're trying to rattle you, honestly. Maybe they think you'll get flustered and spill whatever you know."

"That might work if I actually knew anything." Evelyn walked out to the back porch and stared over the pastures, where three beautiful horses stood, looking peaceful, like all was right with the world. "When are we meeting?"

"In an hour?"

She sighed. "Great." So much for peace and quiet.

Forty-five minutes later, Evelyn pulled into a parking spot across the street from Casey's office, turned her car off, and forced herself to take three very deep breaths. She couldn't afford to have even the threat of another panic attack when she met with the FBI. How guilty would that make her look?

She'd managed to pull herself together, dressing in a pair of dark jeans, a loose blouse, and a fitted blazer along with red heels, hair in a low ponytail. Evelyn somehow looked presentable again, despite how she felt.

She got out of the car, smoothed her hair, and slung her purse over her shoulder. She'd grown accustomed to going places alone over the years, but in that moment, she wished for a friend to help her face whatever was coming in Casey's office.

The brick building at the corner waited for her, and while everything within her wanted to turn and run in the opposite direction, she started toward the corner, where she would cross the street and face her accusers.

As she trudged along, she passed two women, who both nearly stopped walking for all their staring. Neither of them spoke—not to her face— but as soon as she went by, she heard one of them mutter, "I don't care what they say; that is the face of a guilty woman."

Evelyn's heart quickened and her cheeks flushed with fresh pain. She reached the end of the block and waited for the light to change so she could cross, keeping her gaze focused ahead and doing her best not to make eye contact with anyone.

She spotted Trevor walking up the block toward Main Street, accompanied by a woman she didn't recognize. In spite of this woman's presence, Evelyn's nervous heart stilled at the sight of Whit. He might be cold, but he wouldn't be downright mean. She stepped toward the curb, eager for even the appearance of a friend. The light changed to green and she crossed the street.

"Evie? You okay? You look upset."

She glanced at him, then at the woman by his side. Could they be together? She didn't realize he was seeing anyone—not that it was her business—but she could hardly ask him to leave his girlfriend and join her for a meeting with the FBI.

Trevor's words rushed back. He wasn't a part of her world for a reason. Maybe she should get it out of her head that he ever would be. No sense pining away for a friendship she'd destroyed years ago.

"I'm fine. I just needed to get out for a bit."

His brows drew together, but before he could question her, Agent Todd walked up behind him.

"Mrs. Brandt. Good to see you made it."

"Agent Todd." Evelyn stared at the ground as he and his dragon lady partner passed by, walking toward Casey's building.

Agent Todd stopped and faced her. "Don't be too long, okay?"

Evelyn nodded, avoiding Whit's scowl.

Once the FBI agents had cleared the walkway, she took a few steps toward the door. "Good to see you, Whit." She disappeared inside the building, praying for strength to handle this meeting on her own and desperately wishing she didn't have to.

On the sidewalk, Maggie wore an inquisitive expression. "Is she okay?"

Trevor took his ball cap off and raked a hand

through his hair. "I doubt it." He turned in a circle like an animal in a cage, unsure which way was out.

"You seem upset, Trevor. If you need to go—" Maggie stuffed her hands in the pockets of her jacket.

"No, I don't need to go. I just feel like maybe I should." He faced her. "She doesn't really have anyone else right now and we're old friends."

Liar.

Maggie's brows rose. "Jules always seemed to think you wished you two were more than just friends."

Those days were short-lived. Chris had seen to it. Sometimes he wondered if Evelyn even remembered it was Trevor she'd met first.

"Go see if she's okay. Really." Maggie smiled, sincerity in her expression. "She's lucky to have such a good friend."

Trevor knew it was wrong. He had no business butting in and no place in Casey's office for this meeting. But how could he not? Whether he wanted to be or not, he was invested in this.

"Maybe we can get together tomorrow?" Trevor glanced at Maggie, who stood about a foot shorter than him. She was different from other women somehow. Not so serious. She seemed . . . fun. And for the first time in years, he was intrigued to find out more.

The memory of Rachel's face the night he broke

things off with her rushed back at him. It had been four years, but the way he'd felt causing her that kind of pain was as fresh as if it had happened yesterday. He didn't want to risk hurting Maggie like he had Rachel, especially knowing that his feelings for Evelyn were more confusing than ever.

But that didn't mean he and Maggie couldn't be friends, did it?

"That'd be great," she said. "Can I see your phone?"

He pulled his cell from his pocket and handed it to her. She clicked around on it for a few seconds before giving it back to him. "Now you've got my number and no excuse not to use it."

She'd typed in *Maggie the Magnificent,* along with her phone number. He laughed. "That's bold."

"But true." She smirked. "Text me when you want to grab coffee tomorrow?"

He nodded. "Sure thing."

Maggie walked toward the center of Old Town, leaving Trevor standing in the middle of the sidewalk with a dopey look on his face and feeling more confused than ever. Evelyn was being interrogated one level above where he stood, and he'd just reconnected with a pretty amazing girl he probably never even noticed in high school.

The world had a weird way of keeping him on his toes.

Before he could enter Casey's building, a pack of three women bounded toward him, seemingly out of nowhere.

"Trevor Whitney, as we live and breathe. We hardly ever see you in town." Doris Taylor, one of his mother's oldest friends, fluttered her eyelashes in his direction.

"Morning, ladies."

"Who's the redhead?" Ursula Pembrooke. Old. Rich. Cranky. Like the wild-haired lady on all the Hallmark cards. Her voice sounded like someone who'd spent a hundred years smoking—gravelly and rough—but he had it on good authority she'd sounded like that in grade school.

"A friend, Mrs. Pembrooke."

"Awfully pretty friend, Mr. Whitney," Gigi Monroe said. He couldn't be sure, but it sounded like she sighed a little when she said it.

"Ladies, I know all about your matchmaking, and believe me, I am doing just fine."

Gigi took a step and planted herself directly in front of him. "Listen, Mr. Whitney," she said, her voice and face stern. "I don't know what you've heard, but we are more than matchmakers."

Doris stepped up behind her, eyes fixed squarely on him. "That's right, Trevor. We are do-gooders."

Why did he feel like he was in trouble? He put his hands out in surrender. "I'm sorry. I didn't mean to offend you. I just want to make sure you know I'm not looking for any help in the romance department."

"Mmm-hmm." Gigi sized him up. "So why aren't you married?"

"Is something wrong with you?" Doris asked. "You're not sick, are you?"

"Or gay?"

Gigi and Doris gasped at Ursula's question.

"What?" Ursula practically grunted.

"Nothing is wrong with me," Trevor said. "I'm not sick." He looked at Ursula. "Or gay."

Three sets of eyes narrowed on him. "Well, then what?" Ursula said.

He drew in a deep breath. The third degree was not what he needed, especially about his love life. The women seemed to inch even closer, waiting for an answer.

Trevor took a step back. "Don't you ladies have mail to answer? Or a festival to plan?"

"As a matter of fact, we do, but don't change the subject," Gigi said, giving him a bit of breathing room. "I can't believe you haven't been on our radar before now."

"Me neither," Trevor said halfheartedly. These women had matched or attempted to match just about everyone in town over the age of twenty. He didn't know whether he should be grateful or offended they'd never thrown his name in the ring. Did they not think he was a suitable mate for any of Loves Park's loneliest women?

"He is quite good-looking," Doris said to the others before returning her attention to him. "I always told your mother to keep an eye on you." She let out a slight whistle and shook her head. "The damage you could do with those chiseled cheekbones."

"And he's rugged," Gigi said, as though he weren't standing a foot away. "It's obvious you work with your hands. I heard all about the woodwork and the furniture. The paper really should do a story on you."

Trevor held his hands up as if that could silence them. "Ladies, please. I'm just a guy who runs a farm, and I can handle my own dating life."

"You still haven't told us what's wrong with you," Ursula said. "There must be something."

Gigi studied him. "No, I think there's more to our young Mr. Whitney than meets the eye."

Why did he get the impression that once they set their sights, there was no escape?

Just then—as if by the grace of God—the door to Casey's building opened and Evelyn walked out, pulling the ladies' attention off of Trevor and onto her.

"Evelyn, what's wrong? You look upset." They rushed to her, leaving Trevor feeling like the outsider when all he wanted to do was find out if she was okay.

Evelyn looked past the women, eyes locked on Trevor. "They think I'm hiding something. They think I know where Christopher hid the money."

She quickly blinked back tears. Even though Evelyn had turned herself into the picture-perfect politician's wife, Trevor knew her strength only ran so deep. But he remained unmoving. He wouldn't get involved any further. If she needed a ride or a house, fine. If she needed moral support, well, she had three very supportive women all over her right now.

He stood by while the women fawned over Evelyn, hugging her and telling her things were going to be okay. Finally he glanced up, surprised to find her gaze on him again. Something silent passed between them then because they both knew that despite what these well-intentioned "do-gooders" said, everything was not going to be okay. Not for a very long while.

Trevor yanked his focus off Evelyn and fixed it on the passing traffic.

"Have you talked to Christopher? Is he implicating you?" Gigi asked her.

"He hasn't called. I haven't called. I don't even know what I would say. Nothing about him is what he said." Trevor noticed that Evelyn had gone utterly still, like she was unable to move.

"Maybe we should take you home," Doris said. "You look like you might pass out."

Evelyn shook her head. "I'm never going back there again."

"Oh, my," Doris said. "What will you do?"

Evelyn shrugged. "I'm not sure."

She dared a glance in his direction, and what was he supposed to do? Turn her away? She couldn't go home with one of these pick-a-little ladies—she'd never have a moment of peace. She needed to be on the farm and they both knew it.

Trevor drew in a deep breath. "Evelyn's going to stay out at the farm for a while," he said.

The older women turned as one and faced him. "That will hardly do," Gigi said. "The press is all over this story. If they find out she's living with a single man in the middle of nowhere, what will they say?"

Trevor frowned. "Who cares?"

Slowly Evelyn looked up and met his gaze.

"We know the truth, so what does it matter?"

Ursula scoffed. "If only the world worked that way, Whitney."

"I have a guesthouse," Trevor said, though he really saw no need to explain. "It's empty and no one will find her there."

Evelyn nodded. "Thanks, Whit."

He placed a hand on her back and led her away, almost thankful she didn't seem to be fully aware of her surroundings because as he passed the three women, he heard Gigi say, "Ladies, I think we have our next target."

CHAPTER
10

Gigi Monroe watched Trevor Whitney whisk Evelyn to her car. While she didn't personally know Mr. Whitney very well, she did know that he had a kind heart—she could see that in the way he'd befriended poor Evelyn. He would make someone a wonderful husband. Maybe that cute redhead?

"I'm worried about Evelyn," Doris said.

"Why? Because she just left here with the most eligible bachelor in Loves Park?" Ursula asked.

"I'm sure he's simply being a good friend to her," Doris said. "She's married, after all."

"Girls, stop gossiping. Doris is right," Gigi said. "I'm worried about Evelyn too."

"Life is full of disappointments, Gigi; you know that," Ursula said.

She did know that. They all did. The three of them had experienced more disappointment and heartache than an entire town put together, but that wasn't what kept them going. The Valentine Volunteers were as much a Loves Park tradition as the painted wooden hearts on the lampposts and the Loves Park postmark. Their mothers had paved the way, and now they carried on the tradition with gusto.

While Trevor was right about their reputation as the town's premier matchmakers, Gigi knew better. They helped people however they could, cooking meals, cleaning houses, arranging child care—and if a little romance happened along the way, so be it.

Oh, who was she kidding? She loved when the romance happened along the way. It was her favorite part of being one of the Valentine Volunteers.

"Maybe Evelyn needs a project," Doris said, silencing Gigi's thoughts.

"I think the poor girl has her hands full," Gigi said.

"Doris is right," Ursula said.

Doris's eyes widened. "That's the second time in the last three minutes someone has said that. I think this is a banner day for me." She wore a proud smile.

"Evelyn *is* one of us," Gigi said. "She is well versed in all of our duties, including matchmaking, which, I needn't remind you, hasn't been going very well of late."

No, Gigi certainly didn't need to remind anyone of that. The locals were starting to wonder if they'd lost their touch.

"Oh, Gigi," Doris said, "I don't know if matchmaking is the kind of project Evelyn needs right now."

They walked back toward Gigi's Buick, the unofficial transportation of the Valentine Volunteers.

"Nonsense," Ursula said. "There is nothing better to take your mind off your own troubles than sticking your nose in someone else's." She pulled the car door open and got inside.

Doris stood on the sidewalk, clutching her purse. "Why does she always get the front seat?"

"I get carsick," Ursula called before slamming the door.

Doris looked at Gigi, confusion on her face.

For a moment, Gigi felt like the mother of two children vying for position. "Just get in, Doris. I'll buy you a muffin."

They drove toward the edge of town, where Abigail's shop, The Paper Heart, was located.

After a few minutes of pouting, Doris finally spoke. "Just so I'm clear, we aren't matching Evelyn, are we?"

"Doris, Evelyn is married." Gigi looked at Ursula. "Whether we like it or not."

"Not," Ursula said.

"We can't talk like this, girls," Gigi said. "We can't assume Evelyn's marriage is over." After all, couples had made it through far worse, and shouldn't Evelyn at least try to patch things up?

"You saw the pictures, Gigi," Ursula said, leaning toward her. "I don't care how strong she is—that's awfully hard to come back from. And let's be honest; Evelyn really isn't all that strong."

Gigi pulled into the parking lot of Abigail's shop. "God could restore that marriage, Ursula, and you know it."

Doris stilled. "Yes, of course. Time will tell if Christopher is willing to change."

Gigi turned off the engine and grabbed her purse. "None of this is our business. We should stay out of it and just help Evelyn when she needs it."

"Agreed."

"Agreed."

If they were all in agreement, why did it feel there was so much more to be said?

Inside the cozy shop, Abigail met them with their usual assortment of coffee, tea, and baked goods. Tess and Evelyn were the only two members of the group not present, but this wasn't an official meeting, so it was fine if they sat and had a chat, wasn't it?

Abigail half listened, half worked while Gigi and the others discussed their new plan—perfect for pulling them out of their matchmaking slump. As much as she emphasized the Volunteers' commitment to good works, Gigi couldn't deny that they had a matchmaking legacy to uphold.

"We're getting a bad name," Gigi said, "so matching someone like Trevor Whitney is just what we need to get us back on track and restore our reputation."

"Plus, we will need Evelyn's help, and maybe you're right. Maybe it would give her something to occupy her mind," Doris added.

Abigail glanced up from behind the thick wooden counter a few feet away from their table and shook her head.

"Why are you doing that?" Gigi asked, waving a pointed finger toward Abigail.

"Terrible idea." Abigail wiped the counter with a white towel. "She doesn't need a distraction right now, ladies; she needs time to figure out what's next. Her whole world has been flipped upside down."

"Well, so was yours, and you turned out fine," Gigi said, remembering how Abigail lost her store last year only to fall in love, move to a bigger, better space, and watch her business grow, all as a result of what she thought was a terrible tragedy.

"But how is helping us match Trevor Whitney going to help her?" Abigail said.

"Well, we can't do nothing," Gigi said.

Abigail started shaking her head again. "I'm telling you, it's a bad idea."

Doris gasped.

"Are you okay?" Gigi studied her old friend.

"I got an idea."

Ursula groaned.

Doris raised both hands, palms down, as if resting them on an imaginary podium. "The wooden hearts."

They all stared at Doris, who seemed to think her statement was sufficient.

"You're going to have to elaborate," Gigi said.

"We're always saying we're more than just matchmakers. Well, here's our chance to really prove it. The wooden hearts could desperately use an overhaul, and Evelyn is an artist whether she admits it or not."

Gigi couldn't believe it. Two valid points *and* a good idea? Doris really was having a banner day. Loves Park, "the Sweetheart City," carried many traditions, especially around Valentine's Day, and the wooden hearts were a favorite.

The fund-raiser was an age-old tradition in their town, and all proceeds went toward beautifying Loves Park. People could purchase a heart with a personalized message for their loved one, and a team of volunteers painted the messages on the hearts before they were all hung on the lampposts each February. But the current hearts were simple and straightforward—not nearly artistic enough for such a creative community. At least Gigi thought so.

Doris *was* right again. They could commission Evelyn to give the hearts an artistic makeover. And they could hire several other artists to get in on the display, pulling together the creative community and beautifying their city while revitalizing this old tradition at the same time.

When had Doris become so brilliant?

Maybe they could even squeeze a bit of money out of the city to help Evelyn—goodness knows the government had probably seized all of the Brandts' assets and put a freeze on their bank accounts.

She'd seen that happen once in an episode of *Law & Order*, so it had to be true.

"What about that kind of distraction, Pressman?" Ursula asked. "That pass your muster?"

Abigail shrugged. "It's not the worst idea." She walked away to help a customer.

"Girls," Gigi said, her voice just above a whisper. The others leaned in closer, and she continued. "I think we're on to something, and I think I have a way to provide Evelyn with a distraction *and* accomplish the matchmaking of Mr. Trevor Whitney all at once."

Doris clapped her hands together. "I can't wait to hear."

Gigi smiled. "Ladies, we are back. Our so-called slump is officially over."

Now. To figure out how to explain all this to Evelyn.

CHAPTER
11

"I think I need to go see Christopher," Evelyn announced as she entered Trevor's kitchen. It had been almost two weeks since the FBI had stormed her home.

Two weeks of keeping his distance. Of leaving her alone. Of pretending not to pay attention to when she was at the guesthouse and when she wasn't.

Christopher had made bail and sent word—through Trevor—that he needed to stay in Denver to sort through the mess the Feds had made of his life. He'd be in touch with Evelyn as soon as he had some good news.

"Keep her in Loves Park, Whit," Chris had said only hours after being released from jail. "I'll let you know when I need her."

When he wants to look like a dutiful husband, no doubt. Trevor had kept that last part from Evie, telling her instead that Chris was busy preparing his defense.

Which was not, he reasoned, a lie.

Trevor glanced up from his coffee and iPad. "Good morning to you too."

She'd knocked before she came into the kitchen

but hadn't waited for him to answer. Now he could see she must've been too anxious to stand outside for even one extra second.

He poured her a cup of coffee and set it on the table across from where he sat, next to the cream and sugar he'd brought out. It had become a ritual, a small way of making sure she had what she needed, and while she had a coffeemaker in the guesthouse, she still came to the main house each morning for a cup. He wouldn't pretend he hadn't wondered why. "You sure that's a good idea?"

She took a drink. "Why hasn't he called, Whit? Why hasn't he offered any kind of explanation or apology? It's been two weeks. Two weeks in a holding pattern. I don't even feel like I can show my face around town."

Well, he's a selfish jerk.

"The FBI said he's got money hidden, but they don't know where. They're taking everything. The houses. The boat. They even asked for a complete list of jewelry items he's given me the past four years." She looked away. "I think I deserve to know what is going on."

"Evie, what do you hope to accomplish by going to see him?"

She lifted her chin. "I hope to figure out if I still have a husband."

It wasn't a good idea, and he knew it. Chris would spin everything and Evelyn would buy it and she'd be right back under his spell. But it wasn't his place to stand in the way. They were *married*. And as much as it pained him, he wouldn't be the reason she walked away from that.

I just want to be her friend, Lord. I just want to be there for her.

The thought did nothing to comfort him because nothing about it rang true. Great, now he was praying lies.

"You look like you want to say something," she said. Always perceptive, that Evelyn.

He swallowed, then quietly shook his head. "You do what you need to do."

"Will you come with me?"

Trevor stared—a little too intently—at the black coffee in his mug. "I'm supposed to meet up with Maggie later."

Theirs was a casual friendship with the faint possibility of something more. He liked her. She was outgoing and upbeat. And she seemed to like him. A lot.

It was Trevor who held back. No surprise there. Since running into her outside Casey's office, he'd only seen her twice—maybe it was for the best that she lived in Denver. He preferred to keep whatever this was surface-level and nonthreatening.

Evelyn's eyes widened. "Oh, right, of course. I'm so sorry. You should do that." She got up.

"Evie, wait." He would probably regret this. "I'll come with."

"No. You have plans, and I really don't need to heap any more of this mess on you. You are already a saint for letting me stay in your guesthouse. I don't want to get in the middle of your relationship."

Trevor stood. "No, forget it. You need someone to go with you. It's scary out there. I'll call Maggie and reschedule."

Evelyn started to protest.

"It's done."

She let out a sigh. "Thanks, Whit. I'm kind of terrified to go."

He didn't respond.

"Maggie will understand?"

He shrugged. "We aren't a thing. I mean, we're just friends."

Evelyn studied him. Her eyes on him were unnerving. "But you like her?"

He sat back down. "I think your old-lady friends analyze me enough, don't you?"

If he didn't know better, he might suspect those three were following him around. He'd run into one or more of them every time he'd gone to town. Even at the feed store, there was Gigi, claiming to need a bird feeder. He knew better. They were going to try to match him, and there wasn't a thing he could do about it.

She laughed. The first real laugh he'd heard since this whole mess started. "They'll have you married off in no time."

He stilled. He didn't want to be married off.

"It really is a wonder no one's snagged you yet, Whit. You're like every girl's dream. Except for the crabby part." She refilled her coffee mug and walked toward the door. "Thanks for coming with me."

He nodded but didn't respond. He was too busy processing the words she'd just spoken. *"Every girl's dream."*

Stop it.

He could not let his mind wander down that dangerous path. He'd given his feelings over to God a long time ago—the day he found out Chris and Evie were engaged.

Chris had shown him the ring before heading over to Evelyn's to propose, and he was so proud of himself.

"She'll make the perfect wife," he'd said. "She's so into me, she'll do just about anything I say."

Trevor fought the urge to deck him right there. "Is that really what you want?"

Chris laughed. "Of course it is. I'm going into politics, Whit. I've got an image to maintain. Tell me Evelyn isn't the perfect trophy wife."

She was beautiful, elegant, and kind. Of course she was perfect. But there was so much more to her that Chris never even saw. Her creativity. Her free spirit. Her shyness. The way she wrinkled her nose when she laughed. Chris wanted to take all of those things away and turn her into a

Stepford wife. And Trevor couldn't just stand by and watch him do it.

"Are you going to stop seeing the other girls?" Trevor had glared at him.

Chris laughed. "I don't know what you're talking about." He winked. Didn't even squirm. He was so cocky, it wouldn't matter if Evelyn found out the truth. Somehow Chris would explain it away.

Maybe Evelyn would turn him down, Trevor thought. Maybe she'd remember how it felt when she was talking with Trevor and that would make her see there was something better for her. But she hadn't. She must've wanted out of her own house pretty bad to walk into a marriage with Chris.

Either that or she had no idea what her future husband was really like. And Trevor had to admit Chris could turn on the charm when it came to dating Evelyn.

Days after the engagement, Trevor showed up on Evie's doorstep, looking, he was sure, like a lost puppy in search of a home.

"Whit?" She answered the door with a smile, which quickly faded when she noticed his expression.

"We need to talk."

"What's wrong?" Evelyn stepped aside so he could come in, but when he did, he found Chris staring at him from the couch.

Chris stood. "You look like you just woke up, dude." He laughed, clapping a hand on Trevor's shoulder. Of course he was there. They were beginning to plan the wedding of the year, already set for Valentine's Day in Old Town Plaza. The future Mr. and Mrs. Brandt were now the talk of this romance-obsessed town, and nothing Trevor said would change that.

If he told her what he really thought of her fiancé, he'd come off like a jealous jerk.

"Everything okay, man?" Chris's raised eyebrows challenged him.

"Yeah," Trevor said. "Just wanted to give you guys my best."

Chris nodded. "Thanks. Means a lot coming from you."

Trevor gritted his teeth. In the end, he said nothing. He'd even stood up for them at their wedding. Made a speech. Toasted the couple. But the whole night, seeing Evelyn in that dress, watching her leave in Chris's arms, he was filled with regret.

Before she got in the car that would take them o their honeymoon suite, she left Chris for a brief moment and found Trevor standing at the back of a crowd of people waiting to see them off.

His throat went dry at the sight of her. She looked like she'd stepped right out of a fairy tale. "Hey."

She smiled. "I hope this doesn't change anything between us."

It doesn't. It changes everything.

"You're one of my best friends, Whit. I don't want to lose you just because I'm married." She stood on her tiptoes and kissed his cheek. "Thanks for everything."

He said nothing as he processed the way the nearness of her twisted his insides. She walked back to Chris, who stood waiting for her at the car. He leaned in and kissed her, then met Trevor's glare as if to claim his prize, as if to make sure Trevor knew Chris had won.

In the end, Trevor was right—everything had changed. It had to. Trevor stayed home to run the farm and Chris turned Evelyn into the trophy wife he'd always wanted. Over the years, the gap between them had widened as Trevor Whitney removed himself further and further from the world of Chris and Evelyn Brandt. He wasn't strong enough to fully stop loving her, so he walked away.

He hadn't stopped praying for her, though. Or for Chris. He prayed daily that God would get ahold of Chris in the way only he could, that his friend would straighten up and live a right life— if not for himself, then for Evelyn.

Eventually, those prayers became more infrequent as he simply stopped seeing the Brandts.

Evelyn had taken his departure from her life personally, but he played the part of an irritated

116

ex–best friend well. She could never know the truth.

Now, sitting in the silence of his kitchen, Evelyn's presence lingering in the air, he saw how stupid he'd been for so many years. This infatuation he had with Evelyn had kept him from moving on with his own life. She was the yardstick by which he measured every other woman, and it had to stop. In Maggie, he'd met someone worth knowing, and he owed it to himself to see where that might lead.

He'd go with Evelyn to see Chris, but only because he had some questions of his own. After that, it was time for Trevor Whitney to move on. Once and for all.

CHAPTER
12

Evelyn sat in the passenger seat of Whit's truck, staring out the window and worrying. Going to visit Christopher had seemed like a good idea right up until they began to see exit signs for Denver. She'd spent her life in the dark, and now that she was about to shine a light on the truth, she knew why. Not knowing was easier somehow. But it also made her a prisoner, and she wanted freedom more than she wanted comfort.

Christopher's hearing was just around the corner, and so far the media circus continued. Thankfully, though, it seemed no one was aware of where she was staying. How they'd managed to keep that a secret still baffled her. Would the press ever lose interest in the story?

Whit was quiet, as usual. She glanced at him, eyes fixed on the road ahead, jaw twitching like it did when he was deep in thought. If only she knew what he was thinking—ever. Mostly, when it came to Trevor, she had to fill in the blanks. He'd never talked about himself, not even in college when she'd considered him one of her best friends. Not even when his father's health put an end to his own college career and landed him back in Loves Park, which, she knew, wasn't part of his original plan. As the oldest of the three Whitney kids, he'd taken the burden of running the family business while life went on as planned for both his brother and sister.

But that was Whit. Always doing what was best for everyone else.

So different from Christopher, she realized now. Not that it was fair to compare. Christopher had many good qualities, though most of those were overshadowed by the pain he'd caused her.

"Thanks again for coming with me," Evelyn said absently. "I hope Maggie understood."

He didn't respond.

"You did call her, didn't you?"

"Not yet."

"She seems sweet."

He shrugged. "Yeah, she does."

She looked at him. "Just because my marriage is falling apart doesn't mean I can't be happy for you if you've found someone, Trevor."

He gave her a quick glance. "A few cups of coffee and a lunch isn't 'finding someone.'"

"Fair enough." She went back to watching the landscape pass by the window. "But there is the promise of someone."

"There's never a promise," Whit said. "Only a hope."

That was true, she supposed. What was it Whit hoped for? Whatever it was—whoever it was— he deserved it. He'd always been one of the best men she'd ever known, even when they were teenagers, when boys were notoriously foolish. Trevor Whitney walked the straight and narrow, put other people first, and despite his crabbiness, had a heart that always had room to give more.

She'd been living on his property for only a couple of weeks, but his work ethic astounded her. Despite its small staff of about ten people, the farm required long hours—many of them grueling.

She hadn't quite figured out how everything at Whitney Farms worked, but the little bits she'd observed intrigued her.

"You seem to have settled into quite a routine at

the farm," she said, figuring a change of subject was in order. "It's so peaceful out there."

Whit tapped his thumb on the steering wheel. "It has its perks."

"You have cows."

He looked at her, amusement in his eyes.

"I mean, obviously." She folded her hands in her lap. Changing the subject wasn't as easy as it used to be.

"We have horses too."

She smiled, knowing he was making fun of her. "They scare me."

He frowned. "They're gentle. I promise."

"I didn't know you had cows, is what I was trying to say." She'd spent time at Whitney Farms in high school and college, but she didn't remember many animals—just a few stray cats and a dog named Sugar.

"Farming isn't what it used to be," Trevor said, focusing on the road. "We have pretty good success with our vegetables. Lilian makes sure there are no pesticides, and people at the farmers' markets love that. We do a lot of markets all over the state and up in Wyoming sometimes."

She had the distinct impression there was more to this farming thing than she ever realized. How difficult to maintain something so important in a world that had become reliant on prepackaged, instant gratification.

"But we needed a boost, so I started researching

cattle. My dad always said they were more trouble than they were worth, but I liked the idea of giving people an alternative to what they can buy in the supermarket. Now we provide grass-fed beef to over a hundred local families and ten different restaurants in the area."

She stilled. "So you take care of all those cows just to kill them."

He tossed a glance across the cab of the truck. "Is this going to turn into a debate?"

She smiled. "No. It's just sad, isn't it? Doesn't seem to be much of a life."

He fixed his eyes back on the road. "They have an important purpose."

"Blindly going along with the rest of the herd? Every day a little closer to death?" She shook her head. "Not much of a purpose."

He shrugged. "I guess that's what makes them different from us. We get to choose if we want to add purpose to our days."

She didn't know how to respond. If he hadn't meant it as a dig against her, it certainly came across that way. Trevor had made it pretty clear a long time ago he didn't hold her in very high regard, and listening to him talk about his farm, she began to see the vast differences between their life choices. To him, it must look like she hadn't worked a day in her life. Just another human being sucking up whatever she could out of this world. Still, it had hurt, losing him as a friend. He'd always been so kind to her, and despite what he thought of her life now, he'd come to her aid. Oh, he was still irritable, but maybe that was just his way.

She had a feeling there was much more going on with Trevor Whitney than he would ever whisper to a single soul.

"What are you going to say to him?"

Whit's question caught her off guard. "I'm not sure. I heard on the news that if I'm innocent, I'll file for divorce."

He said nothing.

She hugged herself tightly. As if that could comfort her. "I guess I'm waiting to talk to him before I make up my mind."

"You think he might be innocent?" His tone didn't mock. It was a valid question.

Unwanted tears sprang to her eyes. Only a fool would think that. In her heart of hearts, she knew her husband was as guilty as the FBI said. He was obviously a cheater—was it that much of a stretch to believe he was also a liar and a thief? Maybe a part of her had known on some level for a long time. Christopher always seemed to be putting on a show for someone—even when it was just the two of them.

Whit didn't push her to respond. Thankfully. Instead, they drove the rest of the way in silence and reached Christopher's Denver apartment in record time. He parked the truck in the visitors' lot around the corner, but neither of them moved.

"This is the right place?" He looked at her.

She unfolded the little slip of paper she'd pressed into a ball in her fist and reread Christopher's address. So this was where he stayed when he wasn't home. She shuddered to think of all he'd hidden from her behind those four walls.

"I'm not sure I'm ready for this," she said.

Trevor turned off the engine and stared out the window. "Well, you're not alone."

He didn't look at her.

"Thanks for coming with me."

"You already thanked me."

Evelyn stared at her hands, wrapped around the handles of a much-too-expensive purse. "I don't have a lot of friends right now."

She found her words equal parts pathetic and annoying. How had she gone ten whole years making acquaintances and no friends? Everything had always been about Christopher.

They got out and walked toward the front door. Casey had explained that Christopher would have a hearing, which he thought was scheduled for the next day. Evelyn didn't pretend to understand it all, but according to Casey, one thing was clear. When everything was over, prison was very likely.

"He's going to want you at his side," Casey had told her. "It looks better if the public knows the people who love him haven't abandoned him."

She'd wrestled with that—her sense of duty in direct conflict with her emotions. Finally she'd decided she needed to see Christopher in person before she could ever hope to decide on her next step.

Now, though, walking toward the building where her lying, cheating husband had chosen to live instead of coming home to face her, she had second thoughts.

As they neared the door, it happened. First one click, then another; then a cameraman emerged from inside a van—all of them running in her direction. They seemed to pick up additional reporters on the way, like tumbleweeds rolling across a dry desert, and before she knew what had happened, a small crowd approached. Had they been lying in wait? Did they know to expect her there?

Would they ever tire of this story?

She glanced at Whit, who wore his standard irritated expression. For a moment, she wondered if it was her he was annoyed with. But then he put a protective arm around her, pulling her closer as if to ward off the enemy all on his own. "Just keep your head down and don't stop moving."

The questions started rapid-fire, like ammunition from an automatic weapon.

"Mrs. Brandt, are you involved with your husband's fraud?"

"Do you know where he hid the money?"

"Did you know your husband was cheating?"

"Are you and this man having an affair?"

Evelyn spun around and came face-to-face with the woman who'd asked that last question. "How dare you."

"Mrs. Brandt, who is this man you're with?"

Trevor's grasp on her tightened as he led her away and finally deposited her inside the building. The exchange had seemed to rattle even him. "You okay?"

She begged the tears to stay away. "They're treating *me* like a cheater, like a criminal."

He stood a few feet away, watching her. "You've got to ignore them."

Evelyn looked out the window and into the flashing lights of the cameras. "What a mess." Her heart rate kicked up. "What a disaster."

She saw him shift out of the corner of her eye, but then he went blurry. Her breathing became labored and she stumbled backward, leaning against the wall. "How could he do this to me?"

Evelyn's head started to spin, leaving her dizzy and unsteady on her feet.

"You okay?" He moved toward her, helping her to a chair in a nearby lobby. "What's going on, Ev?"

Her breaths came too quickly now and she couldn't respond, her heart racing inside her chest.

I'll never be good enough.

She'd striven her whole life to earn love. As a

child, she'd worked so hard to prove she was worthy of her father's approval, but she always came up short. Somehow she'd fooled herself into believing if she did exactly what Christopher asked, it would be different with him.

But she'd never met his expectations either.

And now everyone in the world knew it. They all knew she wasn't enough for her own husband.

Trevor sat down next to her and leaned in close. She couldn't be sure, but she thought maybe the irritated look on his face had gone away, genuine concern in its place. "Evelyn? What's wrong?" He took her hand in his. She squeezed it—hard. "Hey, it's going to be all right," he said. "Just breathe."

His words hung overhead until finally, after a long moment, her breathing returned to normal. But her eyes had filled with tears again. "I can't do this anymore."

Trevor stayed there for a few more seconds as if assessing whether or not she was actually okay; then he stood, that familiar troubled look appearing on his face. He stared out the window. "You're so much stronger than you think you are, Evie."

His words drew her eyes upward.

Her? Strong? When had he lost his mind?

"I don't feel strong," she said. "Maybe this was a bad idea. I don't know if I can look him in the face after everything he's done."

He didn't respond. Probably didn't know what

to say, he was so filled with pity for the shell of a person she'd become. Even she was annoyed with herself. She took a very deep breath and pushed herself to her feet. She'd come this far—she couldn't leave now. Besides, she deserved the truth.

No matter how much it hurt.

"All right, let's get this over with."

He didn't move. "Are you sure?" The chip had obviously taken up residence on his shoulder. "You didn't tell me the attacks were back."

She shrugged. "It's a recent occurrence."

His stare unnerved her. She pressed her lips together, wishing she were back home, in bed. But then she remembered she didn't really have a home anymore and even her bed would likely end up in some government auction. As if selling their things could repay Christopher's debt.

Evelyn went through the motions of getting on the elevator, pressing the number eight, and riding in silence to the floor where her husband now lived.

The elevator opened, depositing them on the eighth floor, and without thinking, she marched toward apartment 813 and knocked. Hard.

As they heard the lock turning, Whit stiffened, then looked at her. "You okay?"

She nodded, but inside, she felt anything but okay. Christopher appeared in the doorway wearing jeans and a white T-shirt. Whiskers covered his usually clean-shaven face, no trace left of the well-groomed rich kid she'd married all those years ago.

At the sight of her, though, something shifted. His face brightened. "Evelyn?"

She didn't move.

Confusion skittered across his face. "What are you doing here?"

She choked back the tears she'd wadded up and stuffed at the base of her belly. "I came for the truth."

He glanced at Whit, then back to her. "How are you holding up?" He spoke in gentle tones as if not to upset her.

"My husband has been arrested. My home has been invaded. My innocence has been questioned. My dignity has been stolen. And you couldn't even be bothered to call me."

He sighed. "You don't understand, Evelyn. I've been working on something. I'm handling this." He reached for her hand, but she yanked it away.

Anger smacked across Christopher's face. She wasn't behaving the way he wanted, and that never went over well, but she couldn't pretend. Not this time.

"Come in. Let's talk about this."

Evelyn swallowed, but her throat was dry. Did she really want to see where he'd been living? Did she want to know what kind of existence he'd chosen over the beautiful life she thought they'd built back home?

Slowly she took a step into the apartment. There was nothing lavish about it, though it did seem to have all the required amenities. He certainly didn't want for anything, in spite of his circumstances.

They stood awkwardly in the foyer; then Christopher looked at Whit. "Can you give me a minute alone with my wife?"

At first, Whit didn't move, just glared at Christopher like he wanted to rip his throat out. But after a few long, testosterone-filled seconds, he moved farther into the living room while Christopher led her toward the kitchen. The open floor plan allowed her to see that even though Whit was no longer within earshot, he was still watching as if somehow he could protect her from Christopher's weapon of choice: manipulation.

For once, she was prepared for him. Or so she thought.

Evelyn caught a glimpse of Christopher's tightened lips, but he quickly recovered when they were alone.

"You look good," Christopher said, motioning for her to sit down at the kitchen table. How had she not noticed it before? The way he switched emotions so quickly to get what he wanted? He was a master at it—she could see that now.

Sadness hovered above her, waiting to descend.

Was she so foolish to think there was any possibility of a positive outcome to this meeting?

Evelyn set her jaw. "What do you have to say for yourself, Christopher?"

He waved her off. "It's going to be fine. You'll see. No way they can prove I did anything wrong. I'll be back before you know it."

She stared at him, his arrogance spilling out on the table and driving a wedge between them.

"How many were there?"

A dumbfounded look washed across his face. "How many what?"

"How many women?"

He snapped his mouth shut. "I can explain."

"No, you can't. There is no possible way to talk yourself out of this. I saw the photos. The videos. You made a complete idiot of me. You weren't even careful about it."

Christopher leaned forward in his chair and reached across the table to take her hand. "Evelyn. I love you. I never meant to hurt you."

She blinked back fresh tears. "How many were there, Christopher?"

He looked away. "I'm ashamed of myself. I've got a problem. A legitimate problem, but you can't leave me now. I need you at my side if I'm going to recover from everything."

She swallowed.

"I planned to call about this, but now that you're here . . . My lawyer said I should ask you to come to my hearing. It's tomorrow morning. Please. It's going to be a long road, and we have to show a unified front. Having you there would send a huge statement to the judge."

She swiped at a runaway tear, angry with herself for letting it fall.

"Don't cry, babe. You know we're going to get through this."

She leveled her gaze. "Christopher, I know you cheated on me, but did you steal that money?"

He stared back at her, a slight, condescending smirk playing at the corners of his mouth. "How can you even ask me that?"

"The evidence is pretty strong. The FBI has questioned me twice now. They've shown me things—some I don't understand, but they think you're hiding money. They think you took it from the state and you've got it somewhere in some secret account. And they think I know where it is."

He didn't look away, but a calculated loo came over his face and Evelyn knew.

He closed his eyes, lifted his jaw, and opened his mouth to spew a lie that she would've believed only two weeks before.

Closed eyes. Lifted jaw. Lie told.

That was his tell. And in retrospect, she realized he'd used it countless times. The knowledge sickened her.

"I'm innocent, babe. I promise. You'll see. Just don't give up on me yet."

"How am I supposed to forgive you for all those women?"

He squeezed her hand. "They meant nothing to me. You are the only thing that matters. This is our year, remember? Our year to finally become a family. Don't forget everything we're working for."

It chilled her to realize how easy it was for Christopher to lie to her. He hadn't even apologized for what he'd put her through. Did he have any idea how upside-down her world was right now?

Still, she'd been raised to believe that marriage was sacred. It wasn't something you just threw away. Didn't she owe it to him—to herself—to at least try to make it work?

Her mother's words rushed back at her. *It's a wife's duty to support her husband—no matter what.* How disappointed they would be if their daughter ended up divorced and penniless. What a mess she'd made of things.

"I think we're going to have to see a counselor," she said, pulling her hands into her lap.

He stiffened. "You can't be serious."

"How else are we ever going to recover? Are you even sorry?"

"I can be sorry without spewing my feelings to some moron sitting behind a desk," he said. "You know that's not an option for us. I'm a public figure. Besides, I don't need help, Evelyn. I just need you."

She leveled her gaze. "You had me all these years, and it's pretty clear I wasn't all you needed."

His eyebrow rose ever so slightly. Had she dared to challenge him? "I'm not going to counseling. And neither are you."

She paused. "It started again," she said, not wanting to see if there was an ounce of concern on his face. He knew about her panic attacks. Her anxiety disorder. He knew she'd battled them since she was twelve, the last time her whole world fell apart.

"Shut it down, Evelyn," he said, his voice stern. "There are eyes all over you right now."

"Whose fault is that?" She raised her chin and focused squarely on him. For years she'd sat there like a clod, believing every lie he told, or not wanting to admit the truth about the man she'd married—or that she might be partially responsible for the state of their marriage. She'd been pretending. Doing what was expected out of some misplaced sense of duty. And for what?

"What did you say to me?" Christopher shifted in his seat.

"I came here for the truth, and I see it now." Tears rose up again, and it embarrassed her to realize that a part of her had actually been hoping he would give her a reason to work to save their marriage.

Instead, he'd made it clear he had no intention of working for anything.

"What is it you think you see?" His expression turned irritated.

"I see the real you," she said. "You broke my heart. And you don't even care."

He scoffed. "You're so dramatic. You know how important it is that you keep it together right now."

She met his eyes. "Can you promise me you're done with the other women?"

Closed eyes. Lifted jaw. "Of course, Evelyn. There's only you."

Lie told.

She stared at her folded hands in her lap. She had her answer.

And somehow, she wished she could plunge back into the depths of oblivion.

"So you'll come tomorrow?" Christopher's tone had changed again. He thought he'd gotten what he wanted. Thought he'd convinced her he could be faithful. As if a single lie was all it took. How many of those had she fallen for?

He took a strand of her blonde hair and tucked it behind her ear, then leaned toward her and kissed her cheek. "And wear that gray pantsuit I bought you." He gave her a once-over. "You look like you've forgotten who you are." She'd chosen dark jeans and a simple blouse for her meeting with Christopher. She thought it was presentable, but he always had something to say about her appearance.

She said nothing.

"Now go wait outside. I've got to talk to Whit."

Evelyn inhaled deeply, her anger bubbling under the surface. She hadn't felt this kind of hate for over twenty years. Not since she was twelve. The day she realized the world wasn't full of rainbows and unicorns.

She took the elevator down to the waiting area, where she promptly melted into a puddle of stored-up tears.

Life as she knew it was over and she had no idea what to do about it.

CHAPTER
13

Trevor hated that he couldn't hear what Chris was saying to Evelyn. The expression on her face gave nothing away. She'd become harder to read the older she'd gotten, but maybe that was because he didn't know her anymore.

After she left the apartment, Trevor stood and stared at Chris, who hardly looked like an acquaintance, let alone an old friend.

What would he do if Trevor clocked him square in the nose?

"Kind of you to bring Evelyn all the way here to see me," Chris said, sitting back down. "A heads-up would've been nice."

Trevor sat across from him, where Evelyn had been sitting only moments before. He could still smell the faint scent of her, like clean linen.

"Just trying to be a good friend."

"Thanks, buddy."

"Not to you. To her." Trevor clenched his teeth tightly.

"Oh, I get what you're trying to be to Evelyn." Chris sneered at him. "Quite the opportunity you have here."

"Don't be ridiculous, Chris. I've known you both too many years not to be involved in this, and you know it. Besides, you're the one who asked me to keep an eye on her."

"Took that advice to heart, did you?" He glared at Trevor across the table.

"You left her out there alone—do you know what this is doing to her?"

"Her? What about what this is doing to me?" Chris pushed himself away from the table. "Look at me, man."

"You made your bed," Trevor said.

Chris ran a hand over his chin with an irritated huff. "You were always such a Boy Scout."

"That's me, Chris." Trevor wouldn't apologize for believing Chris should reap what he'd sown.

Chris shifted, then leaned toward Trevor. "You know they're after Evelyn. They think she knows where I hid the money."

"You're okay with that?"

Chris shrugged.

Trevor inhaled the stale apartment air. "What makes you think you're going to get away with any of this?"

"I'm innocent, man." But the smug look on his face said otherwise.

Trevor rubbed his temples and let out a sigh.

"I know you're in love with my wife."

He looked at Chris, whose eyes seemed to drill a hole right through him.

"Can't believe you've still got a thing for her after all this time."

Trevor knotted his fists under the table, willing away the desire to reach over and wring Chris's neck.

"You gotta admit, I chose right." Chris leaned toward him as if daring him to lose his composure. "I mean, she is some kind of prize."

Trevor pushed away from the table and swore.

"Nothing pushes your buttons like Evelyn." Chris laughed. "It's been fun watching you squirm. It's like we're right back in high school and all you ever were to her was a really good friend." He punctuated the last three words with a sharp staccato tone. "Wonder how she'd feel knowing you knew about me all along and didn't say a word?"

Trevor's gut twisted. Chris had nicked an old wound—one that Trevor wasn't willing to attend to. He had known about Chris's unfaithfulness, but worse, he'd helped keep his *friend*'s dirty little secrets.

Chris met his gaze. "I'm not going to lose her over this, Whit. Got that?"

"Maybe you should've thought of that before you slept with half the women in Denver," Trevor spat at him. "What is wrong with you?"

"Someone like you could never understand." Chris leaned back in his chair. "These women, they just throw themselves at you. It's impossible to say no."

"I don't know how you can stand to look at yourself, Chris. You're worse than I thought."

"And a whole lot richer too." Chris smiled.

The man had no remorse. No concern for anyone else. He was completely self-absorbed, and the only things that mattered to him were money and power.

"Try not to get too close to my wife, okay?"

"Let her go, Chris. She doesn't deserve this."

"Not a chance." Chris's smirk was enough to make Trevor's blood boil. "I know Evelyn. She loves to save me, to make me a better man. It won't take much to convince her she's the only hope I have at rehabilitation."

"Why are you telling me this?"

"Because I don't want you to get any ideas. Evelyn belongs to me. You remember that."

Trevor had heard enough. He headed out the door without another word, wishing he'd never agreed to come with Evelyn in the first place. Chris was right. Evelyn was his wife, whether Trevor liked it or not, and this whole visit had reminded him of why he'd removed himself from that world in the first place.

He wanted to do the right thing, but from now on, if Evelyn needed anything other than a landlord, she was going to have to talk to someone else. He had to move on with his life or be completely consumed by this situation.

On the other side of the door, he pulled out his phone and found Maggie's number in his contacts.

Dinner tonight? he texted.

Definitely. ☺

Meet me at Barb's at 7?

I'll be there.

Great. It was past time to move on with his life and remove himself from Evelyn's for good.

CHAPTER

14

The ride back to Loves Park was tension-filled and full of silence. Whatever Christopher had said to Whit must have gotten under his skin, but he wasn't talking. Big surprise.

The two men had always had a complicated relationship, one she'd never really understood.

Evelyn wondered why Trevor was friends with Christopher at all.

"I don't even know what to think anymore," Evelyn said, breaking the silence. "He's not anything like who I thought he was."

Trevor drew in a breath. "Maybe he's just lost."

"Why do you always do that?"

He looked at her. "Do what?"

"Defend him. He doesn't deserve your loyalty."

Trevor returned his focus to the road but said nothing.

Anger wound its way through her belly like a snake in search of a cool, dark place to hide. She'd gone to see Christopher because she needed to give their marriage one last try, but she'd left with the distinct feeling he had no intention of changing.

So what now?

Her options ranged from bad to worse. She didn't know what she was going to do, but saying so out loud carried too much weight. Perhaps she'd been turning a blind eye all these years to avoid the very feelings that now smacked her in the face.

After a nearly painful car ride home, Evelyn curtly thanked Trevor for driving and then hid away inside the bungalow.

She took her shoes off and changed into yoga pants, a long cardigan, and a pair of slipper boots. She looked ridiculous, but she was comfortable, and in that moment she had no one to impress.

Something about that fact was wonderfully liberating. She'd spent years in her own house "done up" in case someone stopped by.

The knock on the door startled her. Nobody knew she was there.

She crept toward the living room, angling for a glimpse of whoever stood on the porch. With the side of the house obstructing her view, she inched closer until she spotted Whit's ratty red baseball hat.

She went to the door and yanked it open.

He seemed surprised. "That's a different look for you."

She pulled the cardigan around her. "I'm tired of dressing in those stuffy clothes."

" 'Bout time."

She only stared. "What do you want, Whit?" She hadn't meant for her tone to be so harsh.

He stuffed his hands in his pockets and focused on the porch. "I came to apologize."

"For what?" She knew words—any words—didn't come easily to him. She watched as he avoided looking at her.

"Defending him." Trevor ran a hand over his whiskered chin. "I want you to know I'm not on his side."

She softened. "It's an impossible position for you to be in, and I don't expect you to choose me over someone you've known practically your whole life."

He met her eyes. "But you were my friend too, Evie."

The words took her off guard. She hadn't been the recipient of a kind word from Trevor Whitney since they were in college. She decided not to point that out, though, and attempted to downplay the way it sent a warmth through her that was almost embarrassing. "Well, then you're the only friend I've got." She took a step back. "You wanna come in and watch a movie?"

He lifted his chin, and for the briefest moment she felt like he could see right through her.

Please don't see how lonely I am.

His stoic expression didn't change. "I wish I could, but I've got . . . plans."

Evelyn took a step forward to close the gap she'd left in case he wanted to come in. "Oh, of course. Go."

"And you're okay?"

Evelyn's nod felt a little too enthusiastic. "Have fun."

He lingered for a few more seconds, then finally turned and walked off the porch. She closed the door but watched for a moment as he got into his truck and drove away, realizing that his departure set something off inside her and dragged those unshed tears to the surface all over again.

It took every ounce of strength he had, but Trevor knew spending time with Evelyn that night would be a recipe for disaster. Even if he hadn't made a promise to himself, Chris's words haunted him. Chris planned on winning Evelyn back, and Trevor wouldn't get in the way. Despite all his shortcomings, Chris was her husband, and God could still fix their disaster of a marriage.

He pulled into the alley behind Barb's Diner and parked his truck. Maggie had probably already arrived, and as tied up as his heart was, he had to at least see if their connection could become stronger.

Come to think of it, bringing Maggie to Barb's again was kind of an insult. It wasn't the trendiest option, but it was the first place that had come to mind when they were texting.

She sat in the rear booth, typing on her phone.

He reached the booth and stopped. "Seat taken?"

Maggie looked up and flashed a smile. "It is now."

He slid onto the bench across from her. "Not the most original place for a date, is it?"

Her head tilted slightly and she studied his face. "Is that what this is?" They'd never defined it before.

Heat rushed to Trevor's cheeks, and he felt like an idiot, but before he could stutter a response, she reached across the table and took his hand.

"A date, huh?" She grinned.

"Or not."

"You're not getting out of this one, mister. What you said just made me feel like a teenager again." She squeezed his hand. "I'm on a date with Trevor Whitney." She glanced at the menu.

He watched her for a minute, unsure how to respond. As if being on a date with him was some prize. And yet, if she thought so, who was he to correct her? Her reaction gave him a little ego boost—and who wouldn't appreciate that?

"I thought maybe you were still hung up on Evelyn," she said without looking up from her menu. "What are you going to get?"

Trevor frowned. "What do you mean you thought I was 'still hung up on Evelyn'?"

She set the menu down. "Weren't you?"

"She's married to one of my best friends."

"I meant in high school."

"Oh." He pretended to read the menu. As if he needed a reminder of the single column of options at Barb's.

"How's she doing anyway?" Maggie went back to skimming her own menu, an awkwardness hanging in the air between them.

"She's fine, I guess." Trevor didn't look at her.

"Papers say she's not staying at her house anymore," Maggie said. "Guess I don't blame her. I wouldn't want to be reminded what a jerk my husband was either."

Trevor grimaced. "Can we talk about something else?"

Maggie's eyes widened. "Oh, of course. Yes. I'm sorry. I ramble when I'm nervous. I know you guys are friends and everything."

Regina Ray appeared at the end of their table, took their order, and doled out another healthy dose of flirtation, but Maggie seemed unfazed.

"You've got quite a way with the ladies, Mr. Whitney," she said, a twinkle in her eye.

He waved her off. She had no idea how untrue that was.

As the evening wore on, Trevor forced himself to hold up his end of the conversation. Maggie wasn't difficult to talk to, but his mind kept wandering back to Evelyn. There'd been a time he would've assumed she could take care of herself.

After witnessing her panic attack, though, he wasn't so sure. He'd assumed those had stopped the older she got. Now he wondered if they'd ever actually gone away at all.

In a flash, they were twenty again, sitting on the back deck of the old farmhouse, the summer air unseasonably cool.

By that point, Trevor had two years of college under his belt and he'd settled on a business major with plans of moving to Chicago or New York right after graduation. He was ready to get out of Loves Park for good and see the world—whatever it took to make sure he wasn't sucked back into this black hole of a town.

Never mind that he hadn't told his parents his

plan. They still thought he was majoring in business to improve the family farm.

Evelyn had called on a Thursday, right after he'd arrived home for summer break. At the sound of her voice, all the old feelings rushed back, and before he knew it, they'd made plans to meet at the farm "like old times."

Trevor knew they were just friends. He knew she'd invited Chris. He'd spent the last months pushing her out of his mind. But seeing her undid all the progress he'd made in an instant.

Her hair fell in messy waves past her shoulders, long and loose, driving him crazy. She smiled as she stepped onto the deck. "I've missed you so much, Whit." She wrapped her arms around him and squeezed. He tried not to linger too long, though the smell of her made it hard to pull away.

"Chris is running late, as usual." She gave him a halfhearted smile.

Somehow Trevor didn't mind Chris being late.

She joined him at the table on the deck, eyeing what he'd brought out for her—a brand-new pack of cards. "What are these?"

He grinned. "Rematch."

"You really are a glutton for punishment." She took the cards out of the box and shuffled like a professional card dealer standing behind a Vegas casino table. She dealt and the rummy began.

They'd clocked a lot of hours of rummy waiting around for Chris the past couple of years, even the last time Trevor saw her over spring break. "Just keep her busy till I get there," he'd told Trevor.

Trevor didn't ask any questions and pretended his friend was perpetually tardy, but he wasn't stupid. The truth was, Trevor liked spending time with Evie alone.

So he went along with it, knowing if she ever found out, it would break her heart.

They played in silence, and Trevor tried not to stare at her. She wrinkled her forehead when she was deep in thought and flicked the edges of the cards when she was close to winning.

"You're lucky you get to spend your summer here," she said absently.

"Lucky?" Did he need to give her a list of reasons to prove the contrary?

"It's so inviting. Peaceful."

"Have you met my father?"

She laughed. "Okay, you can relax *after* the chores." He watched her shuffle, then reshuffle her own deck. She kept her head low, her face turned away, but he recognized that look.

"What's wrong, Evie?"

She shook her head. "It's nothing. I'm fine."

He patiently waited until she finally met his eyes. "Things aren't so great in my house right now."

He didn't know much about her home life— just that her dad was a military man who liked everything in order, and she and her mom always walked on eggshells, doing whatever they needed to do to please him.

Evelyn rubbed her temples, her lower lip trembling as she fought back tears. "Today is the anniversary of my sister's death."

Sylvie. Evelyn had spoken of her only once or twice. She'd died in a house fire when Evelyn was only twelve, before her family moved to Loves Park. He supposed there were some things you never recovered from.

Evelyn swiped at the tears that were falling more quickly.

Trevor watched for a full horrifying minute, feeling completely helpless and unsure. Emotions weren't his strong suit and Evelyn wasn't his girlfriend.

But he did care about her, and what she needed most was to know she wasn't alone.

He moved to the other side of the table and pulled her to her feet and into a strictly platonic hug.

She wrapped her arms around his neck and buried her face in his shoulder, letting out the pain she'd been carrying for so many years. He stood, unmoving, and said nothing, choosing not to clutter the moment with vacant thoughts or empty words but simply to let her feel the weight of her pain.

When she pulled away, her cheeks stained with tears, she wore a faraway look. "It was my fault, you know."

"Don't say that, Evie."

"The firefighters came back for us and found me first. I was passed out in the hallway, but Sylvie was trapped." Her voice shook as she spoke.

"Ev."

"You should've seen the look on my father's face when they told him Sylvie was gone. He's hardly spoken to me since. I was never good enough for him to begin with. It was Sylvie he loved. It should've been me, Whit." The words cracked as her breath became shallow, her breathing labored. She leaned forward, struggling to get a deep breath.

"Evelyn? What's going on?"

The look of panic on her face scared him. She grabbed his hand and squeezed it—hard. Was she having a heart attack? Should he call 911?

"You're lost in thought, Whit."

Maggie's voice yanked him from the past, away from the first time he discovered Evelyn suffered from severe anxiety disorder, the first time he truly understood what a panic attack was.

Maggie smiled, but she had to be annoyed he'd been, as usual, a less-than-engaging conversationalist. This whole thing was a bad idea.

"Sorry. Lots going on."

Maggie stared at him over one of the house specials—burger and fries. "You might feel better if you talk about it."

She was wrong. Talking never made him feel better.

"You're really caught up in the middle of this thing, aren't you?" Maggie doused a french fry in ketchup, then tossed it in her mouth. "I bet it's hard, being friends with both of them."

She was perceptive, he'd give her that. Maybe a little *too* perceptive. He didn't want someone dissecting his feelings.

"It's complicated." He sucked in a drink of his chocolate shake and swallowed without tasting.

Maggie covered his hand with hers. "Well, they're both lucky to have you."

Yeah, I'm the guy who's been in love with his best friend's wife since the day I met her. They sure are lucky.

"You seem worried. I mean, I don't blame you. Chris will probably go to jail and no one really knows if Evelyn was involved."

"She wasn't." Trevor turned his glass in a circle.

"But you're still worried?"

Maybe Maggie was right, and he should talk to someone about the situation. Not about all of it—definitely not about his feelings—but he had reason to be worried.

The image of Evelyn slumped in the chair in the lobby of Chris's apartment building, struggling for breath, rushed through his mind. He didn't know much about anxiety disorders, but if it had that kind of hold on her, it couldn't be good.

"I'm losing you again." She ate another fry.

"Evelyn's . . . fragile, I guess."

Maggie's brow furrowed as a confused look spread across her face. "How so?"

"Anxiety. She has these attacks."

"Like panic attacks?"

Trevor drew in a breath. He'd promised himself he was done interfering. "You know what? Forget I said anything."

"Okay. But I would be worried too, Trevor," Maggie said. "I hope you're right and she's not involved with this mess."

"She's not."

Maggie stopped chewing. "But you said you don't really run in the same circles anymore. How do you know that for sure?"

Something inside him sparked, and he fought the need to defend Evelyn. "I think she's just got a lot of stress right now."

"I'm not trying to be argumentative," Maggie said, turning her attention back to her plate. "I just think it's worth considering. It's hard to believe she lived with him all this time and didn't know any of this was going on."

Trevor pushed his half-eaten burger away, his appetite gone.

Maggie frowned. "You're upset."

He shook his head. "I just don't like talking about my friends, is all."

She stared at him for a few seconds, then smiled. "Suit yourself. What kind of dessert are you buying me?"

CHAPTER

15

Trevor never fully recovered from the line of questioning during his so-called date with Maggie, and since he had little to no tolerance for pretending, it had no doubt been obvious to her that he wasn't as removed from the Chris/Evelyn situation as he'd led her to believe. Or rather, as he'd led himself to believe.

He did know one thing, though: he was a lousy date.

The night ended abruptly as he fumbled an awkward good-bye, no promise of another phone call or conversation. She probably thought he was a jerk.

And he was. A jerk with someone else on his mind.

He should've known better. Had his relationship with Rachel taught him nothing? He had no business getting involved with anyone else.

He'd first met Rachel at the farmers' market downtown. Turned out she and her mom and sister never missed one, and when they spotted Trevor, they started making a point to frequent the Whitney Farms booth.

She'd been everything he could've wanted in a

wife—beautiful and kind and smart. She had an infectious laugh that he could still sometimes hear echoing at the back of his mind. He'd loved her in a way, but when it came down to it and she asked him if he was ready to commit to their relationship, he'd hesitated long enough to give her the answer that broke her heart.

The look on her face had nearly killed him. He couldn't let that happen again.

He drove home from Barb's in silence, and as often happened in the quiet of a dark truck, he started to pray. For Evelyn. For wisdom. For forgiveness.

He'd wrestled for years with coveting what Chris had in Evelyn, and he begged God to forgive him almost daily. He'd go long patches without thinking about Evelyn or about what he didn't have, but then he'd see her in the grocery store or read a story about Senator Brandt and his beautiful wife in the newspaper.

Loves Park's reigning king and queen.

"She's not mine to love, God, but I can't abandon her. Not now." The words trickled out as a whisper, and he prayed God would understand the position Trevor found himself in.

No answer came. Nothing that told him to flee. Nothing that told him to be there for her. "I guess I'm on my own, huh?"

On his own with what he already knew—that he had to keep his motives in check, and that meant resisting the urge to tell her to get as far away from Chris as she could. He'd never point out that his old friend didn't deserve someone like Evelyn and he'd certainly never mention that if she'd chosen him that night he'd scored the winning touchdown against Dillon, her life would look very different right now.

"I would've loved her right, Lord." The words shamed him. Who did he think he was, confessing these kinds of desires? Justifying his feelings for a woman who was so far out of his league she practically had a different zip code?

If Evelyn decided to try to work out her marriage, Trevor wouldn't tell her to do otherwise. It wasn't his place. And he didn't want her to regret her decision because of him.

When he pulled into the driveway, he couldn't help but steal a glance at the bungalow. A light was on in the living room and he wondered if Evelyn was all right. Given the circumstances of the day—her panic attack and her run-in with Chris—he thought it would make sense to go check on her.

This time, his only motive was her well-being. *That's okay, isn't it, Lord?*

He wasn't surprised when no answer came. Either God had bowed out of this moral quandary or it was fine to proceed . . . with caution.

Or maybe God had stopped listening to him pray the same things over and over again.

He drove toward the guesthouse, parked in the driveway, and made his way to the porch but stopped before he reached the stairs. In the distance, underneath two sprawling cottonwood trees, Evelyn sat in one of the two white Adirondack chairs that had been in that same spot since before his parents left the farm.

He corrected his course and walked toward her, praying for strength and wisdom with every step that brought him closer.

"Evie?"

She barely moved.

"You okay?"

By the pale light of the moon, he could see she'd been crying, and once again he felt out of his depth. He could still throttle Chris for putting her through this, leaving Trevor to flounder as he tried to navigate the fallout.

"I went to the store tonight," she said, wiping tears from her cheeks. "I just wanted some ice cream."

Trevor sat down next to her.

Evelyn drew in a staggered breath. "When I handed the cashier my card, she took one look at it and threw it back in my face."

His fists clenched—an involuntary reaction to what she said. "What?"

"She said they couldn't accept stolen money." Evelyn's voice shook as she recounted the scene. "She said it loud enough for the people waiting behind me in line to hear her."

Trevor swallowed what he wanted to say.

"It's not enough the FBI has restricted my access to our savings, but people I've known for years think I knew about all of it. They think I was a part of it."

Guilt nipped at him. The fleeting question had entered his mind at first too. Even at dinner with Maggie when the question of Evelyn's innocence came up, he didn't know if he was angrier that she'd asked it or that he'd wondered the same thing himself.

But that was not something he'd ever say aloud.

"It'll blow over. You know how things are around here. As soon as there's something new for people to talk about, everyone will forget."

She sniffed. "I wish I believed that. How many more weeks do you think it'll be before it's safe for me to come out of hiding?"

He shifted in his chair, wishing for words that never came. Comfort, like conversation, was not his forte.

Evelyn hugged her sweater around her more tightly, sleeves covering her hands. "I feel so stupid. I guess I just have some hard decisions to make."

He begged his heart to stop racing and reminded himself of what he already knew. He didn't have the right to want her to leave Chris. He didn't have the right to tell her he never would've done this to her.

It would be wrong. Just like not telling her about his part in all of this was wrong.

So he stayed quiet, as usual.

She pushed herself up out of the chair. "How was your date?"

He was thankful for the cover of night; otherwise she might've seen the red hit his cheeks at the memory of the awkward date and his inability to focus on anything other than his concern for Evelyn.

"Just trying to be a good friend."

Guilt brought up the rear of that thought, as it often did when he wasn't being honest with himself.

Wanting it to be true didn't make it so.

"You like her?"

Trevor faced Evelyn. How he wished he could reach out and touch her. "She's nice, yeah."

She smiled. "Good. You deserve someone nice. Even if you are kind of grouchy." She clapped him on the arm and started for the door. "Thanks for coming to check on me."

"Anytime."

Her presence lingered long after she'd gone, long after he returned to the farmhouse, forcing himself to lie in bed. He knew her words were faulty—he didn't deserve someone nice at all. What kind of man battled thoughts like he did or put his life on hold for a woman who would never—could never—be his?

All those failed attempts at moving on taunted him now, but this time he had to see it through. Because he was pretty sure he couldn't live with the guilt for one more day.

CHAPTER
16

Evelyn had left Denver after her visit with Christopher tempted to rush straight back to Loves Park and file for divorce. He wasn't sorry. He showed no remorse, and he certainly wasn't going to change.

So why did she wake up the next morning—the day of the hearing—with an unbearable burden on her shoulders? How could she abandon him when he needed her most? Yes, Christopher had let her down, and no, he wasn't the man she wished he was, but he was still her husband. If she could help him, shouldn't she?

The pain of his betrayal collided with her overwhelming sense of obligation as she went through the motions of getting herself ready to drive to Denver and take her place at his side.

Christopher's observation of her appearance yesterday had left an indelible mark on her, and she returned to their Brighton Street house to pick up the crisp, tailored gray pantsuit he'd suggested, along with a pair of black heels. Back at the guesthouse, she took extra care with her makeup and hair.

Staring at herself in the mirror, she thought she looked the part. Dutiful, doting wife. Strong and put together, no matter how fragile she felt on the inside.

Fragile, yet angry. And anger wasn't something she usually allowed herself to feel.

She made herself a cup of coffee, poured it into a travel mug, grabbed her purse, and headed out to the car, surprised to find Whit walking up the hill. Embarrassment washed over her. He must think she was such a pushover to even consider going back to Denver after the way Christopher had treated her. And in the exact clothes he'd ordered her to wear.

"You're going," he said when he reached her.

She steeled her jaw. "I am."

She expected him to have an opinion on her decision—or to say something to make her question herself—but he didn't. Instead, he pointed at the coffee mug she'd dug out from the back of one of the guesthouse's kitchen cabinets. "You have enough to get you through?"

"I think so." Gratitude overwhelmed her. He seemed intent on doing the opposite of what she'd expected. What a relief.

But as she studied him, she realized her relief was unfounded. Whit wore his standard pair of old jeans, work boots, and T-shirt underneath an unbuttoned plaid shirt, along with a pained expression.

"What is it?"

He looked past her, down the hill toward the greenhouse, where Lilian was in charge of the organic vegetables.

"You obviously have something on your mind, so just say it."

"What if . . . ?" He sighed. "Do you have some medication or something? You know, in case . . . ?" His worried look finished the sentence for him.

Evelyn nodded. She'd dug out one of her old prescription bottles that still had a few pills in it. Was he actually concerned about her?

He toed his work boot into the gravel drive. "Let me know if you need anything." He squeezed her arm and then walked away, toward one of the barns at the back of the farm.

The weight of his decision not to judge her lodged a lump squarely in the center of her throat. She wasn't accustomed to being accepted without question. How had he managed to do that?

She supposed that's what it was like to have a real friend. Not like those women she spent most of her time with, the ones who had stopped calling the day her husband was arrested.

Evelyn watched as Whit disappeared inside the white barn and, for the first time since she arrived at Whitney Farms, wondered what was in there.

Probably more cows. Did her onetime friend share his secrets with them?

She began the drive to Denver, fighting off the barrage of unwanted what-ifs and whys and *What am I going to do next?* questions. She nearly turned around twice, certain that showing up in that courtroom would make her look like either she condoned Christopher's behavior or she'd been a part of it.

But duty trumped everything else and she arrived at the courthouse ten minutes early, parked the car, and stared at the building, wondering how she'd make it to the courthouse door alone. She'd have to march her way through a throng of reporters, and Christopher hadn't even arranged for his lawyer to meet her there.

She checked her lipstick in the rearview mirror and placed her oversize sunglasses on her face. As if that would hide her shame.

Evelyn stood outside the car for a long moment, visualizing her walk from the parking lot to the door. Years ago, her therapist had told her it would help to visualize uncomfortable situations *before* she walked right into them.

So she did. Over and over.

"It's now or never," she said, smoothing back her hair and forcing herself to put one foot in front of the other. She inhaled. Exhaled. Kept her eye on the courthouse door.

"It's her!" A throng of reporters shuffled their

way toward her, shouting questions intended to garner a reaction.

She ignored them. The cameras clicked in her face as the small crowd circled around her and moved toward the steps of the building. She continued to focus on the door, breathing steadily, wondering why on earth no one had thought to send someone out here to escort her in. She was doing Christopher a favor—the least he could've done was provide a safe entrance to the building. She'd almost made it to the door when, without warning, her heel caught in the crack of the sidewalk and sent her tumbling forward.

She landed on the pavement, her knees taking the brunt of the fall, the contents of her purse spilling out onto the sidewalk. She reached out with her skinned hand and was grabbing a runaway lipstick when one of the reporters dropped to her knees beside Evelyn, raking other escaped items back into Evelyn's purse for her.

Evelyn didn't look up, concentrating instead on collecting her wallet, her phone, and her car keys. She zipped the purse closed, and before she stood, the woman handed her a small bottle of hand sanitizer.

Evelyn took it with a quiet thank-you and glanced toward the woman. She'd already turned her back and begun disappearing into the crowd, but there was something familiar about her. Evelyn couldn't place it.

She tucked the hand sanitizer into her purse and pushed herself up, humiliated, forcing herself to move forward. She couldn't wait to watch that replay over and over again on tonight's news.

Her heart raced, the threat of panic lingering at her edges. She concentrated on the *click-click-click* of her heels on the pavement until she finally escaped inside the courthouse, drawing in a deep breath as the door behind her closed. She spotted the sign for the restroom and hurried in, locking the stall behind her and willing her pulse to slow, her breathing to steady.

When she was unsuccessful, she rummaged through her purse, searching for the medication she should've taken before she ever left Loves Park.

She took everything out but found no pills. She wouldn't have left them behind, would she? An image of her fall outside rushed at her like the bulls of Pamplona.

Oh no.

What if one of those reporters had her medication? They would know she'd been to a therapist, and they'd learn from the date on the bottle that it wasn't a result of Christopher's arrest.

Quietly, she bowed her head in the stall and whispered a prayer, begging God to do for her what the missing medication would have done. "I don't deserve it, Lord, but if you could give me a little help today, I would so appreciate it. Calm my nerves and give me strength."

Her phone buzzed. A text from Christopher's lawyer. **Where are you?**

She shoved everything back in her purse and opened the stall, catching a glimpse of herself in the mirror. On the outside, she looked like a wealthy politician's wife. No one would ever guess that within, she was falling apart.

She found the courtroom where Christopher's hearing was about to begin, rushed inside, and slid into a seat, taking a moment to survey the crowd.

Reporters, mostly, but also a few people who worked for Christopher. One unfamiliar woman sat across the aisle, glaring at her.

A wave of nausea skittered through her. What if this woman was one of Christopher's mistresses? Or one of the people he'd cheated? He had amassed more than his share of enemies. Would they take their anger out on her?

She folded her hands in her lap and drew in a deep breath, praying for the second time that morning. A record for her these days.

Nothing elaborate, just a simple *Help me, Lord. Please give me strength today.*

Two police officers ushered Christopher into the courtroom. He was clean-shaven and wore a suit and tie.

Christopher met her eyes and smiled, warmth in his face. The clicking of cameras behind her pulled her attention from him, and she knew his greeting was only for show. How did he do that? Didn't he tire of always being "on"?

Before he sat, he gave her a barely noticeable nod as if to tell her to do everything she could to make him look better. In other words, don't mess this up. She turned away.

After the judge entered through the door behind the bench, Evelyn listened as the two lawyers argued opposing sides of the case. The prosecutor wanted Christopher locked up. The defense attorney tenaciously maintained his client's innocence.

The prosecutor let out an audible laugh. "Do I need to remind the court of the exploits of our good senator?" He held up what appeared to be photographs. Exhibits.

Evelyn's gaze fell to her hands. She didn't want to risk being accosted with another image of her husband in the arms of someone so very unlike the woman she'd become.

The arguing continued.

"Your Honor," the defense attorney protested, "this man has expressed remorse for his extra-marital indiscretions, but that doesn't make him a criminal."

"No, he hasn't," Evelyn whispered. She twisted her wedding ring around her finger. An upgrade from the original he'd bought her just after college graduation. This one would likely be repossessed, leaving her left hand naked, the way she felt with the contents of her personal life splashed across every news outlet in Colorado.

"You'll notice Senator Brandt's wife is here with us today," Christopher's lawyer continued. "The senator is anxious to get back home so the two can begin counseling and repair their marriage."

He's what?

Evelyn shot Christopher a look, but he was focused on his lawyer. Wasn't it only yesterday she'd asked him to go to counseling? Wasn't it only yesterday he'd rejected the idea as if he were above it?

The judge peered in her direction. "Is this so, Mrs. Brandt?"

She must have looked as startled as she felt when everyone, including Christopher, turned and looked at her. Was it customary for a judge to address someone sitting in his courtroom? She wasn't there in an official capacity. In fact, she wished she weren't there at all.

"Mrs. Brandt?"

Only then did she realize she'd been staring. "Yes, Your Honor?"

"Is what your husband's lawyer said true? Will the two of you begin counseling?"

Evelyn stood because on television that's what people did when they spoke to a judge. Never mind that those people were usually the ones on trial. She glanced at Christopher, the memory

166

of their conversation, the way it had made her feel, still strong in her mind. Her sense of obligation had brought her here, her desire to give her marriage every fighting chance, but the reality was even clearer now. Christopher wasn't going to change. He was still using her to make himself look good.

Their marriage was over.

"Mrs. Brandt?"

She lifted her chin, avoiding Christopher's glare. "I had hoped Christopher would attend counseling with me, Your Honor."

"But . . . ?" The judge squinted at her over thin, wire-rimmed glasses.

"But he refused." Evelyn swallowed, her throat dry, as chatter raced through the courtroom.

"Evelyn." Christopher's tone warned.

Evelyn dared a glance in her husband's direction. He stood, wearing a dark and angry glare. How long had it been since she'd truly defied him? Had she ever?

The judge clapped his gavel. "Sit down, Mr. Brandt."

Slowly Christopher sat, all the while steeling his eyes at her, his misbehaving wife.

Evelyn's hands fisted at her sides as she continued to speak. "Furthermore, my husband has shown no remorse for his actions, and while I have no knowledge of any fraudulent activity, I can only hope he hasn't treated his public office with the same lack of care that he's treated our marriage."

The judge raised a brow, and for a moment Evelyn wondered if he was angry or impressed.

"Mr. Nyquist?" He turned his attention to Christopher's lawyer, who shot her a look and mumbled something about a woman scorned, then shuffled through some papers on the table in front of him.

Evelyn picked up her purse and stepped into the aisle, the room's attention fully on her.

A deafening silence permeated the air as if everyone in the crowded courtroom was waiting to see what the senator's dutiful wife would do after her uncharacteristic outburst.

She slid her ring from her finger and moved toward the small barrier separating the audience's seats from the man to whom she'd wholly given herself. Without a word, she set her wedding ring on the banister between them, willing herself not to fall apart.

She heard the cameras clicking, a dull murmur breaking the silence as she walked out of the courtroom and into whatever new life she'd find waiting for her on the other side of the doors.

CHAPTER
17

"How do you feel, Mrs. Brandt?"

Evelyn had avoided the questions the reporters fired at her as she rushed through the crowd, pretending—for the last time—that she carried with her an unmatched strength and elegance which she most certainly did not possess. But she could not avoid the realization that what she'd just done carried consequences.

She'd sent a message for the whole world to see that she was no longer going to be the wife who turned a blind eye to her husband's crimes or indiscretions.

She sped out of the parking lot and toward the interstate, but once she saw Denver in her rearview mirror, she pulled onto the shoulder, turned her hazards on, and sobbed.

My marriage is over.

Another failure. Blindsided by a life that had chosen to be unkind.

Hadn't she done everything right? Hadn't she become the perfect wife? Hadn't she set aside all her own dreams to help her husband achieve his?

She rested her head on the steering wheel as the tears came fast and furious. She gave herself over to them, allowing herself to feel, for the first time, the pain of her husband's many betrayals, the pain of losing a man she had deeply loved.

The sobs overtook her body, her shoulders shook, and her tears rushed from the depths of her sorrow. She slammed her hand on the steering wheel, anger welling up inside, too great to contain. Another slam, this one accompanied by a scream.

Another scream.

"This isn't fair!" She got out of the car, unsteady on her heels. She took them off and threw them into the ditch. Cars on the interstate slowed to look at her, their drivers astounded, she was sure, at the sight of a perfectly coiffed woman unraveling on the side of the road.

She ripped the gold chain from her neck and threw it on the ground with a shout. "This isn't fair!" Evelyn slammed her hands on the hood of the car with another shout. "Where were you, God? Where were you when he was cheating? Where were you when I was becoming a laughing-stock for the entire world to see?"

She unclasped the bracelets dangling on her wrist and dropped them on the cement, then ripped her tailored gray jacket off and heaved it in the opposite direction.

"Ma'am?"

She spun around and saw a man approaching her. He'd pulled over to the side of the road, a do-gooder with a curious teenager in the backseat, taking a video of her on a cell phone.

Evelyn raised a hand. "Don't."

He held both hands up as if to surrender or calm her down. "Can I do anything for you?" The man inched closer.

Evelyn looked down at her bare feet, then met his eyes. "Yeah, don't ever cheat on your wife."

Small, sharp stones dug into the bottoms of her feet as she made her way around the car and got back inside. What was wrong with her? Was she going crazy? Was this what it felt like to have a mental breakdown?

She sped away from the man on the side of the road, back toward Loves Park to a home that was no longer hers and a life full of empty promises.

Her phone buzzed in the cup holder. Her little display in the courtroom must've hit the news. She turned the phone off without looking at it, knowing that while there were good people in her life, none of them could save her from the mess she'd just made of things.

"How do you feel?"

The question rushed back at her. They'd asked with such exuberance, like excited fans at a rock concert. How did they think she felt? Angry. Hurt. Bitter. Sad. Scared. Alone. Exhausted.

She felt like a woman living in the land of "I don't know," and she was a stranger in this world.

She drove barefoot toward Loves Park, her

thoughts spinning without her permission. She was a grown woman and she'd just had an all-out meltdown on the side of the road. A tantrum that would rival even the crankiest toddler's.

Worse, she couldn't blame anyone else for this humiliation. It was all her own doing.

Evelyn pulled into Loves Park two hours later and made the familiar turn toward the lake as she struggled to formulate some sort of plan in answer to the question that continued to prod her: *What are you going to do now?*

She would ask Whit if he was serious about letting her live in the guesthouse. Just until she got her bearings. She'd find a job. She'd pay him rent.

But as quickly as the thought entered her head, another one replaced it. Who was she kidding? She hadn't worked in years. Her degree in art wouldn't go far in Loves Park—the place was filled with artists already. Why hadn't she thought this through before acting out like she did? Without Christopher, she was nothing.

Fear wrapped itself around her heart and squeezed tight like a blood pressure cuff.

She pulled into the driveway of the lake house on Brighton Street and begged her mind to be still. For the sake of her own sanity, she wished she could go on autopilot for a few months.

The house had sat untouched since the FBI agents had turned it inside out. She stood on the front porch for several long seconds, trying to work up the courage to open the door.

Finally, after a heavy moment of indecision, she pushed it open and walked inside.

Quiet, but not peace, assaulted her as soon as she closed the door. She supposed most of the media had stayed in Denver today on account of the hearing. Good. She could pack her things in solitude.

Upstairs, the sprawling master bedroom beckoned to her. She stood in the doorway, staring at the four-poster bed and wondering if she would ever trust anyone again. How could Christopher betray her like that? Repeatedly? Worse, how could he be so brazen about it? Was he so self-involved that he actually thought he wouldn't get caught?

Evelyn forced the thoughts from her head and moved toward the giant walk-in closet. She opened the doors and stared at the designer clothing and shoes filling the space. One by one, she flipped through the items, intending to pack up only her favorites, but the farther into the closet she got, the more she realized she didn't like any of these clothes.

And she didn't like who she was when she wore them.

She pulled out an elegant black cocktail dress Christopher had purchased for her to wear to a meeting with potential campaign investors.

"These stuffy rich dudes need something beautiful to stare at," he'd told her. "You make perfect arm candy."

She'd laughed at the time, but now the words made her feel cheap, like her only purpose had been to make Christopher look good.

She'd once had ideas and plans and goals—but none of them had stayed with her. Somehow she'd lost herself in her effort to help Christopher. His goals had seemed so much more important than hers anyway.

She dropped the dress on the floor and pulled out a navy-blue pantsuit she'd worn to events meant to target women. She'd played a different role depending on the audience. This pantsuit made her dignified and just a touch out of reach.

"Every woman in the room should look up to you by the end. Give them something to aspire to." Christopher had whispered the words in her ear while fastening the clasp of an elegant string of pearls around her neck.

She dropped the suit on the floor. Pulled another one out and dropped it on the floor.

Outfit by outfit, she went through her closet wondering where the real Evelyn had gone, wondering if she was so far away that she would never find herself again. Each garment landed in a pile at her feet, and as they did, she said good-bye to the persona they represented. But when she reached the end, she didn't have a single outfit to bring with her or a single idea who she was.

She collapsed in a heap and stared at the empty hangers, some of them still swinging.

"I'm not strong enough for this," she said aloud. "God, I can't do this on my own."

She'd always believed that divorce was wrong—how could she admit to herself she'd even entertained the idea? But how could she not? Christopher had left her no other option.

Leaving that ring in the courtroom wasn't a threat. It was a choice. As if her gut had made the decision for her.

But what if that wasn't what she was supposed to do? How did she walk away from the only life she'd ever known?

All those stories she'd heard of women who forgave, who took their husbands back and moved on. Maybe those were the strong women. Maybe leaving was taking the easy way out.

Or maybe those women had husbands who were willing to change. She looked at the other side of the closet, where perfectly pressed dress shirts hung next to pristine pin-striped suits, ties neatly lined at their sides.

Tears sprang to her eyes as the revelation made its way from her head to her heart. What hurt the most wasn't that Christopher had lied or cheated; what hurt the most was that he wasn't sorry. And if he wasn't sorry, he wouldn't change.

And if he wouldn't change, then Evelyn knew

there was no sense trying to save her marriage. After all, she certainly couldn't save it on her own.

But where did that leave her?

Sitting on the floor of a closet full of clothes that represented a person she'd become but didn't recognize. Somehow she knew it wasn't just Christopher's choices that had led them to this point. It was hers too.

And that might've been the toughest part of all.

CHAPTER

18

Casey hung up the phone and stared at Trevor. "I can't believe it." He flipped on the television in his office.

"What now?"

"She wants a divorce."

"Marin?" Casey's wife had just found out she was pregnant. This hardly seemed like a good time to strike out on her own.

"Not Marin." He raised a brow like he had juicy gossip. "Evelyn."

Trevor's heart lurched as Casey turned up the volume. Images of Evelyn entering the court-house appeared on the screen as a reporter explained that when the judge asked the senator's wife if she and her husband would be attending counseling, Mrs. Brandt answered in the negative, removed her wedding ring, and left it in the courtroom beside her cheating husband.

"This is bad," Trevor said. He picked up his phone and called Evelyn.

No answer.

Casey turned down the volume. "You're not kidding. How am I going to write up papers for her to divorce one of my best friends? You know how this is going to go over with Chris."

Trevor took off his ball cap and folded the bill. "Then maybe he shouldn't have cheated."

Casey picked up a Nerf basketball and shot it at the hoop hanging on the back of his office door. "Have you *ever* known Chris to be faithful?"

Trevor cringed. He prayed he never had to admit what he knew.

Evelyn had spent her whole adult life as the subject of town gossip, but none of it had made its way back to her. How was that possible? Did she really live in that much of a bubble? Or was Chris just that good of a liar?

Trevor's stomach turned. Despite his conflicting feelings for Evelyn, he'd been her friend, and a real friend would've told her the truth, no matter how much he didn't want to.

He'd stayed out of it because he wanted her to be happy. Things hadn't exactly gone according to plan.

"I don't want to even think about how Chris is going to respond to this. Doesn't look good, and you know he's all about appearances . . ." Casey shot the ball again. Missed.

"You really stink at that."

"I'm off my game. Marin's nesting. She's driving me nuts."

Trevor snorted.

"I love her, but she's got to stop snoring at night. I can't sleep." Casey palmed the ball. "Did I tell you she wants to name him Jansen?"

"Call him Jan?"

Casey groaned. "Not if I can help it. I hate it. What's wrong with a good, solid boy name like George or Henry or Robert?"

Now Trevor groaned. "It's good you guys are on the same page."

Casey laughed. "What's going on with that Maggie?"

"Dunno."

"Kiss her yet?"

"What is this, eighth grade?" Trevor took the ball. *Swish.* "That's how you do that." He sat on Casey's leather couch, propping his feet on the coffee table.

"I can't believe you. What are you waiting for? You're not getting any younger, you know. Wouldn't you like to have a pregnant wife whose bodily functions wake you up at night?"

He would, actually. Casey had no idea how lucky he was.

"Aw, man," Casey said. "I know that look."

Trevor questioned him with a shrug.

"You're holding out on Maggie because you want to see what happens with Evelyn and Chris."

Trevor groaned. "Don't you start psycho-analyzing me."

"Please. You don't need a shrink to tell you she is the reason you broke up with Rachel. She is the reason you're still single. And she is the reason you're not pursuing this thing with Maggie."

"She's married, Casey."

Casey leaned back in his chair and clasped his hands behind his head. "Right. And you're a good man. A Christian. You'd never do anything to break that up. I know why you stopped hanging out with all of us, man."

Trevor thought getting his wisdom teeth pulled would be more pleasant than this conversation. He'd let Evelyn go a long time ago—he didn't need the reminder of what it had cost him.

He'd seen Rachel not long after he broke things off with her. It was at the farmers' market, where they'd first met. It had taken her some time to come back, but she walked by with her sister, and their eyes met for a brief, fleeting moment before she looked away, visible pain on her face.

Rachel's sister stomped into their booth, stuck her finger in Trevor's chest, and gave him a piece of her mind, which, it turned out, was nothing compared to the knowledge that his indecisiveness had hurt someone he cared for so much.

Nearly a month later, Rachel moved to one of the Carolinas. He heard she got married about a year ago. Did she still hate him for what he'd done?

He'd tried to love her, but something was missing. He hoped she saw that now.

He shook the memories away when he discovered Casey was still talking. "Chris was always threatened by you. He knew how you felt about her, you know."

Trevor didn't reply.

Casey sighed. "Good old Chris. Couldn't stand the thought of you having something he wanted. I think he's been competing with you ever since."

Anger rose in Trevor's chest. "He married her. I guess he won."

Sure felt like a loss on his end.

"Be honest, Whit. Why didn't you ever make a play for Evelyn?" Casey wadded up a piece of paper and shot that at the hoop. Missed.

Trevor didn't want to talk about Evelyn. He didn't need to relive his greatest regret. He did that plenty on his own time.

"Chris must be crawling out of his skin about now." Casey loosened his tie. "He's probably going nuts trying to figure out how to make sure you don't make a move on her now that he's out of the picture."

"Doesn't he know me better than that?"

Casey's glare accused. "Don't tell me you never thought about it."

"Casey, she's Chris's wife." Trevor stood. "That's the furthest thing from my mind."

"Whit, I was there the night you met her." Casey wadded up another sheet of paper. "Chris got in the middle of that on purpose. He couldn't stand it that Evelyn liked you."

The words hung in the air. Fifteen-year-old memories replaying like a movie in his mind.

"I remember how it messed you up when he told us he was marrying her. This isn't just a high school crush, man. You love her."

"Enough." Trevor hadn't intended for the word to come out harsh, but it did. "What good does any of that do now? I've spent the last fifteen years thinking about how I *can't* think about her. Can't think about what a jerk her husband is or how I would never treat her like he does or take her for granted. I've had to remind myself— more than once—that it's not my place to rush in and save her. That I have *no right* to think about her at all."

Casey's eyes were wide. "As long as you're not thinking about her."

Trevor threw the ball at the couch with a thud. "He knew how I felt all along."

Casey stilled. "I'm sorry, Whit."

"Does he even love her?"

Casey leaned back in his chair and kicked his feet up on the desk. "Not enough to take responsibility for what he's done."

Trevor sat on the couch again, elbows on his knees, head down, and sighed. It was worse than he thought. He hadn't fought for Evelyn all those years ago. He'd given her up to someone who didn't even seem capable of loving her at all.

"All I know is I love Marin too much to ever risk losing her," Casey said.

"So what's Chris's next move?"

Casey shrugged. "If Evelyn files for divorce, he's going to try to make you look really bad to her." Casey slid his feet off the desk and faced Trevor. "What's he got on you?"

Trevor sucked in a deep breath and blew it out in one hot stream. He didn't want to think about what Chris had on him. Chris's cover-ups and lies started long before he'd married Evelyn. And Trevor had been an integral part of it all. He wasn't any better than Chris—not really—and to Evelyn, who needed friends she could trust more than anything, Trevor knew finding out the truth would rip open her wounds all over again.

But this time, the betrayer would be him.

CHAPTER
19

An unwelcome pounding on the door of the guesthouse tugged Evelyn from sleep. She'd been doing a lot of sleeping since she told Casey to start divorce proceedings. It had been two weeks since her little display at the courthouse, and the media had finally stopped talking about it.

But the Loves Park gossip mill had not, which meant Evelyn was perfectly fine hiding out in the guesthouse until further notice.

She stumbled to the door and found Whit standing on the porch, looking like a ranch hand in his dirty jeans, a blue plaid shirt, and work boots, that ratty old baseball cap pulled down low, shading his hazel eyes.

"Did I wake you?"

She shrugged.

"It's noon."

"Your point?"

He held up a plastic bag from the grocery store.

"What's that?"

"Ice cream."

"You bought me ice cream?"

"You said you wanted some a while ago, right?"

The shameful scene at the store rushed back.

He handed her the bag. "Lots of chores out here if you feel like getting out of the house." He walked away in the direction of the barns. She stared at the two pints in the bag. Moose tracks and peppermint stick.

He bought her ice cream?

When had they become friends again? Or was this pity ice cream? He probably just felt sorry for her. She had become something of a disaster.

She stuck the ice cream in the freezer as a memory jumped to the forefront of her mind. The summer before freshman year of college. She and Christopher had a date planned—just the two of them—so when Whit showed up at her house, she was angry.

"Did he send you here?"

Whit glanced away. "Got caught up with his parents."

Evelyn sighed. It was always something with Christopher. Sometimes it had felt like she spent more time with Whit—and Casey, when he tagged along—than with her own boyfriend.

"You look good," Whit had told her. "Want to go for a walk?"

"You don't have to entertain me, Whit. I'm fine." She'd never been a very good liar.

"This time next week, we'll all be at different schools. Maybe I'm freaking out about it." He kicked a rock off the edge of her front porch.

She closed the door and joined him outside. "Are you?"

He shrugged.

They walked in silence toward Old Town, both lost in their own thoughts, both on the cusp of "real life"—of getting out of Loves Park and moving on to bigger and better things. They had their whole lives in front of them and no words to process the fusion of feelings swirling around in their minds.

He stopped in front of the Old Town Creamery and smiled.

"Might as well start on that freshman fifteen now," she said, following him into the ice cream shop.

He ordered moose tracks. She ordered peppermint stick. They sat outside and those inexplicable feelings poured onto the picnic table.

"I'm not scared to leave," she'd told him. "I think I'd be more afraid to stay."

Living in her house after her sister, Sylvie, died had been like living with a ghost. Her parents weren't the same. None of them were. And the constant struggle to please her father overwhelmed her.

"I suppose I need to get out on my own," she said, the idea scaring her in spite of what she'd said before.

"To do what?"

"I'm not sure. Something with art, I think. I

want to be an artist." Heat rushed to her cheeks. "Lame, right?" Not many people could make a living as an artist.

But Whit shook his head. "Not lame at all. You should go for it. I think you can do anything."

Now Evelyn wondered if he did remember they'd been good friends once.

Or maybe he wanted to remind her of those words he'd spoken all those years ago. *"I think you can do anything."*

Nobody had ever believed in her like that—before or since. She supposed that's what a real friend did. And yet, she'd traded that friendship for a life filled with acquaintances who'd abandoned her at the first sign of trouble. It shamed her, how she'd miscalculated what was really important.

Dinnertime rolled around, but she had no appetite. No desire to shower either. Instead, she rotated from the Adirondack chairs outside to the couch, where she mindlessly flipped through television she had no interest in, occasionally jarred back to reality by the image of Christopher's face, still captivating audiences with his scandalous ways.

Released on his own recognizance. Awaiting trial. Sentencing. Prison time likely. She didn't even know if he'd returned to Loves Park. She didn't know if he'd gotten the divorce papers. She didn't know anything about Christopher Brandt, and it was painfully obvious she never had.

He would tell her she was weak. And until recently she would've believed him.

Scared? Yes. But weak? Not anymore. At least, she didn't want to be.

Night fell and Evelyn drifted to sleep under the cozy cover of a homemade quilt.

She awoke the next morning and lived the same day all over again. Another week passed, and Christopher started calling from the landline in the home they used to share. She turned her phone off and lay back down on the sofa, but before she could close her eyes, she heard a commotion outside.

What if the reporters had found her? Thankfully, the curtains were closed.

"Evelyn?"

She groaned. It wasn't reporters—it was worse.

"We know you're in there!"

"We came to bring you back to the land of the living!"

She opened the front door and stared at the five very hopeful-looking women carrying an array of baked goods, disposable coffee cups, and a stack of manila file folders.

She resisted the urge to groan but stepped out of the way so they could enter. No sense pretending she had a choice.

"Oh, my, isn't this an interesting look for you?" Gigi said as she passed.

Abigail stopped in front of her and handed her a cup of something warm. "Thought you could use this." More than any of them, Abigail could relate to losing everything. Last year, when she lost The Book Nook, Abigail must've thought her world was caving in too. Did she wonder why God had left her? Did she battle anger and fear and worry and dread? Probably not like Evelyn did. Sometimes her thoughts were so dark they shamed her.

She took the coffee and forced a smile. "Thanks."

"For the record, I was against this 'show of support.'"

Evelyn closed the door. "I had a feeling it wasn't your idea." They moved into the living room, where the other ladies had already set up shop. A tray of pastries and bagels sat on the white coffee table at the center of the room. Ursula and Doris had claimed the oversize armchairs while Tess Jenkins perched on the edge of the couch, where Evelyn had been spending most of her life lately.

"Love what you've done with the place," Ursula said, her tone sarcastic as she surveyed the damage of three weeks' worth of neglect. "Doesn't bode well if you're trying to prove you're *not* mentally ill."

"Ursula!" Gigi's tone warned. Panicked expressions crisscrossed the room.

"What are you talking about?" Evelyn sensed there was something they weren't telling her.

"It's nothing, dear," Gigi said, her tone maternal.

"Tell me," Evelyn said.

"It's all over the news," Ursula said, biting into a donut. "Don't you read?"

"What's all over the news?"

A thick, weighty silence filled the room, Evelyn at its center. "Tell me."

"Honey, sometimes it's better not to know what everyone is saying behind your back," Doris said.

"This is not one of those times, Doris."

"Oh, it might be," Doris replied.

"Someone recorded you," Ursula said. "It's gone virus."

"Viral," Abigail corrected. "A stupid YouTube video."

"Of me?" Evelyn reached for her laptop, but Gigi snatched it before she could get her hands on it. Didn't matter, though. She knew what had happened. The Good Samaritan's teenager had posted the video of her meltdown online.

As if her fall outside the courthouse playing on a continual loop wasn't humiliating enough, now she'd had an all-out viral breakdown.

"That was weeks ago," Evelyn said, wishing she could go hide under the quilt on the bed upstairs, worn threadbare from years of comforting people in their darkest moments.

"The boy said he didn't know who you were until now," Gigi explained. "He posted it right away, but once he changed the headline to include your name, well, that's when the thing took off."

Evelyn smoothed her hair back and plopped down on the other end of the couch while Abigail and Gigi sat on the love seat opposite the two stuffed armchairs. Evelyn couldn't muster an ounce of social grace.

"I don't know why I'm even surprised," Evelyn said, feeling defeated.

"Good thing you don't read the newspaper," Ursula said.

"Ursula!" A choir of exasperation rang out.

"It's fishy," the old woman spat. "And she deserves to know."

"Evelyn, who have you talked to lately?" Gigi asked.

Evelyn frowned. "Why?"

"The newspaper published an article about you."

Evelyn let her head rest on the back of the couch and stared at the ceiling. "I don't want to know."

"They had your appointment records with the therapist in Dillon. And a list of the medications you've been taking," Doris said. "Someone would have to be close to you to find out those things. We didn't even know."

The memory of her fall on the way into the courthouse clamored for her attention. Her pills had never turned up. She'd had to order a new bottle, and it had been ages since she'd needed to do that.

"One of those reporters got ahold of my medication," she said, sure of it now.

"Well, they certainly did their homework," Tess said. "I had no idea about your panic attacks. The anxiety. The stress of being a politician's wife must've done a number on you."

"I've always been this way," Evelyn said mindlessly.

The others stared at her, but she didn't elaborate.

"Lots of people take antidepressants. This hardly seems like news," Abigail said, defensive.

"They're trying to make her look like she's *mentally unstable*," Doris said, whispering the last two words. "You know. Cuckoo." She wound her finger in a circle around her ear and let her eyes cross.

"Doris," Ursula scolded.

"Oh, you're one to talk," the other woman said with a frown.

"You missed our meeting," Gigi said, obviously eager to change the subject.

"Sorry." Evelyn's response was hollow, of course, because she wasn't sorry nor did she even realize there had been a meeting to miss.

"You're still a member of the Volunteers, and we wanted to give you some time to yourself, but we do have work to do," Doris said, sounding falsely chipper.

"Forgive me if I don't feel like matchmaking right this minute," Evelyn said. It all seemed so trite when she thought about it. Pairing singletons, reading love letters, stamping envelopes. Why had she ever joined this group in the first place?

Because Christopher told her to. Why else?

"We have a task that we think is the perfect distraction for you. We waited for some of the chaos to die down, and we feel like the time is finally right," Gigi said.

Evelyn didn't ask what it was because she didn't want to know.

A knock at the door made Evelyn wonder if she was hosting a party and no one had told her.

Another knock. She glanced at the clock. It had been three hours since her last visit from Whit. Odds were that was him on her front porch. He'd been checking in on her every day since she returned from the hearing, always with an excuse to be there. She knew better. He was probably afraid she was going to do something stupid like swallow all the pills her shrink had prescribed.

She wasn't that desperate. Yet.

"Aren't you going to get it?" Gigi wore an inquisitive expression.

"I wasn't going to, no." It wouldn't be the first time she'd tried to ignore Whit's pounding, though even she had to admit it was pointless. He would worry she'd done something stupid and find a way in. He always did.

"Then I'll get it," Gigi said.

Evelyn stood. That would be a mistake. Her best

bet was to convince Whit to leave. And fast. But Gigi was quicker than she looked, and Evelyn reached her just after she pulled the door open, revealing Trevor, who looked less surprised than she expected.

"Thank you for coming, Mr. Whitney."

"I had a choice?" He met Evelyn's gaze. She looked away. What did he think of her in that moment? She'd let herself fall apart under his watchful eye and he had to have opinions about that.

Gigi walked past her, back toward the living room, leaving her in the entryway alone with Whit.

"You okay?" He stopped beside her but didn't turn to face her. As if he could sense her humiliation.

She mustered a nod. He lingered a long moment, then moved into the living room. From nowhere, tears had clouded her sight. She wasn't accustomed to sympathy, especially not from him. She'd learned to live on the other side of his cold shoulder.

She sniffed, wiped her cheeks, and joined her unwanted guests in the living room. They'd already begun talking, and Whit looked as out of place as a cowboy at the prom.

"Have you been out with her again?" Doris leaned forward as if waiting for a juicy bit of gossip.

Whit shifted under her prying question. "This can't be why you brought me here, ladies," he said. "I think I made it clear I don't want any help with my love life."

Gigi's eyes narrowed. "Indeed." She glanced at Evelyn, who stood in the doorway like an intruder. "Evelyn, perhaps we *could* use your help with some matchmaking. We need to be sure Mr. Whitney doesn't ruin this opportunity with Miss Lawson."

Evelyn frowned. "*Mr. Whitney* is doing just fine on his own, Gigi." He'd been gone a couple nights that week, and she had to assume he'd been with Maggie. She knew because she missed the sound of his acoustic guitar filling the darkness with a melody. She often listened from her perch on one of the Adirondack chairs, admiring the music in him, wondering if this was how he expressed himself when words seemed to fail him so frequently. He must love playing enough to overcome his disdain for being around people because she happened to know he was a regular on the praise team at Loves Park Community Church.

Maybe things were heating up with Maggie. That would be good, right? Just because she was miserable didn't mean she wanted her friends to be.

"Uh-huh." Gigi zeroed in on Whit. "But you do have a way of running from commitment, don't you?"

Trevor shifted in his seat.

"We know all about the one that got away," Gigi said. "We want to be sure you don't make that same mistake twice."

Wide-eyed, Doris raised her hand as she spoke. "I'm sorry I told them about Rachel. I felt it was important they knew you gave romance a try for yourself."

More restlessness from Whit.

Gigi must've sensed Trevor's fight-or-flight reflexes kicking in because she quickly raised her voice and announced, "We didn't bring you here to talk about Miss Lawson."

"Though this is a match we approve of," Doris said, winking. "At least we think we do."

Whit fidgeted. Evelyn actually felt sorry for him. He hated to be the center of attention, and these women were ruthless.

Gigi motioned to Evelyn. "Sit down, Evelyn. This concerns you too."

All heads turned her way. Like she said, ruthless. Evelyn sat next to Whit, the only open spot in the room.

"You ever going to wash that thing?" Whit whispered with a nod toward the sweater she'd been wearing for a solid week.

She shot a look at him and noticed the grin tugging the corners of his mouth. She hadn't felt like smiling in weeks, but something about his boyish smile changed that.

Suddenly, thanks to these women, she and Whit were allies.

Gigi's stern voice grabbed her attention. "We've been watching the two of you," she said, sounding like a grade school principal who'd just caught two kids throwing wet toilet paper against the walls in the bathroom.

"And we think you're hiding something," Doris said.

Trevor's eyes widened.

"Not you too." Evelyn groaned. "I don't know where the money is. I didn't know about the women. I haven't talked to Christopher since he got back."

Gigi frowned at Doris. "Probably not the best way to start the conversation in light of current circumstances."

Doris grimaced. "Sorry."

"That's not what we're talking about, Evelyn," Gigi said. "It's come to our attention that the hearts for the Loves Park lampposts are in dire need of an artistic overhaul."

"The hearts?" Evelyn frowned. They'd come all the way here to talk about wooden hearts?

"We have it on good authority that the two of you have talents worth sharing with our community," Tess said, her voice far too chirpy for any hour of the day.

"I don't know what you're talking about," Whit said, leaning forward, elbows on his knees.

196

"Don't be so modest, Mr. Whitney," Gigi said. "Doris told us all about your *extracurricular activities*." She waggled her eyebrows as she said the words. "No wonder you're too busy to pursue a life of love."

Evelyn frowned. "What's she talking about?"

Trevor stood. "I'm afraid that, with the farm, I don't have time for Valentine's Day traditions. Sorry, ladies."

"Mr. Whitney, would you at least hear us out?"

He paused, sighed, then sat back down. Even Trevor's brooding was no match for Gigi's motherly toe-tapping.

"As you know, every Valentine's Day, the people of this community show their love for one another by purchasing wooden hearts that are hung on the lampposts all through Old Town. We paint custom messages on the hearts for the whole town to see. It's a wonderful tradition dating back over forty years and an excellent way to spread love."

"It also raises a good deal of money for the town," Doris said with a nod. "Last year we were able to plant trees along Main Street with the money we made."

"Cut to the chase, Gigi," Ursula said, crumbs on her shirt the only remnant of an annihilated cheese Danish. "You sound like a commercial."

"This year, we want to over. Haul. The. Hearts." Gigi clapped with every syllable as she said the words as if she were talking to a classroom of preschoolers.

Evelyn glanced at Abigail, who gave a slight shrug. "I'm not sure how this concerns me," she said.

Gigi shook her head. "Now *you're* being modest, Evelyn. The city board has agreed to let us come up with a new look for the hearts, and they're allowing us to handle all the particulars." She raised an eyebrow at Whit. "I told you we did more than make matches."

He looked like he wanted to respond but wisely refrained.

"We're looking for something completely new and different. They still need to be made of wood and they still need to be hearts, but other than that, it's up to you two." She punctuated her sentence with a firm nod, then sat down as if her explanation made perfect sense.

"I'm confused, Gigi. What do you want us to do?"

Gigi sighed. "Isn't it obvious?"

Evelyn looked at Whit, who wore the same puzzled expression she imagined on her own face. "No."

The older woman motioned to Trevor. "You're a woodworker. You cut the hearts out." Then she motioned to Evelyn. "You're an artist. You make them pretty. The two of you will make a lineup of example hearts, so people will get excited about placing orders this year."

"Gigi, it's a long time until Valentine's Day." Evelyn would rather have a root canal than help people profess their love to each other on wooden hearts.

"Yes, it is, so you have plenty of time to devise a plan."

Ursula reached for another Danish. "It's not like you've got anything better to do."

Evelyn looked down while the other ladies all chastised their most outspoken member.

"What?" Ursula said. "It's true. Look at this place."

Shame crept into Evelyn's belly. Trevor had opened this home to her and she'd done a terrible job of caring for it. She'd turned it into a prison, and as much as she hated to admit it, Ursula was right. She squirmed under their scrutiny.

"Evelyn, the painted hearts have been such a lovely tradition in Loves Park for so many years. There's something wonderfully romantic about purchasing a heart to have your own personal message inscribed on it as a declaration of love for the whole town to see."

"Sure, but what's wrong with the hearts the way they are?" Evelyn frowned.

Gigi returned the expression. "They simply don't reflect the artistic side of our town. Plain red hearts with white stenciled words? Surely you can come up with something prettier than that—something worthy of this glorious tradition."

Gigi certainly was dramatic.

"I'll think about it, okay?" Evelyn rose. "Now, if you'll excuse me."

"Where are you going, dear?" Gigi also stood.

But Evelyn didn't respond because the truth was, she didn't have any idea where she was going.

CHAPTER
20

After a long walk around the farm, Evelyn expected to return to an empty guesthouse, but as she approached, she could see Ursula sitting on the porch swing out front.

Great.

The old woman stood as soon as she spotted Evelyn. "Took ya long enough."

Evelyn didn't know if she had the patience for Ursula right now. Then again, at least she knew Ursula wouldn't lie to her. That had to count for something.

"Where'd you go? That much walking could kill you."

Evelyn stared at the ground. "I needed to get out of the house."

"I'll say. I opened all your windows. It was starting to stink in there." She followed Evelyn inside, where the temperature had shot up about twenty degrees. It was early June, and the days were warm.

"You do know I have the air on, right?" Evelyn closed the windows in the living room.

Not surprisingly Ursula didn't respond to that. "Do you know why I'm still here?"

Evelyn turned and raised a brow. "How could I possibly know that?"

Ursula narrowed her eyes. "Don't get smart with me, missy. I'm here because I've got something to tell you."

Evelyn waited.

Ursula sat in the plush armchair, crossing her feet at the ankles. Evelyn supposed that was about as ladylike as Ursula Pembrooke was going to get. Never mind she was wearing tennis shoes with knee-highs and a skirt.

"You know my marriage to Frankie is one of this town's greatest love stories."

Evelyn almost scoffed but quickly realized Ursula was serious.

"It's just that nobody knows it is." She leaned back in the chair, and Evelyn had the distinct impression this wouldn't be a quick visit.

"Frankie was a shrewd businessman. Well, you know. He had a lot of enemies, and I guess he was a lot of things to a lot of people." Ursula glanced up. "Not completely different from your husband."

Slowly Evelyn sat across from her.

"Powerful men are always a crapshoot," Ursula said. "But there was one thing Frankie never did, Evelyn." Ursula's trademark scowl had gone soft behind her glasses.

Evelyn held her gaze, almost afraid of what would come next.

"He never cheated on me."

Images of Christopher and those women flashed through her mind. Barely dressed. Smiling at the camera. As if they had nothing to be ashamed of. The memory of his nonchalance about the whole thing had chipped away at her resolve to stay strong. It was as though he didn't even realize the pain and embarrassment he'd caused her.

Or maybe he just didn't care.

Ursula leaned forward. "I know you, Evelyn. You never make a move unless you've calculated it fourteen different ways. You see every possible outcome before determining the best road. But I want you to know you don't have to stay with a man who cheats."

Without Evelyn's permission, fresh tears fell. "I married him, Ursula. I made a commitment." She'd been wrestling with it ever since she left her life on the floor of her closet at the Brighton Street house. She knew her marriage was over, but that didn't keep her from feeling like a failure. And it certainly did nothing to remove the question that permeated every waking moment: *What do I do now?*

"And you honored it, but he didn't. That makes him the failure. Not you."

Sure didn't feel like it. For the past few weeks, Evelyn had been replaying moments from their marriage. What could she have done differently? Was there a way to have kept him from straying? Maybe she'd pushed him too hard to start a family. Maybe she'd complained too much about their life in the public eye.

"Evelyn." Ursula forced her gaze. "This isn't your fault."

She averted her eyes. She wasn't accustomed to Ursula being nice to her. Or anyone, for that matter. Kindness seemed to hide in the corners where she least expected it. First Trevor, now Ursula. Maybe that's what drew the tears to her eyes.

"I mean it. Some men let all that power and money go to their heads. Frankie didn't have a dishonest bone in his body, which is why people didn't like him. It's why a lot of people don't like me."

"It's just because they don't know there's a big heart underneath all those thorns." Evelyn smiled through her tears.

Ursula let out a gruff laugh. "You've got a choice, kid. Stay in the house, mope around, and become the crazy person the media says you are."

"Or?"

"Put on your big-girl panties and make some

hard decisions. I'm all for working out your differences, and if you think your husband wants to change, then give it another go."

Evelyn shook her head. "I think he's got himself convinced he didn't do anything wrong."

"Then he's the one with the mental problem."

Evelyn wiped her cheek and looked at Ursula. "He's not going to change, Ursula. I think he's been cheating on me since before we even got married."

"Then maybe it's time for you to move on."

"I don't have anywhere to go." The words came out in a whisper, accompanied by a crippling fear.

She had never been alone in her life. Christopher had always provided for her. Taken care of her. Did she even know how to make it on her own?

"Well, you've got me. After solving Pressman's problems, I'm bored again. I could use a project."

Evelyn laughed. "Thanks, Ursula."

"Anytime. Especially if there are pastries." She picked up a muffin, took a bite, and let herself out, leaving Evelyn with her thoughts. Evelyn watched as the old woman flagged down one of the farmhands. When she climbed into his pickup truck, Evelyn could only assume she'd demanded a ride home.

She'd done the right thing filing for divorce, even though it wasn't something that happened to good Christians. But lately it felt like nothing in her life was supposed to happen to good Christians. She'd known marriage wouldn't be champagne and roses all the time, but this? She never dreamed this would be her story.

She never dreamed she would consider closing the chapter on Christopher once and for all.

She wondered if God would ever forgive her if she chose to walk away.

And even if he did, would she ever forgive herself?

CHAPTER
21

By mid-July, the media broke the story that a woman named Darby, who lived in Colorado Springs, was pregnant with Christopher's illegitimate child. Evelyn spent that night with a pint of peppermint stick and a spoon.

Despite the fact that she'd made her decision, learning the details of her husband's double life still got under her skin.

"Why do we have to wait the full ninety days, Casey?" Evelyn demanded as if it were perfectly acceptable to take out her frustrations on her poor lawyer. "This is ludicrous."

"This development certainly strengthens your case," Casey said. "But remember, Evelyn, Chris is a proud man. He's not going to roll over. He doesn't like to lose."

"I'm not asking for anything. I just want to move on with my life." As if she had something to move on to. "And he's going to try to make that impossible, isn't he?"

Casey spoke to her in his calmest voice then, reminding her they were getting closer. "Hang on, Evelyn. One day this will all be behind you."

Two weeks later, Evelyn started working part-time at The Paper Heart, in order to bring in a little money, but she generally hid in the back, stocking shelves and staying out of sight. The town had mostly forgotten her, but every now and then something would bring the scandal up again, and she'd have to deal with the stares, the whispers, the finger-pointing.

After one particularly trying morning shift of hiding from Georgina, Susan, Lydia, and the other members of the Loves Park Chamber Ladies, Evelyn returned to the bungalow, anxious for its promised solace.

The knock on the door was unexpected, though the *Loves Park Courier* had leaked her location earlier that week, raising the question, *Who's feeding the paper their information?*

Also worth asking: *Why?*

Evelyn's life was hardly worth reporting on anymore. Aside from work, most days she didn't even leave the bungalow.

She quietly moved toward the door and saw Abigail waiting on the other side.

"I brought you some clothes." She held out a bag of jeans and shirts that would make Evelyn look and feel more normal and less like a wealthy politician's ex-wife. The clothes she'd reluctantly packed up that day she'd raided her own closet did exactly the opposite.

"These still have the tags on them. I just asked for your hand-me-downs." It shamed her that she couldn't afford to go shopping for her own clothes anymore. How would she ever determine who she was if she couldn't dress the part?

Abigail shrugged. "They reminded me of you."

Evelyn hugged her, surprised how the kind gesture affected her. "Thanks."

"One more thing."

Evelyn pulled away, questioning Abigail with her eyes.

"I'm sorry."

Seconds later, four more women burst through the front door, complete with their easel, manila folders, and file boxes. Evelyn looked at Abigail, who grimaced another apology.

"You're looking a little bit better, Evelyn," Gigi said, moving past her and into the house.

"At least your hair is clean." Ursula harrumphed her way to an armchair and plopped down. "Got anything to eat?"

Evelyn excused herself to the kitchen, where

she quickly scrounged together a few snacks. When she returned, she saw a large photo of Trevor pinned to the easel. She set the tray of snacks on the coffee table and sat down.

"What is all this?"

"Your benefactor is in need of our help," Gigi said. "And we're inclined to give it. The man might be well on his way to crotchety, but we think there's a diamond underneath all that mud."

"We have it on good authority he hasn't been out with Miss Lawson in a week and a half," Doris said, slapping a photo of Maggie next to Trevor's and affixing it there with a magnet. "But we think he just needs a push in the right direction."

Evelyn picked up one of the folders and flipped through it. "How do you plan to push Whit?" she asked. "Judging by this folder, you haven't found much dirt on him." That didn't surprise her. The man was private, hated crowds, and spent much of each day in a mysterious red barn she'd yet to inspect.

Maggie's folder was nearly empty too.

"We need your help," Gigi said.

Evelyn tossed both folders back on the coffee table. "Why me?" She hardly saw Whit these days. He was always busy, and now that she had a part-time job, they only really spoke to each other in passing.

"After all he's done for you, it's the least we can do to repay him."

"But if I remember correctly, he asked you not to interfere with his love life." Guilt niggled at Evelyn. She hadn't done anything to help repay Whit. She hadn't pulled a weed or watered a flower.

And while he made the occasional short-tempered remark, for the most part, he put up with her.

Was this really who she wanted to become?

"It's just some harmless digging. We need you to probe him a little—figure out what it is that has him so spooked," Gigi said. "There must be a reason why he's pulling away from her. And doggone it, we need a wedding. Our reputation is at stake."

"I'm not comfortable with this," Evelyn said. After everything Trevor had done for her, she wasn't going to purposely go against his wishes.

Doris let out a sigh. "He's such an attractive, kind man. Plays that guitar at church. All the girls talk about how handsome he is, but he never even looks in their direction."

"Maybe he's holding out for someone special," Abigail said. She looked at Evelyn. "Do you know if there's a woman he's hung up on?"

Evelyn shook her head. "No. I know he dated that Rachel for a long time." That's about all she knew. They dated for a year or so and then they broke up. It would be a miracle if anyone found out why. Whit certainly wouldn't volunteer that information.

Doris slapped Rachel's photo on the board with a thud.

"I don't know why they broke up. I thought they were going to get married." Evelyn stared at the photo of Whit. Where they'd found it, she had no idea. She almost wondered if one of them had taken it without his knowledge because he had that familiar faraway look in his eye, clearly not posing for the camera.

"You need to find out," Doris said. "It's so sad he's still single. And this Maggie might be his best chance at the real thing."

Evelyn sat. "Whit and I aren't exactly close."

Doris waved her off. "You live in his house."

"His guesthouse. He doesn't live here. I hardly ever see him. He's always working around the farm or out back in that barn."

"Making furniture," Doris said with a knowing tone of voice.

Evelyn frowned. *"Farming."*

All heads turned her way.

Gigi looked surprised. "You don't know?"

"Know what?" Evelyn's eyes darted around the room.

"Is it a secret?" Doris asked.

"Hardly." Ursula inspected the cookies Evelyn had set on the coffee table. "If it was a secret, I don't think he would've been on the cover of that business magazine last month."

Evelyn laughed. "Trevor Whitney? On the cover of a magazine?"

Abigail tapped on her phone, then handed it to

Evelyn. She'd loaded a page with the image of a Colorado business magazine featuring unlikely cover model Trevor Whitney.

"I don't understand. Whit runs the farm." Evelyn handed the phone back. "How does that land him on the cover of a business magazine?"

"If she doesn't even know about Trevor's side business, she is clearly not the right person to help make this match," Ursula said.

"Oh, my dear, there's a lot more to Mr. Whitney than meets the eye," Gigi said. "Which is why he could be a wonderful match for this Maggie. It would be a shame for someone with his qualities to go on living such a lonely existence."

"You still haven't told me what is so *wonderful* about him." Evelyn crossed her arms, but her sarcastic statement was met with deafening silence. Panicked expressions raced from woman to woman. She turned and found Trevor standing in the doorway, looking like a lost dog who'd wandered into a den of hungry wolves. Or to be more precise, a pen of cackling hens, which, in Trevor's world, was probably worse.

Had he heard what she said? Her words been so callous, and taken out of context, they must have sounded awful.

Quickly the ladies sprang into action, hiding the information they'd collected about Trevor and Maggie. Doris tore the photos off the board, the magnets falling to the floor with a plunk.

"You look busy," he said quietly. "I didn't mean to interrupt."

"Mr. Whitney," Gigi said, moving toward him. "It's wonderful to see you. We were hoping you and Evelyn might be able to work up some ideas for the new hearts yet this week."

Evelyn looked at him, but he avoided her. He must have heard. What a terrible thing for her to say—as if she couldn't think of ten wonderful things about him herself.

She didn't deserve to be his friend.

"Sure." He backed up, toward the door. "But can you get rid of the rest of that stuff?" He glanced at the folders still in Doris's hand.

The women all froze.

Evelyn had sat in on countless matchmaking sessions, and while Gigi wasn't lying when she said they did other things—many of them good—they did spend a considerable amount of time trying to find perfect matches for the lonely hearts of Loves Park.

Evelyn herself might soon fall under that category, but for obvious reasons, she hadn't sparked their attention.

It hadn't occurred to her before just how humiliating it would be for someone like Trevor—someone who would never willingly draw attention to himself—to walk in and find his face on an easel with a list of pros and cons underneath it.

To have people think he'd only ever fall in love if they intervened.

After he left, Evelyn stood. "That was awful."

"I'll say. You really shouldn't speak so harshly about Mr. Whitney, Evelyn," Doris said. "He's doing you such a favor letting you live here."

"I was talking about your folders and your photos and your list of pros and cons. He doesn't want you matching him. We should stay out of it."

"Yes, but why . . . ?"

"You don't know Trevor."

"I thought the two of you weren't close," Ursula said.

Evelyn rolled her eyes. Leave it to Ursula to throw her own words back at her.

"But you do know him, Evelyn," Gigi said. "So you can be the one to steer him in the right direction. Straight toward Maggie Lawson." She held up Maggie's photo with a smile. "We think you should use the hearts as a way in. Even someone as cold as Trevor Whitney will melt if he thinks someone has made a public declaration of their love for him."

"You want me to lie?"

Gigi frowned. "Of course not. We will convince Maggie to leave him a real, legitimate message. We just need you to play it up with Trevor."

"That's your plan?" Evelyn sighed. Maybe they *did* need her help.

Gigi's brow furrowed. "Do you have a better one?"

"I hate to break it to you, Gigi, but all of this—especially leaving messages on lampposts—is exactly the kind of thing that would have Trevor Whitney running for the hills. There is no way any of it is going to help you in your cause."

Besides, did Gigi know the state of Evelyn's love life? How could they even want her to get involved in this scheme?

"You underestimate the power of Loves Park tradition, young lady," Gigi said. She flipped open one of the folders. "Look at this list of standing messages, some dating back ten, even fifteen years. These are the ones that come in every single year."

Evelyn glanced at the sheet of paper. "This does nothing to prove your point."

"Let me finish," Gigi said.

Evelyn picked up the paper but didn't respond.

"We also get anonymous hearts," Gigi said, flipping to the next sheet in the folder. "The kind too personal or risky to attach to a name. In fact, a couple of those also seem to be standing orders. They come in every year."

"She's still waiting for your point, Gigi," Ursula said.

Gigi shot the other woman a look. "The *point* is I've done my research over the years, and I've uncovered nearly all of the people who've purchased these hearts anonymously."

"I guess the word *anonymous* means different things to different people," Evelyn said.

Gigi scowled. "Anyway, over 85 percent of them are from men exactly like Trevor Whitney."

"I don't believe you," Evelyn said. "There aren't other men like Trevor Whitney."

The other ladies stilled.

Evelyn looked from face to face, replaying the words she'd said. "Oh, stop it. I didn't mean it like that."

"Are you sure? Because that's an entirely different can of worms," Gigi said.

"No, I mean I've never known anyone like him. He's maddening. He doesn't talk. He's kind but mean at the same time."

"Just like Mack Barrett."

"The high school football coach?"

"And one of the sappiest romantics in this town," Gigi said proudly.

"Oh, and Bert McDonald." Doris waved her hand in Gigi's direction. "Tell her about Bert!"

"Bert works construction. Very manly but also quite an accomplished poet."

Evelyn only stared.

"You really shouldn't label people with such stereotypes, Evelyn." Gigi snatched the paper from her hands and tucked it back inside a manila folder, evidently unaware of her own double standard.

"This plan will work. Now here." With a stern

nod she handed Evelyn the binder concerning the hearts. "You and Mr. Whitney can talk about your plan for the new and improved hearts and you can probe him about Maggie. Report back."

Evelyn groaned.

Obviously these women had an agenda, and Evelyn knew from experience that once they'd set their minds on something, there was no changing it.

But as she settled into her spot on the corner of the couch, she happened to glance at Ursula, who hadn't said a word for some time, but who seemed to be intent on assessing the entire situation, and if Evelyn wasn't mistaken, the woman's gaze was fixed on her.

Few things were as unnerving as that.

CHAPTER

22

It had been six days since the Valentine Volunteers had given Evelyn the folders and her mission regarding Trevor's love life.

Six days since he'd overheard her wondering aloud what was so wonderful about him.

Six days since he'd come by to check on her.

She'd blown it. Big-time. She didn't have many friends and she'd managed to run one of them off.

Evelyn pulled on a pair of jeans and a tank top and headed outside to try to find Whit. She had to apologize and explain that she hadn't meant the remark the way it sounded.

But as she approached the house, she saw the entire staff had gathered over by the chicken coop. Farm staff meeting?

She didn't belong there, and yet curiosity got the better of her. She'd never made it out for one of their meetings before. She approached with caution, doing her best to avoid Whit's notice, hiding at the back of the small group of ten or so.

Whit stood at the front, Lilian at his side.

"So you can't keep us all on; that's what you're saying?" one of the guys said.

Whit held a hand up. "No, that's not what I'm saying. I'm just telling you we've plateaued a little. It's time to take a look at how things are running and see if we need to make any adjustments."

Lilian shrugged, perhaps trying to maintain a calm demeanor. "We just need to figure out what we can do to grow. Leveling off isn't good in any business."

"Isn't that why we brought in the cattle? The grass-fed beef is sold before they're even old enough to go to the slaughterhouse," one of the guys said.

"That's been years ago now, but that was a smart addition," Whit said. "Time to see if we're missing any other opportunities."

Evelyn's gaze circled the small team of employees. They all wore the same nervous expression.

Trevor must've noticed. "Guys. This isn't a death sentence for the farm. I'm asking for your ideas, is all. You're out and about more than I am. You're at the markets. Just tell me if anything comes to mind." Whit took his ball cap off and ran a hand through his hair. "Now, let's have a good day out there. Lilian is making her special Italian beef for lunch today in the white barn."

The guys all clapped Trevor on the shoulder or shook his hand before heading out in various directions to feed and water the animals, collect and wash eggs, and water the vegetable gardens. After they left, Trevor finally tossed a glance in Evelyn's direction but didn't approach her.

She was leaning against the chicken coop, waiting for a chance to talk to Whit, when Lilian spotted her and waved. The older woman wore wisdom in the form of deep lines on her face.

"How've you been, Evie?" Lilian said when she reached her. She wore snug jeans, a brown leather belt, cowboy boots, and a white tank top that made her skin look even tanner.

Evelyn smiled. "I'm doing okay. Sounds like the farm isn't?"

Lilian waved her hand in the air as if to swat an imaginary fly. "Hard business. We just want to stay ahead of it."

"Is Trevor worried?" He was deep in conversation with Sutton McIntosh, the livestock manager.

Lilian looked at him. "Who can tell?"

"He is hard to read, isn't he?"

"One thing is sure, though: these guys love him. They'd do anything for him. He's just that kind of leader. Knows how to bring people together."

Evelyn could see that about him. He made people want to be better. Made her want to be better.

"You think he'd be open to suggestions from anyone?" Evelyn asked.

Lilian raised a brow. "From you?" She laughed. "Sure, sweetheart, give it a whirl. I gotta go check on the beans. Have a good day."

She walked away, leaving Evelyn feeling awkward, standing by herself beside a bunch of chickens.

Trevor glanced her way again, finished his conversation with Sutton, and strode toward her. "You're out of the house."

"Good observation." This was harder than she thought. "Sorry I crashed your meeting."

"Sorry to deliver such depressing news."

"You okay?"

He shrugged. "It's my family legacy and I'm not sure how to make a go of it. I've had better days." He started walking toward the pasture. She followed, mostly because she still hadn't worked up the courage to apologize for her thoughtless remark.

His family's legacy. She remembered how important that was to him. It was, after all, the thing that had brought him back to Loves Park.

"I know how much this place means to you."

He continued walking.

"I was there when you found out about your dad's Parkinson's, remember?"

He slowed. "I don't like to talk about it."

Understatement. The diagnosis was what interrupted Trevor's college career, his life plans, and kept him on the farm.

"You never did like to talk about it."

"Don't you have somewhere to be?" He plodded toward the red barn with Evelyn on his heels.

"Your dad would be proud of you, Whit," she said.

He spun around and faced her.

She stopped, backing away. "I'm sorry. I know it's not my place."

Never mind that once upon a time it would've been.

Christmas break, sophomore year of college. That's when Trevor learned about his father. His parents were so concerned about his dad's condition, they'd wanted Trevor home to learn the business before it was too late for his dad to teach him.

She'd watched him wrestle with that decision,

the desire to make his own way conflicting with that need to make his parents proud.

In the end, he'd chosen to stay on the farm. Of course he had. He was Trevor.

He let out a long sigh. "No, it's fine. I'm just having a bad morning."

"I know a little something about bad mornings." She forced a smile.

Her sadness didn't hang like a cloak on her shoulders anymore, but she'd hardly gotten back to normal. She was still refusing to speak to Christopher, ignoring phone calls from her mother, and hiding out in a guesthouse that did not belong to her.

Something needed to change.

He began walking again, this time at a slightly slower pace, toward the greenhouse. "You remember that night?"

She fell into step beside him. "It was the first time I heard you play piano."

"Sometimes that's easier than talking," he said.

If only she could play. She hadn't known until that night that he was such a musician. They were in the music room at Christopher's parents' house—her boyfriend off being Christopher, leaving her alone and empty.

Whit had wandered in looking like she felt, but asking no questions and offering no answers. Instead, he moved to the piano and let his fingers glide across the keys, a haunting melody that seemed to match the mood that had fallen between them. Forlorn somehow. Drawn to watch the ease with which he played, she slid onto the bench next to him. This tall, brooding man seemed to say more with that song than he ever had in words.

Still, she felt like she was privy to something sacred, a side of himself he rarely shared. He stopped playing abruptly, drawing her eyes to his troubled face.

"I'm not going back to school," he announced.

She hadn't responded. She had been able to tell by the look on his face he was still processing it himself.

Looking back now, Evelyn could see what an impossible situation that had been for him. Did he regret his choice?

"I have an idea," she announced, determined to change the subject.

"Oh?" He tugged his hat down lower on his head.

"I don't know if you're going to go for it," Evelyn said.

"Try me."

She pressed her lips together as if doling out the idea in small bits would go over better with him. "What if you created a section of the farm just for people to come out and pick their own vegetables?"

Whit stared at her like she had an arm growing out of her head. "Why would anyone want to do that?" He picked up his pace, focused on the greenhouse.

"Are you kidding me? People love this stuff." She practically had to run to keep up with him. "They like to bring their kids out to learn where real food comes from, and there's something about picking your own food and then going home and making a big meal with it."

"There is?"

She swatted him on the arm. "Ask Lilian if you don't believe me."

Whit shook his head. "I don't know." He yanked an old hose from the side of the greenhouse and pulled it toward the outdoor garden, where he hooked it up to a sprinkler.

"Picture this. We kick it off with a big community farmhouse meal. You could do several each year. Lilian is one of the best cooks in Loves Park—everyone knows that—so you'd have a great turnout. Then we tell people they can get their own delicious box of fresh produce, either prepackaged or pick-your-own, every Saturday at Whitney Farms."

"Would I have to talk to people?" He knelt down at the spigot and the sprinkler shot to life.

Evelyn laughed. "You could let me talk to them. It's the least I can do."

"Pick your own, huh?" Whit squinted up at her. "Is that something you rich people do?"

Her own words hung between them. *"You still*

haven't told me what is so wonderful *about him."* Did she make him feel like she was better than him somehow? It wasn't the first time he'd mentioned the vast difference between their "people."

"Whit, I wanted to apologize for—"

He silenced her with an upheld hand. "I'll think about your idea."

She gave a sharp nod as he stood and headed toward the other end of the greenhouse, where another hose and sprinkler waited to water a second garden plot. Once he'd finished, he walked back to her and stopped. "Anything else?"

"Actually, yes," she said, remembering the other reason why she'd come looking for him in the first place. "The hearts."

He groaned. "Can't we get out of that?" He started toward the pastures now, shaking the fences that kept the cattle from roaming outside their designated area. Evelyn followed doggedly behind.

"Where are you going?" She stopped walking after a minute.

He turned and faced her. "I walk the land every day. The whole perimeter."

"That's nuts."

"Well, I don't usually have company." He continued on.

She jogged until she caught up to him, Gigi's reminders about pushing him toward Maggie echoing in her mind. What did they expect her to do? Outline the good things about a woman she didn't know? She couldn't make Trevor fall in love with Maggie any more than she could make Christopher sorry for what he'd done.

"What's in there?" Evelyn pointed to the barn that sat at the back of the property, the one where he spent so much time.

"Nothing."

She started toward the barn, and this time it was Whit who had to jog to catch up to her.

"You're always out here doing things," she said over her shoulder. "What do you have in there?" She spun around. "You're not a murderer or anything, are you?"

He shot her a look and she laughed, then took off toward the barn.

"Evelyn, come on," he called after her. But he was too late.

She pulled on the door and inhaled the smell of sawdust. "What is this place?"

Lumber in various lengths and widths had been stacked on shelves along one of the walls. Machines, counters, and workbenches, along with half-completed pieces of furniture, filled the main portion of the barn, like islands in a sea of possibility.

"So when Gigi said you were a woodworker, that was an understatement?"

"You've got to be the nosiest person I've ever met."

"Have you met Gigi and Doris?" She gawked for several long seconds, feeling once again like she was witnessing something private and sacred.

And judging by the look on his face, it embarrassed him to share this space. But they were friends, weren't they? He could let her in on this one secret. She took her phone from her pocket, found the image of the cover of the magazine Abigail had shown her, and held it up.

He groaned. "Where did you get that?"

"It's a magazine, Whit! You're on the cover!"

"Don't remind me." He moved past her to the workbench at the back of the barn.

"Seriously, Whit, what is all this?" She watched as he moved around the space, as comfortable in these surroundings as he was out on the farm.

He looked away. "It's not that big of a deal."

"Obviously it is, if you were on the cover of a magazine."

It struck her again how different he was from Christopher. When Christopher saw his face in the press, everyone around saw it too.

Divorced. For a fleeting moment, she'd forgotten. The word popped into her head, bringing with it emotions she would've loved to stuff in a shoe box and bury six feet underground. Once Christopher signed the papers, that status would be official.

"I make furniture. People buy it. It's really not a big deal."

She wandered farther into the barn and discovered, on the other side of the machines, a sort of showroom—only she knew he hadn't set it up for anyone to browse.

"These are your finished pieces?" Evelyn ran a hand across a tall dresser. Dark stain offset aged brass drawer pulls perfectly. Trevor might not be a part of her world, but the people in her world would pay a lot of money for a piece like this.

And that was just the beginning. Behind the dresser were two more, both different styles. Beside those, a bed frame, a headboard, and a gorgeous farmhouse table she would've purchased in a second. If she had any money.

"I have a delivery this weekend."

She walked around to the other side, still inspecting his work. Unlike the shoddy furniture most stores carried, Trevor's pieces were solid and built to last. This table might double as a bomb shelter in a pinch. "A delivery to whom?"

"A store in Denver. They sell my stuff."

At the end of his workbench, tucked underneath a hammer and a can of stain, Evelyn spotted an actual copy of the magazine. Likely someone else had brought that here—she couldn't see him purchasing anything with his face on the cover. She edged it out from under the hammer and stain and read the headline on the front cover.

" 'The DIY Entrepreneur.' "

Trevor groaned. "Put it away, Evie."

She flipped it open until she found the article, which she hadn't read. "What is *Desvío*?"

He took his hat off and rubbed his temples. She didn't care that he was uncomfortable. And for once she would be sure her curiosity didn't run him off, even if it meant she had to get bossy.

"It's the name of my company." He looked embarrassed. This was a big deal; shouldn't he be excited? She paged through the article—a full feature on him, his story, and his company, complete with photos of him working in the barn where they now stood.

Images of completed pieces of furniture in an upscale-looking boutique in Denver stared back at her.

"Why *Desvío*?"

He put his hat back on and leaned against the workbench. "I like the way it sounds."

She shot him a look.

He sighed. "It's Spanish for 'detour.'"

"Detour." So many questions filled her head. She could tell he had stories, and for the first time since they'd parted ways after her wedding, she found herself wondering what they were. "It's really amazing. I guess you aren't so far removed from my world after all."

"About that." He stared at the ground. "I didn't mean it the way it came out."

She held up a hand, mimicking his earlier gesture, then closed the magazine. "It's fine. I was never very comfortable in that world either."

Silence hung between them. Since her life had begun unraveling, Evelyn had started to realize all the ways she'd lost herself. She used to be a person with ambitions and dreams. She used to have convictions to stand by. She used to know who she was. But she'd spent so many years trying to please everyone else, she'd lost her way.

Trevor had those things. He'd always known exactly who he was. How did he do that?

"I can't believe you've been doing all this and nobody knows."

He gestured at the magazine and smirked. "Lots of people know."

But she hadn't known. She bit her lip. More proof of how far out of touch she'd grown from people who used to be her friends. "What's the story behind the name?"

He stuck his hands in his pockets. How the reporter had ever gotten an interview out of this man was beyond her. "If my life hadn't taken that detour, I never would've learned how to do any of it."

"You mean school."

"Right. Remember my dad wanted to teach me how to run the farm before his health made that impossible?"

She nodded.

"Well, he did. But it was here in his wood shop

that I actually figured things out." Trevor's gaze circled the barn. "And this is where I really got to know my dad."

Evelyn filled in the blanks as usual. Imagining hours of quiet moments spent together by a father and a son who didn't need words to communicate.

He set his hand on a plank of wood waiting to be molded into something else—a small piece of something greater.

"I had no idea you were such an artist." She smiled.

"If I remember right, that was always more your thing."

She shrugged. "There are lots of different kinds of artists, Whit." She motioned toward the finished pieces. "This is art."

"I'm just a farmer with a table saw," he said.

"Why do you do that?"

A question played across his expression. "Do what?"

"Downplay your talent. You don't give yourself nearly enough credit. It's like you don't even realize how amazing this all is." She hugged the magazine to her chest. "You don't have to be embarrassed about who you are."

"I could say the same to you." His hazel eyes challenged her.

She didn't like where this was heading. She didn't want to think about all the ways she'd lost herself.

"How long has it been since you painted anything?"

She shook her head. "Never mind."

"Ev, when I left school, I thought my life was over. I had to finish at night while I was working the farm. I missed out on that whole college experience, and I resented it for a long time."

She tossed her hair behind her shoulder, wishing he'd stop talking and yet feeling like what he had to say was important. If it wasn't, he wouldn't be saying it.

"I could've stayed mad. You can stay mad too. You can hide out in the guesthouse and forget how the sunshine feels on your skin. Or you can figure out what you want your next chapter to look like."

She should have known that somehow he'd make this about her. "You think I'm going to spend my days painting, Whit? How is that going to pay the bills?"

He shrugged. "Figure it out."

The words jabbed at her like the perfectly placed tip of a sword.

"My dad never wanted to teach me about woodworking. I had to ask. Because I wanted to know."

But what did she want to know? What did she want to do? Who did she want to become? She didn't have answers to any of those questions.

She just didn't want to feel like she wasn't enough anymore.

"Figure it out."

"Sorry, Ev. But you've been moping around long enough. It's time to dust yourself off and remember what it was you wanted in the first place."

His words smacked at her, but she somehow found the resolve to look at him while she calculated a response. Despite the pointed way he spoke, there was kindness in his tone. The sort of kindness that she desperately needed—no strings attached. Whit didn't want anything from her. He didn't need her to act or dress or speak a certain way.

He only wanted her to be her best self. The version he'd known all those years ago.

Could her detour help her find it again?

"Why are you doing this, Whit?"

"I'm sorry if it's hard to hear, but—"

She shook her head. "No, why are you helping me? Letting me stay here? Is your sense of loyalty to Christopher so strong you feel you have to take care of his pathetic wife?"

"I'm not doing this for him," he said, his voice quiet.

"Then why? You don't even like me." She knew what he thought of her and her way of life. Never mind that he was profiting from people like her with this furniture business he'd built. He'd seen how great her departure from her true self was. That must've been why he'd grown so unkind.

"Is that what you think?" he asked, seemingly confused.

The door to the barn rattled open, pulling their attention away from each other.

Maggie stood in the dim light, and confusion washed across her face. "I'm sorry. I should've called."

Whit cleared his throat, then moved in Maggie's direction.

Evelyn stepped toward the door. "We can finish talking about the hearts later," she said, trying to figure out why she felt like she'd done something wrong.

She reached the door and tossed one mindless glance over her shoulder as she passed Maggie and Trevor, only to find him still watching her. And for the first time in as long as she'd known him, Trevor Whitney looked like he might actually have something more to say.

CHAPTER

23

"That was cozy," Maggie said, her voice accusing. "What's going on with you two?"

"We're working on a project for the city," he said.

She didn't look convinced.

"I didn't realize we had plans today," Trevor said. A roundabout way of asking her what she was doing there.

"I was in town," she said. "Thought I'd stop by and say hi." She ran a hand through her hair. "I should've let you know before I came."

"No, it's fine. Lilian's making a big lunch for the guys. You should stay." Even as he spoke, he knew his tone did not sound persuasive.

Maybe he really was meant to be alone. He was no good at this relationship thing. The truth was, he was thankful Maggie had arrived when she did because having Evelyn in his wood shop threw him off. He craved the solace of this place—the place he came to think and wrestle with God. Evelyn reminded him of past regrets, things he'd prayed through long ago.

Made him think maybe he had more work to do on closing a chapter he thought he'd already ended.

It turned out having Maggie in the barn was a completely different kind of unnerving. He didn't let just anyone in there, and as crazy as it sounded, he didn't know her well enough yet to allow her to invade this space.

But that didn't stop her. She walked over to the furniture. "You *made* these?"

He leaned against the workbench. "I did."

"They're amazing." She strolled up and down the makeshift aisles, touching virtually every single piece. "Really beautiful, Whit."

He nodded a thank-you and started toward the door. "You hungry?"

She followed him outside but stopped a few feet from the wood shop.

He turned back. "Maggie?"

"If I'm getting in your way, just tell me, okay?" She shifted from one foot to the other. "I don't want to make a fool of myself."

He took a couple steps toward her. "What do you mean?"

She kicked at the ground. "What's going on with us? You always seem so preoccupied."

Figure it out.

His own words popped into his head. They'd come out harsher than he intended when he said them to Evelyn. But then they'd always been harsh when his father had spoken them to him too. Dad had no tolerance for Trevor's pouting, so after one too many days of self-pity over the loss of his traditional college career, his father got right up in his face and said, "Look, Son, figure it out. Time isn't on our side here, so if you want to go back to school, tell me now and I'll train someone else."

That was the day things turned around for Trevor, the day he accepted that his life looked different than he thought it would.

Maybe today was a repeat of that lesson.

Maggie stood in front of him, looking exposed and vulnerable. She was putting her heart on the line just by being there. She'd taken a risk even considering a relationship with him. How long was he going to put his life on hold for something that would never be?

"I'm sorry," he said. "I do have a lot going on right now. I'm working on some pretty big changes for the farm."

"And then there's Evelyn." She studied him as if trying to decide whether her words garnered some sort of reaction.

"I am concerned about her, yes," Trevor said. "She's my friend."

"And that's it?"

He took a step toward her. "That's it."

She looked at him, and he wasn't sure if she believed him. "Then why haven't you kissed me yet?"

Casey's similar question rushed back at him. He didn't have an answer for him then and he didn't have an answer for Maggie now.

He'd thought about it, but the memory of the pain he'd caused Rachel always kept him from making a move. "I'm not sure you want to get involved with someone like me, Maggie."

She moved closer to him. "Why don't you let me decide that for myself?"

She was pretty and smart and spunky, and she liked him. She made him laugh. Wouldn't it be better to be with someone like that instead of chasing the ghost of a memory?

He reached out and touched her face. She inched

nearer, her hands on his chest, eyes intent on his own. Slowly she wrapped her arms around his neck and pulled him down to her until their lips met.

Tentative at first, he drew in the scent of her. How long had it been since he'd kissed a woman?

This was good for him. It had to be.

He wrapped his arms around her waist and deepened the kiss.

Of course he should pursue this. He should forget Evelyn and invest in what was right in front of him.

He leaned back for a brief second and studied Maggie's expression. She wore a breathless look as she searched his face. He couldn't process the thoughts tumbling around in his mind, so instead he leaned in and kissed her again.

Figure it out.

He'd been the lovesick fool one too many times and for too many years. Maggie had come along at the perfect moment, just what he needed to keep him from falling back into old patterns and old habits.

This is good.

A stick broke in the distance, and he backed away from Maggie to listen. Could be an animal—a coyote or an elk.

"We should go in," he said, taking her hand. "I'm starving."

She smiled. "Me too."

As they passed the guesthouse, Trevor glanced

at the two Adirondack chairs that faced the mountains. Empty. Evelyn sat outside in one every evening. He knew because he checked for the outside lamp that flickered in the darkness until she went indoors. His way of saying good night.

"Those are perfect," Maggie said, stopping to admire the chairs and the postcard-worthy setting they created. "Did you make them too?"

"They were a gift from my parents," Trevor said, halting beside her. His mother loved those chairs. When she still lived on the farm, they were positioned closer to the main house, but when his parents moved to the retirement community, she'd had one of the farm employees drive them up the hill to the guesthouse for him.

"I know you won't move into the farmhouse," his mom had said. "At least not right away." She gestured toward the bed of his dad's pickup truck. "I wanted you to at least have these here. Somehow it's like your father and I will still be here every night, watching the sun set over the mountains."

A part of him was happy to know Evelyn found solace in those chairs, given what they represented to him. Another part of him could only think of sitting in the empty seat next to her as she sorted through the mess her life had become.

"Trevor?"

Maggie's voice pulled him from his thoughts. "Sorry."

She smiled. "Daydreaming again?"

"Suppose I was."

They were the last to reach the white barn, and when they arrived, the crew let out a shout of welcome. Evelyn stood behind the table, helping Lilian with the buffet-style meal. She glanced up at him but quickly turned her attention to a pan of potatoes.

"Here," he said to Maggie, "let me take your stuff."

She handed him her big, floppy purse as Lilian intercepted her. Trevor set the purse out of the way, but as he did, something caught his eye: a prescription bottle tucked in an inside pocket with the word *Xanax* on it.

He didn't know much about medication, but he thought Xanax was used to treat things like depression. He glanced at Maggie, who stood at the front of the line near Lilian. She was laughing at something one of his employees had said.

She hardly seemed depressed, but he knew it wasn't often easy to tell.

Evelyn, on the other hand, always had an air of sadness about her, though given her current situation, he'd think there was something wrong with her if she didn't. But in that moment, surrounded by the guys who worked his land, cared for his animals, and sold his crops, Evelyn almost looked like her old self again.

She gave him a quick smile, then waved her

hands around the barn at the group that had assembled to eat Lilian's meal. She mouthed the words *community dinner* with a look that said, *I told you so.*

He had to admit she might be on to something. Family-style lunch had become one of their favorite things to do for the staff at the farm. Nothing brought people together like food.

Lilian appeared at his side. "You gonna eat?"

"I'm thinking about it," Trevor said. "Wanted to make sure there was enough for everyone first."

"You kidding? I made enough to feed a small army," she said.

"That's what it takes to feed these guys."

Lilian paused, her desire to say something obvious in the air.

"Say it."

"What?" She looked at him, doing her best to appear innocent.

He gave her a sideways glance. "You forget how well I know you."

She crossed her arms. "It's good to see Evelyn out of the house; that's all I was thinking."

It *was* good to see her out and about. In something other than that tattered sweater she'd been living in. "And?"

Lilian shrugged. "And what?"

"I know that's not all you're thinking. What else is on your mind?"

"She told me about her ideas for the farm."

"And?"

Lilian looked at him. "I think it's brilliant."

Risky was what it was. They had to work twice as hard as commercial farms already just to break even. Throwing in community meals and events would only add to their overflowing workload. "Do you have time?"

"To cook? Sure. I'd make time for this place, Trevor; you know that."

He did know, but he didn't want to take advantage. "But how do we get the word out? That's another full-time job."

Lilian gestured in Evelyn's direction.

"I don't know if she's ready to take on something like that, Lil. Besides, she's working at Abigail's."

"Are you kidding? She's been planning events her entire married life. She's perfect, well connected, and she's got a great head on her shoulders."

That she did.

"I have a feeling she'd make time for this place too."

He drew in a breath. "I'm going to regret this, aren't I?"

Lilian punched him in the arm. "Not a chance, boss. I promise. You just leave it to us and we'll get these dinners off the ground." She shot Evelyn a look and sent her a thumbs-up.

He had to admit their ideas intrigued him. What if it wasn't just his hard work that would keep this farm profitable? What if it was these two unlikely allies who had the right vision for Whitney Farms?

"By the way," Lilian said, turning to face him, "what's up with you and the redhead?"

Trevor glanced at Maggie, who still looked perfectly comfortable chatting with Dale and the others. He shrugged. "Not sure yet."

Lilian leaned closer. "Be careful with that one."

Trevor frowned. "Why?"

"I got a sense about these things," she said softly. "You know I do."

That was true. Lilian did seem to have the innate ability to see through people's facades. "You don't even know her."

"Did I know that Brenner boy your sister brought home from college?"

Trevor groaned. Thankfully, that relationship had been short-lived. Kyle Brenner was the last thing Jules needed and everyone could see it except her.

But Maggie? What could Lilian possibly sense about Maggie?

He brushed her off and moved toward the buffet to see what the guys had left him for lunch, but he couldn't shake the idea that he should listen to his aunt.

He just didn't know why.

CHAPTER

24

A few days later, Trevor's phone rang during his morning coffee. He looked at the caller ID. *Casey.* Trevor's stomach dropped. Why would he be calling so early?

"Dude," Casey said when Trevor answered. "Chris signed the papers."

"He did?" They'd all expected him to keep trying to win Evelyn back, to hold out on her as long as possible. Divorce didn't look good for his case, though neither did a pregnant mistress.

He'd been back in court and all of his assets had been frozen, which meant that Evelyn had nothing but her part-time work at The Paper Heart, free room and board, and Trevor, Lilian, and the Volunteers, who made sure she was taken care of.

It would be only a short time before Evelyn's divorce was final. Trevor's thoughts were interrupted by Casey on the other end of the line.

"Yeah, but . . . man, couldn't you wait another month?"

Trevor frowned. "What are you talking about?"

"Don't play dumb with me, Whit. I read the paper." Casey sighed. "How long has it been going on?"

"Lilian, give me that." He reached across the table, where his aunt was making a shopping list. She shoved the folded newspaper toward him.

He snapped it open. "You've *got* to be kidding."

Lilian stuck her pencil into the back of her ponytail. "What is it?"

He flipped the paper around to show her. There on the second page was a photo of him and Evelyn in his wood shop the other day.

"What in the world?" Lilian took the paper. "Trevor, what is going on here?"

He groaned. "Nothing is going on. That is not what it looks like."

She threw it back at him. "It looks like you're hiding something."

Someone had caught them looking at one another—a pause in their *completely innocent* conversation, he was sure—but even he had to admit, at first glance, the image suggested more than friendship.

"Come on, dude," Casey said.

But before Trevor could respond, Evelyn appeared in the doorway. She held up her own phone, and he cringed at the image on the screen— that same falsely incriminating article, which must also be featured in the *Courier*'s online edition.

"Casey, I'll call you back." He hung up and stared at her.

"Who would do this?" Panic washed over her face. "And why?"

Trevor raked a hand across the stubble on his chin. "I don't know, Evie. I'm so sorry."

Evelyn's head shake seemed almost involuntary. "Someone is out to get me, Whit. Someone is intent on making a story where there is none, and I can't for the life of me figure out why."

She had a point. Regardless of the fact that Evelyn's name had been cleared weeks ago and most of the press had set their sights elsewhere, someone at the *Loves Park Courier* kept dredging up Evelyn's dirty laundry. Her anxiety. Her therapy visits. Her medication. And now her friendship with Whit.

"What are people going to think when they read this?"

Lilian pushed her chair away from the table and glared at Evelyn. "Why is that the only thing that matters with you?"

Evelyn's brows rose.

Trevor had asked Evelyn the same thing many times, but it sounded severe coming from someone else. "Lilian." Trevor put a hand on his aunt's shoulder. "Not now."

Evelyn steeled her jaw. "Go ahead. Tell me what you think."

Lilian sighed. "I think you need to figure out who you are, not who everyone else wants you to be. And that has to be enough. It's enough for the One who made you—why isn't it enough for you?"

Evelyn looked away, hurt.

"Who cares what some faulty newspaper says? What's the truth?" Lilian was on a roll.

Evelyn met the older woman's eyes for a brief moment, then ran out of the room without saying a word.

"Typical," Lilian said.

"That was harsh," Trevor said, wondering if he should go after her.

"She's got to learn, Trevor. Same way we all learned. This stuff can ruin you, or you can use it to make you stronger. That's why God allows it, you know—to stretch us, change us. Get us where he wants us."

Trevor turned away, leaning over the counter. "Why couldn't you say that, then?"

Lilian was silent for a lengthy moment. "You told me you dealt with this."

He spun around and faced her. "What are you talking about? You don't believe that garbage, do you?"

"Of course not. Because I know my nephew would never step over that line."

At least she believed that much.

She held up the paper, the photo taunting him. "But I also know that look on your face."

"Lilian."

"Don't 'Lilian' me. I know you as well as anyone can, Trevor, and this is dangerous territory you're in here."

"I'm fine," Trevor lied. "I just want to be her friend. And I want to figure out who is printing all these lies."

Lilian threw the paper on the table. "Friends, huh?"

"Yes. You know I gave that up a long time ago, Lil."

"Sometimes the heart gets confused," she said. "Convinces you you've surrendered when really you've just shoved the issue down deeper."

Trevor glared at her. He didn't like the implication. He was a man of honor and integrity. He knew Evelyn wasn't his to love, and he'd battled that fact for years. But he'd told God he was done. More than once.

And he meant it, even if his feelings didn't always fall in line.

That was surrender, wasn't it?

"I'll figure out who wrote the article," Lilian said. "Because frankly, I'm pretty angry about that too." She muttered something about Evelyn's fresh start and let the screen door slam on her way out, leaving Trevor face-to-face with the demons of his past and a photo that clearly tattled on every one of those feelings he'd been working so desperately to keep hidden.

CHAPTER
25

Another week and a half later, Evelyn sat at The Paper Heart, listening to Doris read the minutes from the Volunteers' last impromptu meeting, which had been sprung on her in Trevor's guesthouse.

"Can someone else read the minutes?" Ursula said, her voice gruff.

Doris gasped. "What's wrong with the way I read the minutes?"

"You're so slow. Besides, all you really have to say is we told Evelyn to dig up what she could for Operation Whitney/Lawson."

Evelyn glowered. "Is that really what we're calling it?"

Doris nibbled the edge of a cookie. "Perfectly acceptable name. Straightforward, so no one gets confused."

Evelyn didn't bother to argue. "I haven't made much progress." Truth was, she hadn't even tried. After Trevor's directive to "figure it out," she'd had a hard time concentrating on anything but whatever she was supposed to be figuring out. That, coupled with the fallout from the newspaper article all but accusing her of having an affair with Trevor, had pretty much occupied any open space in her head.

The door of The Paper Heart opened and two women walked in. Women she recognized from her charity work around town. When they spotted Evelyn, they looked at each other, whispered something, and walked straight out of the store.

"Unbelievable," Ursula said. "Want me to give them a piece of your mind?"

The familiar pace of anxiety returned to Evelyn's heart. She glanced at Abigail. "I shouldn't be here. I'm costing you customers."

Abigail shrugged. "Those aren't the kind of customers I want."

"How absurd," Gigi said. "It's been months since this whole mess began. Haven't people forgotten by now?"

"Please, Gigi, don't pretend you didn't see the newspaper last week. Someone is determined to keep the Brandt name in the headlines one way or another," Evelyn said.

"I am assuming there's nothing to that story," Gigi said, a question in her voice.

"Of course there's not," Evelyn said, somewhat insulted. "Whit is my friend. You of all people should know that. It's just humiliating knowing everyone is still talking about me."

Her run-in with Lilian had left even more questions at the back of her mind. It did matter to her what people said and thought—was that wrong?

And that crack about caring about only what God thought about her—that would be great if someone could give her instructions on how to do it.

Most days lately, Evelyn felt like a complete failure. It was a wonder she hadn't had another full-blown panic attack these last few weeks.

Ursula harrumphed as she took three cookies from the plate at the center of the table. "Let 'em talk. If you're pleasing everyone all the time, something is off with your integrity."

"What do you mean?" Evelyn asked.

"You weren't created to make everyone happy," the old woman said. "If everyone likes you all the time, you're doing something wrong."

She hadn't thought of it that way. She'd spent most of her life trying to please everyone around her, especially Christopher. What if doing so had compromised who she was?

"The trouble is, it's interfering with a project I've started," Evelyn said.

Tess clapped her hands. "Back to Operation Whitney/Lawson!"

Evelyn shook her head.

"The painted hearts?" Doris asked. "Valentine's Day isn't all that many months away, you know."

"I know, and I haven't forgotten the hearts, but this is an idea I have to help generate revenue for Whitney Farms. However, I need community support." Evelyn turned her mug around in her hands. "Hard to come by these days."

The other ladies stilled at her admission as if they'd realized in that moment what an outcast she was.

"Tell us the plan," Gigi said. "We'll make some calls."

Evelyn noticed her racing heart had begun to quiet. She pulled out her notes outlining her plans for the farm. "I have all kinds of ideas for involving tourists and local families in pick-your-own events, but I think we should start with a Whitney Farms Dinner Night in the white barn."

"You want people to eat in a barn?" Ursula grimaced.

"It's a very clean barn, Ursula," Evelyn said. "We'll set up several of Trevor's big farmhouse tables and serve our community family style, with local food grown right here on Whitney Farms."

Gigi's face brightened. "Evelyn, this is a wonderful idea."

"You think so?"

"Yeah," Ursula said. "You might be more than just some guy's arm candy after all."

Evelyn frowned. "Thanks?"

Abigail smiled. "You know, Trevor could probably sell his furniture there too."

"He would never," Evelyn said. "He's so weird about it."

"Not weird," Doris said. "Modest."

"You're just not used to that quality in a man," Ursula said with a snort.

She had a point.

"Now," Gigi said, "we'll help you with your mission. Are you going to help us with ours?"

Evelyn sighed. She didn't want to invade Whit's personal space, and she knew he was against anyone matching him under any circumstances, but she did have one bit of information she could leak in an effort to quiet her nosy cohorts.

Gigi must've sensed her withholding something. She leaned toward Evelyn and narrowed her eyes. "Spill it, sister."

"I don't know who told you Whit is backing away from Maggie, but I think they were mistaken."

Doris gasped. "What do you know?"

"I don't *know* anything, but I saw them outside the barn," Evelyn said.

"Oooh, a secret rendezvous." Tess sounded thrilled by it. "Tell us more."

Evelyn hadn't intended to spy on Whit that day, but after Maggie had surprised them mid-conversation, she'd taken a short walk to clear her head. On her way back, she'd caught sight of Trevor and Maggie through the trees.

Gigi's expression turned pious. "What were they *doing* out there?"

Evelyn had lingered longer than she should have, but she couldn't help it. She hadn't seen this side of Whit before. He was this quiet, shy friend who never talked about himself unless he was forced, and accidentally observing him with Maggie made her wonder why he had spent so many years alone.

Despite his gruff exterior, he had more decency in him than anyone she'd ever known. Surely other women over the years had seen that.

"They were kissing," Evelyn said, remembering the way Trevor had held Maggie close.

Gigi looked thoughtful. "That's unexpected."

"That's all I know," Evelyn said, trying to push aside the memory of the way Trevor took Maggie's hand and led her away from the old barn, leaving Evelyn to hurry out from her hiding spot behind an aspen tree. She'd felt like a Peeping Tom and had to battle a twinge of jealousy that sprang up at the sight of their intimate moment.

Of course she was happy for her friend, but she wondered why he seemed to have reserved the best parts of himself for other people. Why, when it came to her, was he so withdrawn? He'd certainly been kind to her, but his kindness sometimes seemed forced or obligatory. Had he grown tired of her not pulling her weight on the farm? Had he realized he could command some decent income from the guesthouse if only he kicked her out and found an actual tenant?

"So they're kissing," Gigi said, taking over the meeting again. "I suppose that's progress."

"Definitely," Tess said with a nod.

The others agreed. Evelyn said nothing but happened to glance at Ursula, whose eyes were focused squarely on her like she was a robot programmed to scan Evelyn in search of secret thoughts. Evelyn prayed for a change of subject—and fast. The last thing she needed was Ursula, of all people, figuring out the mess of conflicting emotions running around in her mind.

She stood. "I have to go."

"So soon?" Ursula squinted in her direction.

"I have chores," Evelyn said, though she imagined they knew that wasn't exactly true. "I'll keep you posted if anything else happens."

Gigi followed her to the door. "I forgot to give this to you, dear," she said, pressing what Evelyn could only assume was cash into her hand.

"Gigi, no." Too often lately she'd been the recipient of her friends' charity.

"I insist," Gigi said. "And don't forget the hearts." Gigi started to walk away. "Make them over!"

Evelyn drove toward the farm, relishing the silence of her warm car. Summer was wearing on, and she remembered she'd polished off the last of her ice cream the night before. Ice cream—one of the few indulgences she allowed herself—had become a ritual in the evening, just like walking the farm's perimeter had in the morning. After Whit mentioned it, she tried it for herself. She couldn't walk the whole thing—not yet—but she certainly saw the value of time spent outdoors.

Those walks had turned into her favorite time of day. A time to clear her head and even whisper a prayer or two.

Ever since the last ice cream incident, she'd only visited the store late at night when no one was there and she didn't know any of the cashiers on duty, but it was midmorning now, and the parking lot was full. What if that same clerk was there? What if she refused to serve Evelyn again?

Evelyn pulled into the lot, turned off the engine, and stared at the door. She had to rejoin society at some point. And she had as much right as anyone to be there.

So why did she feel exactly the opposite?

"Figure it out."

She didn't want to be that woman anymore. The one who hid. The one who cared too much about the opinions of everyone else.

She slung her purse over her shoulder and walked toward the front door, holding her head high, yet aware of the stares. Young moms stopped pushing carts to look at her—the senator's wife who'd all but vanished from society had reemerged wearing cutoff jean shorts and a floral top with a pair of brown leather sandals . . . only days after the latest development in her scandal.

A headliner, for sure.

She strode through the aisles, found her ice cream in the freezer section, and was walking back toward the registers when she spotted the clerk who had practically thrown her out of the store. There were three other cashiers working, but in a fit of lunacy, Evelyn chose the rude cashier's line.

She waited as the girl finished with a customer, aware of the line that was now forming behind her.

"Morning." The cashier ran the pint across her scanner without looking up. "That all?" When she met Evelyn's eyes, her face fell. "You're back."

Evelyn smiled. "I am."

"Spending taxpayers' money again?"

"Don't talk to me like that," Evelyn said, surprising herself. Her heart pounded against her chest.

The girl's mouth twisted, and the woman behind Evelyn took a step back.

"I've done nothing wrong, and I won't allow you to treat me like this in my own town. So unless you want me to talk to your manager, you will give me my total, take my money, and kindly shut your mouth."

The cashier stared for a long moment as if trying to decide if this was a dare she wanted to take. Finally she let out a sigh. "It's $4.50."

"Great." Evelyn fished the money out of her wallet and handed it to the girl, who snatched the bills from her hand, ripped off the receipt, and held it out with the change.

Evelyn took it, picked up her ice cream, and strolled out the door as an odd excitement washed over her.

She'd never defended herself in her whole life. She'd spent years working hard to avoid ever having to do so, but she had to admit it felt good.

And she didn't even care if they quoted her on the nightly news.

CHAPTER

26

Evelyn returned to the farm around eleven and resisted the urge to crack open the container of peppermint stick right there and eat the whole thing for lunch. Instead, she shoved it in the freezer and went outside to drink in the day, but the partially open mailbox beside the door caught her attention.

Whit had installed it a few weeks after she arrived so he didn't have to disturb her when he needed to drop off her mail. Thoughtful, she realized now that she held a piece of mail with Casey's return address on it.

Evelyn turned the envelope over and tore it open. She skimmed the letter, but the words *divorce* and *final* were the only ones that registered. Casey must've called in a few favors—the ninety-day "cooling-off period" had barely passed.

Did that mean she was officially single? Somehow she'd begun to think of herself that way the day she left her wedding ring on the banister of the courtroom.

She spotted Lilian near the stables. Her time on the farm had revealed many things, not the least of which was the amount of work it took to keep the place running. Her ideas for the farm were good ones but would require more from people already giving 100 percent.

They would also require teamwork, which was why she wanted to be sure things were okay between her and Lilian.

When Evelyn reached the stables, Lilian stopped brushing one of the horses—Dusty—and squinted in her direction. "You look skinny."

Evelyn glanced down at her body. She supposed it was true. She hadn't been eating well. Some days hardly at all. "Stress is a great diet."

Lilian stroked Dusty. "You need to eat. Can't believe Trevor hasn't forced you to come have lunch with us again."

Evelyn tried not to take that personally.

"Today at noon. Meet us in the white barn." She ran a thick brush along Dusty's back. "I made pulled pork."

"Do you do that often?"

"Three times a week," Lilian said. "Trevor's dad—my brother-in-law—started the tradition with his staff. Said the team who ate together stayed together."

"It must be a lot of work feeding everyone like that," Evelyn said. "But it's a great idea."

"Don't give me any of the credit," Lilian said. "It was all Trevor's idea to carry on the tradition."

That didn't surprise her.

"Can I help out here?" Evelyn asked.

Two men were working in the stables behind Lilian. She glanced their way, then back at Evelyn as if she had no idea what to do with her request. "We're getting ready for the farmers' market this weekend."

Evelyn nodded, hopeful that meant Lilian had thought of a way she could help. It had been too long since she'd felt truly useful. Working for Abigail had been a great distraction, but the job was only part-time, so her schedule was far from booked.

Lilian nodded toward a garden beside the stables. "Do you like weeding?"

She shrugged. "I've never tried it before."

The older woman stifled a laugh, reminding Evelyn again of the gap between their two lives. "Come with me."

Evelyn did as she was told, following Lilian past the greenhouse and down to the garden. By this point in the summer, Lilian's skin had turned a deep bronze, though years in the sun had wrinkled her a bit.

"Here, put these on." She handed Evelyn a pair of gloves. "You just go through each section and pull out the weeds."

She looked at the rows of vegetables, so carefully planted. "What if I pull the wrong thing?"

Lilian put a hand on Evelyn's shoulder. "This isn't rocket science, Ev. You'll be fine."

Evelyn wasn't so sure. She'd always lived by the rules, and Christopher had given them to her. Before they married, it was her father's orders she carried out. She'd spent the past weeks wondering where that left her. How did she move on without instructions?

Lilian knelt beside a bushy green plant. "This is lettuce."

Evelyn frowned. "Really?"

She laughed. "Yes." She gently moved the plant aside and showed Evelyn where the weeds were sprouting. "These are weeds."

Evelyn nodded. She saw the difference. Lilian yanked the weeds away and threw them aside. "You gonna be okay?"

"I think so."

And with that, Lilian returned to Dusty, leaving Evelyn alone to figure out how to weed the rest of the garden.

Slowly, with the sun beating on her shoulders,

Evelyn went to work, praying she didn't somehow mess this up. She knew Whitney Farms had a reputation at the Loves Park Farmers' Market, and she didn't want to be the reason they showed up empty-handed that week.

One by one, she pulled the weeds that threatened their vegetables. She didn't know much about farming or soil or working with her hands, but she knew if the weeds stayed, they would choke the plants, making it impossible for them to grow.

She moved down the row of lettuce and over to another row of something she didn't recognize. Carefully, she determined which greens were good and which were invading the plants' territory. Then she pulled out what didn't belong.

As she worked, Trevor's words rushed back at her.

"Figure it out."

Had he meant them to be harsh? Unfeeling? They jabbed at her now, poking around the open wound of her failed marriage, leaving her to wonder what she could've done to keep Christopher from cheating.

What if she'd been prettier? More adventurous? What if she'd sold out completely to his life in the public eye? Would he have been faithful then?

Their life had been so full of promise.

"You'll never have to worry about money, Evelyn. That means you can stay home and paint to your heart's content," he'd told her the night he proposed. "I can provide for you—a good future." He kissed her. "Let me make all your dreams come true."

She wrapped her arms around him and gave in to his kiss. What he promised *was* exactly what she'd dreamed of, and she loved Christopher. Everyone did. Even her parents eventually came around, though sometimes she wondered if their initial reservations about the relationship had been true.

"You're too young to get married. Don't rush into this. What's the hurry?"

She'd grown so tired of trying to please a father who would never be happy with her. She'd grown weary of trying to make up for all their family had lost when Sylvie died. She could no longer bear the burden of her shame, which only grew every time she saw that look of loss in her mother's eyes.

She wasn't the daughter they wanted, and she knew it.

But the reality of her life after they'd married was much different from the one Christopher had promised.

Only months after their wedding, he'd come home to find her deep in her sketchbook on the back porch. It was a couple weeks after her only solo art show at the Loves Park Gallery in Old Town, and she'd had requests for new work. The first show had been so successful, they wanted her to do another one. They'd written about her in the newspaper, and for the first time, Evelyn felt like a real artist. Her success had awakened another hope inside her—to illustrate the children's book she'd been visualizing for months.

She'd been thankful for the creative boost that gave her the courage to stop dragging her feet, and even more thankful for a husband whose work afforded her the opportunity to stay home and pursue this dream.

But something changed that day.

"This is where I left you this morning." Christopher's tone accused.

"It was a perfect day for sketching," she said, still excited about all she'd accomplished. "The gallery asked for more pieces. I think I might need to look into an actual studio space. Can you imagine?" The thought made her giddy.

Christopher didn't respond.

"I didn't even get to the gallery pieces today." She held the sketchbook up for him to see. "What do you think? Tomorrow I'll be ready to add the ink." This children's book had been a dream of hers, and while she was interested in another show at the gallery, her heart was wrapped up in the idea of illustrating a story, and she had interest from a publisher in Denver.

He drew in a breath, his body tense.

"What's wrong?"

"This isn't going to work, Evelyn." He faced her, hands on his hips. His stance reminded her of her father, who barked orders like the drill sergeant he was, but who had never been anything more than an authority figure to her.

She set the sketch pad down and straightened. "What's not?"

"I thought you'd realize what I need in a wife—and be that."

She swallowed. "I don't understand, Christopher." Her pulse raced. She didn't want to let him down. She didn't want to let anyone down. She'd spent her whole life doing what was expected, making decisions based on obligation—but he'd given her permission, for the first time, to follow her heart.

Was he going to take that permission away?

"I didn't think you'd be so caught up in this art thing, Evelyn. It's not a real job. If anyone is going to take me seriously as a politician, then I need a wife who can play the part."

She felt her shoulders slump at his admission, which sounded a bit like a threat. "You want me to stop painting?"

"I want you to make an effort. Look at you."

Evelyn shrank under his stare, aware of her disheveled appearance, her torn jeans. "I was working today."

He shook his head, expression disapproving. "You have to decide if this—" he waved his hand in the air at her as if she were a visual aid in a speech he was giving—"is who you want to be."

She stood. "This is who I am, Christopher." Her words lacked conviction and she knew it. He knew it. In truth, she didn't know who she was— she'd always relied on other people to tell her.

"I'm going to run for senate as soon as I'm eligible. I want to be the governor someday. If you want to be the woman by my side, then we need to make some changes."

She glanced at the sketch pad, the image of her main character staring back at her. *Silly Lily* would be the story of a goofy little girl who lived her life outside the lines. Evelyn had sketched out plenty of mischief for her character, yet it struck her in that moment that she had no business writing about someone who lived a nonsensical life. She'd only ever lived inside the lines.

"What do you want me to change?" she asked, sadness winding its way around her.

"Your clothes, for starters." Christopher folded his arms. "And I know you'd rather stay home all day, but you're going to have to make some public appearances. Do some charity work, join a board or two. Our life is about public service now."

She swallowed the lump that had formed at the base of her throat and pictured the image she'd drawn of a curly-headed girl with freckles on her nose. She'd fallen in love with her Lily, and Christopher was going to take her away.

"I'll make you an appointment with my stylist. She'll know what to do with you."

She remained under his watchful eye for several long seconds, the kind of seconds that ticked by slowly as humiliation did a number on her confidence. He reached over and grabbed the sketch pad, examining the image she'd finished only moments before.

"This was never going to be published anyway, Evelyn." She read pity on his face as if he felt sorry for her—his naive wife who dared to dream a ridiculous dream.

Who did she think she was, anyway?

He tossed the sketch pad onto the chair and squeezed her shoulder. "Also, I know some of your friends like to call you Evie, but I think we need to insist that they use your full name. Evelyn is elegant and classic." He wrapped his arms around her and softened his tone. "You need to correct them from now on, okay? We can't have the press latching on to anything other than what we want them to."

His unwanted kiss took her off guard. She forced herself to kiss him back, but inside, her stomach wrenched.

Now tears stung her eyes as she continued pulling weeds from around the fragile vege-tables. Tiny weeds that threatened to do so much damage if they weren't removed.

The small sacrifices she'd made along the way

had done the same thing to her life. They'd passed by unnoticed at first, but because they'd gone unattended for so long, they'd grown up taller than she could manage. It hadn't taken long for them to strangle her.

It hadn't taken Christopher long to turn her into the wife he wanted. Compliant. Obedient. Silent.

The life he said she would have was not the life he'd provided. He'd lied to her—and in so many ways that infuriated her even more than the cheating, more than his lack of remorse.

He'd stolen her dreams, but the harsh reality was, she'd let him.

Hot tears streamed down her cheeks as the memory of her so-called ridiculous goals entered her mind. The publisher in Denver eventually stopped calling, and Christopher eventually packed away her sketch pad, replacing it with a date book full of obligations.

Art had been the one thing she'd chosen for herself, and he took it away.

She moved on to the next row and pulled a particularly large and stubborn weed, this one deep and rooted in the soil. As she tugged at it, it ripped open her skin through her flimsy gardening glove. She fell backward, and blood seeped through the thin cover of fabric. She removed the glove to inspect her wound, which stung in its rawness.

She sat, staring at the blood dripping from her palm as tears continued to fall.

"Figure it out."

She'd lost herself. The weeds had grown up around her heart and she'd forgotten everything she'd dreamed of becoming.

"Evie?"

Whit's voice pulled her from the past. She looked at him with clouded eyes, expecting judgment on his face, but found acceptance waiting for her instead. Why would he continue to be nice to her? So many people in town thought they were having an affair—were they treating him like he was some kind of cheater too?

"You okay?"

She wiped her cheeks with her dirt-covered arm. "It's just a cut. I'll be fine." She stood.

He stepped inside the fenced-in vegetable patch and took her hand, inspecting the wound. "Let's run over to the house and clean this up."

"I'm fine, Whit," she said, yanking her hand away. She didn't need him to help her.

"Evie, unless you went shopping for Band-Aids and a first aid kit, there's nothing in the guesthouse that's going to make this fine. Besides, it's almost lunch. Lilian said you're coming?"

She shrugged. "I don't have to."

He just stared at her.

Her hand stung. And he was right. She at least needed a Band-Aid. "Fine."

She followed him to the house, careful to hold her hand away from her clothes, though she wasn't sure why. They were so filthy she doubted she'd ever get the dirt out.

In the kitchen, Whit grabbed a chair and told her to sit in it. "Stay there, okay? I'll be right back."

"You're bossy," she said as he walked out of the room.

"You're stubborn." He returned with a first aid kit. "Let me see it."

She held out her hand, palm up. The blood had pooled around the thin skin where her thumb attached to the palm, and it tingled.

He led her to the sink, turned on the water, and held her hand under it. Then he wrapped a clean towel around the injury and squeezed.

"Ow!"

He shrugged. "Gotta stop the bleeding."

"You have absolutely no bedside manner," she said, trying to ignore the throbbing under the towel.

He looked at her like he wanted to say something but changed his mind.

After a few awkward moments, he removed the towel and gently turned her hand over to inspect her injury. "Can't believe it got you through the glove."

"Pretty useless glove," she said. "Besides, I don't have much of a green thumb."

"It's okay; you've got other talents."

She scoffed. "Yeah, I'm just oozing potential."

He met her eyes. "If you weren't being sarcastic, I would agree with you."

It occurred to her she could probably take care of this cut on her own, but at this point she didn't want to. She missed having someone take care of her, though she never expected it would be Whit.

He rummaged around in the first aid kit. "I've got a few different bandages in here."

She sat quietly, watching him fish Neosporin from the bottom of the kit. He squirted it on her hand. "Rub that in."

She did as she was told.

"What were you doing in the garden anyway?" He found the right-size Band-Aid and tore open the wrapper.

"Trying to *figure some things out*."

Regret twisted his face. "I'm sorry I said that to you, Ev."

"I needed to hear it."

"Not from me."

She lifted her chin. "Why not? We were friends once, weren't we?"

He swallowed but didn't answer.

Silence hung between them, the memory of that day in the barn weaving its way back to her mind. While the newspaper had twisted the truth, it was true they were in the middle of an important conversation at the time. One that had gone unfinished.

"What happened, Whit? Why don't you like me anymore?" The words made her sound like a pathetic, lonely schoolgirl whose best friend played with someone else at recess.

He affixed the Band-Aid to her hand. "You still going to be able to paint with that on?"

The subject change was abrupt and obvious. She didn't respond right away for the threat of tears, her loneliness spilling over like a too-full bathtub. "I'll be okay."

He stood from his chair. "Good. I got you something."

She watched as he moved toward the entry-way and returned with a plastic bag, which he promptly handed to her.

She took it, unmoving. Trevor Whitney bought her a present?

"Open it." His words were quiet like the boy she'd met that night during high school. She missed that boy—her friend.

What was so wrong with them being friends? Why did he insist on keeping an arm's length between them?

She looked inside the plastic bag and found a large sketch pad with an assortment of drawing utensils—charcoal, graphite, markers.

He leaned against the counter, arms folded. "I wasn't sure what you'd need, but I saw some of your sketches for the painted hearts in an old notebook. Thought this would remind you what it feels like to be a real artist."

Unwelcome tears returned, bringing with them that familiar thick, tight knot at the back of her throat.

"Is it not the right stuff?"

She glanced up and found an expectant look on his face. "It's perfect."

The slightest smile danced behind his eyes, but he simply nodded. "Good."

"Thank you, Whit." She stood, the memory of a lost dream swirling overhead. Gently, she took a step toward him, wrapping her arms around him in a quiet hug. "For everything."

He stood still, his body stiff at her touch, that boy she used to know miles away. Finally his hand pressed against her back and he held her for the briefest moment. "Anytime."

The back door flung open and Lilian appeared in the doorway.

Evelyn pulled away from him, and they both turned and faced his aunt, who wore a disapproving scowl.

"So maybe that article was true," she said. "You two are playing with fire."

Evelyn held up a hand to stop her. "You've got this all wrong, Lilian."

But Trevor's aunt only glared at her nephew, and Trevor remained eerily silent.

CHAPTER

27

Another week passed before Evelyn had a plan to present to Whit and Lilian. The Whitney Farms Dinner Night was on the community calendar, but only thanks to some string pulling from Gigi. It angered Evelyn that even after her years of doing good deeds for this community, the people had all but turned their backs on her in her time of need.

They'd even tried to refuse her ice cream!

Thankfully, they still supported Trevor Whitney as his family had been a Loves Park staple for as long as any of them could remember. Gigi didn't say so, but Evelyn knew that was her angle when she told people about the dinner.

Just before it was time to call the Volunteers meeting to order, Trevor sauntered into The Paper Heart with Lilian, that irritated expression on his face. Evelyn's summons had obviously inter-rupted his daily chores, and she'd likely hear about that later.

She didn't care. She had a plan. And it was good.

He looked casual but out of place as he often did in town, which made her wonder if the farm was the only spot that truly suited him.

Doris rushed over to him and grabbed him by the arm, leading him and Lilian to the back of the store, where Abigail had reserved the Volunteers' usual table.

"Oh, Mr. Whitney, you are looking awfully handsome today," Doris said.

Evelyn thought she saw Trevor roll his eyes when Doris wasn't paying attention. She stood at the counter, waiting on the last of their drinks from Abigail, who would join them as soon as her manager, Mallory, returned from her break.

Abigail set a coffee on the tray. "Too bad those rumors about you and Whit weren't true."

"What?" Evelyn asked, confused.

She shrugged. "He seems like such a sweet guy, and he's been so kind to you. I can't help but wonder if there's any truth to what that article said."

Evelyn fully faced her friend, who had obviously lost her marbles. "Abigail, Whit and I are *friends*."

Abigail glanced past Evelyn toward the table with a nod. "Uh-huh."

"He is one of Christopher's oldest friends."

"So?"

"And I'm . . ."

"Officially single."

Evelyn sighed. "Right. Sometimes I forget."

Abigail set another drink on the tray. "All I know is, good men are hard to find, and even you have to agree that Trevor Whitney is a good man."

"He is, but he's so cranky all the time."

Abigail didn't respond.

"Besides, he and Maggie . . ."

She smiled. "Oh yes. Operation Whitney/Lawson."

"We're friends," Evelyn said again. She took the tray and walked toward the table. She placed the drinks on the table and sat down.

"What's wrong with you?" Ursula asked, picking up her latte.

"Nothing," Evelyn said, aware that all eyes were turned on her.

"Your cheeks are bright red," Ursula said.

Evelyn gave an innocent shrug and changed the subject. "Can we get started?"

Abigail joined them, sitting between Evelyn and Trevor, which unnerved her, though she had no idea why.

Gigi cut in before Evelyn could continue. "Before we start, Evelyn, can we just welcome Mr. Whitney and his aunt Lilian to the meeting?" The older woman stood at the end of the table, turning everyone's attention to the uncomfortable-looking pair who had joined them. "Welcome."

"Thanks for having us," Trevor said. "We appreciate it."

"Of course," Gigi said. "It's our pleasure, though we do have one small stipulation."

Trevor frowned.

Why did Evelyn have a feeling they weren't going to like this?

"It's about the hearts," Gigi said, glancing at Evelyn. "We're going to need those plans by the end of the week. Anything you can mock up. We want to reveal the concept to the community at the Sweetheart Festival, but so far, I have a terrible suspicion you haven't begun working on them yet."

Evelyn looked at Trevor. "I started sketching a little, Gigi. It's just been so busy." Not exactly true in her case, but . . .

"I know, and now you can be busy with the hearts." Gigi's smile carried with it a certain finality that told Evelyn the subject was closed.

As such, Evelyn took the floor. She stood and cleared her throat. "As you all know, we're here to plan the Whitney Farms Dinner Night."

"Hear, hear," Ursula said, raising her latte in the air.

They talked through the details Evelyn had outlined for the dinner night, from the invitation design she had mocked up to the menu Lilian would be in charge of. They discussed decorations and budget, parking and prices. Evelyn had spent many evenings figuring out every detail of this event.

After the meeting ended, she expected Trevor to bolt out the door, but he hung around and helped her clear the table.

"You've done a ton of work," he said, picking up two half-empty coffee mugs and setting them on a tray.

Evelyn shrugged. "It's the least I can do."

He stopped and looked at her. "You know you don't owe me anything, right?"

She turned away. "Let's agree to disagree."

He leaned toward her, forcing her gaze. "Ev, I'm not playing that game. We're friends, and friends help each other out. No strings."

"But we weren't friends for so long. I'd become someone neither one of us would ever recognize. I still don't understand why you've been so kind to me, but thank you. And if I want to plan a dinner to try to help the farm grow, let me."

He laughed. "Now who's the bossy one?"

She smiled and directed her attention back to the table.

Someone walked up behind her. Gigi. "Mr. Whitney, we're thrilled to hear there's been some progress between you and Miss Lawson."

Trevor looked startled.

"I know you're awfully private, but we did hear about that kiss outside the barn."

"Gigi," Evelyn said slowly. Had she really needed to specify she was telling them that in confidence?

"What? It's wonderful. He deserves to be happy. He is an eligible single man with a business of his own, and if he wants to kiss Maggie Lawson on his farm, so be it."

Trevor stared at Evelyn.

"I didn't mean to spy," she said, sounding guilty,

like a teenager doling out excuses for her bad behavior.

"Did you mean to tell half the town?" Anger—or embarrassment?—flashed behind his eyes.

Gigi patted his arm. "Oh, don't be silly. We aren't half the town."

But Trevor didn't respond. Instead, he gave Evelyn one last look and made his way to the door.

She knew he hated all of this matchmaking, and she'd fed his personal information—shadily obtained—straight to them. Some friend she turned out to be.

"Oh, dear, I am sorry. I thought he'd be happy," Gigi said, walking away and leaving Evelyn with a pit in her stomach only guilt and regret could've caused.

CHAPTER
28

The next day, Trevor escaped into the wood shop, hoping to finish a table and stop agonizing over his conversation with Evelyn the day before.

He didn't even care that she'd told the meddling matchmakers about him and Maggie, but the realization that she'd seen him kissing Maggie had robbed him of hours of sleep.

The knock on the door came just before he turned on the table saw. He sighed. Only one person would knock before entering a barn.

He opened the door, avoided Evelyn's eyes, and walked back to the saw, horribly aware she was following him.

Not the warmest welcome, but at least he'd let her in.

"Look, I'm really sorry, Whit," she said, setting her sketch pad down on the counter. "They thought you and Maggie were on the outs. Their other idea was to convince her to buy a wooden heart for you. Somehow *that* was supposed to win you over."

She paused, waiting for him to respond.

When he didn't, she pressed on. "I told them that was ridiculous. Someone like you hates things like this stupid tradition, but they don't always listen to me . . ." Her voice trailed off as if she'd run out of things to say. No more words fill the awkward space between them.

He kept his head down as he sanded a plank of wood. "You never told me you saw me with Maggie."

She stilled. "It wasn't a big deal."

He glanced at her but said nothing. It *was* a big deal. His kissing anyone was a big deal. Did she know how long it had been since he'd allowed himself to even consider a relationship with someone? He'd been such a fool.

"Look, I know you're upset with me, but I really am sorry," she said. "Whit, please."

He straightened, hands on his hips, and wrestled for words that never came easily. "I just . . ."

"Can you forgive me?"

"You knew I didn't want them involved in my love life." He decided it was better to pretend that was the issue, not that he was embarrassed Evelyn saw him kissing someone else.

And worse, that she seemed completely unfazed by it.

That should be enough to end his feelings, shouldn't it? But he looked at her, standing in his sacred place, and he knew those feelings were far from gone. They might be getting stronger, in fact, because he could almost justify them as okay since she wasn't married anymore.

So what was it that held him back?

"Can you forgive me long enough to talk about these hearts, at least?" She waved her sketchbook in the air.

"You have ideas, I take it?"

She grinned. "I think it was the new art supplies."

He sighed and pulled a stool over to the counter at the center of his space. "I know you're not leaving, so you might as well sit."

"Gee, what a gentleman," she said with a smile. She sat at the counter and opened the sketchbook. "Wait; did you already start?"

He followed her gaze to the corner where he'd stashed the hearts he'd already cut. "No."

"Then what are those?"

"Those old ladies are rubbing off on you," he said. "You've gotten awfully nosy."

Standing, she picked up one of the hearts and studied it. "I thought you'd do something more straightforward, like from a template."

"Where's the fun in that?" He took her seat at the counter and watched as she set one heart down and selected another.

"They're all different," she said. "Whimsical."

"Whimsical?" *Great.*

"It's a good thing," she said. "The lamppost hearts are so cookie-cutter now. I love these. The way you made them sort of cockeyed and crooked."

"How do you know that wasn't a mistake?"

"Well, if these are mistakes, they're happy ones. I know exactly how I want to paint them."

He cleared a space on the counter, and she put down one of the wooden hearts, then stopped and met his eyes. "You can deny it all you want, Whit, but you are an artist."

He shook his head and returned to his workbench, picked up his sanding block, and did his best to ignore her.

She flipped open her folder, the contents of which kept her quiet for about three seconds. "I can't believe Gigi and her charts." She shuffled through several papers. "She has lists of every heart ever purchased, dating back at least fifteen years."

Trevor looked at her, a knot of panic tied tight in his gut. "Why?"

Evelyn kept reading. "Who knows? Did you hear some of them are purchased anonymously?"

Trevor's pulse quickened, and he imagined this was how guilty criminals must feel when they were being interrogated.

"Gigi has made it her personal mission to figure out who each of the anonymous hearts comes from. I haven't read that list yet." Evelyn turned the page. " 'Tia—You have my whole heart always + forever. Pete.' Aw."

Trevor swallowed, his throat dry. "Gigi tracks down people who want to remain anonymous?"

Evelyn pushed back her long, wavy hair. Why did she do that? It made him crazy. "You know Gigi. Listen to this one." She smiled, then read: " 'Dude. You rock my world. Sal.' "

"Guess it wouldn't be hard to track people down in Loves Park," Trevor said, turning away. Why hadn't he thought of that before? Why had purchasing a heart to let out his feelings each year seemed like a good idea? Ten times.

"I can put faces with most of the ones that give names," Evelyn said. "But some of them do come from tourists. I think that's why the city board's letting us change the overall appearance of them.

To appeal to more people." She turned her folder over. "Look," she said, removing a sheet of paper that had been paper-clipped to the back. "Anonymous. These are the ones I was talking about."

"Why?" Trevor glanced at the evidence of foolish hearts like his.

"Much more interesting." She held up the paper and squinted. "So these are the buyers Gigi hasn't caught."

Thank goodness.

"I'll leave you to it," Trevor said, backing away from the counter. No way he wanted to be in the same room if she was going to start diving into the mystery surrounding those anonymous hearts.

Evelyn watched Trevor leave the barn. The love and romance side of their project probably made him uncomfortable.

"Song lyrics?" Evelyn said to herself. She pulled a pencil from a small pouch and opened her sketch pad. From what she could tell, someone had stenciled a different line from this song on a heart for each of the last ten years. "Wow."

> The very thought of you and I forget to do
> The little ordinary things that everyone
> ought to do.

No melody came to mind, though the words were familiar. The song meant something to someone, and that touched her. As she sketched, she imagined the hands of an elderly couple intertwined. A couple whose love was worthy of documenting and putting on display.

She continued sketching, inspired by the meaning of the lyrics and Whit's whimsical take on the wooden hearts. The ideas came fast and messy at first, but she finally had a clear idea of where these new hearts were headed.

Next she moved from the paper straight to the wooden heart on the counter, and sketched right on it. Her hands moved fast and she didn't stop to question whether or not the idea was good. She just drew, paying special attention to the creative lettering, something she hadn't practiced in years.

When she'd finished that one, another idea came, so she picked up the next heart and did the same thing, using the next line of lyrics from this song that stood for everything love should be—something she now realized she'd never had.

After the frenzy of creating, she sat back, pleased with the results, and feeling for the first time in too long like she'd created something worth showing someone.

But as she looked around the empty wood shop, loneliness—unwanted and unkind—curled up at her feet and begged her attention.

Thanks to Christopher, her whole world was unrecognizable. The trial hadn't begun yet, so at the moment he was still free. And someone told her he'd proposed to that Darby person, so he'd likely end up with a new wife and a baby. An actual family.

The family she was supposed to have.

If the trial went the way he wanted it to—though the odds of that were slim—he would move on as if nothing ever happened.

Either way, she would be left to pick up the pieces. Alone.

She set a hand on the wooden heart and read the words she'd carefully sketched.

You'll never know how slow the moments go till I'm near to you . . .

Christopher had never felt that way about her, had he? He'd probably counted the moments until he could leave her—his quiet, uninteresting wife, who would rather stay home in her pajamas than wine and dine in places where people would take note.

Anger welled up inside her as the humiliation resettled on her shoulders. She'd been so stupid. So blind.

Evelyn held on to the heart, reading and rereading the words she still couldn't match with a melody. Whoever had dedicated them likely did so as a grand gesture of his great love. That kind of love probably never died. It probably wasn't full of lies. And cheating. And other women.

So many other women.

Evelyn gripped the heart with both hands. Without thinking, she heaved the wood against the wall and it landed with a crash. She covered her face with her hands, heat shooting up her spine.

Why had this happened to her? The good girl. The one who did everything right.

"*Haven't* I done everything right?" She said the words aloud. "Didn't I turn myself into the wife he wanted?"

The anger clawed at her, the memory of her revelation in the garden racing back. She knew the problem, didn't she? She'd turned herself into the person Christopher wanted her to become.

And for what? She'd given up her youth—her best years, prime years to start a family—for a selfish man who had never loved her enough to be honest with her.

She'd saved herself for him, never even looked at another man. And he'd taken that gift and spit on it. He'd been reckless and unfeeling.

Evelyn stood.

Maybe it was time she stopped doing what was expected. Maybe it was time she became the person the newspaper said she was. Her loyalty meant nothing to Christopher anyway.

And for the first time in her life, she didn't care one little bit what anyone thought of that.

CHAPTER
29

Trevor got the call around eleven. He'd dozed off on the couch, wishing away the events of the last few days. But after the surprise of a late-night phone call, he was groggily trying to remember what day it even was.

"Whit, it's Dylan Landry."

"Landry, do you know what time it is?"

"Saw in the paper you and Evelyn have a thing going." Voices in the background dulled Landry's words. Probably still at the Royal Pub, his fine drinking establishment. Trevor hadn't been there in years.

"We don't have a *thing,* Landry. Don't believe everything you read."

Dylan let out a groan. "All right, then I guess I should just leave it alone."

Trevor ran a hand over his face, forcing himself awake. "Leave what alone?"

"She's here, Whit."

"At the Royal?"

"Yeah. I know she's an adult and everything, but she looks like she could use a friend."

"Keep an eye on her, Landry. I'll be there in five minutes." Trevor grabbed his ball cap, jogged to his truck, and drove into town, his mind trying to fill in the blanks of what Landry hadn't said. He prayed a silent prayer the whole way there.

Inside the Royal, music blared. The room was dark and there weren't many people left. He caught Landry's eye, then followed his nod to the back, where Trevor could see a guy in a cowboy hat standing much too close to Evelyn.

What was she doing here anyway?

She wore tight jeans and a tank top and . . . were those cowboy boots? She hadn't spotted him yet. Before he could decide what to do, she threw her head back and laughed, then took the cowboy hat off the guy and put it on. She took a drink of whatever he was holding, set it on a table, and wrapped her arms around his neck.

Heat spread within Trevor's chest as he watched this faceless man put his hands on Evelyn.

He took a few steps toward the two of them and found himself standing there, waiting for her to notice him. She didn't.

"Evelyn."

A sleepy glance in his direction was all she gave.

The cowboy straightened. "Back off, buddy. She's having the time of her life tonight." He laid a hand on Trevor's shoulder. "You should go."

Trevor looked at the beefy hand. "Don't touch me."

The guy laughed. "Or what?"

"Do yourself a favor and get out of here," Trevor said. "I don't want any trouble. I just came here to get my friend."

Evelyn leaned over to take another drink, but Trevor pushed it away.

"You're no fun, Whit," she said.

"I don't care, Evie. You're coming home now."

"You can come to my place, darlin'," the cowboy said.

Trevor spun around and grabbed the guy by the shirt. "I gave you a chance, man. Now I'm not gonna tell you again. Get lost."

The guy, wimpier than he looked, held his hands up in surrender. "Fine. She probably isn't worth it anyway."

Trevor wrapped an arm around Evelyn to help steady her, but instead of standing upright, she wound both of her arms around his torso and pulled him close. "Why don't you like me anymore, Whit?"

Her face wasn't even an inch from his, her scent intoxicating. "You need some coffee and a good night's sleep, Evie. Let's go."

But she didn't move. Her hands crept up his back, awakening the very feelings inside him he'd worked so hard to bury.

"I'm tired of always being the good girl," she said.

"No, Evie, you're not. You're just hurt."

She looked at him, her blue eyes the boldest,

most vibrant shade he'd seen. It set him off-kilter, and something inside told him to push her away.

But he couldn't.

"I want to know how it feels to be like Christopher." Her lips brushed against his cheek, sparking his desire. That familiar ache he'd held for all those years rushed through him, and he closed his eyes, inhaling her.

He wanted her. He'd wanted her since the day they met, and now here she was—offering herself to him.

Her lips were too close, too full, not to be kissed.

She stood, hands linked behind his neck, *that* look on her face. And oh, how he wanted to respond. He was weak. His flesh was weak.

She was the only thing he'd dreamed of for the past fifteen years.

"Evie?"

She nestled her face into his neck.

"We can't do this."

"Sure we can. People do it all the time. Ask Christopher. Why should he get to have all the fun?"

"It's not fun, Evie." He took her by the arms, helping her balance as she moved. "Not like this."

She pulled away, her expression angry. "I'm practically throwing myself at you, Whit. And what? You're too good for me?"

"Let's go home, Evie. Please."

"No. I'm not going anywhere with you." She pushed him away, but as she did, she tripped, unsteady, and caught herself on a chair. "Just go."

She swatted Trevor's hand as he reached down to help her up, but he grabbed her hand anyway. Once she was on her feet, he tucked an arm around her and moved toward the door under the watchful eyes of the few patrons left in the bar. "Thanks, Landry," he called as he walked by.

Evelyn glared at the husky bartender. "Traitor."

Trevor practically lifted her into the truck, strapped her seat belt on, and headed toward the farm. Within minutes, she'd fallen asleep.

This was worse than he thought. Evelyn put up a good front, but how could all of Chris's offenses not take a toll on her? How would she ever recover?

And worse, now that he knew what it felt like to have her lips on his skin, how would he?

CHAPTER
30

Evelyn awoke the next day with blurred memories of the previous night accompanying a nasty headache. How had she gotten here?

Judging by the light in the room, it was still morning, and someone had made coffee. If her head didn't feel so heavy, the smell of it might've lured her out of bed. Before she could get up, though, the door opened and in walked Gigi, carrying a tray.

"You're awake." She smiled brightly.

Evelyn sat up. "What are you doing here?"

"Good morning to you too." Gigi set the tray on the nightstand. "Word is, you might need some coffee this morning. And your host wasn't sure it was safe for him to be the one to give it to you."

Evelyn felt her eyebrows draw together. "Why?"

Gigi watched her as if waiting for something to click, and when it did, it landed on her like a cement block thrown from the roof of a ten-story building.

She covered her face with her hands, absolute horror writhing in her belly. "Oh, Gigi."

Gigi held up a calming hand. "We all make mistakes, dear."

Evelyn slowly shook her head, nausea rolling through her. "No. Not like this. Where's Whit?" What had he told Gigi?

"Working, I assume. It's after eight and the Whitney Farms Dinner Night is tomorrow." Gigi sat on the edge of the bed. "He's worried about you, and so am I." She picked up the steaming mug and handed it to Evelyn, but Evelyn wasn't sure she could drink anything right now. She took it between her hands, letting it warm her, then set it down.

The maternal look on Gigi's face caught Evelyn's attention, though she hadn't seen that expression on her own mother since before Sylvie died. Thoughts of her mother ate at her, but she pushed them aside. Didn't she have enough heartache to deal with?

"I'm fine, Gigi," she finally said.

"Dear, you are many things. Fine is not one of them." She let her hand rest on top of Evelyn's. "How are you really feeling about all this?"

Tears sprang to Evelyn's eyes, and as much as she willed them away, in light of Gigi's undeserved solicitude she couldn't keep them from falling. She quickly wiped her cheeks and lifted her chin. "I'm fine."

Gigi's smile was understanding, and while she likely knew exactly what had happened the night before, she didn't seem to have any interest in judging Evelyn.

"Evelyn, have you been praying lately?"

Evelyn didn't reply.

"I am not trying to be bossy, goodness knows, but I'm an old lady who has learned a thing or two about heartbreak." Gigi pulled a throw pillow onto her lap and hugged it for a long moment, seeming lost in thoughts of her own.

"Did your husband . . . ?"

"Oh, goodness, no," she said. "He wasn't that kind of man."

Evelyn bit her lip.

"I'm sorry, dear. I didn't mean that to sound harsh."

She gave a slight shrug. "No, it's good. I'm glad he wasn't that kind of man. I wish Christopher wasn't that kind of man either."

Gigi shifted, turning farther toward Evelyn, a deep line of worry running across her forehead. "I had a miscarriage when I was about your age. I had been praying for a child, and I had waited a long time for God to answer that prayer. Sometimes, when I was praying, I felt like Samuel's mother." She glanced at Evelyn. "From the Bible?"

Evelyn smiled. "I know who Samuel is."

"I thought you might." Gigi folded her hands on her lap. "I was a lot like you. I did what I was supposed to do. I went to church every Sunday and I volunteered in the Sunday school. And I guess in some ways I thought that meant I was exempt from going through anything difficult."

Evelyn had had those feelings. More than once. If she did everything by the book, no more harm could come to her.

A faulty plan, to say the least.

Gigi's eyes turned glassy as tears danced at their edges. "And for a long time after that, I didn't want to pray." Her voice shook as she spoke. "I'm not proud of this."

Evelyn reached over and covered Gigi's hand with hers.

"I didn't talk to God for a year. A whole year. Can you imagine? I grew up in church, and I knew better, but I saw no point in talking to a God who would deny me the opportunity to meet my own child. A child I thought was his answer to my prayers."

Aside from hasty prayers of desperation, Evelyn had spoken to God so infrequently she imagined he didn't even know her name anymore. Oh, she and Christopher had gone to church. Her husband insisted on being involved in the congregation—after all, high moral values were part of his platform. But whenever she was there, she felt the stares. She'd always assumed it as just because of Christopher's local celebrity status, but now she wondered if the people around her were actually pitying her for the things she didn't know about the man at her side.

How many of them had known? How many of those women had Christopher been with?

She shook the thoughts aside and forced herself to focus on Gigi.

"I don't pretend to know what you're going through, Evelyn, but I do know that was the loneliest year of my life."

Evelyn stilled. "It's been pretty lonely around here too."

"But you're *not* alone. Even though you feel a little lost and a lot angry, God has never left your side. He is not the one who betrayed you."

Evelyn hugged her knees to her chest. "I did love Christopher, Gigi."

Tears welled up as Gigi patted her hand. "I know you did."

She quickly regained her composure. "This is all very sweet, but God and I aren't exactly on friendly terms, and after last night, I'm pretty sure he would turn me away if I came knocking."

Gigi scoffed. "Oh, Evelyn, didn't you learn anything all those years sitting in church?" She squeezed Evelyn's hand. "When you are at your worst, that's when God is at his best."

Evelyn nodded, but her heart rejected the words the older woman spoke. It sounded more like a sentiment written on a greeting card than practical, usable advice.

Instead she clung to her own words, words she'd carried with her for years. *I'll never be good enough.*

"None of us is good enough, dear," Gigi said as if she'd read Evelyn's mind. "That's what grace and unconditional love are all about." She smiled. "Though I suppose with a friend like Trevor Whitney around, you've already had an up-close and personal demonstration of those two things."

She frowned. "What do you mean?"

Gigi looked surprised. "Rushing to your aid the day the FBI showed up at your door. Going with you to see your husband in Denver. Giving you a place to stay—" she looked around the room—"a beautiful place, I might add."

Evelyn shook her head. "I think he does it out of some sense of obligation to Christopher."

Gigi tilted her head, sizing her up. "Is that why he came and pulled you out of that bar last night before you could do something you would regret for the rest of your life?"

Warmth rose to Evelyn's cheeks. Gigi really must know all the details of her poor behavior. It shamed her to think of them now.

"I must say, I was surprised, Evelyn." Gigi had switched to scolding mode. "What were you thinking? That's not like you."

Evelyn's mind wandered to the moment she'd had the brilliant idea to slip into Christopher's shoes for just one night. As if that would prove something to him, as if it would make him pay for what he'd put her through. But the sad reality was, he'd already moved on. He didn't care who she slept with.

But Trevor Whitney did. Why?

"So Trevor told you?" Evelyn peered at Gigi.

She waved a hand in the air. "Oh, heavens, no. That boy has a zipper straight across his face. He never tells anyone anything."

"Then how did you find out?"

"I have friends all over this town." Gigi smiled. "But don't you worry; I know how to keep them quiet. This is between you and Mr. Whitney. I imagine you'll have a few things to discuss since I know you're working on those hearts together." She winked. "Remember, we want to reveal them at the Sweetheart Festival. And that's only a few weeks away. Not to mention your community dinner tomorrow night."

Evelyn groaned. "I can't do either of those things now, Gigi. I can't face Whit, and I certainly can't spend all day setting up for this dinner. Can you find someone else to do it? And someone else to finish the hearts?"

The image of the heart-shaped masterpieces she'd created the night before using song lyrics raced through her mind. She loved the way it made her feel to be artistic again. Did she really want to walk away? Give the project to another artist?

Gigi stood. "I won't hear of it. This dinner is your idea, your way to pull your weight here on the farm. You have to see that through."

"And the hearts?" Evelyn stiffened. "I can't stand up on the stage with Whit while you all present our new ideas. Everyone in town thinks we're having an affair."

"But what's true?" Gigi stared at her.

"We aren't having an affair."

She shrugged. "Then that's all that matters."

Evelyn pulled the covers over her head. "Easy for you to say."

Gigi ripped the covers back. "It's not easy for

me to say. But I've learned something in all that praying. And I finally came around and realized God *was* watching out for me, even though I didn't fully understand. There is only one opinion that matters."

Evelyn blinked.

"When you forget that is when things start to go off the rails." She turned toward the door, then faced Evelyn again. "Besides, I hope you aren't planning on letting this thing between you and Mr. Whitney go unattended for too many days."

Evelyn sighed. "The thought had crossed my mind."

Gigi's smile seemed to suggest she thought Evelyn was something of a sad case. "Go find Trevor. Make this thing right so tomorrow night can be a huge success, and then get back to work on those hearts." Gigi leaned in. "And thank him for watching out for you."

Evelyn replayed Gigi's words as the woman shut the bedroom door behind her. She'd said too much in too little time for Evelyn to be able to process it all with her broken heart. Gigi must've learned a thing or two about discipline over the years because she'd clearly put Evelyn in her place, yet Evelyn felt loved, not wounded.

A few minutes later, she heard a truck amble up the drive and watched out the window as it parked near the big white barn. It was full of supplies for the dinner, and she knew she needed to get out there to help set up, but how could she face Whit?

How would she ever face him again?

She tried not to relive the moments that lay foggy at the edges of her thoughts. As much as she wished she didn't remember, she did. She'd all but launched herself at Trevor. Wasn't that what men wanted? It had certainly been a priority for Christopher.

But Whit was different.

She'd likely embarrassed him even more than she'd embarrassed herself.

She watched as Trevor met the truck driver near the barn. If she were smart, she would throw on some clothes and run outside—apology in one hand, thank-you in the other—and beg forgiveness.

That was what she *should* do, but her shame got in the way.

Instead, she paced across her bedroom floor, Gigi's advice still hanging in the air, filling the room with possibility. Yet Evelyn found herself hesitant to reach out and take it. She didn't even know how to pray anymore. Part of her wondered if she'd ever known.

A cocktail of regret and gratitude swirled together at the forefront of her mind.

"Okay, God," she whispered, breaking the silence in the empty house. "It's true. I need help. I'm hurt and embarrassed." She stopped. "And angry." As she said the words, images of her shattered life played in a continuous loop through her head. "And I don't know who I am anymore."

She sat on the edge of the bed, the stillness of the room covering her like a thick blanket. She closed her eyes and drew in a deep breath, knowing Gigi was right. She'd spent years ignoring God's plans and thoughts about her, caring instead about who other people thought she should be, but never measuring up to anyone's expectations.

"I'm sorry, God."

She opened her eyes and saw an old Bible on the dresser. She could only assume Gigi had left it behind. She noticed a sticky note on one of the pages and flipped the Bible open to that spot. She read the verse referenced on the note—Ephesians 2:10.

> For we are God's masterpiece. He has created us anew in Christ Jesus, so we can do the good things he planned for us long ago.

Created anew. What she wouldn't give to know what that felt like.

The room was quiet, but the response wasn't empty. Instead, her head filled with the memory of the way she felt when she was creating. Designing those hearts had awakened something inside her, something she'd shoved aside for too many years.

How had she ever agreed to give that up?

On the table, her sketch pad begged for her attention. She opened it, unsure of where to begin. She had no guidelines, no direction. The possibilities were endless—and yet that reality threatened to paralyze her.

She set the tip of the pencil on the blank sheet of paper and allowed her hand to move. No thinking—just creating.

An hour later, she had four different sketches, and when she finally stopped and took a moment to look at them, what she saw made her realize she had to push her qualms aside and talk to the very person she would much rather avoid.

Trevor Whitney.

CHAPTER

31

Trevor unloaded the rented chairs along with the equipment Evelyn had ordered for their big farm dinner tomorrow night.

He welcomed the busywork, but he knew at any moment she could walk out of the bungalow and he'd have to put on a familiar mask and pretend he hadn't been reliving the previous night's events over and over in his mind.

He'd done the right thing, but he hadn't wanted

to, and that was the part that had him tied up in knots.

So here he was, trying to occupy his mind with work. He needed the distraction of hauling handmade tables from the wood shop to the white barn. Anything to keep his mind from wandering back to the way Evelyn's body felt pressed against his.

Around nine, he'd seen Gigi leaving the little bungalow. He kept his head down in hopes she wouldn't talk to him, but he should've known better. She'd spotted him near the stables, hopped in her car, and drove in his direction.

"This dinner is going to be a huge success," she said with a smile. "Are you warming to the idea of opening your farm to your community?"

Trevor took his hat off and rubbed the top of his messy head. "Do I have a choice?"

The woman had squinted in the morning sun. "Of course not."

He shrugged. "Guess I'll *warm* then."

She eyed him, suspicion on her face. "I hear you're quite the hero, Mr. Whitney."

So Evelyn did remember. His heart dropped. He'd been holding out hope she wouldn't.

"Ma'am?"

"Don't *ma'am* me. My dear friend Dylan Landry told me what happened last night."

Landry. What a bigmouth. "Not sure I know what you're referring to."

She'd leaned toward him then, arm on the car door. "You're a good man, Trevor. I suspect Evelyn thinks so too, though it will likely take some time for her to admit it. What with your pretending to be crabby and all."

Trevor put his cap back on his head and wished Gigi would drive away. He wasn't pretending. Everyone knew he was crabby.

But she kept talking. "Awful good friend you are."

Something about the way she hung on the word *friend* gnawed at him. "Just don't want to see her get hurt, Mrs. Monroe."

Gigi nodded. "That makes two of us." She smiled. "See you tomorrow night, Mr. Whitney, if I don't see you before. And please leave that ratty old ball cap in the house."

After she'd gone, he glanced at the guesthouse. He should go talk to her, make sure she was okay, but he didn't. That was when the truck pulled up—perfect timing, it seemed to him.

He knew he could stay busy for hours around the farm, even after the unloading was finished, and that might be just what he needed to do to keep his mind off Evelyn and the way her arms felt around his neck.

By noon, in spite of her resolve, Evelyn still hadn't worked up the courage to talk to Trevor. She stared at her sketches. So many ideas had poured out of her—ways to make the Whitney Farms Dinner Night not just tasty, but memorable. As if by instant download, she'd sketched an entire layout and design, right down to the white lights in the barn.

If she had any hope of turning the sketches into a reality, she needed Trevor's help.

But every time she approached the front door, something stopped her.

Shame.

She began to weigh her options. Was there somewhere—anywhere—else she could go to disappear for a while?

Her parents lived in Texas, and while getting out of town had some appeal, staying with them did not. As it was, she'd already endured a gut-wrenching phone call from her disapproving mother, outlining all the reasons she needed to reconcile with Christopher.

"We don't believe in divorce, Evelyn," her mother had said. "Your father is just so disappointed in you. Especially since we didn't think you were mature enough for marriage in the first place. Then, once you did get married, you left him at the first sign of trouble."

She'd hung up, regretting that she'd called them back and determined not to ask for their help. No matter what.

Gigi had a sewing room that she'd offered to turn into a guest room, but her house was small and cramped. And with the exception of the awkward tension she felt knowing Whit was close by, she'd grown to love that bungalow. It was more like home than anywhere she'd ever lived.

Besides, she couldn't walk out on Whitney Farms now. Not with these beautiful sketches vying for her attention. More than anything, she wanted to make the event a huge triumph. Not just for Trevor, but for herself.

She hadn't felt that kind of purpose in years, if ever.

She was walking a circle in the entryway, inching toward the window and hoping for a glimpse of Whit, when a knock on the door made her gasp. Panic washed over her.

He'd come to reprimand her, she was sure. And she deserved it. She would take her lumps like a compliant child, apologize, and move on. Even if he'd decided it would be better for her to find somewhere else to live.

She opened the door, but she didn't look up. Instead, she stared at Whit's work boots. They were dirty.

"Hey."

She gave a slight nod, bracing herself for his disgust.

"Wanna see something cool?"

She frowned, then finally dared to look at him. He wore the expression of a boy who'd just created a working volcano in the garage.

"Get your boots."

That was it? No lecture about her poor choices or inappropriate behavior? He was just going to be okay after what she'd done?

She tugged on a pair of rubber boots—a gift from Lilian after one particularly muddy day of weeding. She still smiled when she saw them. With their charming cow design, they were more "her" than anything else in her wardrobe.

She stepped out onto the porch and inhaled the warmth of the day. Summer held on and it was hot, but something about the way the sunlight hit her face as she followed Trevor into the yard filled her up from the inside.

When he didn't turn toward the wood shop, she paused. "Where are we going?"

"Back here. Come on."

She looked beyond him toward the pasture where the cattle grazed. "Cows aren't really my thing." Cute on boots. Pretty intimidating in real life.

He turned and looked at her. "Don't be such a baby. They're harmless."

She scowled. "They're really big, Whit. And their eyes creep me out."

"Fine. Suit yourself," he said, that challenging look on his face. "But you're missing out." He kept walking.

The mountains painted the perfect backdrop to the field, and a small creek ran crooked through the ground. She hesitated for several seconds until finally she decided she wanted to know what it was that he found so cool. What it was that he had to share, even after the humiliation of the night before.

She jogged until she caught up with him. In the distance, one lonely cow lay near a tall bed of grass.

"What's wrong with her?"

"She's in labor." Whit put a hand in front of Evelyn and she stopped moving.

"Should we call a vet?"

He shook his head. "Only if she runs into trouble. Otherwise, she's got this."

"By herself?"

He glanced at Evelyn. "She's strong."

Evelyn turned her attention to the cow as they approached. She moaned.

"I'm not sure I can watch," Evelyn whispered. "I've never seen anything being born before."

Trevor's face warmed into a soft smile. "It's miraculous."

The cow had separated herself from the rest of the herd. She knew somehow she needed to be alone in that moment, and Whit was right—she was strong.

Her name, Whit said, was Jasmine, and the poor girl seemed uncomfortable. Who could blame her? She was about to give birth. Evelyn watched as Trevor spoke in soft tones to "his girl."

Everything he did let her know she wasn't alone.

Funny. He had a knack for that.

"You're good with her," Evelyn said, maintaining a healthy distance.

Trevor stroked the cow's head. "She's a sweetheart."

Evelyn laughed. "Maybe *this* is why you're still single."

His grin radiated shyness. "Could be." He propped himself up on his knees and checked out the cow's backside.

Evelyn turned away. She didn't know if she had the stomach to actually watch this process, and yet something about it held her attention. She found the whole scenario—the sunlight, the pasture, the cattle, Whit—peaceful.

"We haven't always had animals on the farm, you know." Trevor stood. "But they're my favorite part of farming."

"Because they don't talk back, probably." Evelyn crossed her arms.

"Probably."

She laughed, but it felt wrong to joke with him right now. When things were so upside-down.

"Whit, I—"

"Hey, can you kneel over here?" Trevor glanced up. "I think she might need some help."

How he knew this, she didn't understand, but she did as she was told despite her fear of this oversize beast.

She glanced at Whit, who tended to Jasmine with the care of a concerned father, a role she hadn't seen him play. She'd expected his brutal judgment, but he'd said nothing to her about the way she'd behaved.

Evelyn stayed close as Jasmine demonstrated her strength over and over again, never giving up. That sweet mama cow did what she had to, and about an hour later, a tiny calf emerged and staggered to his feet, looking like Evelyn felt—dazed and confused.

Her life had become something she didn't recognize, and in her sadness, she'd decided it was a good idea to turn herself into the very thing she despised. Still making small compromises that conflicted with the instincts she'd been ignoring for years.

How had she gotten so far off track?

She watched the baby steady himself. He was fuzzier than she expected and maybe even kind of cute. Trevor, still on his knees, gave Jasmine a bit more attention, but there was a certain pride on his face that made Evelyn smile.

He was one of a handful of people in the world who hadn't completely abandoned her, and she'd gone and messed it up. Surely he felt the tension between them.

"You must be disappointed in me." Evelyn stood and brushed dirt from her jeans.

He squinted at her. "Why?"

Her inhale was long and slow. "I'm sorry about last night."

Whit got up, his vintage-wash red T-shirt clinging to his chest and showing every muscle built from hours of hard work. She braced herself for the piece of his mind he was about to give her.

But he shrugged. "Don't worry about it."

"That's all you have to say to me?"

"I have a really bad short-term memory." He smiled. "But I do know we missed lunch, so do you want to go eat something?"

She watched as he patted Jasmine one more time. "Good job, mama." Then he turned to her. "Turkey and cheese? Or are you more of a peanut butter–and-jelly girl?"

She smiled. How he could think about food after what they'd just witnessed, she would never know, but she didn't ask any questions. She had a feeling that, given the chance, she would learn many things about Trevor Whitney that weren't at all what she thought.

And as she sat at his kitchen table, she felt compelled to find out what those things were.

CHAPTER
32

Gigi parked the Buick in the lot in front of The Paper Heart and stomped inside. The phone call that morning from Dylan Landry had been a surprise, but it wasn't just Evelyn's behavior she had to deal with.

"What's this emergency meeting about, Gigi?" Ursula barked from the table in the back. "And you better be treating us to Danishes."

Gigi nodded at Abigail, who returned the nod, then moved toward the pastry counter to accommodate their crankiest member's tremendous appetite. Gigi joined the others at the table. "Ladies, we have a problem."

Doris raised her hand but spoke before she was called on. "Shouldn't we wait for Evelyn?"

"I didn't invite Evelyn," Gigi said.

Abigail set a tray of pastries on the table and pulled up a chair, and Ursula snatched the cheese Danish. "These are my favorite," she said.

"Why ever not?" Doris asked. "She's one of us."

"Because Evelyn is part of the problem."

Now she had their attention. She gave them the highlights of her phone call with Dylan Landry, grazing over the specifics of Evelyn's behavior as best she could. But she should've known the others wouldn't stand for vague innuendo.

"She was drinking?" Ursula winced.

"In a bar?" Tess frowned.

"With a cowboy?" Doris shook her head. "Was he cute at least?"

"Doris, that is not the point," Gigi said. "The point is, she was hurting."

"She's lost," Ursula said. "Still doesn't have any idea who she is."

Gigi knew Ursula was right. And if Evelyn continued down that path, she'd never find out.

"She's been playing a part for years," Abigail said, sipping her mocha. "Maybe we could cut her a little slack?"

"Of course we can," Gigi said. "Slack has already been cut."

"Did she go home with this cowboy?" Tess asked, biting into an apple fritter.

Gigi drew in a breath. "Thankfully, Dylan Landry had the good sense to call Trevor."

Ursula's narrow gaze zeroed in on Gigi. "Trevor Whitney?"

Gigi shrugged, nonchalant. "She does live on his property. That's not a secret anymore. Mr. Landry was under the false impression he and Evelyn were romantically involved."

"Trevor rescued her in the middle of the night?"

Gigi wouldn't tell them the rest. Not about that. Not about Evelyn throwing herself at him.

Not about the look she saw on Trevor's face that morning when she questioned him about it. And certainly not about her suspicion that she had uncovered the reason for his decision not to marry all these years.

"There's more to the story, ladies," Gigi said, trying to get them back on track.

"More than Trevor Whitney playing the part of a knight in shining armor?" Tess asked.

"He's such a good boy," Doris said with a grandmotherly smile.

"Mr. Landry observed more than Trevor pulling Evelyn out of the bar," Gigi said.

A collective frown appeared on the other four women's faces.

"He said there was a reporter present."

Doris gasped. "Documenting her indiscretions? Poor Evelyn."

"That's not the worst of it," Gigi said, staring at the table. "She was a petite redhead with freckles on her nose."

The other women stared at her until realization settled over them one by one.

"Maggie Lawson is the one keeping Evelyn in the news," Gigi said.

"What did you just say?"

The voice came from behind them, and Gigi spun around in her chair, knowing she had no way of keeping this secret any longer.

"Evelyn." Gigi stood and took a step toward her.

"Trevor's *girlfriend* is the one who reported those things about me? About us?" Her eyes widened and she dropped into a seat at the table.

"I blame myself, dear," Gigi said. "I don't know how we missed it. We should've been more thorough."

Evelyn shook her head as if replaying a memory. "She was at the courthouse. The day of the trial. It must have been her. I fell, and a woman helped me pick everything up and put it back in my purse."

"You didn't recognize her?" Gigi asked, retaking her seat.

"I didn't see her face, and I'd only met her once. But after that I couldn't find my medication. She must've taken my pills."

Gigi didn't like this one bit. How they had attempted to match such a sweet, kind man with such a devious woman she would never understand. Maybe they *had* lost their touch.

"How do I tell Whit?" Evelyn looked up. "I think he really likes her."

Gigi had a sneaking suspicion he wouldn't be too broken-hearted, but she didn't voice that just now. No sense confusing the situation even more.

"You have to tell him," Tess said. "If his girlfriend is a liar, you owe it to him to be honest."

"I don't want to hurt him," Evelyn said. "Not after he's been so kind to me."

"It will be a momentary hurt," Gigi said.

315

"You can't wait," Abigail said. "You don't want this thing with him and Maggie to get any more serious than it already is."

Evelyn sighed. "I suppose that's true. Think what kind of pain the truth could've saved me all those years ago." A sadness washed over her face. "I'll tell him, but after the dinner. I think he's nervous."

"And you?" Gigi asked.

"I'm excited." Evelyn pulled a large sketchbook from her purse. "Gigi, after you left, I got some ideas. That's why I came in, actually. Abigail, do you think you could help me decorate the barn?" She laid four sketches on the table, and the others leaned in to get a closer look.

Evelyn had clearly been inspired. She had a plan to transform that white barn into something completely beautiful.

Gigi watched as she outlined the whole idea for the rest of them, amazed by the transformation her young friend had undergone. That morning she'd been emotionally beaten and bruised, and now she was bubbling over with purpose.

It never failed to amaze her what God could do with a willing heart.

"This plan is perfect," Abigail said. "Of course I'm in."

"We all are," Doris added. "I can't wait."

"Me neither," Evelyn agreed. "It's the first time I've felt like maybe I'm doing something special."

"You've been planning events and parties for years," Tess said. "Give yourself some credit."

"True, but my heart was never in it, and honestly, I never felt like those kinds of events were really me. Does that make sense?" She tucked her drawings back inside her sketchbook.

"Maybe God is going to take all that training and use it now," Gigi said. "For something that makes your heart leap. God's in the dream-making business, you know."

Evelyn paused. "I *don't* know, but I want to."

"You're off to a good start, dear," Gigi said. "Pay attention and stay open, and your purpose has a way of finding you."

Evelyn met Gigi's eyes and smiled.

Friday evening, Trevor stood in front of the mirror, wondering if he should shave. How was a farmer supposed to dress to host a community dinner?

In all the years he'd been running the farm, he'd never done anything like this, and he still couldn't believe the number of tickets they'd sold. He owed it all to Evelyn, who'd planned it from beginning to end, and those Valentine Volunteers, who'd helped them overcome the hostile opinions of some members of the community.

They'd spent the entire day hanging white lights in the barn and the trees that surrounded it. Glass jars she'd converted into lanterns hung from the low branches of the trees and sat at the centers of all the tables, many of which were set up outdoors just to make room for everybody.

Lilian had been cooking all day, dishes made entirely from farm-raised meat and homegrown vegetables. Soon people would be able to pick their very own produce right here on the farm.

While he'd resisted these ideas at first, even he had to admit Evelyn had had a stroke of genius when she suggested them.

Lilian appeared behind him, looking more dressed up than he'd ever seen her in a long skirt and loose white top.

"You look fancy."

She hitched up the skirt just above her ankles to reveal cowboy boots. "I'm still your favorite aunt underneath all this pretty." She grinned, then glanced at Trevor's clothes. "Is that what you're wearing?"

"I'm not putting on a tie," Trevor said.

"Cargo pants and a button-down are hardly dressy," Lilian said.

"I'm wearing sandals." He smirked.

"Wait till you see Evelyn. You're going to feel like an underdressed fool."

He could only imagine.

Lilian smacked his arm. "Get it together. Your girlfriend is out there too."

Maggie. He hadn't seen her in days. In fact, he hadn't even called her. They'd all been so busy getting ready. And if he was honest, he'd been so focused on trying to stop thinking about Evelyn, he'd stopped thinking about everything but work.

Shouldn't things be moving more quickly with Maggie? Shouldn't they be more serious than they were? He'd never been much of a casual dater, but even he had to admit that's exactly what they were. Casual.

He was walking toward the white barn, thankful for the perfect weather, when the sound of voices coming from inside stopped him. The door was ajar.

He inched closer, careful to be quiet as he did.

"How long did you think you'd get away with this?"

That was Evelyn. What in the world was she talking about?

"Just until I could prove the truth."

And that was Maggie. The two of them didn't even know each other—what could they possibly have to discuss?

"I don't know what you think you know, but I did nothing wrong. I would've told you that if you'd asked me, but instead you dragged my friend into this and made fools of both of us."

Trevor frowned.

"In my experience, guilty people aren't forthcoming with questions from a reporter," Maggie said. "I knew if I was going to be the one to break the other side of the Christopher Brandt story, I had to do it like this."

"You had to lie?" Evelyn raised her voice. "Did you even think about who you were hurting when you wrote those things?"

What was she saying? That Maggie was the one responsible for the stories about Evelyn? About her anxiety and her medication? About their supposed affair? Maggie had dragged both their names through the mud—and Evelyn knew about it?

His jaw tightened.

"Oh, please," Maggie said. "Everyone knows there was no way Trevor was going to fall in love with me or anyone else."

Trevor darted inside, catching their attention and stopping Maggie from voicing her theories on his feelings for Evelyn aloud.

Both women spun to face him.

"Trevor," Maggie said.

"Is it true?"

She took a breath. "I can explain."

He looked at Evelyn, wearing a blue sundress and looking horrified at the sight of him. "And you knew about this?"

She turned away.

"Well, I guess the joke's on me then."

"Trevor, please," Maggie said. "I know how it looks, but I really like you. I never wanted you to get hurt."

He put his hands on his hips and leveled his gaze. "I'm not hurt, Maggie. But what were you thinking? Why would you do this?"

"I didn't mean for it to get out of control," she said. "And I really didn't mean to like you so much."

He glanced at Evelyn, who focused on the ground.

"You should go, Maggie."

"Trevor, please."

He faced her. "Go."

She lifted her chin as if to reposition her dignity. "Fine. But you and I both know you were just looking for a reason to walk away from me." She looked from Evelyn to Trevor and stormed off just as Gigi, Doris, and Ursula arrived.

"Whit." Evelyn moved toward him.

But he took a step away. "Evening, ladies. Welcome to Whitney Farms."

CHAPTER
33

Evelyn wished she could turn back the clock. If only she'd told Whit the truth about Maggie as soon as she got home from The Paper Heart. If only she hadn't accused Maggie the second she walked in the barn.

She watched as, without so much as a glance in her direction, Trevor welcomed his guests to the dinner she'd planned and executed. He mingled and talked like a person who actually liked to entertain, and she had to hand it to him—he pulled it off.

"This is such a wonderful idea, bringing the community together like this," said one of the ladies Evelyn recognized in face but not in name, stopping Trevor with a hand on his arm.

He stiffened at her touch, likely anxious to get this thing over with, but forced a smile and a polite thank-you.

"Everything is just *lovely,*" another woman said.

At that, Evelyn expected a glance, a smile—something—but he only nodded and moved on.

Lilian's slow-cooked roast beef with rosemary potatoes was received with requests for her secret recipe, which, of course, she refused to give.

Evelyn would've asked Trevor how he felt about the whole event, but he avoided her all night long, and that made her sad.

She hadn't even had a chance to tell him how she'd felt about planning that evening. How it awakened some sense of purpose inside her and gave her so many other ideas to help the farm grow.

And while the dinner was, as a whole, a huge success, the victory was empty because she couldn't share it with Trevor.

• • •

Days passed and Trevor and Evelyn still hadn't spoken about Maggie. They settled instead into a distant working relationship. With the dinner event behind them, they both turned their attention to the Sweetheart Festival and the rebranding of the wooden hearts.

Whit cut the hearts out and left them on her front porch, but the days of him knocking and checking on her were gone.

She'd set up a makeshift studio in the sunroom and spent most of her time there, transforming his blank wooden hearts into works of art.

Never mind that she had no idea if anyone else would see them that way. She supposed she would find out at the Sweetheart Festival dance when Gigi unveiled their plans for all of Loves Park to see.

Loves Park, which still hadn't forgiven her.

She shoved the thoughts aside, reminding herself again to focus instead on what God thought of her. That she was good and lovely. That she was a *masterpiece*. Created anew.

She'd written the Ephesians verse on a note card and hung it on her bathroom mirror so she wouldn't forget the message that comforted her when she needed it most. As an artist, one word stuck out to her. A creator had to be quite pleased with his creation to call it a *masterpiece*. Was it really possible God saw *her* that way?

• • •

Saturday morning, two weeks after the dinner event, the sound of voices outside woke Evelyn early. She peeked out the curtains and saw Trevor and Lilian, along with two farmhands, loading the truck for the farmers' market.

She hadn't been out in a few days, and the thought of spending the whole day at the farm alone didn't make her happy. She dressed quickly—jean shorts, a tank top, and a loose white button-down—pulled her hair into a long side braid, and hurried outside.

She approached the truck as Lilian pegged Trevor in the face with a carrot, teasing, "Yoo-hoo. Earth to Trevor."

He picked up the carrot and turned to her. "Do you really want to start something with me?"

She grinned. "You're not so tough."

"What do you think you're doing?" Evelyn called as Trevor lifted his arm to toss the carrot back.

He spun around, but she didn't see kindness in his face.

"I poured a lot of love into those carrots, Whit. Don't you dare turn them into weapons," she said, hoping somehow they could move past her bad decisions.

He dropped the carrot. "Sorry."

"You're out of your art cave," Lilian said, shooting Trevor a dirty look.

"I needed a break," Evelyn said. "Can I come with you guys?"

"To the market?" Lilian asked.

She shrugged. "I've never been."

Lilian glanced at Trevor, who said nothing, then back at Evelyn.

"I don't have to come," Evelyn said, feeling like an intruder.

Lilian hopped down from the bed of the truck. "Don't be ridiculous. We would love the extra help." She reprimanded Trevor with a look. "And like you said, you poured a lot of love into these vegetables."

Evelyn found herself at a loss for words. Trevor must've really liked Maggie to be this upset about her betrayal. And Evelyn's.

"You'd be doing me a huge favor," he finally said. "Give me someone other than her to spend the day with."

Slowly Evelyn met his eyes and forced herself to hold them. "Okay, then."

Lilian held up a half sheet of paper. "Plus, you can help us push this pick-your-own-vegetables day. It was your idea, after all."

Evelyn smiled. "You're actually doing it?" She glanced at Trevor, but he didn't say anything.

"The dinner went so well, I've already got another one on the calendar," Lilian said. "We figured we should give all your ideas a try."

An unfamiliar feeling of accomplishment

bubbled at Evelyn's core. She'd been forced to plan parties and gatherings for years and hated every minute. Somehow, planning this event, giving back to the people who had embraced her when she was at her worst, brought with it a whole new significance.

Maybe Gigi was right. Maybe all those years of social events would serve her well. She thought back to the mornings she'd spent with her sketch pad and wondered if God could take the very thing she'd loathed about her life in the public eye and turn it into something with meaning. She'd asked him to reveal her purpose, hadn't she?

And what was it Gigi had said? *"Pay attention and stay open"?* What if this was all part of it— the reason she was here? In the quiet moments between pencil lines and brushstrokes, her mind always wandered there, searching for a way to pull the weeds that had grown up around her life, strangling her abilities and pulling her from anything God might've had for her.

Trevor got in the truck and started the engine. The passenger door swung open, and Evelyn stared at the bench seat. Three people would make for cramped quarters. Best if she sat by the window, Lilian in the middle. Trevor probably wanted as much distance between them right now as possible.

Lilian gave her a light push. "You get in, Evie,"

she said. "I forgot my phone inside." Lilian took off for the house, leaving Evelyn peering into the truck.

Trevor glanced at her but quickly faced forward. She pulled herself onto the seat, and seconds later Lilian emerged from the farmhouse, carrying the phone she probably had in her pocket all along.

Trevor's aunt wouldn't likely put up with their tension for much longer.

"Scoot," Lilian bossed, hopping up on the seat beside Evelyn.

Evelyn moved next to him, her body tense as Trevor started toward town, country music on the radio, Lilian humming along.

"Thanks for letting me tag along with you guys," Evelyn said. "I've never sold anything at a farmers' market."

Lilian popped a piece of gum in her mouth. "Why not? You could set up a whole booth with your artwork."

"People sell artwork at the farmers' market?"

Lilian laughed. "Just you wait and see."

Evelyn kept her eyes on the road. "I guess I will."

Lilian shook her head. "How is it possible you've never been before? You've lived in Loves Park since high school."

"Christopher thought they were too 'home-grown.'"

Lilian gasped. "What's that supposed to mean?"

Evelyn shrugged, her shoulder bumping Trevor's. "Who knows with Christopher?"

They pulled in near what appeared to be their booth space.

"I don't care what your rich ex-husband thinks, Evie," Lilian said. "This market is the heart of this town. If he had any sense, he would've realized that a long time ago."

There were a lot of things he would've realized a long time ago . . . if he had any sense.

Evelyn and Trevor began unloading their *homegrown* vegetables, which they carried from the truck to their booth's table, box by box. More than once, she paused to take a look around. It was a shame she'd never been to the market before.

It felt right, her being there, and she decided the new Evelyn would love to be a part of the homegrown community of Loves Park.

There. A decision she made all for herself— and not because anyone told her to.

Baby steps, but it was still progress.

"Once it's all set up, we'll have to walk through," Trevor said.

"Really?" She faced him. He would do that with her?

"You'll love it. There's all kinds of vendors. Art, jewelry, candles, food."

"I always wanted to come," Evelyn said, grabbing a basket of cilantro. "But Christopher was so concerned with public perception."

"Wouldn't the public perceive you were out to support your town? Buy local and all that?"

Another shrug. "Yes, but he had himself convinced local meant cheap. And nothing about Christopher was ever cheap."

Trevor watched her for a long moment, then went back to hauling boxes of vegetables.

"We brought a lot," Evelyn said, picking up another box.

"The market brings in a big crowd," Lilian said. "Thanks to you, we have more vegetables than we normally have. Should be a good market for us." She smiled.

"Thanks to me?"

"Yeah. With you tending part of the garden, those vegetables have been thriving. Haven't you noticed?"

She hadn't noticed. She'd been too focused on not messing up the plot of land they'd put in her care.

"Get ready," Lilian said, nodding toward the front gates of the market. "Here they come."

Evelyn couldn't believe the number of people who'd turned out so early on a Saturday morning. The booth was instantly busy, and while Trevor carried, lifted, and hauled, Evelyn mostly tried to stay out of the way.

Lilian mingled, took money and made change, and occasionally asked for Evelyn's help, which she was happy to give. By noon she'd decided she liked being at the farmers' market and she loved feeling like a part of Whitney Farms, whether she really was or not.

"We should have a lull now," Lilian told her. "Mind straightening the front table?"

Evelyn nodded and did as she was told. She started by rearranging the berries, stacking them carefully so shoppers could see how appealing they were.

She smiled at the thought. She used to believe diamonds and pearls were beautiful, but now it was berries and radishes that captivated her.

"Evelyn?"

She looked up. "Lydia." She tucked her hair behind her ears.

How long had it been since the FBI had interrupted their luncheon at her house on Brighton? How long since she bore the weight of this woman's judgmental stares across the table? She swallowed, her throat dry as cotton.

Lydia leaned in but did nothing to quiet her voice. "What are you doing here?"

Evelyn looked at Trevor, seated on a crate. He picked up an apple, took out his pocketknife, and cut off a chunk.

Lydia did a slow turn toward him right as he glanced their way. She raised a brow. "Oh, I see."

"I'm just helping out," Evelyn explained. "I weed the garden."

"Is that what you're calling it?" She raised a brow. "I read about you two."

Evelyn moved behind the table of berries as if that would put a safe distance between her and this barracuda.

Lydia shrugged. "I say good for you. Christopher has always been a slimeball. Isn't that right, farmer?"

"His name is Trevor," Evelyn said.

He took another bite of his apple, still regarding them, but said nothing.

"Does Georgina know you're having a fling with the farmer?"

"I'm not having a fling." Evelyn sounded defensive.

Lydia laughed. "That's right. I read that pitiful retraction in the paper. Did you pay for that?"

Evelyn's shoulders sank.

"Wait, I forgot. You're broke." She pulled a twenty-dollar bill from her pocket. "I'll take an assortment of vegetables. I'm nothing if not charitable."

Evelyn took a step back, wounded.

Lilian snatched the bill from Lydia's hand, bagged up the vegetables, and shoved the sack into her arms. "Thanks."

Lydia glanced at Trevor again. "When you're done with the farmer, Evelyn, send him my way." She winked at him and walked off.

"What a horrible woman," Lilian said. "Did you used to be friends with her?"

"I think she slept with Christopher," Evelyn said.

Lilian spun around. "What?"

"I was a fool for so long. It's silly to think none of these affairs began until he started spending time in Denver. Isn't it?" She turned to Trevor.

He didn't reply.

"Is it okay if I go for a walk?" Evelyn asked.

Lilian squeezed her arm. "Of course." She looked at Trevor. "Trevor will go with you."

"You don't have to," she said. The last thing she wanted to do was burden him with her sudden, inexplicable sadness. Oddly, it wasn't the loss of her relationship with Christopher that currently gnawed at her; it was the loss of her friendship with Trevor.

He stood. "No, it's fine. I'll show you where to get the best fancy coffee drink."

"That would be good. Fancy coffee is my favorite."

He tossed his apple core into the garbage and joined her in front of their booth. As they walked, people stared. People whose faces she recognized sneered at them. She caught words like *affair* and *fraud* and *criminal* as they were whispered on the wind.

People hadn't accepted her innocence, and clearly some of them still thought she was having an affair with Trevor.

She knew that people had only come to the

dinner event because of their loyalty to the Volunteers and the Whitney family, though she had to admit, she'd hoped it would smooth things over somehow. It hadn't.

She inched closer to Whit, wishing for the solace of his friendship, but knowing she'd put quite a dent in that.

They reached the coffee vendor. "Fancy coffee," he announced.

She gave him a sad smile. "Maybe this was a mistake."

He faced her. "You can't stay hidden forever."

She sighed. "It's easier." A tear streamed down her cheek. What she wouldn't give to be hidden right now.

Whit reached over and swiped the tear with his thumb. She closed her eyes, expecting him to walk away, but he didn't. His hand lingered there on the side of her face, his grip tightening ever so slightly, fingers tangled underneath her long braid.

She leaned in to his touch and opened her eyes, but before she could decipher the look on his face, a voice behind her claimed her attention.

"Well, well, well. Isn't this cozy?"

Evelyn straightened at the sound of Christopher's voice. She spun around and backed into Whit.

She hadn't seen him since the hearing, and now he stood right in front of them, wearing jeans and a polo, carrying a bag of homemade kettle corn.

"What are you doing here?" Evelyn's heart raced.

Christopher wore a smug expression. "Brought Darby out for some fresh air."

He nodded toward a booth across from where they stood. A leggy, pregnant brunette wearing not nearly enough clothing perused the goods at a jewelry table. She picked up a necklace, turned to Christopher, and waved. "I want this."

He smiled. "Anything you want, babe."

Evelyn's jaw went slack. "You brought your . . . your . . . *her* here?"

Christopher returned his attention to her. "My people thought it would be good PR. Make everyone forget she wasn't my first wife to begin with. Once they see the pictures of our beautiful baby girl, they'll stop thinking about the circumstances surrounding our marriage."

"So it's true. You're marrying her."

Christopher looked at the brunette. "She's got a few things to learn, but she's going to be the perfect politician's wife." He winked at Evelyn. "Maybe you could train her?"

Trevor placed a protective hand on Evelyn's back. It steadied her. "How are you even out here, Chris? Aren't you confined to your house or something?"

"I have friends in the DA's office," Christopher said. "This case could be tied up for years. I'm a free man until a judge says otherwise. Sounds to me like I might walk. This whole thing will be over by Christmas."

Not a chance. Evelyn had seen the evidence against him. Was Christopher delusional? She turned away, feeling like her safe place had been invaded. For most of his life her ex-husband had avoided these small-town events, and he picked today of all days to check one of them out. How did he even have money to give his girlfriend "anything she wanted"?

Christopher looked back and forth between her and Trevor. "So I read the paper. What exactly is going on here?" His eyes narrowed. "Surely you're not looking at my misfortune as an opportunity, Whit."

Evelyn took a step toward him. "Don't pretend you care. I can't believe I ever thought I loved you."

Christopher's face mocked. "Ouch."

Evelyn backed away just as the brunette— Darby—strolled toward them.

"Be careful with this one, Whit," Christopher said. "She's feisty."

"Back off, Chris," Trevor said.

"No, *you* back off." Christopher's voice threatened. He stepped toward Darby. "Hey, beautiful. Did you get what you wanted?" He wrapped an arm around her and sauntered off in the other direction.

Evelyn watched as Christopher greeted people in the crowd as if nothing had ever happened.

How was it possible they all seemed perfectly accepting of him, but so many of them had completely turned on her?

Trevor moved in front of her, blocking her view of the man who'd practically ruined her life. "How about that coffee?"

She nodded, thankful that despite the turn this day had taken, at least she and Trevor were on good terms again.

But as they stood in line for their fancy coffee, the image of Trevor's face—when she'd opened her eyes before Christopher's interruption— came back to her, kicking up nerves in her belly she hadn't felt in years. And she had no idea what to do with them.

CHAPTER
34

Later that night, Evelyn curled up on the sofa, pushing aside the feelings at war inside her head. Seeing Christopher had brought forth unwanted emotions, and she replayed the day's events like a movie in her mind.

Of course the trial was dragging on. Of course he was walking around free as a bird with a new soon-to-be wife and a baby on the way. Of course he had money from who knew where for kettle corn and handmade necklaces when she was scraping pennies together for the basic necessities so she didn't feel like a complete charity case.

But what she didn't expect was not to care.

Seeing him with that Darby person had only confirmed that she'd done the right thing. And somehow even that made her feel guilty.

Around dinnertime, the knock at the door sent panic racing through her as usual. While she and Whit had eventually been cordial, their friendship was anything but intact. He'd shown her kindness and she'd allowed him to look the fool.

She'd hurt his pride.

She checked her hair in the bathroom mirror and then quickly realized how ridiculous that was. What did she care if Whit saw her with messy hair? It was just Whit.

But when she opened the door, it wasn't Trevor waiting for her.

"Christopher."

He smiled. "May I come in?"

She hovered there, her body protected by the door. "Why are you here? Isn't your girlfriend going to miss you?"

His expression patronized. "That probably really bothered you, didn't it?"

She drew in a breath. Arguing the truth would be completely pointless. His ego would hear nothing but what it wanted to hear. "What do you want, Christopher?"

337

He tilted his head, took her in. "You look good, Evelyn, but when are you going to come home?"

She frowned.

"You didn't think our divorce was actually going to last, did you?"

She swallowed hard. "Of course I did. You're planning to marry someone else. Someone who is going to have your baby."

He moved away from the door, toward the porch railing. "I know. That's what my campaign manager wants me to do."

"You signed the papers," she said, following him. "Without protest."

"I thought it would be a wake-up call for you."

She knew he was egotistical, but was he insane too? "I'm not interested in playing games with you anymore."

He approached her. "But I love you, Evelyn. I always have." He pulled at the end of her sweater, tugging her closer to him.

She looked at Christopher, searching within herself for some trace of affection for him, but came up empty. It was like a lightbulb had gone on and she'd been awakened to the truth. The only question she had now was why it had taken her so long to see.

He pushed her hair back, away from her face, eyes locked on hers.

Before she could pull away, the sound of footsteps at the side of the house grabbed her attention. She turned toward the noise and saw Whit standing in the yard, carrying a stack of wooden hearts. He looked away from her, toward Christopher.

"Or have you already moved on?" Christopher said.

Evelyn glanced at Whit, who stood for a long moment and finally set the hearts against the front steps before heading back the way he'd come.

"Don't be ridiculous," Evelyn said. "Whit used to be your friend."

Christopher laughed. "And what do you really know about him, Evelyn?"

She steeled her jaw, a certain defensiveness coming over her. "What's that supposed to mean?"

"He's not the Boy Scout you think he is."

"I don't think he's a Boy Scout," Evelyn said. "I think he's a good person."

Christopher laughed. "Whit has secrets, Evelyn, just like I did. You're not going to ever find someone who doesn't, so you might as well admit that what we had was working." Christopher leaned against the post, relaxed and calm. He thought he had her in the palm of his hand—she could see it on his face.

Regret twisted inside her, her stomach hollow. "How can you say that?" Evelyn fought tears. "How can you say what we had was working?"

Christopher straightened. "We were always

good together, Evelyn. We can get back to that."

"You're having a baby with another woman."

He waved her off. "We can have our own baby."

She shook her head. "I can't believe you."

"I need you, Evelyn, and you need me. The public has always responded well to us as a couple."

Evelyn couldn't remember a time she'd ever been so stunned. He didn't want her back as a wife. He wanted someone to make him look good in the polls. As if she could even do that after he'd destroyed her reputation. "Did someone make you realize Darby isn't marriage material?"

"She's fine. I can work with her. But why choose someone else when I've already got you?" He stepped toward her and took her hand. "I'm lost without you, Evelyn. You always knew how to make everything okay."

Tension radiated through her entire body. "I can't be that person for you anymore, Christopher."

He leaned his forehead on hers. "I'm scared."

She took a step back and surveyed his face. Perhaps that was the only honest thing he'd ever said to her.

"Of what?"

He turned away. "Prison. Loneliness. Losing. I don't know how to do any of this without you."

A tear escaped without her permission. She brushed it away. "You broke my heart, Christopher. You humiliated me."

"I know. I'm so sorry." He looked down. "I thought you knew."

She felt her eyes go wide. "You thought I knew you were cheating on me?"

He shrugged. "Babe, I'm away for weeks at a time. You didn't think I was spending them alone? I mean, you know what I need."

She only stared.

"I can do better."

"You don't think you did anything wrong, do you?"

He sighed. "Evelyn, don't do this. Don't lecture me about morals right now. I'm a powerful man. I have needs. I thought we understood each other."

"Why did you really come here?" Evelyn backed up, arms over her chest. "Was it to try to win me back? Because you're doing a really poor job."

"I just thought after spending all these weeks out here on this farm, you'd be ready to return to the real world."

"In the house that's no longer ours? Wearing clothes you picked out for me because you wanted me to play a part?" She shook her head. "I can't believe I didn't see it before."

"What?"

"You don't want a wife. You want a puppet. Someone who will do exactly what you say when you say it."

"It never bothered you before. I gave you a good life."

"You gave me a lie," she yelled, surprising even herself. "I deserve better than a lie."

"Did Whit tell you that?"

"Whit has nothing to do with this!" She shouted the words, angry at herself for losing her temper.

"Don't think I don't know the truth here. You're all high and mighty with your code of honor, but you two are no better than I am."

"You don't know what you're talking about."

"And you don't know the truth about Trevor Whitney." He straightened. "You think I'm despicable for the way I live my life, but he's got plenty to answer for."

She turned away. "I don't care how Trevor Whitney lives his life, Christopher."

He moved close to her, too close, and leaned in even closer so she could feel his breath on her neck. "I don't believe you."

"I don't care," she whispered. She squared her chin and straightened her shoulders. "I deserve better than this."

He scoffed. "Fine, Evelyn. Have it your way. Keep hiding out here on this disgusting farm." He moved back. "I'm finished with you anyway."

She swallowed. "Get out of here."

His laugh mocked her. "I'm already gone."

She stood on the porch, watching as he hurried to his car, started the engine, and peeled away.

When she turned to go inside, she had the distinct impression that Trevor was still at the side of the porch, just out of sight but well within earshot.

And she wondered if she'd ever trust anyone again.

CHAPTER 35

Trevor spent the next two days avoiding Evelyn. The hearts were all cut out and his collaboration with her was over. So should his feelings be.

If only it were that easy.

He hadn't meant to eavesdrop on her conversation with Chris. In fact, he wished he'd just gone back to the house, but something in Chris's eyes wasn't right, and he couldn't walk away without making sure she was okay.

"We going to this thing?" Lilian stood in the doorway of the kitchen, interrupting Trevor's thoughts.

He groaned. "It's not like I have a choice."

"Well, you look great." She grinned. "Picking up Evie?"

He grabbed his truck keys off the counter. "It's just you and me tonight."

He felt her eyes on him but walked outside anyway. He didn't need a lecture about how he should at least offer Evelyn a ride to the Sweetheart Festival dance. They were a team on this wooden heart revamp and they were friends—or had been for a little while, anyway.

He knew all those things. He'd been battling the unwanted thoughts all day long. In the end, he decided he couldn't offer her a ride because he couldn't sit next to her in such a confined space. He couldn't inhale the scent of her or drink in the thought of her. He couldn't deny these feelings he'd been working so hard to eliminate.

Especially not after Chris had planted the seed that her good friend Trevor might not be so good after all.

Because he wasn't good. He was lousy. And both he and Chris knew it.

Lilian opened the passenger door of the truck and stared at him.

"You coming?" he asked without looking at her.

"You really aren't going to go pick up Evelyn?" She was probably glaring at him.

"Let's pretend you already gave me the lecture and now we're at the part where you get in the truck and go to this ridiculous dance. Anyway, Evelyn probably left already."

She didn't move for several seconds and then finally pulled herself up into the seat.

Trevor focused on the road and not on the huffing and puffing Lilian sitting next to him.

Chris probably couldn't stand the fact that

when he'd seen Evelyn that day at the farmers' market, she wasn't the broken woman he no doubt thought she would be. In fact, spending time with her at the market, even Trevor had noticed she seemed to have turned a corner.

Maybe it was the overwhelming triumph of their community dinner, which he had to admit had been a bigger hit than he'd expected. It would be months before they saw any real change in their profits as a result, but they were creating multiple streams of income, which was how he planned to keep the farm profitable into the future.

She had to feel pretty good about that, didn't she?

But what if that conversation with Chris knocked her back to the sweater-wearing hermit who never left the couch in the guesthouse?

Worse, what if she realized Trevor wasn't a "Boy Scout"—as Chris pointed out—and she packed her things and moved away? Leaving Loves Park in the rearview mirror once and for all?

Lilian let out a particularly vocal sigh. "This just isn't right, making her come by herself. I don't care how uncomfortable you feel."

The statement pinged Trevor's conscience. He knew she was right. Saying it out loud didn't help.

He did his best to ignore his aunt as he drove through town. The Sweetheart Festival had been a weeklong event, though Trevor had barely noticed. Old Town Loves Park had been decked out for the occasion. From a scarecrow-building contest to a caramel apple–dipping station to a small makeshift café serving pulled pork and apple cider donuts, this town looked for any chance to celebrate, and they'd done a good job getting locals and tourists to come out and show their support this year.

Tonight, though, the town would shed their jeans and boots in favor of semiformal attire. Not exactly Trevor's cup of tea.

Someone had decided Abigail's store and the outlying land were the perfect location for the dinner and dance that night, and when they pulled into the patch of field designated for parking, Trevor had to admit that someone was right.

He supposed the luminarias leading up to the main entrance were a nice touch. Inside, the white lights hanging on the ceiling also added a certain charm women loved and men tolerated. He knew most of the people milling around in the barn, but he found himself scanning the crowd for one person.

And the thought of her made his palms sweat.

"Oh, Mr. Whitney, thank goodness." Gigi bustled toward him, her voice loud over the music blaring from speakers near a small stage at one end of the room. "You certainly did take your time getting here. The presentation is in just a few minutes."

He saw a number of the plain wooden hearts he'd designed decorating the walls. He had to admit, they'd turned out better than he hoped. When he got the idea to stain thin slats of wood with several different finishes and affix them to heart-shaped plywood cutouts, he wasn't sure if he'd even like them.

As he studied them on the walls of The Paper Heart, he decided he did.

"These hearts you made are a huge hit—and people haven't even seen the painted ones yet." Doris had joined them. "You're quite the artist, Trevor."

"Did Evelyn come with you?" Gigi asked.

Lilian scoffed.

Gigi frowned. "She brought her painted hearts here earlier, but I haven't seen her since."

Trevor shook his head. "She didn't come with us."

He hoped Evelyn hadn't backed out. He certainly didn't want to stand up there in front of the whole town by himself. Though maybe that would be preferable to standing beside Evelyn. At least if he was alone, he had a better chance of not thinking about the softness of her skin or the smell of her hair.

He should've found out how she was doing after their run-in with Chris—after his visit to the farm. What kind of person abandoned a friend when she needed him most?

"Follow me," Gigi said, looking at Trevor. "Doris, you go find Evelyn."

But their search ended when they turned around.

Evelyn stood a few yards away, near a side entrance lit only by the dim white lights hanging above. She wore something blue, turquoise, like the color of the ocean in an ad for a cruise. Her eyes were that same color, and for a moment, he said a prayer of thanks it was too dark to see them. He might buckle under their boldness. Her blonde hair was long and loose. He wanted to touch it.

Doris let out a quiet "Oh, my. She's beautiful."

Gigi, barely at Trevor's shoulders, looked up at him, her gaze too intent. He could feel the words she wasn't saying. He had to give her credit—the woman had a knack for figuring out matters of the heart.

Thankfully, she said nothing. He forced himself to look away.

Evelyn finally caught sight of them. He could see her walking toward him out of the corner of his eye, and when he dared a glance in her direction, he noticed she refused to make eye contact. Just as he thought. Chris had gotten in her head.

It was what he deserved. She might have kept the truth about Maggie from him for a few hours, but he'd been hiding the truth about her husband for years.

When she reached their small circle, he turned

away. He couldn't face her. If she knew the things he'd been thinking—the way her nearness had set something off inside him—he would be the one cowering in embarrassment. Not the other way around.

Gigi reached her hands out to Evelyn, pulling her into a hug. "We're so glad you're here. I took a peek at the hearts. They're absolutely perfect. I knew the two of you would create something wonderful together."

Trevor glanced at Evelyn—a reflex—and she did the same. They both looked away immediately. His mouth had gone dry and his throat felt raw. He drew in a deep breath. If Gigi had figured out the truth about his feelings, how much longer did he think he could keep it from Evelyn?

Never mind he'd hidden it for years.

His stomach flip-flopped. How could he keep pretending? He'd given her up the day she married Chris. But the day the divorce went through, a new battle had begun. Knowing she was no longer married had knocked over the main barrier to his feelings.

"Going to get a drink," he said, walking in the other direction, guilt tugging at the corners of his mind. But he hadn't been secretly wishing for Evelyn's marriage to fall apart. In fact, he'd even prayed God would bring conviction to Chris so he could be the kind of husband she deserved. So why had Trevor's love for Evelyn returned?

"Three minutes, Mr. Whitney," Gigi said.

Three minutes wouldn't be enough time to calm himself down. He walked to the punch table and, for the first time since high school, wished there was something stronger than sugar in that punch. He took a cup and drank, eyeing the door.

Before he could decide, he heard tapping on the microphone. The music stopped and a little old lady wound her arm through his. "Gigi sent me to get you." Doris winked. "Thought you might get cold feet."

He stifled a groan and let himself be led to the front of the room, where Gigi had taken the stage, Evelyn only a few feet away.

"Get up there," Doris said. "Gigi's orders."

Gigi waved Trevor up. Like a child, he did as he was told, telling himself this would all be over in a matter of minutes and he could go home.

He stood next to Evelyn. He scanned the crowd of faces, but none of them seemed to register. The only thing he could think of was how close he was to the woman he loved.

But then he'd always been close, and it had never been enough.

His tie squeezed his neck like a noose, his palms wet. He contemplated making a run for it.

The microphone looked awkward and unbalanced in Gigi's hand as she addressed the audience. "We're so happy to see you all here as we close out our Sweetheart Festival, and we're very excited because we have a surprise for you."

She glanced at Trevor and Evelyn before continuing. "Now, some of you may have read the little exposé in the *Courier* about my dear friends, Trevor Whitney and Evelyn Brandt."

Trevor's heart dropped. What was Gigi doing?

"But I can assure you, there was a misunderstanding. As you probably guessed, these two are not romantically involved. They were simply working together on a project for our fair city at my request."

Beside her, on a screen, a picture of the Main Street lampposts appeared.

"As you all know, we do love the tradition of our wooden hearts, but being such an artistic community, we thought perhaps we could come up with a bit more creative version this year to celebrate our town's great love affair with love."

A smattering of applause worked its way across the room. Trevor shifted. He had no interest in being the poster boy for the Sweetheart Festival, and yet here he stood.

"Enter Mr. Whitney, the woodworker, and our dear Evelyn, the artist."

More clapping. Was this what it had taken for the town to view them more favorably?

"We've asked them to reimagine our tradition, and we think you're going to love what they've come up with. Before I show you, I want to tell you one of my favorite things about being a

Valentine Volunteer is that I get drawn in by some of the stories we see come our way." She smiled. "For example, about ten years ago, we received an anonymous request for a special wooden heart from someone here in this very town."

Heat rushed to Trevor's face.

"And what we've found is that every year since, this same anonymous request has come in, but every year has been a different line from the same song lyrics. It's been so many years, we've almost got the entire song on hearts. There's something so intriguing about a mysterious love story," She paused and glanced at Trevor, but he avoided her eyes.

"I never mentioned this story to Evelyn, but it just so happened to be the one that inspired her artistic reimagining of our age-old tradition."

Nausea rolled through Trevor's gut. This *just so happened* to be the story? Was the universe playing some cruel, cosmic joke on him? *God, have you been ignoring all my requests for help on purpose just to humiliate me here in front of the entire town?*

"Now, with Trevor's help, she's re-created these beautiful hearts in an effort to show you what our new painted hearts campaign is going to look like. Our lampposts are truly going to be works of art." Gigi spun around. One look at Trevor and she lowered her microphone. "Are you okay, Mr. Whitney?"

He nodded. A lie.

Evelyn stared over the crowd. Probably better. He didn't need her turning his way. Not right now.

Gigi addressed the audience again. "Ladies and gentlemen, we are thrilled to reveal the masterpieces created by these two local artists. Trevor has provided the wooden cutouts, and Evelyn, the painted words. I think you'll agree the combination of both is stunning."

She nodded to Doris, who tugged on the end of a rope, loosening the large canvas backdrop that hung in front of the new hearts. The backdrop fell to the ground, revealing Trevor's hearts, which looked nothing like they had when he'd turned them over to Evelyn. She'd transformed them with her flawless artwork.

Never mind that each of the ten hearts behind them spelled out the lyrics to the song that had been playing the night they met. Trevor remembered because high school parties rarely featured the music of Nat King Cole.

Someone had accidentally turned on Chris's dad's stereo and let it play through almost the entire song before the mocking began and the music was changed.

But in Trevor's mind, it had been the perfect sound track for the events of that evening. Seeing Evelyn like that, dimly lit by the pale moonlight. Working up the courage to talk to her. Deciding in that moment he could actually love her, though he knew it was a ridiculous notion given the fact that they'd only just met.

He routinely left out the part of the memory where Chris swept in and stole her attention the way he always did.

It had seemed like a good idea, purchasing one of the hearts that first year they were married. His way of expressing a love that could never be. The one indulgence he'd allow himself where his feelings for Evelyn were concerned. But now? Seeing all of them on display like this—not just one at a time on a Main Street lamppost—he realized the error of his thinking. If anyone ever found out . . .

If Evelyn ever found out . . .

Her discovery of the things he'd kept from her for Chris's benefit would be one thing. Her discovery of his feelings would be something else entirely.

Gigi allowed the applause to die down before finishing. "Feel free to peruse the hearts for yourself and get an early start on ordering your own custom sign this year. They will take longer to prepare, as you can imagine. Now, why don't we ask our two artists to lead us in a celebratory dance as we return to the evening's festivities?"

Trevor's stomach plummeted to the floor. She couldn't be serious.

Gigi set the microphone in its stand and faced

them. "I hope you don't mind me putting you on the spot. I thought it would be a lovely touch."

Right. *Lovely.*

"I've asked the band to play the song painted on the hearts. I hope that's okay." Gigi walked toward the stairs. "Come on, you two."

Trevor swallowed, then gestured to Evelyn. "After you."

She didn't meet his eyes. Instead, she walked past him, down the stairs, and stood waiting.

All around the room, guests focused on the two of them, and Trevor thought for the first time he might be in more danger of having a panic attack than Evelyn. He met her on the floor. "You okay with this?"

She stared into his chest. "Let's just get it over with."

She seemed to have taken a page out of his playbook. The two of them had settled back into a friendship, but now that Chris had planted the seed that she couldn't trust Trevor, she'd pushed him a healthy arm's length away.

Plus, he hadn't exactly been kind to her after the whole Maggie fiasco blew up in both their faces.

A lifetime of regret swirled together with a week's worth of the same, leaving Trevor without words.

He walked to the center of the room, aware she followed close behind. Dim lights shone around them as the band waited for them to take their spots.

Trevor extended his right hand. Eyes still cast downward, she took it, stepping toward him and allowing his left arm to rest at the small of her back. Her free hand found his shoulder and the crowd went quiet.

Kate Willoughby, the doctor's sister, stood at the center of the stage, one faint light illuminating the side of her face. The first line of the song rang out through the barn, her voice melancholy. Seconds later, she strummed an easy chord on her guitar, and Trevor and Evelyn slowly started to move together.

> The very thought of you and I forget to do
> The little ordinary things that everyone
> ought to do

The words haunted. The tune tortured, drawing him back to that night. The night he found her— the night he lost her.

He inched closer and drew her in. He could feel his defenses weaken at her nearness. He wanted to fold her into himself, to have the right to hold her.

Around them, other couples began to dance, but he kept his face low, near hers. If he could've absorbed her pain, he would've. Without question. He wanted to tell her the truth—all of it. And he wanted her to be okay with it—all of it. He wanted to make her understand that everything he'd done, he'd done for her.

Kate reached the second chorus and another singer added harmony.

But Evelyn's feet stopped moving, and her grip tightened ever so slightly.

Then, for the first time since the embarrassing evening before, she lifted her chin and gazed into his eyes.

She knew.

The song must've awakened a memory because the way she looked at him, the pieces falling together, it was clear Evelyn Brandt had discovered the secret he'd hidden since he was seventeen years old.

Her hands slipped from his as she stepped back. Confusion filled her face.

"Evie." He reached for her, but she moved away, stepping slowly out of the light and disappearing into the darkness.

As always, inches from his reach.

CHAPTER
36

Evelyn raced out of the barn, but when she reached the parking lot, she remembered she'd gotten a ride over with Abigail. She circled through the cars like a rat in a cage. Trapped.

She felt—not saw—Whit emerge from the barn.

"Evie?" She turned as he walked toward her, sending her mind back years, the memory of the melody begging for her attention.

She searched his eyes for an explanation.

"What's wrong?"

She shook her head. "Don't. Don't pretend."

He drew in a breath and let it out as he turned away, raking a hand through his hair. "Evie, please."

"It was you."

He brought his hands to his hips, stared at the ground. "Don't do this."

She took a step forward. "Me?" Her laugh lacked amusement. "I painted those lyrics, nothing more than words. I never looked up the song because I didn't want to think about some happy couple celebrating Valentine's Day. Not this year."

But she had thought of them, hadn't she? She'd allowed her mind to invent a love story so beautiful it almost convinced her that one day she could know how it felt to be loved without condition. How had she been so foolish?

He looked at her. "How happy could their story be if the hearts were purchased in secret?"

Her stomach lurched. "But I know that song, don't I, Whit?"

All the words he hadn't said hung in the air. He watched her in silence for so many seconds, she had her answer.

The song had been playing the first night they met. She would've forgotten it, but he'd also played it for her on the piano the night he told her he wasn't going back to school. The night Christopher interrupted their conversation. The night something unspoken passed between them—something she quickly dismissed.

"I know that melody."

He kicked a rock. Sighed. "Listen, can we just forget about it? I don't know what you think you remember but—"

She moved toward him, quickly, and stopped inches from where he stood. "You don't get to do that right now."

He closed his eyes and drew in another breath.

"It was you. You bought the hearts." She stilled. "For me." She'd whispered the words, the reality of them settling on her shoulders, tears filling her eyes. "Why?"

He walked away from her, but she followed him.

"Are you leaving?"

He yanked his tie loose and wove through the parked cars, stopping at the sight of Jerry Yates, an old classmate who spent most of his days drunk.

Jerry spun around. "Whit!" He glanced at Evelyn. "I knew the paper got it wrong about you two." His words slurred together like butter melting in a pot. "She is *way* out of your league." Jerry laughed. "Am I right, Evelyn?"

Trevor moved past Jerry until he reached his truck, parked near the exit for a quick getaway.

Evelyn followed. "Stop."

Finally he faced her. "This is no good, Evie, and you know it. Just let it go."

She searched his eyes. All those years of her marriage, she'd thought he despised her. What if she'd gotten it wrong? "I can't let this go. Explain it to me."

He had one hand on the door of the truck, the other fidgeting with his keys. "I can't talk to you tonight."

She moved to his side, her back to his truck, and forced him to turn. He didn't look at her.

"Trevor?"

"Just don't."

"I know you played me that song," Evelyn said. "I remember it now. You played it the night Christopher found us in the music room. He thought something was going on between us, didn't he?"

Whit stayed focused on his own feet. "He always thought something was going on with us, Ev."

She frowned. "Why?" And why hadn't he talked to her about it?

"Because he knew . . ." Trevor groaned, clearly unhappy they were even having this conversation.

Evelyn waited for him to finish his thought, silent.

"How I felt about you." He brought his eyes to hers. "Okay? He knew. And that's why he asked you out in the first place."

Tears clouded her vision. "What are you saying?"

He inched closer, the bulk of his body shielding her from the cool autumn wind. A foggy memory of the night at the Royal invaded her mind, and that familiar shame along with it. Why had he pushed her away? If he had feelings for her, wouldn't he have acted on them?

She could see years of pain locked up in his expression.

His thumb brushed across her cheek. "Evie," he whispered.

She held his gaze. He'd been there all along, hadn't he? And she assumed he'd been paving the way for Christopher, but what if that was never Whit's plan?

She leaned against the truck. He inched closer, hands pressed against the vehicle on either side of her. She lifted her chin, and he studied her for a long few seconds as if memorizing every bit of her.

"Why didn't you ever say anything?" The words nearly choked her for the lump that formed in her throat.

He shook his head. "I couldn't. Chris was my friend. You were happy. I couldn't have made you that happy, Evie."

She reached up and touched his face. "Do you really believe that?"

He leaned into her, eyes closed, the weight of his internal battle visible on his face.

Finally, after a conflicted moment, he replied. "You could never be happy with someone like me." He shifted her aside and pulled away. "You *are* out of my league."

With one motion, he opened the truck door, got in, and started the engine, leaving her standing in the middle of the parking lot surrounded by cars yet completely alone.

CHAPTER
37

Trevor sped away from the store on the edge of town, his mind reeling. Now what? The horror on her face—how did he ever expect her to trust him again?

He stepped on the gas and cruised toward the lake. When the truck came to a stop, he found himself sitting in front of Chris and Evelyn's mansion.

As usual, he sat on the outside, staring at what could never be. Anger flashed through him like electricity, much different from the jolt he'd gotten when Evelyn had touched his face. He'd wanted to kiss her, and he didn't want to be gentle about it, but he couldn't.

She didn't belong to him.

In his mind, she was still Chris's wife. He'd accepted it. He'd wanted the best for them. Wanted her to have the husband she deserved— even if it wasn't Trevor.

But Chris had gone and screwed that up, hadn't he?

And Trevor could've predicted it from the start. Yet he'd said nothing. Some friend.

Trevor saw movement inside the house. Chris was home. Moving on with his life as if nothing was wrong, as if nothing had ever been wrong.

He gripped the steering wheel and his knuckles whitened.

He killed the engine, got out, and trudged up the sidewalk. He didn't knock on the door, just pushed it open and went inside.

"Chris?"

The man appeared from the doorway of the living room, frowning with his whole face. "What are you doing here, Whit? Don't you have wives to steal?" Ice cubes clinked in his glass as he waved his hand at Trevor.

Whit slammed the door. "Who do you think you are?"

He laughed. "That's rich coming from a farmer who never left his parents' house. A farmer who had to wait till I was finished with the woman he loved before ever getting a chance with her." He turned, but before he could walk away, Trevor grabbed his arm and spun him back around.

"Don't walk away from me, Chris."

Chris looked at Trevor's hand, still grasping his arm. "Get your hand off me."

"Or what?"

Chris glared at him. "Evelyn thinks you're such a saint, but we both know the truth."

"Shut up," Trevor said through gritted teeth.

"You knew all along." Chris pulled out of his grasp. "How many times did you lie for me? To your beloved *Evie?*" He snorted. "If you were half a man, you would've told her the truth, but you didn't. You lied. Covered it up. Gave me alibi after alibi. You're just like me."

He walked into the living room and Trevor followed. "I heard what you said to her," Trevor said.

"Isn't it just like you to hide in the shadows and listen to other people's conversations?" Chris stopped at the center of the room. "Do you want me to tell you what it was like being married to her? What it was like to touch her whenever I wanted?"

Trevor's hands trembled. "You never deserved her."

"Maybe, but I still had her. Over and over again." He lifted his glass, but before he could take a drink, Trevor slapped it out of his hand. It shattered on the floor.

"What are you going to do—defend her honor?" Chris smirked.

"It's about time someone gave you what you have coming to you."

Chris raised an eyebrow. "*You're* going to do that?"

Trevor responded with a right hook to Chris's cheek. He stumbled back but quickly found his footing. When he did, he lunged at Trevor, tackling him to the ground. Chris got in a few hits, concentrated near Trevor's left eye, before Trevor regained control and fended him off with three punches to the gut and two across the other side of his face.

"Enough!" Chris yelled, pulling away.

Trevor dabbed his bleeding brow with the sleeve of his shirt. "No, it's not. Not by a long shot." He moved toward Chris, who stumbled backward.

"I'll leave her alone, Whit."

Trevor stopped, eyes locked on Chris.

"I'm done with her anyway," Chris sneered.

Trevor grabbed him by the shirt with both hands and threw him into the entryway, where he crashed into a small table, a crystal bowl shattering on the ground. "You're not even worth it."

He opened the door and strode outside, feeling no better than he had when he arrived. Obviously beating the tar out of someone wasn't a good remedy for anger. And he was angry. At Chris, yes, but mostly at himself.

He got back in his truck and, for the second time that night, peeled away, just in time to see Chris stagger forward and close his front door.

Trevor drove toward home, his head throbbing and his eye swelling. He hadn't been in a fight since high school when some idiot stole from their table at the farmers' market. He'd mortified his mother that day, but he wasn't about to let anyone steal what she'd worked so hard for.

He'd been protecting people his whole life, and now he wondered why he'd been so careless with his own heart.

Chris was right. He was pathetic.

"Didn't I do what you asked?" He said the words aloud. Unconventional prayers were his specialty. "I honored her vows. I stayed out of it. I even asked you to bless their marriage."

No, he hadn't done so willingly at first, but he knew it was the right thing to do, so he'd prayed for Chris and Evelyn. Prayed his feelings would subside. And they had, to some extent—only to reemerge stronger and more powerful than ever.

If only he'd told her the truth in the first place. If only he hadn't covered for Chris over and over again.

But he was a coward. He'd let his feelings cloud his judgment.

"Why didn't you take these feelings away? Bring me someone else to love? Let me live my life?" He slammed his fist on the steering wheel. It hurt. His hands were already sore from the beating he'd given Chris, something he was sure would humiliate him in the morning.

"What am I supposed to do now?" The words nearly choked him. He hit the steering wheel again, pulling the truck into his driveway and cutting the engine. "What am I supposed to do?"

He stilled, the reality of his lack of direction washing over him like a cold shower. He stared at the house, illuminated by moonlight. As he got out of the truck, he saw motion on his front porch. Evelyn stood and moved toward the stairs. She'd been sitting on the swing, waiting.

And he'd returned, bloody and embarrassed with no idea what he was doing.

Love without condition.

The words raced through his mind, but he shoved them aside. He'd *been* loving without condition. For fifteen years. And what had that gotten him?

A black eye and a chip on his shoulder.

He didn't want Evelyn to see him. Not like this. She'd ask questions and he'd have to tell her the whole truth about his juvenile actions and listen to a lecture about what an idiot he was.

And he couldn't give her answers to her questions about those stupid painted hearts either. He didn't have it in him. Not tonight. He didn't even know why he'd continued to have the lyrics to that song stenciled and displayed for the whole town to see.

He'd done his best to force himself to get over her—handed it over to God and everything—but he'd never stopped buying the hearts. Why?

She walked toward him and he hovered near the truck, unable—or maybe unwilling—to face her. When she reached him, she stopped.

He was thankful it was dark out, even if the moon did threaten to tattle. He leaned against the truck, trying not to imagine what his face looked like.

She said nothing.

After several beats of silence, he lifted his chin, daring to meet her gaze. Yep. She was looking at him.

Now what?

"Do you want to see something cool?"

He only stared.

"Follow me." She started walking. When he didn't move, she turned. "You coming?"

Didn't she have more to say? He did as he was told, wondering how long he could conceal the cuts on his face. Or go without aspirin.

She led him over to the Adirondack chairs, where she'd set out two blankets. "I thought you were going to miss it, but I think you're just in time."

"For what?" He watched as she sat down.

"Look up."

When he did, he saw the chairs had been shifted slightly to face the full moon. "What am I looking at?"

She grabbed his hand and tugged him onto the chair. "Sit."

He did, but when she didn't let go of his hand, he lost focus. Was she going to let him off the hook? Just like that?

"You're not looking," she said, smiling at him.

He followed her eyes upward and realized it was a rare lunar eclipse. A blood moon. He hadn't seen one in years. "That's amazing."

"I thought you would like it."

They sat in silence, and the pain in his head began to subside. He'd gone to Chris's house to fight for Evelyn's honor. Or maybe just to let off some steam. He was angry and he'd acted like a fool.

He glanced at her. She knew all about that, didn't she? Maybe that's why she offered him grace. When he didn't deserve it.

"I have ice cream inside," she said. "Want some?"

He nodded, still trying to find some sense of balance.

When she returned with two bowls, she handed him his moose tracks and studied his face.

She frowned. "What happened to your eye?"

So much for the cover of darkness.

He took the bowl, set it on the arm of the chair, and turned away. "It's nothing."

Evelyn stared at him, waiting for an explanation. "Let me look at it. Inside."

He had the distinct feeling his grace had just ended. Why did he act on his anger? Why did he ruin what might've been a perfect beginning?

Trevor walked into the guesthouse and winced when she flipped on the light in the entryway. When she saw his face in full light, she gasped. "What on earth?"

She rushed past him, and he heard her rustling around in the kitchen. The water came on. "Get in here."

Okay, bossy.

Sheepishly, he walked into the kitchen, where she ran a cloth under the cold water.

"Sit." She studied his face. "What happened?"

She pressed the cold cloth against his eye. It hurt. He didn't want to tell her what he'd done.

At his silence, she sighed. "Never mind. It doesn't matter."

He waited while she dabbed his cheek with the

cloth, wincing occasionally because she certainly wasn't being gentle.

"I was so mad at you when you left tonight," she said, cleaning his forehead with the cloth.

"I'm sorry. Are you trying to take it out on my face?"

She looked at him. "Does that hurt?"

"Do you see the blood?"

"Sorry. I'll be careful." She proceeded more gently. "I was mad. If you sent those hearts in, that means you lied."

If she didn't have hold of his face, he would've turned away.

"Lies are the last thing I need in my life," she said. "You know that."

"It's complicated, Evie," he said, his voice quiet.

She stopped dabbing and stared at him. "Is it?"

He studied her eyes, bold and blue as the color of the dress she still wore. "You said you *were* mad."

She nodded.

"Past tense?"

She shrugged. "I started thinking about how rude you always are. Cranky and kind of mean, you know? Like an old man with a No Trespassing sign at the end of his driveway. You put up all kinds of signals that everyone should leave you alone."

He said nothing. She couldn't possibly understand why he acted the way he did.

"When it first started, I was so irritated. I mean, I always thought we were friends." She walked over to the sink, rinsed the cloth, then turned off the water and faced him. "But tonight I realized it all started after Christopher and I got married."

"You really don't need to talk about it—"

"Yes, I do," she interrupted. "I thought you couldn't stand me. Because things were different with you and Christopher. He was acting all stuck-up and I was the annoying wife who got in the way."

He shook his head. "That wasn't it."

She waited until he finally looked at her.

Trevor shoved his hands in his jacket pockets. "You've always deserved so much better."

Her eyes looked glassy, wet. "No, I don't."

He forced himself not to look away. "Evie. Yes, you do."

"Why didn't you say anything sooner?"

Because I'm a coward. Because you fell in love with my best friend. Because I'm no good for you.

But he said none of those things. Instead, he simply stared at her, heart racing.

She moved closer, eyes still on his.

"Evie, I can't."

She touched his face as if seeing him for the first time. He inhaled the clean smell of her skin. She wanted him to say words he'd never allowed himself to say. Words that tormented him every single day of his life, even on the days he'd convinced himself he was over her. Had he ever truly given his feelings to God? Or was he walking around with this bitterness because the answer had always seemed to be no?

Regardless, he'd been hiding these feelings for years. How could he dare to speak them aloud?

She was off-limits. Had so recently belonged to someone else. And Chris was right—Trevor couldn't give her what she needed. Besides, if she ever found out the things he'd hidden from her, she wouldn't just walk away—she would hate him forever.

And yet, standing here, this close to the woman he loved, he felt unable—or unwilling—to move.

"Tell me, Trevor."

"What do you want me to say?" Didn't she know how hard he'd worked *not* to say it?

"The truth. Tell me the truth."

The thought of it tortured him. All the truths he'd kept hidden from her. Where did she want him to begin?

"You don't want me to do that."

She inhaled a soft breath but only spoke with her eyes.

Slowly he wrapped a hand around her back, horribly aware of his pulse. If she knew how she turned every sane thought in his head into a jumbled-up mess, she'd run the other way.

But just for a moment, what if none of that mattered? What if he allowed himself the fleeting thought that they could be together? That she could love him the way he loved her?

"I—"

She watched him, searching as if daring him to continue.

"I'm not very good with words." He drew her closer, stood and pressed her body into his. She didn't move, only watched as he sorted out this moment for himself. And then, when he couldn't untangle his thoughts anymore, he took her face in his hands and brought his lips to hers.

As the realization settled in that it might be okay to kiss her, he pulled her nearer still, held her tighter, kissed her deeper. She tasted sweet like strawberries and she smelled like home.

The kiss became rushed, years of longing catching him off guard.

He pulled away. "I'm sorry."

She leaned into him, clung to him, desire racing between them. He held her for a long moment, soaking in every ounce of her, allowing himself the fantasy that she could ever feel about him the way he felt about her.

And while a part of him knew it was just that—a fantasy—another part of him wholly surrendered to the idea because now that he had her in his arms, he wasn't sure how he'd ever move forward without her.

But even as the thought entered his mind, another one replaced it. He'd kept other things from her, things that had hurt her. He could've spared her so much pain, but he'd been too selfish. He wasn't any better than Chris.

Gently he disengaged himself. "This isn't a good idea, Evelyn," he said.

Her face fell. "Why do you do that?"

"What?"

"Push me away. You can't even tell me how you feel. Instead, you're just going to close yourself off. Again."

She didn't get it. She never would. Because she didn't know the truth.

"I should probably go." *Because clearly I don't have a lot of willpower when it comes to you.*

Trevor turned away from the pain in her beautiful blue eyes. He couldn't stand the thought that he was the one hurting her tonight.

But it made no sense to prolong the inevitable. She deserved better than Trevor and his years of deception. Plain and simple. As he walked past her and out the door, his hand involuntarily moved toward her as if by some magnetic force. But he was too late.

He'd made his decision a long time ago. He wasn't good enough for her then and he wasn't good enough for her now, especially with all their history.

Best she came to that conclusion sooner rather than later. She'd said it herself. Lies were the last thing she needed in her life.

But that night, when his head hit the pillow, he couldn't deny the knot in his stomach—a knot that drove him up and out of bed more than once—because somehow, Trevor feared walking away was the biggest mistake of his life.

CHAPTER
38

Through her tears, Evelyn tossed all of her belongings into the only suitcase she had and stuffed it in the trunk of her car. As she pulled away from Whitney Farms, humiliated at Trevor's second rejection, she realized she had nowhere to go.

She drove aimlessly toward town, wondering how things had gotten so far off base. Earlier this evening as she'd stood in the middle of The Paper Heart, that song echoing from the speakers, it had all swirled back, like a circle of leaves kicked up by an autumn breeze.

She remembered. Trevor's lanky fingers moving over the piano keys as he hummed that melody— the familiar song she couldn't place. And that's when she knew.

But with the knowing came so many new questions.

Why hadn't Trevor said anything?

Was it true Christopher had only pursued her because he knew about Whit's feelings?

And perhaps the most pressing: Had Christopher ever loved her at all? Or was she simply a prize to be won?

After nearly an hour, she rounded a familiar corner, driving along the lake until she found herself sitting across the street from the house she'd shared with Christopher. The house where he probably lived with his pregnant girlfriend— or was she his wife now?

She parked her car and watched in the stillness of night. It was late. She should just go check herself into a hotel or, even better, drive straight out of town. And yet she found herself here.

Why?

She turned the car off and looked at her key ring. Unless Christopher had changed the locks, she still had a key to the front door. She got out and walked up the sidewalk until she reached the porch. She stood for several minutes, trying to decide if she even wanted to know the truth.

But if she didn't ask, how would she ever move on?

She drew in a breath, stuck the key in the lock, and opened the door.

Christopher emerged from the study, probably concerned that someone had opened his front door at midnight. She stopped moving. His lip was swollen and his face red and bloodstained.

Whit.

At the sight of her, he softened. "I knew you'd be back."

She shut the door behind her. "I came here to get something I didn't have in the whole ten years we were married."

He frowned. "What is it?"

"The truth."

He rolled his eyes. "Evelyn, in case you can't tell, your boyfriend already worked me over tonight. I don't have the energy to fight with you too."

"I'm not here to fight. I just want to know one thing."

He put his hands on his hips, heaved a heavy sigh. "What?" He did nothing to hide his annoyance.

She forced herself to move toward him, begging God to give her strength to stop trying to please other people all the time. It didn't matter anymore if Christopher was happy with her. *She* wasn't happy with *him*.

That had never mattered before. But now it did. Now she realized she had the right to an opinion of her own.

"In high school, did you ask me out because you knew Trevor wanted to?"

He raised a brow. "Is that what he told you?"

"He didn't tell me anything. I'm trying to figure out what's been going on for the last fifteen years."

Christopher strolled past her into the living room and sat down on the sofa. "Why don't you ask him?"

She followed him. "I'm asking you."

"What difference does it make?"

"It makes a difference to me."

He leaned into the couch, spread his arms across the back, and stared at her, head tilted as if sizing her up. "What do you want to know?"

"The night we met, I spent most of the time talking to Trevor. He was the first person at school who was nice to me."

Christopher scoffed. "Yep. Trevor Whitney, the nice guy. Worked out real well for him."

Evelyn ignored him. "He liked me, didn't he? And you knew it."

He inhaled, then narrowed his focus on her. "Yep."

"A few days later, you asked me out. Is that why? Was it just some kind of weird competition for you?"

"You were new and mysterious. And stunning. You should've heard the way everyone talked about you when you first showed up."

She folded her arms.

"All the guys wanted you. That made you more interesting, I guess. And there was no way I was going to let someone else have you. Not when I was sure I could."

"But you knew how Trevor felt."

"Everyone knew, Evelyn. Just like everyone knew about what I did when I wasn't with you." He stood, a smugness washing across his face. "Well, everyone except you, I guess." He shook his head. "Once the mystery wore off, what was I supposed to do? You didn't really expect me to only have you for the rest of my life?"

The words stung like an electrical shock zapping her off-kilter, but she forced herself to keep her balance.

"I think you're jealous of Trevor."

Christopher laughed. "I'm jealous of Whit. The farmer who still lives at home. It took him six years to finish college, Evelyn." He rolled his eyes.

"And he had parents who cared for him and never worried about his public image. They loved him anyway. He has a very successful business you probably don't even know about, and more than anything, he's perfectly comfortable in his own skin. He knows what's really important."

"Right, because those are things I'm after."

Evelyn watched him, and for the first time since the FBI invaded their home all those months ago, she began to feel something she never expected to feel for her ex-husband. Pity.

"You've been searching for contentment your whole life, Christopher," she said. "I know because I've been searching too. And I think you had me convinced that it was all wrapped up in status and power and money. But you know what Trevor Whitney has always known that you and I failed to realize?"

He didn't respond to her rhetorical question.

"Those things only complicate the search for peace. I know you couldn't stand the fact that Trevor liked me, so you got in the middle and you made sure we would never be together. Because in your mind—even if you didn't realize it— Trevor already had everything you wanted."

Christopher ran a hand over his chin. "Is that right?"

"I know I made mistakes too," she continued. "I was so caught up in the promises you made, in the way you turned heads and how everyone responded to you. I wanted out of my parents' house, and the life you offered won me over. I was too influenced by everyone else's opinions to make a single decision of my own."

"Great, Evelyn," Christopher said. "I'm glad you've had this epiphany."

Months ago, she would've stopped talking at his sarcastic comment, but she had more to say. "Trevor is content with who he is. I've never had that. I was so busy becoming who you wanted me to be that I forgot who *I* wanted to be. And honestly, Christopher, I don't blame you completely for our failed marriage. Maybe if I'd been more willing to demand your faithfulness, none of this would've happened in the first place."

"Maybe you're right, Evelyn. Maybe Whit is the guy for you."

"That's not what I said."

He moved toward her, stopping only a few inches from where she stood. "And maybe, just maybe, he's kind and good and honest."

"He is." Her words were barely a whisper.

"Or maybe he's been a part of this thing all along and you were too blind to see that either."

She stepped away, but he closed the gap between them.

"Who do you think helped me hide everything I was doing while we were dating, Evelyn? Who do you think lied to you when I was late because I had a 'previous engagement'? Oh, he was more than happy to step in as a fake boyfriend when I was out having the time of my life, but how much could he really care about you if he'd stand by and let you marry a man who hadn't been faithful to you one single day of his life?"

The words rushed at Evelyn like a flood. "What are you saying?"

"He's not your friend, Evelyn. He's always been my wingman. He even pretended one of the girls I was with was his girlfriend once. In fact, I couldn't have done it without good old Whit." He ran a hand up her arm, wrenching her stomach.

"I don't believe you."

"Well, ask him then. He's known from the beginning, and he never said a word. How can you ever trust someone who would allow you to be so hurt?"

She moved away from him but backed into the table next to the sofa. "You're the one who hurt me, Christopher."

"If you say so. Forget that he kept you occupied a few times when we were dating until I could *finish* with other girls. Oh, he always hated it, but somehow it worked for us. He got to pretend he was dating you and I got to be a man."

"You're disgusting."

"And you're naive. Trevor Whitney is no better than the rest of us, so take him off that little pedestal and stop feeling sorry for his tortured heart. This isn't some Shakespearean play. It's just life, Evelyn. You made your choices and he made his. Tell me, how will you ever recover from them?"

She started for the door. "I feel sorry for you," she said, hand on the doorknob.

"Don't. I don't need your pity. I'm going to be just fine. I always am."

Evelyn faced him. "You've been surrounded by people your whole life, Christopher, and you're the loneliest person I know."

She pried the house key from her key ring and set it on the table in the entry, then walked out the door into the crisp autumn night.

CHAPTER
39

"She's gone." Lilian's words hung in the air.

"What do you mean?"

But he knew. He knew the second he awoke, face throbbing, the memory of his unwise choice to pay Chris a visit the night before lingering, the pain of his unwise choice to push Evelyn away tormenting.

"She's not at the guesthouse anymore. Her car is gone and the closet in the bedroom is empty." Lilian glared at him. "What did you do?"

He turned away. "What makes you think it was me?"

But they both knew better. He stared out the window at the guesthouse, mining the regret from the dark part of his soul. He couldn't walk down this path with Evelyn until she knew the whole truth about what he'd done—or not done—over the years.

Then, if she still wanted to see if there was something between them, at least he'd be moving forward with a clear conscience.

"She found out how you felt, didn't she?"

He hated that Lilian knew how he felt, but at least he'd managed to keep his foolishness regarding the wooden hearts to himself. Until last night, that was. If she discovered that embarrassing tidbit, his aunt certainly would have chastised him for clinging to someone who was married to someone else.

Never mind that he hadn't been "clinging." He knew Evelyn belonged to Chris, and he was completely fine.

But he saw now that was a lie he'd told himself. And unfortunately, he'd only made things worse.

He'd been awake most of the night, replaying that kiss over and over in his mind and attempting to pinpoint what it was that he was so afraid of.

He walked past Lilian and up to the guesthouse. Evelyn's scent still hung in the air, but the bungalow was, as Lilian said, empty. Where had she gone?

He tried calling her cell, but there was no answer.

He walked through his chores that morning with a vague connection to reality, wondering what his problem was in the first place. He'd been pushing her away for so many years, maybe he didn't know how to stop. And maybe she'd forgive him for lying to her.

By noon, he decided he couldn't pull one more weed, feed one more animal, or fix one more broken barn door. He drove to town, where he saw the remnants of the Sweetheart Festival hanging throughout Old Town. Community volunteers worked to clean up the streets, and while Trevor should've stopped and helped, he didn't. Instead, he drove past all of it until he reached Casey's house in a neighborhood about three blocks from the lake.

Casey knew more about the way Trevor felt than he ever let on, but more than that, he had a wife. And the opinion of an unbiased woman might be what Trevor needed right now.

Marin answered the door, her face free of makeup, her hair pulled off her face. "Whit? What are you doing here?"

"Came over to talk to Casey." No need to reveal his true intentions yet. "Is he home?"

Marin opened the door wider, then took a step back so Trevor could come in. The smell of something cooking on the stove filled the air.

She closed the door behind him. "He's watching football." She led Trevor into the living room of the small two-story. "Even though he's supposed to be putting together the crib we just bought."

Casey looked up when they entered the room. "Hey, Whit. Did you come by to watch the game?"

"No, but I'll help you with the crib if you want." He winked at Marin.

"Did she call you over here to make me feel guilty?" Casey's tone teased.

Marin put her up hands. "I think it's divine intervention. His visit is unprovoked."

Trevor held his ratty red ball cap, folding the bill. Casey stood and studied his old friend. "All right, let's go. Broncos are losing anyway."

They went upstairs and into a small room with pale-green walls and wood floors. "Marin painted it two weeks ago. She thought blue was too cliché."

"Looks good," Trevor said.

The crib lay in pieces on top of a soft striped rug. Trevor knelt down and took inventory of the parts. Casey sat in a rocking chair in the corner. "Why are you really here?"

Marin walked in just in time to hear the question. She carried two glasses of lemonade. He resisted the urge to make a remark about her belly. If he remembered correctly, her due date was quickly approaching and he knew better than to draw attention to her size.

"For us?" Casey said.

She raised her eyebrows at him. "One of them was going to be for you, but from the looks of it, you have no intention of working up a sweat. So they're both for Trevor." The smile that punctuated her sentence dripped sarcasm.

Trevor grinned but kept his head down, fitting pieces together. "Actually, Marin," he said, "do you have a minute?"

Casey stood. "I don't know whether to be proud or hurt. In all the years I've known you, you've never needed a woman's opinion for anything."

Trevor moved on to the second leg of the crib. "Well, now I do."

Marin took Casey's seat. "We've got all day, Whit." She smiled. "What's up?"

"Evelyn," Casey said. "Finally divorced, cheating Chris out of the picture. You're wondering if you should make your move."

Trevor groaned. "Not exactly."

Casey's eyes widened. "You made your move?"

Marin smacked his leg. "Will you let him talk?"

"You were at the dance last night." Trevor started on the third leg of the crib.

Marin sighed. "It was really beautiful. Made me feel like a teenager all over again."

"A knocked-up teenager," Casey laughed.

She smacked him again. "Whose fault is that?"

Casey waggled his eyebrows at her. "All mine, baby."

She turned her attention back to Trevor. "I love the hearts you two made."

"Yeah, well, those hearts are the reason I'm in this predicament." On to the fourth crib leg.

"Did you mess something up?" Casey said.

"You could say that."

"Did you find out who bought the hearts with the song lyrics? Spoil some surprise? Crash a romantic fantasy?"

"Now who isn't letting him talk?" Casey quipped.

"You could say that too." Trevor kept his eyes on the task at hand.

Marin gasped. "Who? We were all guessing last night."

Trevor flipped the crib over and stood, then hung his head. He was no good at this talking thing.

"You?" Marin studied him. "You?" She did nothing to hide her surprise. "But you're so . . ."

"What?" Trevor frowned.

"What she's trying to say is that around here, people think you're kind of cold. Standoffish," Casey said. "Like, the least romantic person in town."

"Evelyn said that too."

"So you've been buying hearts to profess your love to Evelyn Brandt for ten years?" Marin's face reminded Trevor of a Disney princess.

Trevor groaned again. "It sounds really pathetic when you say it like that."

"No, it's wonderful and romantic. Did she just melt when you told her?"

"Not quite." Sparing as much detail as possible, Trevor explained the whole mess. The moment she found out about the hearts, the moment he showed up at Chris's house and got into a fist-fight with his former best friend, the moment he realized he hadn't buried his feelings for Evelyn as well as he'd thought, the moment he found himself kissing the woman he loved, then lastly—and most regrettably—the moment he pushed her away.

Marin stood. "Who knew you were such a romantic?"

Casey put a hand on her shoulder. "You're married, remember?"

She laughed. "Why can't you be more like Trevor, Casey?"

Casey shot a look at Trevor. "Well, that's not something I ever thought my wife would say."

Marin shook her head. "I had no idea, and I bet Evelyn didn't either. But you love her, and she's not married anymore. So what's the problem?"

Trevor put the finishing touches on the crib and took a step back. "Crib's done."

"Good grief, you're like a magician," Casey said. "I've got a dresser in a box in the garage."

Marin raised a hand and Casey stopped talking. "Don't change the subject."

Trevor drew in a breath. Here was the ugly part. The truth. "I've been lying to her for years."

"But she'll understand. It sounds like she already does."

"Not only about my feelings." He glanced at Casey, who looked away. "About Chris."

Marin frowned. "What do you mean?"

Trevor glanced up at the ceiling as if it were the most interesting thing in the room. "I knew about the cheating. Even before they got married."

He could feel disappointment settle on Marin's shoulders.

"I know. I'm worse than Chris," Trevor said.

"No one is worse than Chris," Casey said.

"I pretty much helped him cheat on her," Trevor said.

Marin waved her hand in the air. "What do you mean you helped him cheat on her? Like, you found him girls? You gave him a place to go? What are we talking about here?"

"In high school and all through college, Chris always had other girls. He'd call and tell me he was held up and ask me to keep Evelyn company until he could get there."

Casey had known. He'd even encouraged Trevor to tell Evelyn the truth, but when he tried, Trevor chickened out. Didn't want to be one to tell her that kind of news. Didn't want to be the guy who broke her heart.

Some friend. He told himself he just wanted her to be happy, even if he wasn't the one she chose. But it was selfish and he knew it.

After a long pause under Marin's watchful gaze, she finally sighed. "They were just kids, Whit. And so were you. You couldn't have known he was still cheating on her after they got married."

Trevor said nothing.

"You knew?" Marin evidently had no skill at hiding her emotions. Whatever she thought was clearly painted on her face.

"I thought everyone knew. It's not like he was discreet."

"Why didn't you tell her?" Marin's face fell.

"I tried to once, when they'd just gotten engaged." Trevor stilled at the memory. "Went to her house, knocked on the door—almost got the words out—but when I realized Chris was there, I took it as a sign."

"You didn't try again?" Casey's wife almost looked personally hurt by his admission.

He could only imagine how Evelyn would look when he told her. Because he would tell her. He had to.

"I didn't want to be responsible for the fallout." He shook his head, regret racing through his veins. "I went to Chris instead. He promised he would stop all of that. But I knew that wasn't true."

"Don't beat yourself up because Chris was a lousy husband," Casey said. "It's not your fault."

"There's more." Trevor sighed, the memory still fresh. "A few years ago, I saw him out with someone else." Lilian had an egg delivery to make at a hotel restaurant in Dillon, but she got sick and Trevor went instead. After he unloaded the eggs, he walked through the restaurant to find the manager and instead he found Chris, cozied up with a leggy redhead, hidden in a corner.

The worst part was Chris hadn't even pretended to be sorry. He sauntered over to Trevor and tossed a glance at the woman, whose dress was so tight it looked like it might cut off her circulation.

Heat rushed to Trevor's face, and he fought to restrain himself.

Chris had grinned. "Whit. How ya been, man?"

Trevor looked pointedly at the woman.

"Business meeting," Chris said.

"What kind of business is she in, Chris?"

He smirked. "Don't you worry about that."

Trevor glared at him.

"You look so serious, Whit." He laughed. "Have you seen Evelyn lately? We're thinking about having a baby. She's so happy." He squeezed Trevor's shoulder.

Trevor bit back words Christian men didn't say.

The restaurant door popped open and Evelyn walked in, confusion on her face when she saw the two of them standing together, mere feet from the table where the redhead sat, swirling a cocktail in a tall glass.

Evelyn frowned as she approached. "I thought I'd come surprise Christopher at his conference, but what are you doing here, Trevor?"

Chris didn't even stutter. "Just finished up our last seminar and stopped in here for a drink when I ran into Whit."

"What are the odds?" Evelyn glanced at the woman at the table, who watched the three of them. She stood and walked toward the group.

Chris put a hand on Trevor's shoulder. "Yeah. I was just going, actually."

Trevor glanced away, disgusted by how easy it was for Chris to lie to his wife.

"Evelyn, this is Whit's girlfriend, Janine," Chris

said, giving the redhead a push toward Trevor. She got the hint and wrapped an arm around Trevor's waist.

Chris laughed. "Whit, you're so tense." He glanced at Evelyn. "We should leave so Janine can help him with that."

Evelyn looked at Trevor, then at Janine. "I didn't know you were dating anyone."

Trevor met her hopeful eyes. "It's, uh, new."

Coward.

Evelyn smiled. "Well, have fun."

Trevor nodded but turned away, disgusted by how easy it was for *him* to lie to her.

"She's gonna hate me," Trevor said now, pushing the memory to the back of his mind, where he wished it would stay. He looked at Marin and Casey.

Marin moved toward him. "It's not great, Whit, but it's not a deal breaker. You need to tell her the truth and then see if you can move past it."

Casey groaned. "Terrible advice."

Marin spun around. "You knew too, didn't you?"

"Yes, but I'm in love with you—not Evelyn."

She huffed impatiently. "What is it about Christopher Brandt that everyone is so afraid of? He's a small-minded, narcissistic, pig-headed man on a power trip. And he doesn't deserve your loyalty. Or Evelyn's."

Marin was right. For whatever reason, they'd all been overawed by Chris since they were kids.

Somehow that translated to bad behavior on his behalf—and it had to end.

She took Trevor's hands and looked at him with the same concern his mother used to have when she would give sage advice. "Put this down, Whit. It's not yours to carry."

The words dangled in the air, daring him to take them to heart. He wanted it to be true—that he didn't have to drag all of this around with him anymore. Evelyn's marriage had ended. She was mostly free of the man who'd betrayed her.

"I have to tell her," Trevor said, his voice quiet.

"Then you need to eat some of Marin's chili before you go." Casey led him out of the nursery. "As last meals go, it's not a bad choice."

They walked downstairs and into the kitchen. Trevor watched as Marin and Casey maneuvered together like a couple performing a perfectly choreographed slow dance. "I hope you guys know how lucky you are."

Casey glanced at Marin, whose face lit with a soft smile. "We don't really believe in luck."

"Yeah, I know." Trevor didn't believe in luck either. He believed in a God who would help him navigate the consequences of the choices he'd made up to this point.

Marin laughed. "You're lucky too, Whit. You just don't know it yet."

He hoped so. As he ate, he said a silent prayer that he would find the courage to finally tell the truth, and he hoped that somehow it really would set him free.

CHAPTER
40

Evelyn stood in the loft above The Paper Heart, admiring the way the light filtered in through the many windows facing east, perfect for catching the morning sun.

"What do you think?" Abigail Pressman stood at the top of the stairs; below them was the store she'd filled with unique treasures, hand-painted furniture, and one-of-a-kind artwork from Loves Park's most prominent artists.

But the loft? Empty.

"It's an incredible space," Evelyn said. "Peaceful."

"So." Abigail smiled. "Do you want it?"

Evelyn frowned. "What do you mean?"

"I heard through the grapevine you were looking for a studio space." Abigail had been through quite an ordeal with her previous business, but now it was as if losing her prime real estate in Old Town was always part of the plan. She seemed genuinely happy, as though she'd found some-thing Evelyn had only ever dreamed of.

Her purpose.

"I'm not sure who told you that. The only painting I've done lately is the hearts." But that didn't mean Evelyn hadn't thought of it. She'd lost so much of herself, she had a feeling painting might be the only way to figure out who it was she was supposed to become in the first place.

And yes, she was still on the hunt for peace, the kind she'd glimpsed at Whitney Farms.

"Surely you don't want to stock shelves forever," Abigail said. "I was thinking you could work up here, and we could set up art workshops for kids, parents, whoever wants to come." Abigail watched her. "It would give you some time to decide what's next."

Evelyn looked around. The loft, in the old barn that was currently Abigail's store, was certainly large enough for a small group of people to come in and paint. And there would still be plenty of room for Evelyn to work during the week. Her children's book sketches were long gone, but she'd begun reimagining them. It would be wonderful to have a place to bring *Silly Lily* to life.

She looked at Abigail. "You would want me to teach them?"

"Why not?" she replied. "People would love to take art classes from the woman behind those painted hearts."

Had Abigail forgotten what was still being said about her around town?

"I'll think about it."

"Okay, but don't think too long," Abigail said. "Sometimes you have to stop thinking and just *do*."

"Is that what you did?" Evelyn asked. "With the store?"

Abigail started down the stairs, motioning for Evelyn to follow. "Not exactly. I overanalyzed that situation for too many weeks."

Evelyn watched as Abigail steamed milk for two lattes.

"But I learned that sometimes when we're busy looking for open doors, we forget that the closed doors are just as important." She handed a cup to Evelyn.

Evelyn took a sip.

"Sometimes the doors that close lead us to something better."

"I'm not sure that's true when it comes to marriage." She thought about what Christopher had told her about Trevor. She should've gone straight to Whit and demanded the truth, but she didn't. Maybe she hadn't wanted to know the truth. Instead, she'd been camping out in Gigi's guest room for three weeks, under the old woman's watchful eye.

Trevor had called every day, and every day Evelyn ignored the calls, deleted the voice mails, and tried to stop reliving the moment he'd finally kissed her, then pushed her away.

And while she'd decided there was a good chance Christopher was lying about Trevor helping him, there was still his rejection to sort out. His mixed signals. His unkind kindness. It would be easier to hate him if she still thought he was only a boorish, angry man with a grudge against the world, unhappy with the hand he'd been dealt.

But he wasn't any of those things.

She shook the thought away. Regardless of whether he'd helped Christopher betray her, he had kept things from her. Important things she had a right to know. In some ways, that was harder to swallow. She'd been wrestling with her conflicting feelings for three straight weeks, wallowing in self-pity and wishing she could disappear from her life for a while.

The fact that she even stood in The Paper Heart at all was something of a mystery. She certainly hadn't wanted to get up that morning. Perhaps it was Gigi's incessant knocking that had drawn her out of bed.

"All I know is what happened to you was unfair and devastating," Abigail said. "I felt like losing my store was unfair and devastating too." She looked at Evelyn. "I know it's wrong of me to compare the two, but that store was my whole life."

And Christopher had been Evelyn's.

"Losing it gave me the chance to start dreaming

again." She put a hand over Evelyn's. "Maybe it's time for you to do that too."

Evelyn stared at their hands on the counter. She'd been doing that for three weeks. Holed up in Gigi's house, sketching, making lists, getting ideas. Dreaming of a life without a facade, free of expectations and obligations—caught up, instead, in whatever God had for her and hopeful that one day she could accept the gift of his grace.

What she wouldn't give to help Trevor and Lilian with the next community dinner. If plans held, it would be coming up soon—would they try to do it without her?

Could she blame them if they did? She wasn't taking Whit's phone calls, so how would she know?

The door opened with a start, drawing their attention.

"Glory be! It's cold out there," Gigi said, rushing inside, Doris and Ursula close behind. "You girls ready to get to work?"

"Doing what?" Evelyn took another sip while Abigail set about making drinks for each of the ladies and Tess, who had a knack for tardiness.

"You didn't tell her?" Doris stared at Gigi.

"Probably didn't want to hear her complain," Ursula said, plopping down at a large table next to the counter. "Got any food back there, Pressman?"

Abigail shot her a look. "I've only got two hands, Pembrooke."

Ursula frowned, eyes narrowing underneath bushy brows. Since the two had teamed up in business, they'd formed this odd, mutually sarcastic relationship. The others knew better than to get in the middle of it.

"Do you want to tell me what's going on?" Evelyn asked. "Is this about the hearts? I only did the prototypes. They're finished now."

Gigi and Doris exchanged a worried glance.

"We have a job offer for you," Gigi said.

"Why?" Evelyn asked.

"Because you're broke." Ursula set her elbows on the table. "Money is a great motivator."

"And I know you don't want to sleep in my sewing room forever," Gigi said.

Well, that was true. Evelyn moved over to the table, where the others had begun to sit. "I'm listening." As much as she hated to admit it, Ursula was right. She was broke. And while Abigail's offer was a kind one, and something she would certainly consider, it wouldn't provide enough to live on.

Gigi smiled with her whole face like a child with a secret she couldn't wait to tell. "The city is looking for an artist in residence," she said, rummaging through her purse. She pulled out an envelope and slid it across the table toward Evelyn. "They want you. Apparently we aren't the only ones who believe in your talent."

"I don't understand," Evelyn said. She peered

at the walls of The Paper Heart. A variety of artists were represented, all different mediums. How would Evelyn ever compete with these people? It had been years since she'd painted seriously— and she had a lot of catching up to do.

"Don't do that," Ursula said, mouth full of the blueberry muffin Abigail had set in front of her moments before.

"Do what?" Evelyn asked.

"Analyze it." Ursula squinted at her. "Pressman does the same thing. Sometimes you have to stop thinking and just do."

Evelyn glanced at Abigail, who shrugged. "Told ya," she said.

"I'll consider it," Evelyn said.

"Right, because you have so many other appealing offers." Ursula popped another bite in her mouth.

Doris and Gigi both chastised her for her honesty, but Evelyn found it refreshing. At least she knew Ursula would tell her the truth, which was more than she could say for Christopher. Or Whit, for that matter.

The thought stung. She missed the peacefulness of the farm. She missed walking the perimeter, keeping her distance from the cows. She missed *him*. But none of that mattered now. He'd rejected her, kept things from her, and that was what she needed to remember—otherwise, she'd find herself hurt all over again.

Maybe Trevor Whitney was the closed door Abigail was talking about.

"What is there to think about anyway, Evelyn?" Gigi asked. "I've been authorized to make you this offer."

"Won't other artists be interested?" Evelyn asked.

"The committee asked for you," Gigi said. "They were so impressed by what you did with the hearts and doubly impressed by the community dinner you organized and decorated for Mr. Whitney."

There had to be a catch. Evelyn knew firsthand how unpopular she was with committees in this town. She frowned. "Why all of a sudden does Loves Park need an artist in residence?"

"Overthinker." Ursula spat it like a swearword.

Gigi shrugged. "I'm not sure. The mayor called and said after your work with the hearts, they started thinking of many other ways someone with your talent could be of service to the community. They're willing to give you a chance."

Doris nodded in agreement. "They haven't done much updating around here lately. Someone with your creativity and artistic eye is just what Loves Park needs."

Evelyn couldn't deny the offer intrigued her, but she still had questions. Like why was the city suddenly willing to create a position and offer it to her? It was only a few months ago they were accusing her of being a part of defrauding Loves Park with her criminal of a husband.

"Stop thinking so much, Evelyn," Tess said, finally joining them after rushing in late. "This is a good thing. Could be an answer to prayer."

Evelyn couldn't disagree, though frantic half thoughts called up in moments of despair hardly counted as prayers . . . right?

But that wasn't accurate, was it? Prayer had become a regular part of her morning routine. Could Tess be right? A tangible answer to prayer?

"While you ponder this incredible opportunity to work for the city of Loves Park *doing what you love* . . ." Gigi's words were pointed. Evelyn took the hint, but Gigi continued. "We need to talk about the opening of the painted hearts exhibit tonight."

Evelyn groaned. The city council had been so impressed by the prototype hearts, they'd decided to add them to the museum as a display of the importance of the romantic tradition in their town. Apparently tourists loved that sort of thing.

"Would you rather discuss why you've been sleeping in my spare room instead of Trevor Whitney's guesthouse?" Gigi asked matter-of-factly. "Or perhaps why you won't take his phone calls?"

"Ooh, yes," Doris said, leaning in toward Evelyn. "Let's talk about that."

Evelyn set her coffee down. "Let's not."

"I've been asking her for days," Gigi said. "The first night she showed up with a suitcase, she looked far too disheveled for questions, really. Hair was a mess. She'd clearly been crying."

"I'm still sitting here," Evelyn said, though she had a feeling this was a repeat of a conversation these women had already had.

"Odds are she and Mr. Whitney had some sort of fight," Doris said. "But he's so kind and so good, I can't imagine why you would want to pick a fight with him."

Evelyn shot Doris a look, but before she could respond, Ursula pushed herself away from the table. "She probably overanalyzed him too."

"Maybe she's upset that we did such a terrible job of matching Trevor. We obviously didn't do our homework on that Maggie," Tess said.

"Oh, we haven't given up on Mr. Whitney," Doris said. "Now that we've discovered him, we won't rest until we find him a suitable companion. Tess, have you done any digging into those other names I gave you?"

"What other names?" Tension squared Evelyn's shoulders.

"Possibilities to match with Trevor," Tess said. "I should have details by our next meeting."

Gigi held up a hand. "Ladies, please."

"Yeah, Gigi wants to complain about her new housemate," Ursula said.

"I am not complaining," Gigi said. "I'm known

for my hospitality. I only wish our Evelyn trusted us enough to share the truth with us." She turned to Evelyn, finally acknowledging she was still sitting beside her. "Ever since the night of the Sweetheart Festival dance, something has certainly been bothering you. We only want to help."

Evelyn saw the concern in Gigi's eyes. She circled the table slowly, noting worry on all of their faces. She originally assumed this group of women was like every other group she'd joined at Christopher's request, but she'd been wrong. After all she'd been through, she counted these ladies among her very small circle of friends, and they deserved the truth. But Evelyn couldn't talk about any of it. She was far too humiliated to admit she'd trusted not one but two of the wrong men.

"So what do we need to do before the painted hearts exhibit opens?" she asked.

Later that night, Evelyn stood in the lobby of the Loves Park Museum working up the courage to go inside. Thankfully Evelyn wouldn't need to get on a stage, and according to Gigi, Trevor wouldn't be in attendance.

Still, Evelyn would be asked about the artist-in-residence position. She would be expected to mingle. She needed to be kind, polite, and charming. It smacked of the life she'd left behind.

The outer door opened, cool air rushing in. She turned and saw Abigail with her fiancé, Dr. Jacob

Willoughby. Her friend looked so happy, it was hard to believe that her own closed door had once seemed like the end of the world.

Would Evelyn ever feel that way about her old life? Would she ever look back, thankful for the pain she'd endured the day the FBI showed up at her door?

More importantly, would she ever find herself in the rubble left behind?

She'd tried to stop overanalyzing it all, as Ursula said, and simply pay attention to when she was comfortable and when she wasn't, but she had trouble trusting herself, even when her guard was up.

"Evelyn?" Abigail moved toward her, Jacob close behind. "What are you doing out here? You're the woman of the hour."

Evelyn forced a smile. "Just working up the courage."

"I'll hang our coats," Jacob said. "Then we'll all go in together."

Evelyn nodded. It would be preferable not to go it alone. She drew in a breath.

"You're not going to have a panic attack, are you?"

For the first time, Evelyn realized it had been weeks since she'd taken her medication—and the same length of time since she'd suffered an attack. In spite of her circumstances, she'd remained at peace.

Somehow she didn't think it was a coincidence

that her anxiety lessened when she started praying again.

"I've been thinking about what you told me," Evelyn said.

Abigail raised an eyebrow. "What did I tell you?"

"Not to overthink everything."

"You've been thinking about not overthinking?" Abigail grinned. "That's a good strategy."

Evelyn laughed.

"Ursula hangs around The Paper Heart a lot," Abigail continued. "Sometimes she just randomly shouts advice like that at me while I'm trying to work. She's brash, but she knows her stuff."

Evelyn nodded.

"You don't have to tell me," Abigail said. "But why *did* you move out of the Whitneys' guest-house? My understanding was that Trevor let you live there for free. What's really going on?"

But before she could answer, the door opened again, this time revealing an all-too-familiar silhouette. Trevor stopped, eyes glued to Evelyn. It had been weeks since they'd seen each other. Weeks since he'd rejected her, weeks since Christopher had told her he'd been a willing participant in her husband's betrayal.

Now, standing there, stunned, she didn't know how to feel. She'd told herself the time apart would clear her mind, but she was still waiting to find that elusive clarity.

When Jacob returned from the coatroom, he moved toward Whit, stretched out his hand, and said something about how good it was to see him.

"Are you okay?" Abigail whispered. "You look pale."

Evelyn turned away. "I'm fine."

Jacob and Whit approached, stealing Abigail's attention and leaving Evelyn feeling exposed. "We can all go in together," Jacob said. "It's probably going to be a bunch of blue-hairs in there anyway."

"I resent that, Dr. Willoughby," Gigi said, appearing as if from thin air. "It's us blue-hairs that keep you in business." She opened the door to the gallery. "Hurry up, you slowpokes." And just like that, she was gone.

Abigail giggled, linking arms with her good doctor. "She told you."

Jacob and Abigail moved together, in unison, in a way Evelyn and Christopher never had. They were equally in love. One of them wasn't working harder than the other.

Was it wrong of her to wish for that? Regret twisted through her, wrapping itself around her heart. With Jacob and Abigail in front of them, Trevor and Evelyn also fell into step.

As they moved into the dimly lit gallery, his hand brushed against hers and the memory of his kiss haunted her mind.

"I've been calling you," he said, walking through the crowd, face forward.

Mayor Jensen Thompkins approached them. "It's so good to have you both here. You've breathed new life into our little tradition. And, Evelyn, we are so thrilled to have you as our artist in residence. We have big plans for you."

Evelyn avoided Trevor's eyes. "Actually, Mayor Thompkins, I haven't officially accepted that position."

He regarded her for a long moment. "Well, I'm afraid if it isn't you, we won't have the money to work with, and we've already begun brainstorming the areas where we could use your artistic skill. Someone suggested painting the ugly electrical boxes around town. The metal ones on the street corners. And someone else was hoping for painted pianos all throughout Old Town."

Trevor towered over both of them, and while he pretended not to listen, Evelyn had the distinct feeling he was paying attention.

"There are so many artists in town. I'm sure any one of them would jump at this chance," Evelyn said.

"I'm sure. Which is why it's positively baffling that you're still thinking about it." The mayor squinted at her. "The anonymous benefactor who is supplying the funds to make this position possible was very clear. He or she wanted it to be you. Or nobody. Please don't let it be nobody, Mrs. Brandt."

She shook his hand, and he walked away, but he'd done nothing to shed light on any of this.

"What was that all about?" Trevor asked.

She met his eyes, but then Christopher's words rushed back at her. *"He's known from the beginning, and he never said a word."*

She didn't know what to believe anymore. The only thing she knew for sure was that she was better off alone.

On the other side of the room, she spotted Ursula, wearing a long skirt with a long tunic top and a pair of running shoes. "Will you excuse me?"

Trevor put a hand on her shoulder, stopping her. "Before you go, there's something I need to talk to you about."

She forced herself to be brave. "We really don't have anything to discuss, Whit."

"It's important."

"What do you want to tell me? That you knew the truth about Christopher all along and never bothered to say a single word to me about it?"

For a split second, he looked like someone had smacked him across the face.

So it was true. The realization stung. Christopher had been lying for as long as she'd known him, but this time she would've preferred he not tell her the truth.

She forced herself to pretend not to care, though inside, her heart was breaking. "I know all about it already, so if you came to apologize, you're too late."

"You've got to let me explain," he said.

An ache formed deep in the back of her throat. "I can't believe I actually thought you might be different." Evelyn raised her chin as if that would make her appear stronger. "You really had me fooled, but the truth is, you're just like Christopher. You're all the same."

Evelyn felt a hand on her shoulder. "There are a few people who would like to speak with the artist," Gigi said. "I'm sorry to interrupt, Mr. Whitney."

Trevor shook his head. "It's fine, Mrs. Monroe. I shouldn't have come." He walked away, leaving Evelyn standing there, on the verge of a full-on panic attack, and yet, with Gigi's hand to steady her, her pulse began to slow.

"What's going on, Evie?" Gigi asked, her voice quiet.

Evelyn faced her. "First, you."

The old woman frowned. "Me what?"

"Tell me the truth. Was it you and Ursula who concocted this artist-in-residence plan? The mayor told me whoever is funding it requires that I be the artist. That hardly seems right."

"Why ever not?" Gigi asked. "Look around. Your art is exciting. It gets people talking."

For a moment, Evelyn allowed herself to scan the crowd. Gigi was right. People *were* excited. So excited they were already ordering their own painted hearts. The plan had worked—a tradition that had nearly been forgotten was reborn, and Evelyn had a lot to do with that.

Evelyn and Whit.

She turned back to Gigi. "You didn't answer my question. I know Ursula is richer than the queen of Sheba."

"That might be true, dear, but I can assure you, this was not our doing. We do think it's perfect timing, and frankly, we're happy to put you to work, but we are not the ones footing the bill."

Evelyn frowned. "Then who would do this for me?"

"The senator?"

Evelyn shook her head. "No. He's living on a fixed income that amounts to almost nothing, at least by his standards. Besides, he's got himself believing I'm the bad guy. He would never do something like this."

"Well, I don't know then," Gigi said. "Ask the mayor if you want. Or just be thankful someone had the good sense to believe in your dreams. Goodness knows you certainly don't."

Evelyn's only response was silence.

"Now, what in the world is going on with you and Mr. Whitney?"

Evelyn sighed. As if she had any idea how to answer that question. But she could tell by the look on Gigi's face that anything but the truth wasn't going to satisfy the old woman.

CHAPTER
41

Trevor walked a circle in the parking lot outside the Loves Park Museum. He hadn't even walked through the exhibit, his shame and regret too heavy to carry under Evelyn's watchfulness.

Actually, that wasn't right. Evelyn appeared to be watching everyone except him. In fact, she didn't seem at all interested in anything he had to say.

She already knew. He should've told her days ago. Years ago. What an idiot!

Trevor started back toward the door but lost his nerve halfway there. He turned around, avoiding the stares of a young couple walking toward the building. He probably looked like a lunatic with all his back-and-forthing. He should leave. He should go home to the farm, where it was quiet and Evelyn was nowhere to be seen.

But then, the farm was quiet. And Evelyn was nowhere to be seen.

Was he going to roll over just like that? Let her believe whatever lies Chris had fed her?

Oh no. What exactly had Chris told her? Could it be even worse than the truth? And how could he just let her go on believing it?

He had to tell her the truth. The real truth.

"Whit?" Casey hurried toward him, Marin right behind. "What are you doing out here, man?"

Trevor shoved his hands in his pockets.

"Did you tell her?" Marin's voice was hopeful. She'd been married so long she'd forgotten how miserable falling in love could be.

"Didn't get a chance," Trevor said. "Chris got to her first."

Casey clapped a hand on his shoulder. "Sorry, man."

"Yeah. She never wants to see me again." Trevor turned toward his truck. "I'm just going to go home."

"Don't be a coward," Marin said. She moved around him, planted her feet, and stared him down, barely reaching his shoulders. "What have you got to lose?"

Trevor stared out into the darkness of Old Town.

Marin waited until he finally glanced at her. "If she never wants to see you again, then you have nothing to lose." She took a step toward him, eyes angled upward, forcing his gaze. "Stop hiding your feelings, Whit, and go after what you want."

He glanced at Casey, who offered nothing but a half shrug.

Marin started for the museum door, then stopped, turned back, and stared at Trevor. "Well?"

He kicked a rock beneath his feet and began moving in her direction.

Marin was right. He didn't have to stand back and watch his life happen in front of him. He could actually become a part of it every now and then.

Besides, she was only saying what he already knew. He had no reason not to tell Evelyn the truth. And he wouldn't find a bit of peace until he did.

He drew in a deep breath and followed Casey and Marin to the door. As he walked through, Trevor suddenly felt the stranglehold of his collared shirt, too tight for his neck.

"You look like you're going to puke," Casey said, taking Marin's coat.

"That's about right," Trevor said.

Marin put a hand on his arm. "You really love her, don't you?"

Trevor ignored the question. The last thing he needed was Casey's wife romanticizing his feelings for Evelyn. They weren't romantic. They were pathetic. And the only reason he was standing there at all was because he didn't want her taking Chris's word on everything he'd done, even if it was accurate. If anyone was going to explain the truth, it was going to be him.

Why, then, did he feel like he might lose his dinner?

Trevor opened the door to the gallery and walked inside. The crowd had grown in the twenty minutes he'd been outside, and as he searched for Evelyn, the occasional pat on the back or "Good job" required his attention.

In a corner, away from the crowd, Evelyn sat at the center of a small group of women. The older ladies who seemed intent on ruining his life caught his attention as he approached, and the closer he got, the clearer it became that they weren't happy with him.

What have I got to lose? he reminded himself. He didn't care what these women thought anyway. It had always only been Evelyn's opinion that mattered to him.

He reached the table and stood for a long moment. "Evie?"

Five pairs of eyes darted from her to him and back again. His stayed fixed on Evelyn, who barely moved.

"Can we talk?"

"Oh, Trevor," Doris said, standing. "I'm so disappointed in you."

He drew in a deep breath. "Evie, I only need five minutes."

Finally Evelyn turned. "Fine. You have three."

"Can we go somewhere else?" He looked around the circle of women staring at him. "Please?"

She stood, then without a word, moved past him through the crowd and out into the lobby. As if pulled by a magnetic force, he followed, working out in his mind what he might actually say to her once they were alone.

Not a single word came to mind.

She led him through the lobby to an empty room off to one side—an exhibit that had been closed for the evening—and for a brief moment, he thought the crowd would've been less intimidating.

When she finally stopped moving and faced him, she nearly knocked the wind out of him. In this light, in that red dress, hair pinned off to one side, her beauty was enough to make him buckle.

But the icy look on her face pulled his head out of the clouds. She was angry. And rightfully so. He'd pushed her away. He'd failed to be up-front when that was what she needed the most. He'd loved her the wrong way.

How did he fix that?

"Maybe this was a bad idea," he said, raking a hand through his hair. *But what have I got to lose?*

"Great. Can I get back to my friends now?" Evelyn didn't move, just stood in front of him, looking painfully beautiful and somewhat displaced. "I don't really have anything to say to you anyway."

He saw the pain in her face. His rejection had hurt her. Maybe this wasn't the right time to add insult to injury. What if what he had to say hurt her even more?

"Would you let me explain?"

She put her hands on her hips. "I can't read all of your mixed signals. The night we met, I thought you might turn out to be someone really special in my life. And you were my best friend for so long."

The words scratched at him, years of regret stinging his skin like a swarm of hornets.

"But after I got married, I saw only glimpses of that boy. It was like you traded in this kind personality for one that got colder and more distant with every year."

"I didn't behave well, I know."

She laughed. "Then you came to my rescue when this whole mess with Christopher blew up in my face, and in a moment of weakness, I threw myself at you. You rejected me flat."

"I was there, Evie. I don't think we need to relive this."

"But we do. Because a few weeks later I find out you've been purchasing wooden hearts anonymously in my honor. For years."

He forced himself not to look away.

"Years." Her voice trembled, but she found her resolve. "And I thought maybe I could overlook that. Maybe it was even romantic."

"Please, let me say this before I lose my nerve—"

"I don't want to hear what you have to say, Whit. I don't need you to let me down easy or whatever you've got planned. I'm fine. I just need to move on with my life."

He stopped her as she passed by, intent on walking away from him for good. With his hand on her arm, he stood still, facing the opposite direction from Evelyn, her nearness threatening his courage.

She tensed at his touch. "Just let me go."

He closed his eyes. "I've loved you since that first night I met you."

Evelyn relaxed slightly, but he didn't—or couldn't—look at her.

"There *was* something special between us, but I was a farmer's kid and Chris was the rich son of a real estate mogul. I could offer you a pickup truck and he could offer you the moon. I couldn't give you the life you deserved, and I knew it."

She didn't move or speak. She just stayed at his side.

He studied the floor. "Chris knew how I felt, but when he got you in his sights, I realized I didn't have a chance."

"Why did you think that? Do you think I'm so shallow I only care about power and cars?" She turned to him.

He didn't move. "Chris was Chris, and I was me."

"You should have given me a chance to decide, Trevor."

Really? "I almost told you how I felt once. That night in the music room when I played 'The Very Thought of You' for you. The night Chris walked in." Had she felt the tension between them that night, or had he only imagined she did?

"But you acted like you hated me for so long," she said quietly.

"It was easier that way. Being your friend was the most wonderful, horrible thing I ever did."

She stepped in front of him. "So the hearts—that was, what?"

"My one indulgence. Just for me. Made me feel better somehow. Reminded me there was someone out there worth loving. Even if I couldn't have her."

"I never knew, Trevor," she whispered.

"I'm not finished," he said. He raised his head until their eyes met.

"This is the part that's going to hurt, isn't it?" she asked.

He nodded, drew in a breath. "I want you to know that anything I ever did or didn't do, I did for you. Because I never wanted to risk seeing you hurt. But also . . . because I was afraid."

"Just say it," she said.

"You were right. I did know about the women. I did cover for Chris—many times."

"Like the night I surprised him at that restaurant in Dillon? That woman. She was . . . ?"

"Not my girlfriend."

She stood unmoving, blinked twice, and then slapped him—hard—across the face.

He grabbed her hand. "Listen to me. If I had told you then, you would've hated me. Chris would've talked his way out of it—told you how

I felt about you and made me seem like a liar."

"You can't possibly know that."

"You know it too."

She looked away.

"Or you would've believed me, and then I would always be the guy who gave you the news that broke your heart."

"Your decision wasn't about me, Whit," she said, tearing up. "It was about you. You were afraid my reaction would hurt you, so you didn't tell me the truth."

Silence was his only response.

"Well, congratulations, Trevor. You made me love you before showing me who you really are." She wiped her cheeks dry. "And for that, I don't think I can ever forgive you."

He reached for her, but she was just out of grasp, and within seconds, she'd vanished from the room—and probably from his life—forever.

CHAPTER
42

It had been a month since the night Evelyn walked out of the museum, certain her anger toward Trevor Whitney would never, ever subside.

At least she'd been right about that.

She paced around the loft in The Paper Heart, admiring the work of her students. It was her second workshop that week, and both had been full. This artist-in-residence thing had its perks. After she rejected the benefactor's money and made it clear to the mayor she worked only on her own terms, she'd agreed to take the position.

"There's not money in the budget without the benefactor," he'd told her.

"I will raise the money myself," Evelyn said. "With each event or fund-raiser, I'll propose a modest wage from those I'm serving, but I won't be anyone's charity case."

He almost looked impressed with her, and she had to admit, it felt good to be the one calling the shots for once. Never mind that there were days she did wish she had the security of a steady paycheck. Still, she was making her own way, doing something she loved that also helped to pay back the city her husband had stolen from. And it seemed her community was finally beginning to forgive her.

What more could she ask for, really?

"Miss Evie?" A girl named Sadie raised her hand. "Can you show me how to draw her hair?"

Evelyn smiled, then knelt beside Sadie, sketching examples that would be perfect for her version of *Peaceful Girl in Boat*, the painting Evelyn had walked them through, step-by-step.

"Evelyn?" Abigail stood at the top of the stairs. "We're ready for you when you're finished."

"Five more minutes."

After the last student walked out, Evelyn stacked her sketches together and piled them in her sketchbook, but not before catching a glimpse of a nearly perfect illustration of Silly Lily putting lipstick on her dog, Beefcake. She smiled. Sometimes when she worked in that sketchbook, she thought of the day Trevor had given it to her. He'd practically tossed it at her, he was so uncomfortable showing his kind side. More than once, she almost threw it away, but it now represented the closed door that led her here, to a place where she'd begun to find happiness. It was as if God had set her up perfectly, knowing she'd find her purpose eventually. He'd been so patient with her while she figured it out. She still had a lot to learn, but one thing was certain: God could take even her deepest pain and turn it into something beautiful.

When she joined Abigail downstairs, she was taken aback to find not only the other Valentine Volunteers but Georgina Saunders, Susan Hayes, and Lydia Danvers. They hadn't been to any of these artist-in-residence meetings—what were they doing here?

After a brief hitch in her step, Evelyn forced herself to keep walking until she reached the large table.

Mayor Thompkins shook her hand. "So good to see you again, Evelyn. I trust you've been busy."

She held up her sketchbook. "I have what you

asked for." Sketches for the mural in the children's wing of the hospital. She'd worked hard on them, and she'd even come up with ideas that excited her. How long had it been since she'd been excited about anything?

"Wonderful." He turned to the group. "Shall we begin?"

Evelyn moved to the other side of the table and sat.

"My, you certainly have embraced your free spirit, Evelyn," Georgina said. "Too much time out on Whitney Farms, I would say."

The other ladies laughed. Evelyn glanced at Abigail, who scowled at the pompous old woman.

Evelyn smoothed the peasant blouse over her jeans, hugging her loose sweater around her midsection. Had it been only moments ago she'd felt more herself than she had her entire adult life? Why did the presence of these three women threaten to take that feeling away from her?

"How have you been since they seized your home?" Georgina's question, shrouded in the cover of worry, niggled at Evelyn. Christopher's crimes had finally caught up to them these past few weeks.

She lifted her chin. "I've never been better." Oddly, it wasn't a lie.

Georgina raised a brow. "Seems a rather callous response now that your ex-husband is surely on his way to prison."

"Well, we all know what the Good Book says," Gigi said, obviously trying to steer the conversation. Gigi was wonderful, but she was no match for Georgina—and Evelyn knew it.

"Love your enemy?" Georgina wore a trying smile.

"You reap what you sow." Gigi folded her hands. "So shall we discuss what we're actually here to discuss?"

Mayor Thompkins cleared his throat. "Ah, yes, the mural." He turned to Evelyn. "What a wonderful new project for our artist in residence."

Evelyn smiled. "I'm excited about the project, but I am quite busy with the painted hearts. With all the publicity and the new design, we've nearly doubled the number of hearts to be painted this year, and Valentine's Day is only a couple months away."

Georgina scoffed. "And you're painting them all yourself?"

"No, of course not," Evelyn said. "Not all of them. But I am overseeing the other artists."

Georgina waved a perfectly manicured hand in the air as if brushing away a cobweb. "I don't understand why we can't find a different artist for this mural project, Mayor Thompkins."

He frowned. "Evelyn does a beautiful job, Georgina. This is the very reason we have an artist in residence."

She squinted across the table at Evelyn. "Yes,

tell us about that. How did that position come to be? I didn't see any applications."

Evelyn stilled. Even she had no idea how it happened. She continued to suspect Ursula or one of the other Volunteers, but she'd had no luck in proving it, and Gigi didn't lie well. Something told her that if one of them was behind it, she'd have found out by now.

"That's really not why we're here," the mayor said. "Didn't you have ideas for the mural?"

"Of course I have ideas," Georgina said. "But I'm not sure a criminal's wife who may or may not have stolen money from our city is the person to carry out those ideas. Besides—" she narrowed her gaze on Evelyn—"do we even know if she's really that great of an artist?"

The words stung, pulling Evelyn back to all the times she'd been humiliated, rejected, and put in her place by these ladies. Even when she was one of them, she was always striving to be more. It had only been in recent months she'd even realized how much time she'd wasted working so hard to be liked by people who didn't like anyone but themselves.

Why did their opinions matter to her at all?

Her heart began to speed up—only slightly, but a warning signal that maybe she should get out of there. She wouldn't recover from the embarrassment of a panic attack. Not in front of this group.

Georgina stared at her as if waiting for a

response to a question Evelyn didn't know she had asked.

Evelyn stared back for a long moment, and the words came to her like a whisper. *Be anxious for nothing.* Her soul clung to the idea that she, of all people, could ever not be anxious. It was a verse she'd found only a few weeks before, when she was putting the finishing touches on her painting of the girl in the boat. A girl she'd sketched at least twenty times, a girl who'd stopped searching for peace and purpose because she'd found them.

Evelyn glanced down at her hands, the image of them pulling weeds in the Whitneys' garden rushing at her, reminding her of those small compromises she'd made through the years and how they'd turned her into someone she didn't like or ever want to become again.

But wasn't she becoming the girl in the boat? Couldn't she experience a peace and a newfound sense of purpose in using her gifts to better the city, to encourage children, to do what she loved?

Rest in me.

God loved her for who she was—not because she was smart or beautiful or talented. Just because she was *his*.

She owed it to the Lord, and to herself, to focus only on his opinion and not to allow Georgina or Christopher or anyone else to steal her focus again.

"Evelyn, are you okay?" Gigi reached over and put a hand on her shoulder.

"I'm fine, Gigi. Thank you." She smiled.

The mayor—the only man in the room—quickly surveyed the others at the table as if unsure whether he should proceed. He'd clearly lost control of his own meeting. "About that mural . . ."

"It's for the children's wing of the hospital," Georgina reminded them.

"That's perfect given Evelyn's whimsical style," Gigi said.

"There are a lot of hospital donors who are going to want to approve of these plans, Mayor Thompkins." Georgina's face was firm.

As if her body had been taken over by an outside force, Evelyn stood. "I would love to do the mural for the children's wing of the hospital. I already have several ideas of what we could do and how we could involve not only trained artists, as Georgina suggests, but children. Children whose hearts are pure and loving and kind. Children who never seem to hold a grudge or judge one another. At least not until they see adults doing those things."

Georgina's eyes widened.

"But I will only agree to do this project on one condition." She squared her jaw, aiming her gaze at Georgina's. "I have the final say." Even Evelyn couldn't believe she'd spoken the words aloud. "I'm a talented artist, Georgina, whether you want to believe it or not. I studied for years, and while I wish I hadn't taken such a long break from painting, I have every confidence I can create a mural the hospital, the doctors, the donors, and the patients will all love. I'm happy to do this as part of my artist-in-residence duties; however, I will not be micromanaged."

She slid her folder of sketches toward the mayor. "Feel free to look over my ideas and let me know what you think. Now if you'll excuse me, I have some hearts to paint."

CHAPTER
43

Trevor had just returned from welcoming Casey and Marin's baby, a surprise for everyone since it wasn't a boy after all. He didn't hold the little girl but congratulated his friends, then left the hospital with an aching sense that there were some very important things missing in his life.

He'd finished sweeping out Dusty's stall when he heard a car kicking up gravel outside. He moved toward the door of the stables and spotted Gigi Monroe's enormous Buick ambling up the hill. If only he hadn't parked his truck outside the stables, he might've had the perfect hiding place.

He considered making a run out the back, but he knew Gigi well enough to be sure she wasn't leaving until she got what she came for. And as she stepped out of her car, he had a feeling whatever she came for involved him.

When Doris and Ursula appeared on the other side of the car, he nearly ran for the hills after all. Gigi he could handle, but the three of them together? He'd rather wear a suit and tie and parade himself down Main Street.

He stood at the entrance to the stables, watching as the women approached him. Gigi gave Trevor a knowing nod. Why did he feel like he was about to be reprimanded for something he didn't even realize he'd done?

When she reached him, she shoved a plastic container his way. "I made you some cookies. Snickerdoodles. Those are my favorite."

He took the cookies. "Thanks."

Ursula nudged him. "You gonna share?"

He handed her the container.

"Those aren't for you," Gigi said. "If I wanted you to have those, I would've given them to you in the car."

Ursula responded with a crunch.

"Did you just come here to bring me cookies?"

Gigi shook her head. "No." Then her face took on a worried expression. "Have you spoken with Evelyn?"

He leaned against the doorframe. "Not since the night of the museum opening."

The three women exchanged a knowing look.

Knowing to them, anyway. He had no clue what it meant.

"Gigi, do you have something you need to say?" Trevor asked. "Because you look like a balloon with too much air in it."

Doris raised her hand before she spoke. "She heard what you said."

He frowned. "What I said when?"

Gigi let out a long sigh. "That night at the museum. I was right outside when you and Evelyn were talking in that room."

"She didn't bother to clear her throat or anything because she secretly wanted to eavesdrop," Ursula said.

"That is not true." Gigi looked down. "I admit I should've made my presence known, but I didn't want to interrupt."

"I wish you would've." Trevor's hands found his pockets.

She peered at him with that same pitying look he'd seen a hundred times. It must be easy to feel sorry for the guy who had no wife, the one who'd spent most of his years trying awfully hard not to love a woman he had no right loving.

"I just had no idea, Trevor," Doris said.

He didn't respond. He'd tricked himself for years into believing he'd pretty much gotten over Evelyn—he was the biggest fool of all.

"I suspected," Gigi said. "After that night you rescued her from the Royal."

Doris gasped. "Why didn't you say anything?"

Gigi gave Trevor a sad look. "For once it didn't feel right to interfere. At least not after my attempt at matchmaking Trevor and Maggie failed so miserably."

Trevor groaned. "Let's not do this, ladies."

"I'm worried about you," Gigi said.

"That why you made me cookies?"

She shrugged. "I bake when I'm worried."

"I'm fine."

"I don't think so. You've missed the last two Sundays at church. The music isn't the same without you."

Doris shook her head. "It's really not. Last week we had a tone-deaf worship leader who knew only four chords. Also, I think he might've been older than me."

"Snap out of it," Ursula said. "You look like you're in mourning out here."

Trevor shifted. "You can't mourn the loss of something that was never yours."

"Have you tried talking to her since then?" Doris's eyes were hopeful—too hopeful. He hated to be such a disappointment to so many people.

He turned back toward the stall, found the broom, and went over the floor he'd finished sweeping moments before the Volunteers arrived. "She won't return my calls."

"She's painting at The Paper Heart and leading

art workshops. Somehow Abigail got the idea that she needed studio space," Gigi said.

Trevor kept his head down. He could feel them watching him.

"And the city made her the official artist in residence." Doris moved in next to Gigi.

"Evelyn swears Ursula is behind the whole thing," Gigi said.

Ursula cackled. "She thinks I'm much sweeter than I am."

He shrugged. "Wouldn't be the first time you surprised everyone." Ursula had helped Abigail open her new store, after all.

The women responded by stepping still closer to him. When he finally looked up, he instantly regretted it. What were they, some kind of mind readers?

He groaned. "Don't say anything."

Gigi and Doris let out what could only be described as a squeal.

Ursula only nodded. "Good on ya, kid," she said.

"I mean it," he said. "I don't want her to know it was me."

"We won't breathe a word," Gigi said. "But why keep it a secret?"

"She rejected the offer. She obviously didn't want my help," he said.

"Do you know what you've done for her?" Gigi asked.

He didn't. How could he? He hadn't seen her in

over a month. The guesthouse haunted him, the farm mocked him—the whole world felt empty since she'd gone.

Gigi smiled. "The other day, she actually stood up for herself. It's like she just needed a reminder of who she was." She reached out and took his hand. "You did that for her simply by giving her that push."

"Don't mistake her wanting to do things for herself as a rejection," Ursula added. "She's finally figuring out who she is."

"Good," Trevor said. "I spent a lot of years thinking she'd changed. And not for the better. Turns out she was just a little lost."

"I think we're all a little lost in our own way." Gigi squeezed his hand. "But I've known Evelyn a long time, and she seems very different to me now."

"Don't you see?" Doris said, her eyes shining. "You've given her another chance at being happy, at finding her place."

"You should do the same for yourself," Ursula added.

He walked away. "You ladies give me too much credit. All I did was put the bug in the mayor's ear. Told him all the ways Evelyn could help him accomplish his goals for the city."

"It got the ball rolling, Mr. Whitney, and now she's more content than we've ever seen her," Gigi said, following him.

Evelyn's decision to reject the money he'd offered stung somehow, as if she'd knowingly rejected him. But these crazy old women were right—Evelyn needed to stand on her own two feet.

"I don't take any credit for her happiness," Trevor said, knowing that all he'd caused Evelyn over the years was grief. If she'd found strength through this whole situation, she'd come by it on her own.

"Why must you punish yourself?" Gigi asked. "What's so bad about you?"

"You were there. You heard."

"Yes. But I don't think that's it." He felt her watching him but kept his head down.

Gigi sighed. "I thought *Evelyn* was stubborn. The two of you are quite the pair."

"No wonder you never ended up together— you're both too nice." Ursula sounded disgusted.

He went back to sweeping. "I let her marry him."

"It's not your fault that they got married. Or that he cheated. You can't take on their burden as your own." Doris and Ursula circled around him, closing in like the walls in Willy Wonka's chocolate factory.

"No, I had my chance. It's too late." His sweeping had become hurried and useless. "Can we just drop it?"

Doris put a hand on his arm to stop him from

moving. "Tell me you don't love her, and then we'll drop it."

He paused. "You know I can't do that."

Three pairs of eyes watched him. "Then tell us this," Ursula said. "Isn't she worth fighting for?"

"Of course she is, but you don't understand." He stared past them, toward the guesthouse that Evelyn had turned into a home. How empty it all seemed since she was gone. "She deserves better than me."

"Oh, hogwash." Ursula gave him a shove.

Trevor righted himself.

"That is a fool's response," she said.

Doris looked genuinely afraid.

"I have three words for you, Whitney." Ursula took a step toward him, poking him square in the chest. "Figure. It. Out."

He didn't move. "What did you say?"

"You heard me. You've had fifteen years to convince yourself she deserved better. Fifteen years to talk yourself out of it. Told yourself she was someone other than the girl you knew. She's not. She never fit in with all those rich, hoity-toity types."

"Now, that's true. Something about her always seemed different," Doris said with a nod.

"You think you're going to get a gaggle of chances, or what?" Ursula glared at him from behind her large-framed glasses.

"No, I just told you. I had my chance."

"You aren't listening!" She threw her hands up. "*This* is your chance."

"Mr. Whitney," Doris said, her tone calm to offset Ursula's tirade. "What Ursula is trying to say is that this is where Evelyn belongs. Out here. With you."

He shook his head. "She doesn't want me. Especially not after she found out what I did. I lied. That's a felony in her book. The worst kind of crime."

"She'll get over it," Ursula said.

Gigi scolded her with a look, but Trevor wondered if anything—or anyone—could ever shut that woman up.

"I appreciate your concern, ladies, but some things just aren't meant to be."

They stared at him, hopelessly, helplessly defeated.

"So that's it, then?" Gigi asked. "Nothing more to be said?"

He shrugged. "I put the whole thing in God's hands a long time ago." Surely they wouldn't argue with God.

Gigi's face turned sour as if she'd just gotten a whiff of a carton of milk well past its expiration date. "No, you didn't."

Now Ursula and Doris sent her a chastising look, but it was obvious the supposed leader of this little band of matchmakers had no intention of backing down. She took a few steps toward

Trevor. He stood unmoving, waiting for her to unload whatever it was she had on her mind.

Gigi looked as though the revelation was coming to her that very moment. "If you'd really given this thing over to God, would you have ordered those hearts every single year?"

Trevor felt the surprise hit his face. "What do you mean?"

"Giving it over means letting it go. You found a way to hold on to it all this time. You never really gave this thing to God."

"Oh, my," Doris said. "She's right."

"No, she's not," Trevor said, searching for a valid line of defense. "No one even knew who bought those hearts, especially not Evelyn."

"But you knew, Mr. Whitney," Gigi said quietly. "And that's the point."

Trevor leaned against the door of the stable and sighed. He'd convinced himself all those years ago that he'd let her go—but Gigi was right. He never really gave his feelings over to God. Not wholly.

What did that say about him?

"It might be time to surrender, Mr. Whitney," Gigi said. "Truly and completely surrender. You may've thought you did that, but unless you were willing to accept that the answer might be no, you didn't."

"What do you mean?"

"You held on. You tried to stay in control. If

you'd really surrendered, you would've accepted that the answer was no and moved on. It's time to surrender now."

He ran a hand over his stubbled chin. "So you don't think I should make a grand gesture to try to win her back?"

"They might," Gigi said, looking at her friends. "But I don't. Maybe for once it's better if we don't get in the middle of this and you accept that if it really is meant to be, God will see to it. Lay it down." She touched his arm. "Once and for all."

They started out toward Gigi's old Buick, but before she opened the passenger door, Ursula turned around. "It's not weak, you know. Surrendering." She squinted in his direction as if sizing him up all over again. "Takes a whole lotta strength to give the thing you want most over to God, not knowing whether he will give it back to you. And it takes a lot of faith to mean it."

She gave him a final once-over, then climbed into the car, which drove away, leaving Trevor with nothing but thoughts he didn't want and a sad kind of regret he knew he could only pray away.

Hours later, in the quiet solace of an empty farmhouse, Trevor replayed the words over and over. *Surrender. Lay it down. Figure it out.* How had he failed so miserably?

He tossed and turned, battling questions he knew he couldn't answer and realizing all the ways he had not surrendered. He'd exited her life but kept one eye on her at all times. He'd clung to that ounce of hope and rushed in when she was in need. Was it possible he'd done the right thing for the wrong reasons?

He got out of bed and shuffled to the kitchen, got himself a drink of water, and stared out the window at the empty guesthouse.

"What do you want me to do, Lord?" The words came out angrier than he intended, but then he had been angry lately, hadn't he?

He had finished the water and set the cup in the sink when that one word popped into his head again. *Surrender.*

That was it. If he and Evelyn were ever going to be together, then God would have to work a miracle. Evelyn would have to forgive him, come to him. It would have to be her idea. No more gestures or painted hearts. No more love songs or romantic memories.

Finally, once and for all, he was giving up the one thing he wanted more than air. Because he could finally see that if she wasn't God's will for him, then he shouldn't spend time loving her in that way.

He plodded back to bed and tried—failed—to drift off to sleep. Somewhere between two and three in the morning, Trevor finally sat up in bed and rubbed the tired from his eyes. "God, I mean it this time. I'm laying this down."

Trevor vowed in that exhausted moment to let this go. To really let it go. And that meant no more clinging to shreds of hope.

He knew women liked men who were strong, but he'd been strong all this time and it had gotten him nothing. So he chose a different kind of strength. The strength of surrendering. Of trusting God's will.

But as he lay back down, he prayed a simple, final prayer. "Please let it be your will . . ." And he drifted off to sleep.

CHAPTER
44

Evelyn sat outside the office of literary agent Alexandra O'Dell, clutching her portfolio with both hands. When Doris had let it slip that her niece was an agent in Denver, Evelyn did something she never would've done before.

She asked for a favor.

"I have a book idea," she'd told Doris, feeling naked at the admission.

The other Volunteers all looked at her, and she waited to hear the many reasons it was silly. Frivolous. Unlikely. But they said none of those things. Instead, her confession was met with encouragement and support.

"What's the story about?" Abigail had asked, joining them at the table.

Evelyn hesitated.

"We're safe, Evie," Abigail said. "We want this for you."

And Evelyn believed her. She spent the next hour telling those women about Silly Lily, the girl with a knack for mischief. She told them about the grumpy neighbor who had no tolerance for anything childish or fun. She explained how Lily had a dog named Beefcake, who inadvertently led the curly-headed girl to the yard of that neighbor, where Lily single-handedly brought joy and happiness into the old lady's life.

She flipped to the last illustration, where the little girl rushed over to the old woman and gave her a hug.

She leaned back. "Is it dumb?"

Gigi put a hand on Evelyn's. "Of course it's not dumb."

"Who's that supposed to be?" Ursula pointed at the picture of Lily and the old woman. "She looks familiar."

Evelyn smiled. "I don't know what you mean."

Ursula picked up the image and squinted at it. "Are you saying I'm cranky?"

Amused glances crisscrossed the table.

"Is this what you think I look like?" Ursula held the picture up next to her own face. Evelyn didn't want to brag, but she'd captured the very essence of the woman sitting across from her.

"You're missing the point, Ursula," Gigi said. "At the end, the old woman has a heart of gold."

"Yeah, it's just buried under a pile of cow poo," Doris giggled, barely glancing up from the phone she held in her hands.

Tess spoke before Ursula could respond. "Doris, what are you doing over there?"

Doris's forehead wrinkled in concentrated confusion. "My grandson changed the settings on my phone. I can't find Alex's number."

Tess took the phone from her, pressed a few buttons, and returned it.

"How'd you do that?" Doris stared at the phone in her hands.

"Magic," Tess said. "And isn't your grandson seven years old?"

Doris shrugged. "He's very advanced."

She'd called Alex and told her about Evelyn's book, though Evelyn had cringed a little at her pitch, which was long and meandering. In the end, Alex had agreed to meet with Evelyn, and while Evelyn was thankful for the favor, sitting here now, she thought she might throw up.

An office assistant offered her coffee while she waited. Evelyn politely declined. She fidgeted. She thought about leaving.

Anxiety bubbled underneath her surface, begging her attention.

She closed her eyes, drew in a deep breath, and

forced herself to focus on the words that had calmed her more in the last few months than anything else ever had.

Be anxious for nothing.

God, please calm my weary heart. She prayed the words silently, knowing he heard them.

"And the peace of God, which surpasses all understanding, will guard your hearts and minds through Christ Jesus . . ."

"Evelyn Brandt?"

The woman's voice startled her, but as she nodded a hello, she realized her heart rate had slowed and the knot in her stomach had considerably less of a hold on her. She stood and extended a hand to the petite woman with a blonde bob.

"I'm Alex," she said. "Come on back."

Evelyn followed her to a small office and sat across the desk from her.

"So you know my aunt Doris?"

Evelyn smiled. "I do. She's very sweet."

"She reminds me of a bird."

Evelyn laughed.

"In a funny way. Not a mean way." Alex flicked her hand in the air. "Oh, you know what I mean."

Oddly enough, she did. "I appreciate you taking the time to see me."

"Let's see what you've got."

An hour later, Evelyn left Alex's office feeling like she'd just made a friend. She probably should've been looking for a business partner, but she'd unknowingly had one of those for ten years of marriage, and she'd decided she didn't want to do business with anyone unless she liked them.

And she liked Alex.

Thankfully, Alex liked her too. She'd offered to represent her and to get to work trying to sell *Silly Lily* to publishers. Would it be easy? No. But it didn't matter. Evelyn had taken the first step toward following her heart—and she couldn't put a price on that if she tried.

As she drove back to Loves Park, she realized her excitement was short-lived. She wanted to pick up the phone and tell someone about her meeting, her revelations, her dreams—but the person she wanted to tell was the same person she'd given up talking to.

Trevor's betrayal had hit her hard, so why was she even considering dialing his number? She'd determined not to get involved with men who lied or told half-truths ever again.

That evening, she walked into The Paper Heart for a meeting of the Valentine Volunteers. Gigi and Doris rushed toward her as soon as she came in.

"We've been waiting for you," Gigi said, handing her a warm drink. "To celebrate."

Doris scrunched her nose. "I called Alex. The suspense was killing me."

Evelyn smiled and let Gigi pull her into a maternal hug. "Congratulations, dear."

"Thank you," Evelyn said, saying a silent prayer of thanks for the unlikely friendship of these women.

"We want to hear all the details." Gigi ushered her to their usual table. "But first, we have some business to attend to."

As Evelyn sat at the table, she discovered they had their easel out, and Trevor's photo was on it again.

"What are you doing?" Evelyn asked.

"It's almost Valentine's Day," Tess said. "And if you don't want Trevor Whitney, we've thought of about ten other women who would."

Evelyn felt her eyes widen. "What does that mean? If I don't want him?"

A quiet beat passed around their circle. "Gigi was eavesdropping again," Ursula said.

"Oh, I was not," Gigi argued. "I might've accidentally stumbled into a conversation I wasn't meant to hear, but that is not eavesdropping."

Evelyn frowned. "What are you talking about?"

Gigi sighed. "That night at the gallery showing of the hearts. It's been a while now, and I didn't want to say anything because you've been doing so well."

Evelyn only stared.

"We know about you and Trevor," Tess said matter-of-factly.

Evelyn shook her head. "I don't know what you think you know but . . ."

"We know he loves you," Abigail said. "And we thought you loved him too."

Evelyn put her hands up as if that could stop this conversation. "I think you've been misinformed."

Their collective glare unnerved her. No one spoke, but she had the feeling they'd pieced together a lot more of this story than she ever wanted them to know.

She compacted her lips. "So you want to match Trevor?"

They stared at her. She knew this game. They were trying to get her to admit to something she was determined not to admit. Or feel. Or even consider.

Trevor Whitney had no place in her future.

"Let's see who you've found for him," Evelyn said.

Their confused expressions told her this wasn't what they'd expected.

Tess stuttered as she rummaged through a file, then pulled out a small stack of photos. She affixed them to the whiteboard with small black magnets, moving slowly as if waiting for Evelyn to protest.

She didn't.

Instead, she led the discussion about the pros and cons of each young woman they'd found as a possible match for her old friend Trevor Whitney. Some she discarded as too young, too old, too *experienced*. When she finished, they were left with three possible options.

"There. Any of those women would be great for Whit," Evelyn said. "Now, ladies, if you'll excuse me, I've had about all the matchmaking I can handle for one day."

CHAPTER
45

Sadness overwhelmed the solace of the loft above The Paper Heart. Evelyn thought she'd put up a great front, but her heart had protested with every word.

She didn't want the Volunteers to match Trevor. Not that she didn't want him to be happy—she did. She just wanted him to be happy with her.

And she hated herself for it.

He'd been so awful, the way he'd hidden Christopher's unfaithfulness. How would she ever trust him again?

She took out one of the wooden hearts she'd kept from the Sweetheart Festival and stared at it for a long time. He'd made this. His hands had cut the wood slats and stained each individual one. He'd created something beautiful out of some-thing ordinary.

He had a knack for that.

She certainly felt beautiful when she was with him. Yet she knew she was the most ordinary of all.

She pulled out the messages she had left to paint and sat at the table. Some she'd assigned to other artists. Some she'd kept for herself. All new messages passed through her as artist in residence, but so far, she hadn't seen any come in with the lyrics to their song.

She rolled her eyes. *Their song.* Like they had such a thing.

She flipped through the newest messages as if double-checking might change the fact that Trevor hadn't purchased a heart this year. Why would he?

"Evelyn?"

She spun around in her chair to find Ursula standing at the top of the stairs.

"You scared me," she said.

"I get that a lot."

Evelyn watched as the old woman lumbered over to the patchwork armchair Evelyn had positioned in one corner of the room. She plopped down, and Evelyn wondered how many people it would take to get her back up.

"This thing between you and Mr. Whitney," Ursula said. "It's annoying."

Evelyn frowned, thankful for the space between her and Ursula. Not that it did anything to protect her. "There is no 'thing' between me and Trevor."

"Don't think you're fooling anybody with that charade downstairs."

"You were all intent on matching him," Evelyn said, picking up her pencil. "I only thought I should do my part since I'm the one who knows him best."

She could sense the old lady eyeing her. Suddenly she felt like the little girl she'd created for her children's book, a girl who cowered at first from the mean, crotchety old woman who lived down the block.

She dared a glance at Ursula.

Yep. Still watching her.

"Do you have something to say?" Evelyn asked, pretending to sketch on the wooden heart.

"You're right. You do know him best, which is why I find it suspicious that the three women you settled on are the exact same three we all discarded on the first pass."

"What are you talking about?" She stopped fake sketching and looked at Ursula.

"It was a test," she said. "You failed."

"I have no idea what you're—"

"Stop. You're embarrassing yourself." Ursula sank deeper into the chair. "We set you up. You picked the three women we knew were a terrible match for Trevor Whitney, just like I said you would."

Evelyn pulled her hair into a low ponytail and fastened an elastic around it. "I think you're mistaken. I discarded women who were too old or too young or—"

"Too likely?"

She met Ursula's eyes.

"You have yourself convinced you're better off without that man, and maybe you are."

Evelyn looked away.

"But what if you're not? What if you've forgotten all the good things he's done because you've chosen to pay attention to the one small thing he did wrong?"

"It was not a small thing," Evelyn said, her voice shaky.

"You got hurt." Ursula hugged her bigger-than-a-toddler purse. "I get it. But how much of that hurt can really be blamed on Trevor?"

Evelyn squeezed the bridge of her nose to keep from crying. She didn't want to dredge all this up. Not today—a day that had started off so well.

"I know you know the answer," Ursula said, scooting forward in the chair. "He's probably not going to come calling again, so maybe now it's your turn to make the gesture."

Evelyn lowered her hand. "I can't do that."

"Why?"

"I told him I didn't want to ever see him again."

"And?"

Evelyn sniffed. "And I meant it."

The old woman squinted at her. "You're a terrible liar."

"I'm not lying."

"You think you're not, but how many times have you gone over those hearts looking for the one Trevor purchased for you?"

Boy, they really did know everything, didn't they?

"That kid has done an awful lot to show you how much he cares about you." She scooted forward again. "It's your turn now."

Evelyn scrolled through a mental list of memories—all the times Trevor had been there for her. It started years ago, in high school, and it carried all the way to just a few short weeks ago.

She was angry that he'd kept the truth about Christopher from her, but was it possible he had done it—in part, at least—for her? She couldn't say how she would've reacted if he'd said anything all those years ago.

"I'll think about it," she said, hoping it was enough to get the old woman out of her studio.

"Great," Ursula said. "And if Gigi asked, I was never here."

Evelyn frowned.

"She won't believe me when I tell her I wasn't meddling, which we all agreed not to do."

"Weren't you?"

"Not when God tells you to make a point." Ursula raised her brows. "And he did, in case you're wondering."

Evelyn had a hard time believing God would

use Ursula to make a point, but stranger things had happened.

"I won't say anything," Evelyn said.

"Good." She paused. "Now, can you help me out of this chair?"

CHAPTER
46

A week before Valentine's Day, Evelyn hurried to get ready for a meeting at the hospital to discuss the mural for the children's wing.

She hadn't heard from the mayor since their last meeting, but she assumed he'd accepted her terms.

Evelyn pulled on a pair of fitted jeans, an ivory camisole, and a burgundy jacket with cuffed sleeves. Her burgundy ballet flats and a chunky bracelet completed the outfit and had her feeling ready to stand up to Georgina all over again if she had to.

She drove to the hospital, Ursula's words running through her mind. To her dismay, she'd thought of little else all week. She'd finished all the painted hearts thinking about them. She'd gone to bed thinking about them. She'd woken up thinking about them.

And she hated that this crabby old woman knew the truth before she even knew it herself.

Regardless, she'd determined not to act on feelings that would probably only end up hurting her again down the road. Instead, she busied herself with her work. Not that she could call creating art "work." Despite so much of her life having fallen apart, she had to admit she was happier than she'd been in a very long time.

Mostly happy, anyway. With a bit more time and distance from Trevor Whitney, she'd be even happier.

She parked the car and made her way inside, where she was met by the mayor, the Valentine Volunteers, and a woman named Tonya, who was a member of the hospital board.

As she followed the group to the elevator, she leaned toward Gigi. "No Georgina?"

Gigi winked. "She wasn't invited to this meeting. It's only for more *creative* types."

Evelyn smiled.

They reached the children's wing and, as a unit, made their way down the hall. While they walked, Evelyn took notes on the colors and structure, falling a bit behind the rest of the group. Ideas began to jump into her head, and as they did, she sketched and scribbled, wondering if there was more she could do in this wing than paint a mural.

What if this children's wing had a mascot? What if Silly Lily were more than a character in a book? What if she could come to life and spread her silliness, her happiness, her joy among those who needed it even more than a crabby old neighbor?

"Evelyn?"

She turned and found the rest of the group watching her. How long had they been doing that?

"I'm sorry," Evelyn said. "I just got an idea."

"We would love to hear it," Tonya said. "So far every idea you've had has been right on point. In fact, we love the sketches so much, we'd like you to paint a mural on each floor of the hospital."

"Me?" Surely this was some kind of joke.

Tonya smiled. "You're quite talented. And once we received Mr. Whitney's recommendation, we knew we had the right artist."

Evelyn frowned. "I'm sorry; what did you say?" She scanned the other women's faces for any sign they knew what Tonya was talking about, but they all looked as confused as Evelyn felt.

Tonya continued. "When he created the artist-in-residence program, he mentioned you to me. The mural was his idea."

"I don't understand," Evelyn said, her voice quiet.

The mayor shifted, then leaned in toward Tonya. "Evelyn wasn't aware of Mr. Whitney's involvement in her position with the city."

Tonya's eyes widened. "Oh, my. I am so sorry if that was not for public consumption. I only assumed everyone knew how generous he's been."

Evelyn tried to process what she was hearing. "It was Whit?"

Gigi moved toward her and draped an arm across her shoulders.

Ursula folded her arms. "Told ya."

Evelyn couldn't wrap her brain around what they were saying. It wasn't possible that Trevor had been the one to dream up this position for her, that he'd offered to foot the bill. She'd been so cruel to him—why would he go out of his way to drop her name to these people?

"Evelyn, all Mr. Whitney did was point out the obvious," Mayor Thompkins said. "That you have a gift our city has greatly benefited from."

"No, Mayor Thompkins. That's not all he did," Evelyn said.

Trevor had given her a second chance—one she'd pursued without him. He'd let her go, but he'd clearly given her a gift for the road.

"If you'll excuse me . . ." Evelyn stumbled backward down the hall toward the elevator.

She heard them call after her and prayed they would cover for her with Tonya. She didn't want to ruin her chances to impact the community by helping out at the hospital, but in that moment, she had something else she needed to do.

Her mind wandered as she drove out to the edge of town and then kept going. When Whitney Farms came into view, her heart pounded a quickstep in her chest. She forced herself to keep going, no matter how much she wanted to turn around and forget she'd just heard anything Tonya and the mayor had said.

She reached the farmhouse, but she could see Trevor's truck parked near the old red barn. His wood shop, his quiet thinking place.

Was that where he'd gotten the idea to invade her entire life?

She parked next to his truck, took a deep breath, and got out of the car. She nearly lost her nerve as she reached the door, but she forced herself to push it open before she could chicken out.

Inside, that familiar smell of sawdust filled her nose. She looked around, but the shop appeared to be empty. Another deep breath. Maybe this was stupid. She should go. She could resign the position and move away.

Never mind that she loved her job. Never mind that while it might've been Trevor's idea, she had been the one to make it into something that gave her meaning.

"Evelyn?"

She turned and found Trevor standing in a doorway that led to the makeshift showroom in the barn. At the sight of him, she nearly forgot why she'd come.

"What are you doing here?"

She swallowed, remembering. "Why didn't you tell me you were the one behind my position with the city?"

His face fell. "You weren't supposed to find out about that."

"Well, I did."

He wiped his hands on the rag he was holding, then tucked it in his back pocket. "Would you have taken it if you'd known?"

"Of course not."

He shrugged as if now she had her answer.

"You tried to pay my salary."

He shrugged again. "You rejected my offer."

"I wouldn't allow any of my friends to pay my salary."

"Is that what we are? Friends?"

The question smacked at her. She had no answer. How had they gotten here? He'd become the most important person to her, yet they weren't even speaking. He'd shown her unconditional love, and she'd cut him out of her life completely.

He walked away.

"Are we done talking?"

He didn't look at her. "I'm not very good with words."

That line—the same one he'd said the night he kissed her—hung between them.

"What am I supposed to do?" she asked.

"Whatever you want, Evie." He picked up a clean rag and ran it over a table he'd built. It was beautiful, but she wouldn't say so. Not when she was this angry.

"You're unbelievable."

"Listen, you've got a good thing going. It seems like you've got it all figured out."

"Well, I don't," she said. "But I'm trying. And I don't need your charity to do it."

He sighed. "Why won't you ever let anyone help you anymore?"

She glared at him. "I'm sorry, Whit, but your so-called help broke my heart, so you'll understand when I tell you that, as much as I love it, I don't feel right keeping this position with the city. It's time for me to find my own way."

He stopped wiping the table and held her gaze for several long seconds. "I just wanted you to believe in yourself—in that girl I fell in love with all those years ago—the way I believe in you."

She started to speak but quickly changed her mind. She didn't know how to soften when she was determined to stay angry with him. She didn't know how to melt in his arms and say thank you because she did believe in herself now. She'd rediscovered who she was, without the mask, without the strangling need to please everyone around her. She'd discovered she didn't need to compromise anymore. She could make decisions for herself.

She was happy and more herself than she had been in years. The fact that Whit was partially responsible for that didn't make it less true.

So why did she stand there like a stubborn child, unwilling to relent?

Because she couldn't bear the thought of needing someone like that ever again.

"Good-bye, Whit," she said, unmoving.

He didn't respond. Instead, he watched her as if trying to determine if there was anything left between them.

And as she turned and walked out of the wood shop—out of his life—she had the undeniable feeling that she'd just used up her last chance with Trevor Whitney.

CHAPTER
47

As Evelyn sped away from Whitney Farms, tears stung her eyes.

What was wrong with her? She'd just thrown away the only good relationship she'd ever had because she couldn't forgive Trevor. He'd forgiven her for choosing Christopher, for turning into an unrecognizable person, for taking advantage of his goodness, for throwing herself at him in a moment of drunken weakness, and finally for breaking his heart.

She had, hadn't she? She could see the pain of a broken heart in his eyes. Trevor wasn't the same man he'd been a few months ago, and she was to blame.

She drove to town and stopped in front of the museum, where their hearts were still on display.

Inside, she headed straight to the exhibit where the story of the Loves Park painted hearts was told by way of an overhead speaker and a not-so-professional voice-over.

Evelyn stared at the hearts she'd painted. Lyrics to a song that had come to mean so much to Trevor—but that she'd failed to recognize until recently. How little attention she'd paid, and yet he cared enough to remember each year.

"What I wouldn't give for Barry to love me like that," a lady standing a few yards away said to the woman beside her.

"Men like this don't exist, Shirley," the other woman said. "I think the city made it up as some kind of brilliant tourism scheme."

"Quit ruining the romance, Mary Sue. Just because our husbands would never do it doesn't mean no one would."

Mary Sue waved her off. "Fantasy."

"It's not fantasy," Evelyn said quietly.

"Pardon me?" The one named Shirley turned to her. "Did you say something?"

Evelyn stared at the hearts. Trevor had given everything for her—for nothing but heartache in return. "It does exist. He does exist."

The women laughed. "Well, do you want to give him our numbers?"

Evelyn brushed away a tear. "Not a chance, ladies," she said.

She found the museum manager, an old woman

named Joan who bounced when she walked.

"I have a favor," Evelyn said, apparently getting a knack for this asking-for-help thing. "I'd like to borrow the hearts."

Joan's thin eyebrows crumpled. "You mean you want to take them out of the museum?"

"Yes, but I'll return them, I promise."

Joan tilted her head as if contemplating. "Fine. You are their creator. I suppose it would be silly for me to tell you no."

"It would, wouldn't it?" Evelyn smiled. "I'll get them later today. First, I have some painting to do."

Trevor had one plan for Valentine's Day. Get out of town. He'd arranged for Lilian and Dale to handle everything on the farm for a few days, and he planned a long weekend of doing a whole lot of nothing but being away from the romance mess that was his hometown.

After his final run-in with Evelyn, he guessed he had his answer. He'd asked God to be clear, and the Lord appeared to have answered. In spades. So far every decision he'd made concerning Evelyn seemed to be the wrong one.

And he was tired of caring so much.

He threw his clothes in a duffel bag, filled his thermos with coffee, and hauled his gear out to the truck. He hadn't been camping in ages. Too busy with the farm and the woodworking. But he needed to clear his head, and nothing would do that like the great outdoors.

As he finished loading up the truck, Lilian's car sped around the bend and came to a stop beside him. "Have you been out there?" She looked panicked.

"What's the matter—has Loves Park exploded into a pile of love dust?"

She glared at him. "Whit. This is serious."

"What is it?"

"Just drive into town. You need to see it for yourself."

"No, I don't," Trevor said. "I'm going *out* of town before this place sucks me into all of its Valentine's Day madness." The last thing he needed was a reminder of what he *didn't* have.

She stood in front of him and put her hands on his arm. "Trevor. This is important."

He took a step back. "All right, now you're starting to worry me. Is everything okay?"

"Just go."

He huffed as he got behind the wheel of his truck. "I'll be back."

He pulled out of the driveway, mind spinning with the possibilities of what could have Lilian so rattled. Last time she'd been this worked up, Evelyn's home was being invaded by the government.

He flipped on the radio and a familiar tune filled the cab of the truck.

"The very thought of you and I forget to do . . ."

No. Way. What were the odds that this of all songs was on the radio at that precise moment? He glanced down and discovered it wasn't the radio at all. It was a CD. He popped it out and looked at it.

Someone had drawn a single heart on the front of it in thick black marker.

Were they mocking him?

He turned his attention back to the road, but something else quickly stole it again. Ahead, on a telephone pole along this old country road, was a painted heart.

The hearts were only hung on Main Street. How had this one gotten all the way out here? He slowed down.

Not just any heart—one of Evelyn's hearts. One of the hearts she'd painted with the lyrics before she'd discovered the truth.

As he drove, he counted six, seven, eight, nine hearts, all attached to the telephone poles on one of the most rural roads in Loves Park.

The tenth and final heart came into view.

Who had done this? And more importantly—why?

Some sort of cruel joke to remind him of how he'd screwed everything up?

He continued toward town. He'd go to the museum and find out why the hearts were no longer on display. He'd demand they be taken down so he didn't have to be tortured by their existence anymore. He didn't need the reminder of all he'd lost.

Even if he never really had it in the first place.

But as he reached the final stop sign before Main Street, a different image caught his eye.

She wore a puffy turquoise ski coat, skinny jeans, and gray boots. A multicolored stocking cap covered her head, leaving her long blonde hair flowing out the bottom. She looked like something out of a dream.

He slowed the truck to a stop on the side of the road. She seemed . . . hopeful.

In her hands, she held an eleventh heart. Identical to the others, but the final words of the song had been painted on this one.

It's just the thought of you
The very thought of you, my love

He stared at her for several seconds, unsure of how or why she'd done this. He'd lost her, hadn't he? The second she walked out of the wood shop, he'd given up—once and for all.

He turned off the engine and got out of the truck, walking toward her.

She appeared to have a difficult time holding his gaze.

"Nice heart," he said.

She smiled. "You weren't going to leave the song unfinished, were you?"

He glanced away.

"I thought it was time for me to meet you halfway."

He had no reply.

"You've always been there for me. Always. It's time I was there for you in return."

"How did you do all this?" Trevor waved his hand in the direction of all the other hearts.

"I'm the artist in residence of Loves Park," she said. "I have a lot of pull."

He laughed. "Good to know."

"Besides, I wanted to make a point."

"That you're crazy?"

"That I love you."

The words floated there, full of promise and begging his attention, but he couldn't believe them. He'd imagined this moment a thousand times, yet now that it was here, it felt surreal. Like a dream.

"Did you hear what I said?" she asked. The admission had exposed her. He understood that risk, and he knew how difficult this must be for her. Probably the kind of admission she didn't want to make, but there she stood—her heart literally on the line.

"I did."

"I want you to have this." She held the heart out in his direction.

He took the painted heart, eyes locked on hers.

"I want you to have my heart."

Trevor cupped her face in his free hand, a world of emotions rushing through him. "You already have mine." He brought her closer, searching her face and finding something there that he'd given up on a long time ago.

"Nobody has ever loved me the way you have, Trevor."

"And nobody ever will." He leaned in and let himself fall into her kiss as she drew herself nearer to him, reminding him without saying a word that God really did answer prayers.

Often when you least expected it.

He tugged himself away, still holding her, brushing her hair away from her eyes and getting lost in their deep blue for a long moment. "You are the answer to all my prayers, Evie."

She softened, drawing him closer again. "Thank you for loving me. I know it wasn't always easy."

"I couldn't help it. Believe me, I tried." He took her face in his hands and pressed another soft kiss on her lips.

As he stepped back, he heard a car behind him. He turned and saw Gigi's old Buick speeding their way. It came to a screeching halt, kicking up gravel dust, just inches from the tail of his truck.

The three old women got out and trudged toward them.

"You ladies have something to do with this?"

Trevor called out, holding up the painted heart.

"No, Mr. Whitney," Gigi said. "This was all Evelyn's idea."

"But we are happy we get to cross you off our to-be-matched list," Doris said. "Hardest match ever."

Trevor frowned.

"We're not so hard," Evelyn said. "We just needed a little time."

"I'm just happy I don't have to watch you two continue to mess everything up." Ursula slung a wide bag over her shoulder. "That really gets old. You are both so dense."

Trevor wrapped an arm around Evelyn, the two of them laughing at Ursula's honesty, at the truth in it, at their own happiness.

"It is good to see you both smile," Gigi said.

He glanced at Evelyn, who was looking at him. "You're stuck with me now," he told her.

"Thank goodness." She smiled. "Because I can't imagine going one more day without you."

He kissed her forehead, pulled her close, and thanked God that while their story hadn't followed the path he originally wanted, it had all led him here, and *here* was exactly where they both belonged.

A Note from the Author

When I first had the idea for *Change of Heart*, I knew it would be difficult to write. Essentially, I thought, the book is about a man who's in love with a married woman. Tricky for someone writing Christian fiction, no?

But as I began to peel away the layers, I started to see that while this is a part of the battle my hero faced, it's only a part—and at its core, this book is about surrendering our will to whatever God has for us. Even when the answers aren't ones we want to hear. Even when everything seems to go completely wrong. Even when every choice we make seems to be the opposite of what we should've made.

I'm not very good at surrendering.

I've lived a fairly self-sufficient life, but in the past few years, I've realized that this isn't a badge of courage I want to wear. I don't want to be the one who has everything all figured out because it leaves no room for God to work in me. I would much rather readily admit I have no idea what I'm doing and can't do any of this life stuff without him.

My prayer for this book is that it will not only give you a few hours of peaceful escape, but that it will also help you, dear reader, take a look at the regrets you've been carrying with you and finally lay them down. No matter what story you're telling yourself, the truth is our choices don't define us—thankfully.

And while the human heart tends to be fickle, God's heart toward us never changes.

I pray you rest in his unending grace.

Courtney

Acknowledgments

To Adam. My rock. What a gift, this love of ours. I am so thankful for every moment with you. Thank you for always encouraging, keeping me on the right path, and helping me get over myself. You + Me.

To my kids, Sophia, Ethan, and Sam. Watching you grow into really awesome young people has been my greatest joy. Thank you for not grumbling too much when I make you unload the dishwasher and for being totally okay eating cereal for dinner when I'm on deadline. My prayer is that you always know how very loved you are, and that no matter what, you rest in God's grace and lean in to his purpose for your lives. I love you.

To my dad. My forever hero. I look up to you more than you know. Your wisdom and faith inspire me every single day. Thank you for being there for me.

To Sandra Bishop. I will always be so grateful for your belief in me.

To Stephanie Broene and Danika King. Thank you for pulling the good stuff to the top. For being such an important part of this process. For being kind in your critiques and generous with your praise. It is pure joy that I get to work with you both.

To Deb Raney. I couldn't ask for a better mentor and friend. I am so glad we sat next to each other at that ACFW breakfast all those years ago. You are a true gift.

To Ronelle Johnson. For your graciousness in answering my questions and helping me make sense of legalities that pretty much make no sense. And just for being one of the kindest, sweetest, and most generous people I know.

To the Grove Girls. God has brought such sweetness to my life through each one of you. I am forever grateful.

To my Studio kids. You bless my socks off every single time I watch you shine. Never stop believing in yourselves. . . . I never will!

To the Michael Nyman station on Pandora and every instrumental movie sound track that has filled my earbuds. I love you.

About the Author

Courtney Walsh is a novelist, artist, theater director, and playwright. Her debut novel, *A Sweethaven Summer*, hit the *New York Times* and *USA Today* e-book bestseller lists and was a Carol Award finalist in the debut author category. She has written two more books in the Sweethaven Summer series, as well as two craft books and several full-length musicals. Courtney lives in Illinois with her husband and three children.

Visit her online at www.courtneywalshwrites.com.

Discussion Questions

1. Bit by bit, Evelyn sacrificed parts of herself to become the model wife Christopher wanted—she gave up her goals, her individuality, and even her clothing preferences. If you knew Evelyn, what advice would you give her once she realized all she'd lost?

2. When Christopher and Evelyn got married, Trevor did his best to hand his feelings over to God. However, he still faces a years-long struggle to move past his affection for her. Describe a time in your life when obeying and trusting God was more of a lengthy, challenging process than a onetime decision.

3. After Christopher's crimes and indiscretions come to light, Evelyn is shunned by most of her community even though she was not involved in his actions. Have you ever been scorned or left out by your family, friends, or community? What was your response?

4. Trevor's woodworking company is called *Desvío* (Spanish for "detour"). What is the significance behind that name? Has your life

ever taken a turn that was different from what you expected? What happened?

5. Trevor knew about Christopher's infidelity years before it became a news story. But he chose to keep it from Evelyn, even colluding with Christopher to help him cover up some of his affairs. Why did he do that? What would you have done in his shoes?

6. After Evelyn's night of drinking too much at the bar, Gigi leaves her a note with Ephesians 2:10 written on it: "For we are God's master-piece. He has created us anew in Christ Jesus, so we can do the good things he planned for us long ago." Why do you think Gigi chooses to share this particular verse with Evelyn? Why is it necessary to become a new creation in Christ before we can do the good things God has planned for us?

7. In chapter 34, Evelyn reflects, "Of course [Christopher] was walking around free as a bird with a new soon-to-be wife and a baby on the way. Of course he had money from who knew where for kettle corn and hand-made necklaces when she was scraping pennies together for the basic necessities so she didn't feel like a complete charity case." What do you do when life doesn't seem fair—

when things appear to work out well for the "bad guys" but not for the innocent? How can you encourage and support your friends and loved ones when they face situations like this?

8. Trevor chooses to finally and completely surrender to God's will in chapter 43. But he still prays, "Please let it be your will . . ." Have you ever found yourself in a similar situation—deciding to follow God wherever he wants you to go but still hoping his will aligns with your desires? What was the outcome?

9. By the end of the book, Evelyn realizes that "God could take even her deepest pain and turn it into something beautiful." Think of an example from your life—or the life of someone you know—where this was true. How can this reality impact the way you view difficult circumstances?

10. In *Paper Hearts*, the first book in this series, the people of Loves Park express their affection through anonymous notes written on cutout hearts. In *Change of Heart*, it's painted messages for the whole town to see. Can you think of a creative way to tell a loved one how you feel about him or her?

Center Point Large Print
600 Brooks Road / PO Box 1
Thorndike, ME 04986-0001 USA

(207) 568-3717

US & Canada:
1 800 929-9108
www.centerpointlargeprint.com

REFLECTION

If I had walked under
another tree last night
I might have missed
the golden ladder
propped against the sky.
Then there would be
no cause to wonder
at hallucination
or mirage—
no need to question reason
destination
or wisdom of ascent.

Yet in so small an orchard
it was inevitable perhaps
to see from any angle
the ripened fruit, brightened
by the ladder's glow.

I'd like to know
what led me in the grove
to such a vision.
I should have touched
a rung, or picked a plum
trusted imagination and my eyes
and climbed.

Instead
I try to analyze.

VULNERABILITY

There are no savage horns
to sound arrival of the enemy
no drums that beat
to warn of the encroaching
stranger
who may lift the tent flap
in the sweaty night
and ease himself inside.
The councils are disbanded
and ineffectual sentries
dwell within.
A heightened rhythm
of the blood
comes too late to alleviate
the danger.

NEIGHBORHOOD

A view of split levels
and other brick and
mortar assembly line
dwellings out my
writing window
might just as well
be cabbage
or a stand
of sweet corn
blocking out the predictable
vegetables in their fields.
The muses issuing forth
from Meadowdale
and Idlebrook inspire
tract poems with
rows of beans and peppers
neatly lined
just out of sight.

TRANSPOSITION

Love darkens with the night
or the imagined night
as midnight forces
converge.
At noon
behind a desk
behind a business smile
the eclipse begins.
Pupils dilate
responding to diminished light;
afternoon candles flicker,
licking the blackened walls.
Were you to prick my finger then
blood would run dark as burgundy.

MENDING

Some scars lie on the surface
like roadmaps, pointing directions
where the surgeon or some accident
left markers of pain.
Tissue is different there,
sometimes through several layers.
Running a finger along those lines
deep cells have faint recall
of the original wounds. Healed properly
they fade blood red to lighter
than the surrounding flesh,
desensitized.

Others are harder to identify;
invisible, unsutured,
they lack air and medicants
to ease the healing.
Bleeding at intervals
ragged cuts open and close
with the rhythm of seasons.

IN RESPONSE TO A NEW LOOK AT THE NATURE OF HUMAN INTELLIGENCE

His sleek neck bends and ripples
as he turns to catch me in his beak.
Fear commands from hollow bones,
from cells that know an enemy
better than the bamboo home he's learned.
He'll travel human perches
only by necessity
disdaining offers from a hand that grasps
to blunt his wings,
then proffers bits of apple
in amends.

Gray feathers lift and stretch
touching the bars
that keep us out.

We have evolved
beyond this plumed, orange dappled creature
chained to jungle patterns.

We can reflect.

We read of others who have walked our paths
and fallen prey to tigers,
then take the same trails
thinking
as claws tear pale flesh red
of the UPI reports
that will go out tomorrow.

SURRENDER

The crest of the wave lets me glide
with the raft, holds me high
in the sun, stinging salt in my eyes,
in my hair, in the wind,
in the water that makes me believe
I can ride to the end of the world
on the edge of the sea.

The crash of the surf
as it breaks unexpectedly
sends me down to the sand
where I scrape knees and arms
on the grit of the floor.
Then thrusting my body out of the water
I give myself back.

I learn to expect to be flailed,
to go under, to fight for my breath,
to be beaten.
I seek to go down
under power that is greater than mine,
to feel ragged rocks tear my skin.

FLUX

I lie still, submerged,
each muscle disciplined
to resist disturbance.
A drop from the tap
sends waves
silver magnified
to redistribute shards of light;
designs kaleidoscope in chrome.

Unable to sustain the image
I relent
let water undulate over skin
warmed pink
sink deep
until hair fans the surface.

Eyes closed
I feel new patterns in the making.
Rivulets, directed by a twitch or sigh,
trickle from emerging flesh
as water laps the air.

COMMUNICATION

Plants wither and die when I sit in their rooms
too long.
Whether I water or not, croon, play Beethoven,
or humidify, they wilt in corners;
vines too tough to be conquered by cement-dry soil
grow limp in my presence. Days later
leaves yellow and fall.
I speak to the schefflera behind my yellow chair;
neither pleas nor threats make any difference.
Words fall on deaf leaves
tuned to my pulse;
their brittle responses break on the floor.
Bare stems and drying leaves need no decoding.

CAESAREAN

A slice from crotch to navel
split the bursting belly
reluctant to yield.
Needles half suppressed
incessant pain
while water gushed
in cruel imitation
of the end
to clear the blood
and give a better view
to the butcher
who hacked methodically
then pulled skin
carelessly together
leaving a red gap
ten years later
matching sunburn carved
in arcs accentuating
symmetry.

PENALTY

Spindly legged insects
move spasmodically through the morning air
delicate creatures
transformed by Allhallows Eve
from young girls
gathering sweets at midnight.

Too late in years and hours
to walk as children
too soon for beauty
they wake to spread their awkward limbs
in silent rooms,
to fly from men
who leave legs scattered carelessly
wall to wall.

FLIGHT

Our shadow glides over the water
like the shadows of clouds
drifting across the sun.
The ripples are continuous
unbroken, undisturbed by our coming and going.
We penetrate the layer above deliberately
like a syringe into white flesh,
proud of our deftness, then
disappear into the blue above the blue
so that the lake's surface
darkened in shallow patches
glimmers evenly again,
the reflection temporary as insight.

LOSSES

Passing through a town
where tulips faded early
in the heat
I bought ivy from a man named Alfred P.
and thought of you.

Some year
after we have all escaped our winters
you will pass where stunted blossoms
grow neglected
clouds of color
taking the shapes of memory
blurred by design
buffeted by wind.

I preferred the promise to the hyacinth.
Did you know that red ones die more slowly?
It blackened hard like cooled blood.

SHOW ANIMALS

Our eyes are tiger wild
pulled to green slits
as we are jostled through tunnels
to cages
where we claw and scream
yellow curses into night.
The stripes on our backs are invisible;
ulcered welts turn inward
lining bellies with trenches
where meat pulped by our juices
urges the blood to flow.

Lids droop,
taut muscles quiver quiet.
Tranquilizers break our pacing
into irregular segments.

We suppress the urge to tear.

DISCOVERY

Under deep green camouflage
wild strawberries hide;
trees crease the sun,
leaves slide across each other
gently in the wind.

Tall grasses bend
to hold the green impression
where we lie
tasting swollen fruit
that runs like sweet blood
from our summer mouths.

ON BEING A POET

In summer
green dominates the landscape;
the petunias and geraniums
in my baskets
are crowded out by leaves;
tall stalks keep the sun
from coming through my windows
while trees cast speckled shadows
on the glass.

There is not enough green in the land
to camouflage my reds—
(I have been the clay covered thinly
with a layer of fragile grass)
nor to cool the yellows
penetrated deep
and lodged beneath my skin.
I suspect by now
my bones have taken a persimmon tinge.

In fall I'll match the world
and for a time
deceive that season;

for now
green might as well enjoy
a tentative supremacy.

SICKNESS

The hours rattle against each other
uneasily, like rowboats tied to a dock
where even small waves jostle them
roughly together.
Sometimes night becomes day
unexpectedly,
cracks like lightning,
is night again.
Events are slides in a cheap projector,
one jerked back and forth, repeated
until it jars loose and is replaced
by another, focused differently.
There is no pattern.
When the sun shines
I see the sharp edges of things—
spikes of barren trees, profiles of strangers.
In moonlight, fields of wildflowers
hesitate into view,
white blossoms reflected in the patch
of pale light
soft before dawn.

ACCOMMODATION

His bulbs die in their beds.
Hot winter days tempt them
to life, opening dry bodies
too soon. Carolina shifts
warm into cold into warm;
rain trickles down slowly
before becoming sleet
which freezes the upper layer,
sealing it off.
Last year's yellows
rot darkly into themselves,
reds split open, bleeding away
their color. The tulips,
the daffodils, the hyacinths
all flatten in their clumps,
softened before real spring.

A wife
dressed in light jacket
to keep out the chill April air
tackles the yard on a weekend.
Shovel, rake, hoe, basket
are brought from the closet.
She digs around the tree
where dirt, spongy and damp,
turns over easily;
sees bulbs, still discernible
by their shapes, black against
the brown earth; chops
one after another for fertilizer,
turning them into the ground.

July: radishes and carrots
spread luxurious green stems
above the earth. Tomato plants
hang heavy with early fruit,
skins split by rapid growth
even before they ripen.
The garden flourishes.
Peas swell in their pods,
beans bend the vines with slender
massed weight.

She gathers her fruits and vegetables
one by one
to make a summer salad,
cuts radishes into flowers,
petals and stuffs tomatoes,
arranges green cylinders
in an elegant pattern
and serves her husband
(who has forgotten the bulbs)
a platter of artful blossoms.

DECORUM

I bend mutely, unlike the willow
who sings and sighs her felt beauty
through the neighboring trees.
Mine is not a supple leaning
but follows a predictable curve.
If I should moan as breezes
sift through my hair
touching this body like remembered hands
on soft, remembered skin
my neighbors in their yards
would be solicitous
or, recognizing joy in those unseemly sounds,
cluck cluck and shake their heads.
They would be right.
Old women have no business
unbuttoning their dresses
on spring mornings
or going barefoot in the garden
waiting for rain.

TRANSFUSION

Wine sky is colored by the heat of day
melting through red toward black.
We drink it slowly
as the liquid in our glasses,
fearing fragile dreams
will drain with day.

Twilight seeps into our blood—
we refill transparent goblets
again and again
perpetuating purple into dawn.

DEAF GATHERING

Hands chop air into words
that disappear in silence
as faces in the circle nod
and soundless laughter
fills the room.
Ideas penetrate
through straining eyes;
fingers transmit electric images
over invisible wires.
Evening extends the quiet—
lamps illuminate the singing,
shouting hands
less crisply lucid,
each drink increasing animation.
Voiceless desires murmur
in delicate gestures;
sensitive fingers
pulse messages into the night.

INTOXICATION

Words are balloons
filled with helium.
I am attached
to a basket beneath
and ride
to their rhythm
and rhyme
their unrhyme
and touch
their caress
their control.
I am wafted from
verb to verb
am battered by images
tossed upside down
and retrieved.
I desire the assault
of lightning
near-drowning
in storm changing
currents
the thunder of fear
in my ears
the risk of the fall.

THE PLANTS

Fuchsias would not survive.
Their pink lips dried like the orifices
of old women, soft skin shrunken,
tender petals inverted, faded
gray, sickly as age.

Established coleus, meanwhile,
sprouts new growth.
Embryo leaves unfold to multicolored
arrogance, elaborately fringed.
They curve and twist to maximize
the touch of fingers
on their velvet surfaces. Small flowers,
violet deepened to purple,
burst from the top.
In a room of ivy and fragile blossoms
the eye is drawn
to jagged leaves,
young, bright, and beautiful.

LEA

Then she seemed strange
living on raw edges
of the shale
we had smoothed to comfort.
Experiments in pain
shocked casual strangers
drawn to the compulsive flow
of her unnatural narrative
before its tightening to fiction.
Exaggerated gaiety
rattled above despair,
lasted until pills ran out
or were consumed too fast.

We knew more—
coped in complacency
hooked rugs, read horoscopes
over doughnuts and coffee.

Caught in the spokes
of a wheel revolving on rocks
into air
she was spun into shadows
unable to speak
in a voice we could hear
without hearing the voices
whose echoes we all
had successfully drowned.

STERILITY

My cries come back on the wind diminished—
wrenched like water from the lungs of drowning men,
mere pools beside the sea.
They lose their force in the surrounding moans
of air and earth like lovers in abrasive union.

This hill, these trees, the darkening clouds
are priests, deaf and impotent,
who offer nothing.

The gods neglect their duties;
wine turns to vinegar, then to rain
that will not be absorbed
but taunts the spring with cruel promise.

INGÉNUE

It is not a matter simply of forgetting lines—
halfway through this second act
I doubt the play, cannot remember
who the playwright is. Did I write this script
or did somebody contract me
merely to act the part?
Too late to flee
my only recourse is to improvise.
Was that the plan?
"Love, love, I implore you to . . . "
To what? Is he my lover?
The cue—"This lacks the proper balance."
No help.
"I bring you flowers—or did you bring them
to me?"
I fumble for a vase, arrange red paper tulips.

As laughter fills the room like steam
I rise absurd
wondering when the curtain will come down.

CAVERN

The dark does not escape through my mouth
when I smile.
Bats fly behind night widened pupils
tenants
squealing their displeasure
seeking roosts in narrow passages.

Light leaks in through dots in eyes
nearly closed against the sun.
The bats, disturbed,
scratch at the walls
wings pulsing in the summer heat.

MIRROR

Smash the glass
and watch the
fragments
scatter.
Where once was
face
the pieces lie
in startled
new arrangement.
A glint of sun
fastens
upon a cheekbone
spare
while in the corner,
nostril wide
as in surprise,
a silver
sliver
shines.
Chin and
eyebrow—
temple, line—
disparate elements
discomposed,
potential masks
made infinite.
Pick up a piece—
perhaps an eye
of liquid
green.

Faced with blank glass
it reproduces
terror
error
hopeless
hope.
Relax the lid
and let it
rest.
Focus
upon that damp
tired eye
and
reassess.

STORM

I will not be Freya
but Thor's mistress
hurling myself with fury
into defenseless trees.
Riding shafts of fire
and crushing rain
I slam against windows
streaking them
in dissolved white
energy;
steam rises from hot earth
at my assault.

In the aftermath
wind carries empty clouds
west—
black sky continues black
and I do not return.

GENERATION GAP

The gold we guarded in our thighs
melted
needs to be recast.

The young choose silver
alloyed like flatware
three percent
for strength.
They are practical,
these girls who know
that chastity
is its only reward.

We saved
for 14 karat lives—
then learned what Frost meant
(more or less)
when he said:

Nothing gold can stay.

INTERIM

The halfway world
between midnight and morning
wraps nakedness in mist—
dreams obliterate
distinctions
awaken without waking
until bleak dawn
pressing white
forces in the light.

AMERICAN GIRL

Starched collar white
from careful bleaching
circles shiny plaited
hair hanging
shoulder length
soldier straight
not too long to be
a nuisance.
Piano lessons Saturday
at half past ten
demand an hour each
day along with bath
and brushing hair and
teeth and prayer at
meals and now I lay
me down, it's eight
o'clock.
At twenty-one remembering
to change her linens
once a week
forgetting European
hungry children
leaving half her soup
she goes to choir
and feels the music
only in her
fingertips.

COUNTY FAIR

girls   half lidded like snakes

iridescent under midway lights

move softly
undulating through the crowds

sway to music that swells and dies
as they pass each teeming tent

lathered horses pace the track
three times around

one breaks stride   the driver curses
pulls him out

children beg for rides in whines

as sweating young men move
against the flow

to brush the sleek hipped girls

DISEASE

I pull the tired sheet around my neck
and turn to sleep again where sleep and dreams
are dull as stone.
Before the nurse comes in
I fall to where the sky is blacker
than this winter morning, cold before the sun
as rain is cold
crystallizing without warning
aging the season in white folds
as I age here.

You come through clouds
trailing the injection
bringing hothouse flowers
to deceive me into spring.

PATERNITY

The old man squats
beside the flower
bed in January,
lights his pipe
and waits, as water
trickles
from his hose.
He guides the nozzle
with a trembling hand,
helping the
artificial member
spew its liquid
onto the ground.
Satisfied,
the old man takes his
hose and goes inside
to wait for the first
signs of life.

JELLYFISH

Swept onto an indifferent beach
the translucent jellyfish
begins its dying labor
as the embryonic brain
visible through colorless layers
of swollen sac
floats laconically
in the heaving sphere.
Tentacles are withdrawn
deceptive in their nearly still
defenseless posture.
Curious men toss sand
that slips, grain by grain,
from its shimmering back,
kick tentatively
at the untentacled side
rolling it farther up the shore.
Other spectators take turns
at the death watch
before returning
to the gathering of skeletons
too long dead
for response to be rooted
deeper than in color.

FIRST BABY

She lies
propped on a pillow of hospital muslin
with stenciled numbers, blue on white,
identifying military property.
By now she has forgotten
half the agony,
terrified hours
when white draped strangers
charted pain.
Perhaps in sleep
when memory is unrepressed
she almost wakes to escape
being wrenched apart again.
But in the day
when flowers come
and visitors and telegrams
she smiles, and lying still
to minimize reminders
sharp between her legs
shuts out the hot white lights
the gasps for scant relief
cold stainless steel
hard sterile hands.

ABSENCE

a snuffed candle in a small room
its thin black trail weaving uncertainly upward,
odors of wax

red evenings when the sun diffuses warmth
over the land

I remember your finger drawing a pattern on my thigh

nights of counting stars,
leaning from windows, dreaming

coffee on summer mornings

absence of pain

RETURN

They still come
lines etched only slightly deeper now
to wear linoleum patches
with their feet
choosing the same stools daily.
Laura, dish towel wrapped
around her aging head,
grunts a greeting on good days;
on bad she chooses not to speak
but slaps change on the counter,
shuffles out.
One year she sent a Christmas card,
surprised the lot by wishing cheer,
will not allow
the weather to be criticized:
God knows his business.
People never can be satisfied.
Marianna, glassy eyed at 12:00
before and after
orders two full dinners
to get her through the afternoon
at the competitor's where
she scrubs the floors, cleans rooms.
She calls to Fred
(whose name is really Fritz—
she's never known the difference)
and shrilly asks for pie,
puzzles at gentle teasing,
stays an hour.
The teacher who retired

years before the official time
shakes dice and looks
as if his bones should rattle too.
He pays for the plumber's coffee,
allows the break from rest to last
as long as there are men
to play the game,
remembers war and feels shrapnel
under old skin.

Once I poured their coffee,
passed the dice box,
passed the time.

Like figurines carved in stone
or photographs
or memories
they remained
while I trudged out of snow,
flew from the patterned rhythm
of their days
to unregulated change.

CHARLESTON

I planned to walk again
among historic sites
where traditions stand unchallenged
but sit instead in the empty courtyard
sipping coffee, watching water drip
over the fountain's edge
onto pink and green caladiums
glistening in late morning sun.

Yesterday
wandering among old shuttered homes
enclosed by iron fences
I felt the strength of years—
survival against sea storms
that must have battered their determined walls
a hundred times.
The quiet town invited me
to cobbled walks and formal gardens;
the dignity of age and custom held me.

Later, in the harbor,
affected by salt air
and drinks mixed to a sailor's taste,
my Viking blood called raucously
from cruiser to staid shore
in defiance of a past where traditions are not mine
though I would choose them.

This morning
tired from last night's revelry
I am caught between the fountain's gentle splash
and the impelling crash
of hard Atlantic waves
against the rocks.

DOWNBEAT

1

Van Gogh from a distance
gets out his sidewalk paintings
early.
He pulls his straw hat down
keeping even gentle morning sun
from cancered skin.
Both ears intact
half an eye is scarred
on mottled flesh.
Unlike the other
a woman drove him only
to New Orleans;
he mentions alimony,
strokes a slightly ragged
red-gray beard
and sanely sells
his summer tourist art.

2

As the voodoo lady gathers fallen plums
in Jackson Square

an old guide in the cathedral
points to priceless figures
stained glass
frescoes
Italian statues
Bishops under a velvet altar

and runs his fingers along
the sacred pews.

The lady
draped in black
expressionless
eats each plum
with great deliberation.

A box for contributions at the rear
is flanked by books for sale.
God needs help with maintenance;
photographs
histories
prayers for the faithful
line the shelves.

Escaping rain
the people plunk donations in the box.

The lady finishes her dinner
bows demurely to St. Louis
and offers to trade
some of her magic for his.

3

Near the square
the market tempts old men
heavy lidded
from their corners.
Where bars are interspersed
with bakeries

beer and bread
waft from alternating doors
meeting vegetable odors
across the street.
Hanging baskets line the balconies
where women lean to wave
drinking chicory in early hours
before heat
sours morning smells
and wilts bright fragrant flowers.

BALANCE

Trees bend with the hill
downward
spread thick branches to break
their suspended fall.
Inside the building floors are level.
Elevators move straight up and down,
less dizzying than the adjustment of vision.
This room
perpendicular to the sky
planted at awkward angles with the earth
glasses me from the sun, the green
askew across my window.
My cubicle is safe.
In the intoxicating air
devoid of boundaries
I would slide to the edge of the world
where moths light precariously
and grope their way back.

DREAMS

The days wind down
wind down,
the slow grind of a defunct windmill
catches their rhythm,
moves air slowly.
Clouds pass under the sun
defining intervals.

A cock crows in the August dark,
fences heave and splinter in the rain,
dry gray under August sun.
Cats slip under, away from cows,
to look for milk in pans.

In the city
the squeal of metal
against metal
echoes the old pump.